I0822495

Du Rose Paradise

K T BOWES

Join Me

I have a reading group which you're very welcome to join.
You can do that by signing up on my website ktbowes.com
In return, you'll receive four free eBooks sent to your inbox and an email from me once a month.
I'd love for you to join us.

Love from Kate x

Dedication

For Dr Rox and her special number 30.

1

A greeting - kia orana

The unnatural blue of the sky soared above her and she blinked, as though seeing it for the first time. Each fresh day paraded before her a set of new experiences and Hana promised never to take the vibrancy of life for granted. "This is paradise," she sighed to herself, stretching and flexing her pale toes against the white sand. A groan cut off her enthusiasm as she used her stomach muscles to lie back on the hairy tartan blanket beneath her. The novel in her right hand thudded to the sand with a muted hiss of closing pages, and Hana pressed her fingers against the pain blossoming from her side. It engulfed her thighs and her chest before she wrestled it back under control. Her sense of gratitude faded.

She abandoned her novel and remained on her side, relieving the pressure from the healing knife wound. Her fingers shook as she cushioned her head with her left hand. It had been a month since a skilful surgeon repaired the damage to her liver. A month since she counted her blessings on the cold tiles of a bathroom and watched her blood pool beneath her. Just a month.

Hana sighed and closed her eyes. Sometimes it seemed a lifetime ago, time playing tricks on her as it alternated between distancing the event or hauling it into yesterday with dizzying speed. The same powerlessness broke over her like a wave. She couldn't help herself. Her fragility reflected at her from the white foam of the lapping tide, as though it crept onto the shore to claim her. If Logan hadn't searched for her, uneasy about her length of time in the bathroom, she'd have bled out alone. If Bodie hadn't just finished an intensive first aid course.

If. If. If.

The thought of never seeing Phoenix's coy smile, Wiri's frown or Edin's pout, filled her with a bone deep misery. And to never again experience one of Mac's wholesome hugs as he wrapped his spindly arms around her neck fit to stop her breathing; unthinkable.

She sensed herself disappearing into a void of despair and reached for a lifeline. Hana practised the breathing technique, which the physiotherapist taught her. Slow in through her nose before whooshing the air from between her lips as though expelling her memories of the event. The sunshine stroked her bare shoulders, adopting a maternal role as it pressed its lips over each of her freckles with a scorching kiss. Hana's heart rate evened out, settling over the next few minutes of concentration. The pacemaker beneath her left collar bone had defibrillated her heart after the attack. Blood loss and a slowing pulse had activated its latent purpose, an unexpected benefit of the old implant. The surgeon who fitted it years ago had perhaps imagined Hana's heart stopping of its own accord as it once did. Even he, with his godlike status, could not have foreseen a near fatal stabbing.

The back of Hana's right elbow prickled, the sun intensifying the threat to her porcelain skin. She needed to apply more sunscreen, but lacked the energy or inclination to shift position again. So she lay on the tartan rug and burned.

"Are you okay?" Bare feet with hairy toes appeared in front of her, startling her from a shallow sleep. Hana exhaled as her pulse rate hiked again with the heightened fear reaction she'd grown to detest.

"Fine," she replied, "thanks."

A grunted reply issued from above, and then the sand in front of her face shifted. A scarred knee dusted with blond hairs folded next to her. "You don't look okay," the voice said.

Hana bit back her groan and used her left elbow to lever her torso into an upright position. She took extra care when twisting herself to sit on the tartan blanket. "I'm fine," she said again, hauling her light summer dress over her head and drawing it down to cover the exposed scar. She prayed the intruder didn't ask questions about it. She imagined the door of heaven slamming in her face and her prayers discarded as he drew his blond brows into a line.

"What's the scar from?" He made it sound casual, but Hana responded to his enquiry as though he'd marched through her front door without an invitation and crapped on the doormat. The tee shirt covered her bikini top, but staring at the scar meant he'd also taken in her stretch marks and the thread veins snaking across her right thigh.

"Accident," she replied. Her fingers scrabbled for the novel and drew it free of the sand which shrouded it. She lifted it by the cover and gave it a shake. Granules the hue of raw sugar poured from the fold and bounced against the rug. Hana dropped the book into the tote bag at her side. "I should go," she said, shielding her eyes with her flattened hand. "My husband is due back soon."

The man's lips twisted. He hugged his knees to his bare chest and nodded. The start of a middle-aged spread hung over his green board-shorts, but it didn't detract from his boyish handsomeness. He brought an air of smugness with him as though he'd grown used to women giving him an easy pass because of his looks. He seemed younger than Hana, possibly mid forties. She sighed as her familiar internal monologue suggested he'd had an easier ride. "I saw him leave earlier. Did he go snorkelling?"

Hana frowned. Despite the heat, Logan Du Rose had left wearing his uniform of a white tee shirt, jeans, and cowboy boots. His clothing hid a rented wetsuit because his extensive scarring prevented him from changing on the boat, but this man couldn't know that. Her lips parted, and she stared at him without replying. He waved a nonchalant hand. "The van picked him up from the reception. Hosking's Dive Tours. His assistant left a wetsuit for him on your porch last night." He chuckled. "Your bloke is a big guy. They don't get many tourists over six feet tall wanting to rent a wetsuit. I think they broke out a new one just for him."

"Right." Hana offered a definitive nod. She shifted onto her hands and knees and pushed herself upright. To her horror, the inquisitive man snagged a corner of the rug and flapped it to release the sand from its gathered folds. He took time turning it into a perfect square before tucking it under his right arm.

"I'll walk you back to the resort," he stated, his blond fringe bouncing against his eyelashes.

"I'm fine," Hana protested. She held her hand out for the rug, gesturing towards the tote bag at her feet. "It'll fit in there." Her eyes widened as he lifted that too and clamped it under his arm with the rug. The fabric straps bumped against his ribs. "I'm okay to walk just across the road." Her tone held panic, and she gnawed on her lower lip. Her imagination readied a scenario where he accompanied her to the villa and demanded entrance. It added in a fictitious link to the woman who'd stabbed her, and Hana's pulse increased to send her blood thudding through her eardrums. She gulped air and ordered her feet to run. They refused, her body sick with the rush of adrenaline when the holiday had promised rest and relaxation. She closed her eyes and sent anxious vibes to her husband, knowing he couldn't hear and wouldn't come. Yet.

"I'll walk with you." The blond man turned his body, his feet seeming to lag as he faced the shallow rise of the beach towards the road.

"No!" Hana's breath locked in her chest. "I'm fine!" Hysteria edged her voice. She snatched the bag from beneath his arm, ensuring she had the villa key and her useless phone. Abandoning the rug, which plunged into the sand, and ignoring his startled expression, she ran up the beach and across the road.

Out of breath before the entrance to the resort. The sign waved in the gentle breeze. Paradise Villas.

Hana felt not only out of breath, but also out of options.

Just out. Of everything. And she had been for a while.

2

Alone - anake

The emptiness of the villa seemed to mock Hana's anxiety as she locked the door and leaned against it. But her mind taunted her with the man's easy access if he really wanted it. He owned the resort, which meant he also possessed a master key. Hana's fingers trembled as she used the shiny metal chain to add another layer of security. "Well, it *was* paradise," she grumbled to herself, her voice echoing back from the minimalist décor of whitewashed walls and high gloss kitchen cabinets. It didn't seem like paradise any more.

Hana looked down at her dainty feet, noticing the sand still collected between her toes and dotted across her insteps. Sweat beaded over her brow as she turned to inspect the doormat. Spots of blood followed her in a circle. She groaned, resting a hand against the door to examine her feet. "Great!" she sighed with a giant exhale. So far, she'd lost the tartan picnic rug and her flip-flops. "Not bad for the first day," she rebuked herself.

A hot shower removed the excess sand and a plaster from her suitcase sealed the tiny cut to her right foot, which she'd earned running across the gritty road. Hana changed into a light summer dress after pressing gauze over her scar. She banged sand from her novel into the sink and settled on the bed to read. It galled her how easily she allowed others to shatter her peace, and she read the same two pages over and over without understanding. In defeat, she sat the book on the night-stand and rested against the pillows.

For the first time she could recall, she missed the distraction of a television.

The holiday in Rarotonga had seemed like a magnificent idea. Her brother took charge of the children for a whole week, assuring Hana he would cope. And he would. That wasn't in doubt, especially with her mother-in-law tagging along as his back-up. The stabbing had knocked Hana out of action for a month already, and her family had stepped into the breach without complaint. Leslie Du Rose seemed in her element as the doting grandparent, coming alive as she did school runs, after-school activities and endless packed lunches for the four Du Rose children. After her brother, Mark's, considerable persuasion, Hana had loaded a suitcase with summer dresses and a bikini and hoped the break would bring healing. “Day one,” she murmured to the matt white ceiling.

The island’s isolation made an internet connection both expensive and unreliable. Few resorts provided a television, as the single local channel held little interest for anyone but the island’s permanent residents.

Hana sent her mind back to that morning. She’d held Logan’s hand as they walked to the communal seating area for breakfast. For the first time in months, she’d experienced the heady excitement of freedom. The child-free holiday meant they could work off a different timetable, one not dictated by meal times and school hours. Hana had drunk fresh orange juice and eaten mango and pears for breakfast. Until the blond resort owner plonked himself down at their table and pumped them for information.

“Du Rose?” He’d frowned and cocked his head. “You’re the ones who own a hotel in the north island of New Zealand, aren’t you?”

Logan’s thigh had tensed beneath Hana’s palm as she’d sipped her ginger tea and peered at the man over the rim of her mug.

“I’m a high school teacher,” Logan had replied. He hated people prying into his life, and Hana sensed even in that brief interaction that he already disliked the man. She’d taken her cue from her husband, trusting Logan’s heightened intuition. They hadn’t had time to discuss it before Logan left to catch the shuttle to the dock and she'd headed to the beach.

Hana lay on the bed with her arms by her sides. There were only two flights a day to the island, and they'd arrived on the later one the night before. It took an astounding two hours for their fellow passengers to clear customs and security, and they fell into the double bed after midnight. Hana yawned as tiredness caught up with her. She closed her eyes and listened to a group of wild hens scratching in the dust outside, little grunts and burbles issuing from contented throats. Despite her best intentions, she slept.

Arguing woke her. Disoriented, Hana blinked at the unfamiliar room and frowned. The villa vibrated as though after some kind of shock, and it took a moment for her to recognise her surroundings and place herself on holiday within them. She yawned and inhaled the villa's stuffy air. Perhaps an earthquake. She lifted her phone from beside her on the bed and peered at the screen for a notification. Nothing. Then she groaned. No phone signal and no data.

"Keep your voice down!" a male voice hissed. It came from beyond the rear wall of the villa. Hana tilted her head back to study the upside down view of a high window above the headboard.

"You shafted me!" Another male voice responded, the tone acerbic. "You didn't tell me you brought more of it onto the island last night! I suppose you planned to shift it without me knowing."

"No!" The first voice held a placatory tone. "You didn't need to raid our villa while we ate breakfast! I would have given it to you later today."

"Keeping it in your suitcase isn't a smart plan. It needs to stay hidden until we can switch it. This is as good a place as any. No one will look for it here."

"Whatever!" The base notes of the man's scoffing carried through the wall to Hana. Her tingling nerve endings warned her of danger, but it vied with her budding curiosity. Ignoring the pain from her side, she clambered onto her knees, intending to peek through the high window. She couldn't quite reach and rose on tiptoes, needing to stand on the pillows to see through the bottom edge of the glass.

Two men walked away, giving her a rear view of their mismatched heights. She recognised the shorter one as the resort owner, his blond hair glistening in the sun's harsh rays. The taller man had the build and colouring of a Cook Islander. He wore flip-flops on his tanned feet and his shorts hung low on his buttocks. He walked with a listing gait, the resort owner scurrying along beside him. Hana twisted her lips and watched them navigate between the villa sitting perpendicular to hers and the one next to it. She held her breath and ducked down as the resort owner's head turned. His shoulders followed until he looked back at the window. Hana cursed as the curtain twitched with her sudden movement. Embarrassment flamed her cheeks, though she doubted he'd seen anything other than the curtain swishing. She reasoned he'd put it down to a through draught.

But the conversation perplexed her as she boiled water for a drink and collected food from the fridge to make lunch. Her hasty late night retrieval of supplies from their suitcase meant she'd forgotten the bread. It lay nestled in the bottom of the case between a floral summer dress and Logan's crisp shirts. Distracted, she set about fixing their clothes onto hangers in the bedroom and filling the drawers with underwear and toiletries. The click of the kettle reminded her of her former task.

Rarotonga's enticing pamphlets hadn't warned about the need to boil all water and use bottled product for teeth cleaning. Residents of the island were immune to the bugs inhabiting the surface water from streams and springs within the catchment valley. Tourists weren't so fortunate. The last thing Hana needed after her surgery was a stomach upset. She used the tea bags she'd brought with her and the carton of long-life milk from the fridge. Then she sat on the deck to force down the simple meat paste sandwich and the drink. The heat sapped her energy, and she picked at the food, tearing off the crusts and persuading herself to swallow the bite sized squares which remained from the rubble. Her mind kept flicking back to the overheard conversation. She wondered what the resort owner had brought onto the island and why he'd hidden it. Drugs, she reasoned, and sighed. "None of my business," she soothed. But her visceral reaction to the man hailed a warning she wouldn't ignore.

A wild chicken pecked at the edge of the shared lawn, its beak darting against the dusty earth. Hana crumbled the crusts and the remains of her sandwich and scattered it onto the scrubby grass. She realised her mistake within seconds as the cockerel lifted its beak and squawked. The thwack of wing muscles and flutter of feathers surrounded her as at least fifty chicken friends joined it to fight over the impromptu feast. Hana abandoned her tea and the empty plate and ran inside and slammed the front door. She rested her forehead against the laminated notice which said, 'Please don't feed the wild animals. ESPECIALLY the chickens.'

3

Visitor - manu'iri

Hana opened all the windows, grateful for the mosquito screens which kept the flies and the chickens from entering. A decent draught funnelled through the villa and she returned to her novel. She groaned when sand cascaded from the fold into a crease in her dress.

The chickens scattered as she flung open the front door again and brushed the debris onto the deck. An indignant cockerel studied her with its head on one side, a single beady eye severe and unblinking.

"Hiya!" A woman's voice set the chickens scrambling further afield, their warbling shrieks accompanying their haphazard directional chaos.

Hana looked up and gave the fabric a last brush. "Hi," she replied, frowning in the porch's shade to identify the visitor. She relaxed as she recognised one half of the couple from the villa adjacent to hers. A reluctant smile crossed her lips.

"I noticed you on the flight over here," the woman said. She stepped onto the porch and halted. "You're with the really tall guy." She presented her observation as a statement and not a question, leaving Hana with a simple nod in response. "Hallie." The woman reached out, offering her hand. Hana took it, stifling a yawn as she contemplated the peace of her villa and the waiting, sand free novel.

"Nice to meet you," she replied, the moment growing awkward. "Do you have everything you need?"

Hallie winced. Hana regretted her question, which held a silent implication that she might provide anything lacking. Flyaway mousy hair lifted in the breeze like a static haze, and Hallie's rumpled skirt and blouse gave her a dishevelled appearance. A lack of confidence created a woodenness which morphed into wide waves of her arms as though she engaged in an overcomer's silent mental battle with it. Her frame appeared slight, but she carried extra weight, which settled around her hips and bulged through a skirt a size too small. "I don't suppose you brought any sugar with you?" she asked. "Jared rented a car from a friend of Craig Henderson's, but we need to catch the bus to collect it later. Then we can grab some supplies from the Avarua District." She twisted her pretty features into a grimace. "I packed sugar in our suitcase, but the milk carton leaked and soaked it. I just spent the last hour hand washing most of our clothing. It's a pity because I caught the bus into town earlier, but didn't realise I needed more or I would have got it then." She heaved out a ragged sigh and peered at the chipped paint on her fingernails. "Happy holidays."

"Come in." Hana relented and stepped aside, allowing Hallie to proceed into the villa at a rush. She halted just inside the door and peeled off her worn sandals. Matching polish graced her toes, displaying what her fingernails had originally looked like. "Tea or coffee?" Hana walked into the kitchen and lifted the kettle, inspecting the water level.

"Coffee please. Two sugars." Hallie ran a hand through her tangled nondescript curls. She frowned and dragged a band from her wrist, which she used to corral her hair into a ponytail. She sank into an armchair which faced the kitchen. "Do you always travel in business class?"

Hana frowned, surprised at the question. She emptied more water into the kettle from a bottle and snapped on the lid, depressing the button to make it boil. "No," she replied, replacing the bottle back in the fridge. Her tone held a warning. She didn't intend to discuss Logan's financial status with a random acquaintance.

"It looked nice up there. You got wine and everything." Hallie cocked her head. "Jared booked an aisle seat because otherwise he literally needs to wrap his legs around his neck to get comfortable." She grinned, as though wanting Hana to appreciate the stranger's great height. "He's just over six feet tall. Like your husband."

Hana turned away and drew mugs from an overhead cupboard. Logan would tower over Jared by a head. She'd never seen him, but wondered about the accuracy of Hallie's tape measure. No one else on their flight had bumped their nose on the overhead lockers. She didn't have the heart to destroy the woman's illusion. Or the energy for irrelevant point scoring.

Hallie took the mug of coffee with enthusiasm and slurped the hot liquid. "Perfect," she mused, her eyelashes fluttering closed with enjoyment. She lifted her chin and peered across at Hana's mug. "Oh, what's that?"

"Herbal tea. Lemon and kawakawa." She hadn't realised how much she would miss coffee. But the lobe of her liver, which her attacker sliced with a sharp blade, meant a changed lifestyle to hasten its healing. No toxins such as pain pills or alcohol. Indefinitely.

Neither she nor Logan had sampled the wine in business class which had so interested Hallie.

Hana took a mental stock of her unsociable attitude as the silence stretched between them. She released a heavy sigh and began again. “My brother bought the holiday for us as a gift. My husband upgraded the flight because it’s meant as a recovery break for me after an illness.”

“Oh.” Hallie sat forward. “Sorry. I didn’t mean to pry. Jared says I’m socially awkward. He hates how I get two sentences into a conversation and drop my guts.” She gave a nervous laugh, and Hana relaxed. She settled back on the two-seater sofa and sipped her tea. It wasn’t so bad, she reasoned. She’d drunk it before through choice and the taste hadn’t changed just because she’d run out of alternatives.

“It’s fine,” Hana said with a smile. “My husband calls it verbal diarrhoea. It’s quite endearing.” She winced at the implied rudeness of the statement and apologised. “I meant it in relation to my daughter, not to you. She has a terrible crush on our local vicar and can’t seem to stop herself babbling whenever he’s around her.”

Relief flooded through her as Hallie nodded. “Yeah, that’s me. And the more nervous I am, the worse it gets. I got stopped on the expressway for having a broken tail-light last week and ended up telling the police officer my life story. She made the mistake of asking if I had children and that unleashed a whole diatribe about how Jared fires blanks and IVF had failed four times. And now this." She flapped her hand in front of her but didn't elaborate further on what she meant by *this*. "Anyway, she didn't ticket me, but only because I think she wanted to get away from me."

Hana smiled, and the mood lightened. She sensed Hallie's embarrassment at the retelling of her mortifying story and dodged the issue at its heart. Her soul ached for couples struggling with infertility. But as a woman with four children by two fathers, all of whom were accidental, her sympathy always contained a note of weakness. She switched to their arrival on the island instead. "It was strange coming here in the dark and going straight to sleep. I don't know how Logan crawled out of bed to go snorkelling this morning." She'd wanted a slower start, but he'd insisted she eat breakfast before he left.

"Oh." Hallie brightened, her features sharpening. "That's where Jared went. So they're probably already acquainted." She leaned back in the armchair and kept hold of her mug as though needing the coffee-hit as a lifeline. Hana didn't enlighten her. She'd only brought the decaffeinated version.

"Perhaps." Hana imagined Logan making friends and dismissed the notion. Her husband would remain pleasant but aloof. He permitted so few people into his inner circle she doubted Jared would gain entry at a first meeting. She leaned forward at the memory of the argument she'd overheard. "Did you see the resort owner at breakfast?" she asked.

Hallie cocked her head. "We didn't go for breakfast, but Jared's known Craig for years. They shared a student flat in Auckland. He stays with us when he visits the mainland. I let him share my booth at the Auckland travel show. It was at the showground this year." She shrugged and took another sip of her coffee. "I always come to this resort, so he gives me the biggest villa. Jared rarely visits because he works. Or at least, he did." Her brows narrowed as she considered the root of Hana's question. "Why?"

She formulated her reply with care. "No reason." She dismissed the aura of concern with a forced smile. "I just saw him out here earlier and recognised him from this morning."

Hallie wrinkled her nose. "Blond, muscular, bit of a surfer looking dude?" A mistiness crossed her hazel irises until they appeared unfocussed. She didn't wait for Hana to confirm her impression. "Yeah, that's him." She cleared her throat. "He bought the resort about ten years ago. Since then, we've had all kinds of global problems which have affected the tourist industry." She lowered her voice. "A cyclone ripped up the other side of the island last year and scared away the tourists. Craig said he almost went bust. I'm not sure how he clawed things back again, but he told me he'd salvaged it."

Hana nodded but kept her suspicion about his potential drug running to herself. "That's good." She thought of Logan's hotel in the mountain and the similar issues they'd had. Leasing the property had immunised them against the potential losses of a declining industry and become a hidden blessing. The event management company had absorbed all the economic hit and not their family for a change. But Hallie was right. Things had improved, especially on the conference scene.

"Do you work?" Hallie rushed on, not waiting for an answer. She dipped forward in a curious action and pressed at a spot beside her navel. "I'm a travel agent. We get subsidised holidays in exchange for recommending resorts to customers. Jared thinks Craig gives us the biggest villa because they're friends, but it's not the real reason. I've sent him heaps of business over the years."

"Right," Hana replied. "I think my brother stayed here with his husband towards the end of last season. He booked it for us, so we're just grateful for the break. We haven't explored yet. We had a boat tour booked for next Wednesday morning, and he thought Logan might enjoy snorkelling. He arranged a diving expedition for next Tuesday but the company switched it to today. They didn't have enough numbers, so they merged two diving trips."

Hallie gave an enthusiastic nod. "Yes, the Ellie Marie had a major refit after the last cyclone. They can do overnight and weekend tours now. I think they lost a lot of trade while she was out of action. She needed almost a rebuild. What about you? Didn't you fancy diving or snorkelling?"

Hana licked her lips and paused. Lying required far too much effort, and she'd already realised Hallie had no filter. The truth then. "I had surgery a month ago. My brother's a doctor. He didn't think I should try squeezing into a wet suit and swimming in the sea just yet."

"What sort of surgery?" Hallie's hazel irises gleamed with the scent of gossip, and Hana regretted her candidness. "I had an accident and damaged my liver. It'll take time to heal." As though in agreement, the scar tissue beneath her right rib twinged. It sent stabbing sensations like tiny pins rocketing up her side. She shifted position and set her tea on a nearby table.

"What sort of accident?" Hallie leaned forward in her seat.

Hana sighed and resolved not to further fuel her inquisitiveness. "A painful one," she concluded. "Would you like a biscuit with your coffee?"

Hallie cleared her throat and for a moment, desolation seemed to reflect through her irises as though pulled from her soul. She touched her stomach again, a light, tentative flutter of her fingers. "Yes please. I don't suppose you have any painkillers, do you?"

Hana turned away with an ironic twist of her lips. "Oh yes," she said with a sigh. "Enough to sink a battleship." And she couldn't take any of them. She turned back to meet Hallie's gaze. "Paracetamol or Ibuprofen?"

"Both," she replied.

4

Pest - ‘ē

Hallie exhausted Hana with her continual questions. She figured Jared had the patience of a saint as the woman drew in another scant breath before launching into a vivid description of her mother-in-law’s friend’s sister’s house in Auckland. “You’d love it,” she gushed, knowing nothing of Hana’s personal preferences. “It’s huge, and it overlooks the ocean. They’re loaded.” She downed the mixed medications with a gulp of her coffee, but her fingers still fluttered over her stomach when she thought Hana wasn’t looking.

“Nice,” Hana managed, her smile drooping at the thought of her own vacated villa on the mountain. She cleared her throat, sorry when she cut Hallie off mid-sentence despite waiting for an appropriate break. Hallie’s temporary pause included a grab for the last biscuit. “I need to walk to reception,” Hana lied.

"Oh. What for?" Hallie spoke around her crunching.

Hana's mind blanked. "Leaflets." Her voice rose at the end of her sentence. "Lots of leaflets."

"About activities?" Her interest piqued, and she spread her hands. "What do you need to know? I can sort you out with any of the local trips and get some sweet deals. Is there something particular?" She clapped her hands together, cascading crumbs onto the tiled floor. Her eyes flared with a curious brightness. "Oh!" she exclaimed. "Our husbands are probably already friends. We could do stuff together!"

Hana made a non-committal sound in the back of her throat, reluctant to merge their holiday with someone else's. She imagined Logan's dismay at Hallie's constant chatter and doubted he'd given Jared more than a cursory nod. Logan didn't collect friends. He had his immediate family and a tiny group of men he'd consider brothers. Many acquaintances suffered disappointment at having pushed to join his inner circle and grazed their chins on the solid brick wall with which Logan surrounded himself. Once ejected, he permitted no one to re-enter.

Hana rose and collected the empty mugs and the plate which contained only crumbs. She dumped them in the dishwasher and lifted the villa's key from the counter. To her surprise, Hallie took the hint and stood, brushing more crumbs onto the floor. "I'll walk across with you," she said. "Craig lets me use his internet connection to pick up my emails."

"Oh." Hana pursed her lips. Her gaze strayed to her mobile phone charging beside the microwave. "Do you think he'd let me contact my brother? Logan said I could hotspot from his phone, but I'm not sure how and I think he took it with him. I need to let my family know we've arrived safely." She didn't voice her other motive. Leslie's haphazard child-minding could go either way. Phoenix and Mac would behave, but Wiremu and Edin could wrap the elderly woman round their pinkie fingers between them.

Hallie wrinkled her nose. Her lips flattened into a severe line. "I don't think so. It's a special favour to me." She reached out with fingernails painted the colour of ripe mandarins. She clasped Hana's forearm with over familiarity and gave it a solid squeeze. "Please don't mention I told you about it. Craig's quite unpredictable, and I don't want him to stop the arrangement."

"Okay." Hana nodded. Her brother, Mark, had warned her about the lack of connectivity before they set off, but the reality seemed harder to process than she'd imagined. She missed her children's cheerful voices and craved one of little Mac's famous bear hugs. Her stomach knotted and her excitement drained through her feet. She shouldn't have accepted the gift, not when she felt safest at home.

Home.

The word taunted her with its irony. It drew the mountain and the hotel into its embrace. And after all, the stabbing occurred at home.

"Are you coming?" Hallie cocked her head and stared at Hana. She nodded in response and searched for the flip-flops she thought she'd left on the porch. It took a moment for her to realise she'd abandoned them on the beach after Craig's intrusion. The key dug into her palm as she clicked the front door closed behind her. A light push proved the lock had engaged.

Sunshine beat down on her auburn head as they walked between the villas and skirted the crystal blue water of the swimming pool. A muscular man with tanned skin swam long, lazy lengths, his easy stroke appearing effortless. A woman sunbathed on a lounger, a floppy hat protecting her face from the glare. Magazine pages fluttered against the light breeze, clicking like the strange elaterid beetles which inhabited the island. Hana followed Hallie's circuitous path, the grass warm beneath her bare feet.

"Do you have any advice about the island?" she asked, forcing herself to act interested.

Hallie turned to face her and her expression grew serious. Her lips pursed for long enough to make

Hana drag her feet. "Just be careful," she advised, her tone loaded. Her lips pulled back from her teeth in a snarl. "There's corruption here." She lowered her voice. "Nobody is who they say they are."

Hana remained on the path as Hallie stepped ahead of her. It seemed such a strange warning and with no back story, it left her confused. After a moment's delay, she jogged to catch up with the other woman, the slight activity already making her sweat.

They rounded the corner of the last building and Hallie skidded to a halt. Hana ran into the back of her with a grunt of pain. "What's wrong?" she demanded, gripping her side and staring past Hallie to the empty through-road. The reception office occupied the building across the street, two sides formed from floor to ceiling glass windows. It jutted into the visitor's car park as though glued to the side of the main house like a child's attempt at cardboard architecture. A scooter leaned drunkenly in the only occupied space, a police logo emblazoned on the side.

Hallie's complexion paled, and she held her breath as a female officer emerged through the reception door and clambered onto the bike. She didn't bother with a helmet, firing up the scooter and buzzing out through the resort's tree lined entrance. Her pale blue uniform sleeves fluttered against her brown arms as she turned right and sped away. The bike's husky buzz resembled a hairdryer as it echoed back to Hana's ears. "Are you okay?" Hana asked, rubbing her side.

Hallie turned to her with a fake smile plastered onto her lips. "Yeah, just the local cop. I can't remember her name, but she's nice."

"Right," Hana murmured. So nice she wanted to avoid her. They stepped across the molten tarmac at a fast pace as Hana avoided burning her soles. A bell clanged over the door of the reception as Hallie opened it wide.

"Hello!" Hallie burst into the snug space as though arriving home. The frigid air from a wall unit took Hana's breath away. She closed the door behind her with difficulty and stood back to observe the luke warm greeting meted out to Hallie from the woman behind the desk. A sign on the inside of the door glass offered a cash withdrawal service. It swung in the breeze from the air conditioner. "This is my new friend Hana." Hallie seized her arm and yanked her alongside, disregarding Hana's awkward stumble and her hiss of pain. Hana braced herself against the counter.

"Is there a problem?" The receptionist's pencilled brows narrowed as though she hated her on sight, and she peered at Hana through penetrating blue eyes the colour of Antarctic ice. The plunging neckline of her uniform blouse finished level with the white bow clinging to a lacy bra. Two peachy breasts peered from within the fabric like twin voyeurs in their world. The lace struggled to hold them and Hana bit her lower lip to distract her from their unnatural bounce. The woman appeared older than Hana, but her smooth, coconut sized breasts didn't match her wrinkled chest and neck.

"No. I'm fine, thanks." Hana shook herself free and pointed towards the wall of shelving, which contained activity brochures. "I just wanted some information leaflets." She escaped Hallie's grasp and sought sanctuary on the other side of the narrow office. The woman behind the desk observed Hana with a hard expression, which contained too much animosity for a first encounter.

"I'll just be in the office checking my emails," Hallie trilled. She flounced around the counter and into a room behind the desk, oblivious to the tight-lipped glare it induced from the receptionist. Hana reached for a leaflet about pests, attracted by the image of a beautiful tree with bright red flowers adorning the cover. The glossy paper gave off a chemical scent, confused by the lemon air freshener mounted on the wall above the rack. Hallie's laughter filtered through the open doorway, met by quieter male tones.

With Hallie out of the way, Hana smashed and grabbed from the rack, not paying much attention to the spoils. "I'll just take these," she announced to the receptionist, keeping her voice low. "Thank you."

"Oh, Mrs Du Rose." She ground to a halt with one hand on the door handle, the other clutching a wad of leaflets. Turning back to the counter, she blinked in confusion at seeing only the receptionist when she'd heard a male voice. Then Craig bobbed up from behind the woman like a Jack-in-the-box. He dumped her abandoned rug and flip-flops on the counter. "You dropped these on the beach," he said, his brows drawing into a line.

"Thank you." Hana forced a smile onto her lips and collected them into her arms, ignoring a leaflet which fluttered to the floor. On the front cover, a boat roofed from coconut leaves shimmered on an azure sea, dolphins surrounding the grinning tourists in the water. She used her right foot to push it closer to the counter in a pretence of not realising she'd dropped it. Craig narrowed his eyes at her. "I called by with them, but you didn't answer the door."

Hana swallowed. She considered the shock awakening, and the argument she'd observed between Craig and the other man. Perhaps his knocking had disturbed her initially. She feigned ignorance. "Sorry. I went straight to sleep. Then Hallie popped round to borrow some sugar."

Craig shot an irritated glance towards the office behind him. His gaze strayed to the receptionist, and they exchanged a look. The hidden meaning evaded Hana, and she concentrated on her escape. She eased the heavy door open and a wall of humidity slapped her in the face. Another leaflet cascaded to the carpeted floor. Hana emitted a squeak of surprise as the weight of the door disappeared, almost pitching her over the threshold at speed. She put her arms out to save herself and dropped a flip-flop and more leaflets. "Sorry!" she gushed. "I didn't realise you'd got the door for me." The warm air stole her breath, and she stepped outside. Craig followed her out, closing the door behind him. He bent to retrieve the leaflets, frowning at the one about pests. Hana quailed as his lascivious gaze grazed every square centimetre of her legs from ankle to thigh as he rose. "You're interested in biodiversity?" He blinked in the sunlight, his blond fringe falling into his eyes. A deft movement set the pile on top of the tartan rug and he bent again to grab the single flip-flop.

"Yes," she lied.

Craig studied her for a long moment. The silence stretched between them as the awkwardness grew. "Du Rose," he said in a musing tone. "Why did your husband tell me he's a schoolteacher?"

Hana swallowed. "Because he is." *And a farmer. And an investor. A brilliant mathematician. And unequalled in bed.* But she added none of those accolades out loud.

Craig shook his head. A vibrant floral shirt covered his torso, the buttons opened to reveal curly blond hair across his pectorals. "Maybe, but I know he also owns that hotel near Auckland," he said, his tone grave. "I read an interview he gave in a magazine after it won a tourist award a few years ago." He lifted his hand and ran it through his damp curls. The humidity hiked around them like a cloying fog. "I want some advice." His muddy brown irises sparkled in the light as he fixed his gaze on Hana. "I'll pop round later."

Hana ground her teeth in her jaw as anger set a fire in her painful stomach. "Please don't," she said, trying to add politeness to her request. "We're on holiday. We both need to relax and not think about work for a while." Her words hid a fathomless understatement.

Craig shrugged, not deterred by her refusal. "Well, it's important," he persisted. "I could use some consultation on this place." His arm waved in an expansive arc to encompass the resort.

"Right." Hana sighed and edged past him, avoiding the sharp gravel which bordered the hot paving slabs. He didn't assist her by stepping aside, watching with casual interest as she navigated him and set off along the path towards the swimming pool. She paused before crossing the resort's narrow lane, dropping her flip-flops to the hot asphalt and pushing her feet into them. Her soles still burned and tingled with the memory of the heat even after they ceased contact with the road. When she shot a glance behind her, she found Craig still watching, his features scrunched and his expression unreadable.

5

Love - ʻinangaro

Logan returned in the early afternoon. His black fringe hung in a curtain over his eyes, flattened by the salt water from his snorkelling. He settled on the armchair after closing the screen door, obliterating the dent in the cushion left by Hallie's exit. "How was your day?" His grey eyes observed Hana as she poured bottled water from the fridge into two glasses. Her hand trembled as she sensed him studying her.

"Not as peaceful as I'd hoped," she replied, keeping her tone light. She pursed her lips and considered the day's chance meetings, the information clashing and clanging in her head. When she thought about repeating it to her husband, it all amounted to nothing. It occurred to her she'd begun labelling the resort manager as Creepy Craig. It seemed disingenuous when he'd only ever tried to help her. Hana swallowed and turned, the condensation from the glass seeping over her fingers. She handed it to Logan with a smile.

Too late.

Her perceptive husband cocked his head. "How so?" His casual tone belied his interest. He'd scented the faint tang of smoke and mirrors and would dig until he uncovered the source of her disquiet.

Hana sank onto the two-seater with a sigh. She sipped her drink and considered her reply so as not to betray her neuroses. "My side hurt," she confessed. "I went to the beach to read and laid down wrong. It pulled the stitches and made me miserable."

Logan wrinkled his nose in sympathy. "It's early days yet," he soothed. "That surgery was serious stuff." He pushed the fingers of his right hand through his hair, leaving his fringe sticking up like a cockerel's plume. "Are you afraid?"

His question stymied her and the glass wobbled in her hand. "What?"

"Of her. Are you afraid she'll come back for a second attempt? Or visit the house while we're away?"

"No!" Hana gasped. She half rose, the scar tissue tugging as she sank back into the cushions. The glass tipped as she set it on the coffee table between them, and water sloshed onto the mottled wooden patina. She pressed her fingers into her eyes. "I never thought of that." Her chest rose with the increased rapidity of her breathing, and she darted a glance at the open front door protected by the fly screen. She imagined undoing the morning's labour with their clothing by slamming it all back into the suitcase.

She jumped and squeaked as the sofa depressed next to her. Logan's muscular arm slipped around her shoulders, and he pulled her legs across his. He exercised extreme care as he eased her into his lap. "You didn't need to think of it," he soothed. "Because I already did."

Hana tilted her head back to stare at him. Her irises swam with ready tears, but he held her gaze without discomfort. His confidence infused her with safety, and she licked her lips before speaking. "Is David Allen watching over them?"

Logan's mouth twisted, and he paused for a moment before replying. "Yes. But they're not at home. I arranged for them to have a holiday, too." Hana blinked without understanding. Horror filled scenarios filed through her mind.

"Holiday?" Her voice rose. "But they have school. Leslie can't cope with all four of them away from the house!"

"It's fine." Logan lifted his hand and brushed his index finger over her forehead. "Dean and Mark have them in Hamilton. If a paediatrician and a trauma doctor can't manage them for a few days, then it's a poor show. Your brother made it a condition of this trip. He wants time with our kids."

"But what about Leslie?" Hana's jaw hung open.

Logan's smirk provided the first sign of amusement. "Yeah, she keeps surprising me. We all thought she'd confess everything the first second she got you by yourself." His lips turned downward in veiled approval. "But she didn't. I rented an eight-seater and David drove them all down to Mark's yesterday after we left for the airport. He'll stay with them all week and run security. No one would expect the whole family to decamp to Hamilton and we figured they'd be safest there. Your son tracked the bitch who stabbed you to a motel in Northland. She can't stay loose for too much longer. He's got all her accounts locked and guys watching her premises. It'll be over by the time we get home."

Hana pitched forward and rested her temple against Logan's collarbone. She'd always underestimated his strategic abilities. He thrived on the buzz of planning and successful execution. She could have saved herself the raised heart rate if she'd remembered that. He dropped his chin and his bristles grazed her cheek. Never still, his fingers smoothed the soft fabric of her dress over her thigh.

An unexpected stirring disturbed Hana's musing, the sensation like weightlessness in the pit of her stomach. The woman's blade had already robbed her of a month of her life, and she braced her hands against Logan's chest and pushed herself upright. He blinked in surprise at the unexpectedness of her kiss. His lips tasted of warmth and sea-salt. The lingering scent of sun cream mingled with the rubber of the wetsuit. Hana imagined him stripping out of its tight wetness, peeling it from his powerful limbs like a second skin. She wondered where he'd done it, imagining him hiding his Adonis' body in the darkness of a pitching on-board bathroom. She pushed her fingers beneath the hem of his tee shirt, earthing herself against the plates of defined muscle encasing his stomach and chest.

A frenzy seized her fingers, forcing them to dance as she raised Logan's tee shirt with an unaccustomed roughness. She tore at the fabric, hearing the seams ping with the release of tiny stitches. Her kisses spread across his brawny chest, from left to right, until her lips found the raised bud of his nipple. The tang of sun cream jarred against her tongue. She heard the click of a surprised breath, followed by a familiar exhale. Hana wanted normality like an addict tasting the heady bloom of cocaine after a painful absence. She couldn't reclaim the endless days her attacker had stolen, but she could prevent her from taking more.

Hana's scar tugged and ached as she raised her arms above her head. In an unspoken duet, Logan lifted the hem of her dress until it cleared her head. He dropped it onto the floor beside the sofa, a fire flaring behind his irises. Experienced fingers popped open the clasp of her bikini where it nestled between her breasts. The garment fell apart; the straps cascading from her shoulders to reveal her pale, delicate skin. They trapped her arms by her sides, and she shrugged herself free until it landed carelessly on the rucked fabric of her abandoned dress.

Logan's left arm slipped beneath her thighs, his other braced against her spine. He edged forward on the seat and rose. The sinews and tendons tightened in his neck as he lifted Hana into the air. She weighed so little since the attack, and she saw the blink of shock in his eyes as he took a tentative step forward and turned. "I love you," she whispered, pressing her lips to the dip where his neck met his collar bone. His scent collected there, second only to the space at the side of his nose before the curve of his angular cheek. Hana inhaled and sighed, his presence enveloping her in a familiar cocoon of cosseted safety. She kissed the soft hollow again, feeling a jerk as he raised his heel and kicked the outer door of the villa closed behind him. It clicked against the screen door and the metal rattled.

A movement in her peripheral vision caused Hana to glance at the window behind the armchair. The half-closed curtains pulled across the glass had lessened the sun's harsh glare. The top of a blond head showed in line with the level of the windowsill. A man's head, attached to a body moving with a smooth, lazy gait. He navigated the edge of the deck, and Hana held her breath as footsteps clattered up the stairs to the front door. The sharp rap echoed through the villa, seeming to bounce off every surface like an unwelcome claxon raising an alarm.

Logan cursed, but didn't deviate from his course to the bed. He raised an eyebrow at Hana's wide, fearful eyes and his lips curved upwards into a grin. She'd held the bow and released the arrow of desire. Nothing would get in its way. Not even Creepy Craig.

6

Mortality - mate

"Are you hungry yet, kōtiro?" Logan rolled onto his stomach and rested his outstretched arm across Hana's chest. The biceps filled with strength, raised veins pumping blood from his heart as he kept the arm flexed to avoid crushing her. Hana clasped his hand, grateful he'd deviated the familiar action at the last second from her painful stomach.

She pressed a kiss over his knuckles. "Maybe." Her brow furrowed as she waited for signals from her digestive system. It neither confirmed nor denied her tentative question, still sulking after the emergency surgery. "I'm not sure," she admitted. Then she groaned. "Oh no. The lady next door popped in to scrounge some sugar. I forgot to give it to her."

Logan wrinkled his nose. "Ah, you made a friend already," he joked.

Hana widened her eyes until her irises resembled glittering emeralds. "More like death by interrogation. She's a travel agent who's won industry awards for giving clients the perfect, tailor-made holidays." Her lips curved into a reluctant smile. "It's probably only possible because she finds out everything about them, from their underwear preference to their deepest, darkest fears."

Logan turned on his side and braced his elbow, resting the heel of his hand against his cheek. He released his left fingers from Hana's grasp and stroked her chin with his thumb. "She can hold all that data in her head but forgot to take the sugar with her? Or do I smell a pretext?"

Hana shrugged. "Perhaps." She twisted her lips in a mischievous smirk. "I think I'll introduce you both. You're a wall of mystery and guaranteed to drive her absolutely crazy."

"Bring it," Logan retorted.

"Oh. Her husband went on your dive boat, apparently. Jared. I don't know their last name."

Logan stared at the ceiling as he ran through a mental image of their gathered faces. His head shook from side to side and he frowned. "I don't remember a Jared, but I didn't memorise their names. The captain took a group photograph at the end. He's emailing it to all of us."

"How very chummy. Let's print it off and stick it to the fridge at home. Logan and pals." Hana mocked him shamelessly, releasing a shriek when he jerked as though to tickle her. He changed his mind in the last second, perhaps mindful of her scar, and pushed himself to a sitting position.

"Well, I'm starving," he announced. He tilted his wrist to check his watch. "It's almost three o'clock now and the buses run until four thirty. Why don't we get dressed and see if we can catch one that goes past the supermarket? We can travel clockwise to Avarua and catch the last anticlockwise bus back here?"

Hana groaned and threw her arms out to her sides. She stared up at the ceiling. "I don't think I can move that fast anymore," she grumbled.

Logan shrugged. "It's that or a nine kilometre walk each way."

"Or a sandwich."

"I'll carry you," Logan promised, his expression sincere.

Guilt bubbled in Hana's chest, condemning her recent abstinence from anything remotely stressful. The family had closed ranks following her surgery, wrapping her in care and indolence like a warm blanket. She suspected Mark's gift of the holiday contained a hidden agenda. He wanted her to draw a line and step over it.

"Okay," she agreed. She lifted an index finger and bopped Logan on the end of his regal nose. "But I'm having a quick shower first."

They stood in the sweltering temperature by the faded sign which showed Paradise Villas still had six vacancies. The bus didn't arrive. Locals tore past on scooters, only a few wearing helmets. They showed no interest in the idiots standing in the full sun with the heat wave, which caused them to shimmer in the glare from the hot tarmac. Logan glared at his watch as though holding it responsible for his discomfort. He raised his cowboy hat and grunted before turning to Hana with his eyes downcast in apology. "It's not coming," he stated, disappointment filling his voice. "I forgot everything here runs on island time."

Hope budded in Hana's chest. If the bus didn't come in the next ten minutes, they wouldn't have long enough in town to shop and catch the last one home again. She'd bet top dollar that the final driver on the schedule ran on time in anticipation of his day's end. She turned to Logan to offer soothing condolences, which she'd try to fill with sincerity. But her stomach ached, and she imagined sitting under an umbrella next to the swimming pool, a soft breeze kissing her bare legs as she dipped her toes in the cool water. "I brought bread for a sandwich," she began. But Logan's expression of alarm stole her words. She saw his arm shoot sideways, and he snatched at her forearm, his nails digging into the soft flesh as he hauled her towards him. Her lips parted in a scream of ready fear, muffled by the fabric of his tee shirt.

A wave of damp heat engulfed the backs of her calves, a metallic scent shrouding her. Rubber screeched against the asphalt, grit peppering her legs. She left a line of lipstick on the front of Logan's shirt, which would only depart with stain remover. The mark would irritate him until he consigned the garment to the dustbin. Just like the one soaked in her blood and which she'd never seen again. Hana's head bobbed back on her neck like a dandelion pappus, and she noticed the purr of an engine behind her. Logan's arms stiffened around her, the muscles of his chest growing taut as he readied himself for a confrontation. It took a moment for her to realise he'd saved her from a traffic accident. Or at least his expression said he believed he had. His lips flattened into an angry line and he pushed her behind him.

"Hiya!" The familiar lofty tone jarred with the severity of the situation. Hana turned to see Hallie wearing a sun hat and waving at her from the front seat of a red convertible. Her other hand kept the hat clamped to her crown in a death grip. A floral fabric hair tie hugged her left wrist in a pre-emptive strike against her flyaway hair, which would poof if she removed the hat. The brim cast her face into shadow, but the puffiness of the skin beneath her eyes betrayed either hay fever or a bout of tears.

A line of black exhaust fumes belched from behind the vehicle. A solid man occupied the driver's seat, his hair black and his skin a healthy russet.

"Sorry!" Hallie called. "Didn't mean to scare you. We've borrowed this car from a friend of Craig's. Fancy a spin?"

Logan's body language suggested he fancied taking the car and the occupants and hurling all three into the sea. Hana delayed answering, concentrating on her breathing and praying for her fluttering heart to settle. She rested a steadying hand on Logan's forearm and offered Hallie a watery smile. "We're waiting for the bus." Her voice wobbled.

"It's broken down," Hallie replied. She shouted over the spluttering of the engine. The bonnet shook as though housing an escapee demanding release. A rusty mechanism held a fabric hood against the boot. The original black had faded through exposure to sand and salt to a dull grey. Hallie appeared thrilled with the vehicle, though Hana doubted it capable of passing a Warrant of Fitness on the mainland. "Come on!"

Hallie trilled. "It's fun. We'll give you a ride to the Avarua District. There's a great pub which overlooks the ocean."

Hana contemplated a lazy evening by the pool, punctuated only by the effort of picking sand from the pages of her novel. And then she imagined Logan lying next to her, his fingers moving in an endless dance of suppressed boredom. She wouldn't relax, not really. Not while she knew he'd only travelled here for her. Guilt overtook common sense in a game fixed long ago by loaded dice. She sighed and nodded, stamping her reluctance underfoot as she turned towards the vehicle. "Thanks," she said, towing Logan behind her with her tiny hand gripped around his forearm like a fly on a drum. His feet moved with deliberate slowness, his boot soles scraping against the grit. "This is Hallie," she stated, her tone dull. "I told you she visited this afternoon."

Logan blinked with acknowledgement, and his set jaw told her he didn't want to get into the car. But Hallie bounced from the passenger door and fiddled with mechanisms which groaned as she forced her seat forward so the headrest touched the dashboard. "I'll sit in the back," she squealed, pushing herself through a narrow gap to slump behind her husband. Hana didn't look at Logan again, knowing what she'd read in his disapproving expression. But she understood him well enough to predict he wouldn't allow her to leave with strangers, especially one who drove like a maniac. She slid through the gap left by the bowing passenger seat and sat next to Hallie, twisting her body to search for a seatbelt.

By the time she'd secured herself, Logan had relented and bent his long legs enough to take his place in front of her. He slammed the passenger door and dragged a seatbelt across his body. Jerky movements and the stiffness of his neck warned Hana of his latent irritation with her. She pursed her lips and tried to ignore the sense of risk rising as nausea into her chest. Neither Hallie nor her husband bothered with seatbelts as the vehicle took off with a stamp of a heavy foot on the gas. Logan's cowboy hat pitched from his head in protest at the standing start, and Hana caught it in her lap. She shouted to him she'd got it, but the wind snatched her words and threw them over her shoulder. Squealing tyres and a throaty cough from the engine covered her hysterical laughter.

7

Swindle - ʻakaviki

Logan Du Rose appeared to outsiders as a risk taker, but his analytical nature loaded the dice and mitigated the effects. Danger only gave him a buzz when he defeated its outcome with a series of strategic manoeuvres and pure courage. He knew his limits, and Hana understood that about him.

As Hallie's husband weaved the convertible along the main road, he grew distracted by the stunning beaches he pointed out along the way. Hana sensed Logan's tolerance waning. The rigid tilt of his head told her all she needed to know.

Jared dumped the car in a supermarket car park on the edge of the district, activating the central locking and hauling his shorts up one-handed. Hallie fussed with her short dress next to him before wrapping a tentative arm around his waist. She leaned in close to whisper to Hana as they stood by the vehicle. "He's gorgeous, isn't he?" she cooed, her irises glittering like river water kissed by the sun's rays.

Hana glanced sideways at her husband and nodded. Beautiful but deadly in too many ways to list. She sensed his disapproval breaking over her head like a foaming surf. Her life contained an unhealthy mixture of responsibility and hazard. She'd been stabbed and left for dead on a hotel bathroom floor, yet she still lost her head with little encouragement. Her chest tightened as she anticipated Logan's disapproval. She'd almost left her children without a mother, and him like a right shoe without its pair. Her heart clenched, and she shivered despite the baking sun spreading kisses through her red hair. Getting into a car with a maniac seemed foolish now. The warm breeze and Jared's chaotic disregard for road rules had caused the heady excitement to abandon her.

"No, Jared, silly." Hallie slapped Hana's forearm without reservation. She pursed her lips and shot Hana a glare which contained a hidden threat, as though she envisioned her swapping Logan for Jared in her dreams. Her eyes narrowed and she reached up to secure the floral scrunchie keeping her wispy curls secured. She divided the ponytail in half as though wishing to permanently rent the hair from her head. The yanking action forced the daffodil speckled fabric closer to her scalp in an action which appeared masochistic.

"Right," Hana answered, not willing to commit to either confirmation or denial. It seemed rude to admit Jared wasn't her type. And then there was the other thing. She'd seen him before.

"Grab what you need from the supermarket. It closes at six. Meet us at the bar on the waterfront for a swift half before we drive back. We'll take the scenic route and show you the island." Hallie's chest gave a sharp hitch before covering her mouth with her hand, and Hana stared harder at her. Not hay fever then, but tears. At some point in the last few hours, Hallie had cried until her heart broke, her chest muscles still reacting to her distress.

"Thanks," Hana gushed, raising her voice to cover Logan's heavy sigh and expletive. A wave of pity sent a knot into her throat, though she knew she couldn't help her. Hallie attached herself to Jared's right elbow like a limpet as they turned and ambled towards the supermarket. In the distance Hana saw her drop her grip and put distance between her and Jared as though unable to continue the charade any longer.

"Ride home with them? Over my dead body," Logan intoned. He dropped his chin and glared at Hana through the tops of his eyes. She swallowed and handed his hat to him.

"What do you propose, then?" she asked, her tone light.

"Catch the last bus like we planned." He turned away from her and traced the couple's steps towards the bustling store.

Hana caught him up, her handbag bumping against her left hip. She'd looped the strap over her head to avoid it catching her scar, but its bouncing action still ricocheted through her body. "You know Jared from your dive," she said, her tone conversational. Her heart sank as he frowned and his head shook from side to side.

"Do I?"

Hana gnawed on her lower lip. Logan's irritation bowled over her like a wave. He stopped dead and Hana ran into his ribs, grunting in pain and clasping her side. The fire left his eyes. "Sorry," he acknowledged. He placed his giant hands on her shoulders in a natural reaction of care, as she floundered for a minute. She bought herself time and exploited his sympathy.

"No," she conceded. "I'm sorry. I got in the car despite already knowing the quality of his driving. You wanted to go to the shops, and I needed to please you. It seemed the only alternative in the moment with the bus out of action."

Logan lifted his left shoulder in a shrug. "Fair enough." He pressed a kiss to her forehead.

The supermarket accepted New Zealand dollars and Logan had drawn cash from the bank before they left for the airport. The island relied on supplies shipped from the mainland and the prices reflected the hassle. Hana blinked at the cost of a few groceries and watched as Logan drew notes from his wallet. The cashier broke his hundred dollars into smaller denominations and handed him the change. The words, "Thank you," hung from her lower lip as she bounced her hand once in confusion. Cash shuffled in her palm, her bent thumb keeping it in place. A trolley bumped Hana's left hip as the customer behind grew restless.

But Logan shook his head. He plucked the five-dollar note from the woman's hand but rejected the twenty. "It's fake," he said, leaning back in distaste.

Her lips parted, and her brown eyes grew round. A band held her curls away from her face, creating a false bulge above her eyebrows as the skin pulled too taut. "What?" she whispered, and stared down at her hand. The note rose and fell as though breathing, threatening to fly away without the pincer of her thumb holding it in place.

"It's fake." Logan raised his voice and jerked his head towards the offending note. "It doesn't look right."

"You gave it to me." She licked her lips and stared at the customer behind Hana. "You gave me a fake."

Logan's jaw tightened, but he didn't react. The woman shoved her hand towards him, fear in her eyes. The implications of the counterfeit note ran through her mind as though on a film reel. Her fear created a heady tang around the gathered queue as she sought to dodge the coming blame. Logan shook his head, his mana covering him in its familiar authority. He didn't alter his body language, but he didn't weaken either, holding his ground. "I gave you a hundred," he stated, his words clear and concise. "If I passed you a dodgy twenty, why are you trying to give it back to me?"

"Because it's fake." The girl's eyes widened to show the whites, her chin wobbling and her mind betraying her with its erratic thoughts. Hana would have felt more sympathy for her if she hadn't flipped the blame onto Logan.

The queues on either side of them slowed as the other cashiers craned their necks to observe the origin of the drama. An unhealthy ache blossomed outwards from Hana's scar as adrenaline pumped through her bloodstream. Her mind fast forwarded to the potential outcome of the stand-off. Police. Accusations. Denials. A local resident's word against theirs. It played out before her in slow motion, the island uniting behind the cashier. She knew how it worked because their township would behave in the same way. And had done.

She sighed and dropped to the ground in a crouch, bracing her soles against the tiled floor and clasping her arms around her stomach. But that single action unpicked Logan's resolve and split his loyalties. She saw the indecision in his eyes as he glanced down at her in alarm. "I'm fine," she said with a sigh, waving up at him from her position near the floor. "We don't want hooky money. Tell her to call the cops. I need to sit down, anyway. A bench in a cell is as good a place as any."

8

Deceive - pikika 'a

But the bench in the cell gave her no comfort. And Hana hated how the police officers separated her from Logan. It also freaked her out when they referred to it as prison. Which it was. And fully occupied.

Shiny vinyl encased the foam over the bed and it creaked as she moved. Old sweat and urine seemed ingrained into the concrete walls around her and she regretted leaning sideways and sniffing the mattress. "Yuk!" she hissed, realising she no longer wanted to remain sitting on it. So, she paced instead, round and around, until she grew dizzy.

"You okay?" The female voice echoed, and Hana whipped to face the door. A narrow opening revealed kind hazel eyes with laugh lines creasing their corners.

She nodded at the officer and then shook her head. "Not really." She sighed, clamping her arms around herself and moving towards the door. "We arrived last night, went to buy groceries, and got arrested for possessing fake cash." She shrugged. "You must have checked the security cameras by now. And the people in the queue behind us heard my husband refuse to accept his change because he recognised the fake."

"All in good time," the officer replied. A frown lined her brow. "You cold? Need a blanket?"

Hana paused and tuned into her body for long enough to notice herself shivering. The windowless cell concealed the time of day, and a chill had crept into the room. She nodded. "Thank you. Can you tell me if my husband is okay?"

"He's fine. Please step away from the door."

Hana skittered into the corner without touching the walls. An illusion of unreality and displacement misted her vision as keys clattered against a heavy lock and the hinges creaked.

"Blanket." The officer stepped into the cell and tossed a folded square onto the mattress. The room echoed with the dull thud punctuated by a creak as the vinyl accommodated its weight. Her pale blue shirt held creases like knife blades in the sleeves, and she brought the scent of clean soap and floral shampoo into the room with her. Damp hair pulled into a tight ponytail gave her head an egg shape, which jarred with her circular face. An armoured vest stressed the illusion of roundness. Dumpy legs poked from the bottom like scissors.

Hana ran a hand through her hair, distracted when her fingers tangled in the curls. The happy blush of her afternoon romp with Logan seemed a lifetime ago. Unfairness and resentment lit a fire behind her navel.

The officer's tone held neither anger nor sympathy. "I'll bring you a snack soon. Tea or coffee? Any allergies or dietary limitations?"

Hana shook her head. "I don't intend to stay here long enough to eat," she replied, her tone clipped.

The officer raised a dark eyebrow. "We'll see." She turned away.

"Are there any embassies here?" Hana swallowed, the foolishness of her question evident in the officer's widening eyes.

"Rarotonga has a free association with New Zealand. Why do you need an embassy?"

Hana ground her teeth until her jaw ached. "I'm a British citizen," she said, claiming her dual nationality for the first time in over three decades. "We're the victims of an attempted crime and of a wrongful arrest. We're at least entitled to see a duty solicitor."

The officer's face softened, and she dropped her chin, her lips flattened into a sad line. "I understand," she said. "Keep warm and I'll bring in some dinner soon." She turned away and the creaking hinges signified the definite end of the conversation.

"My husband is a haemophiliac," she gushed, rushing towards the door. "It's a blood disease."

The door clanged, and the officer's kind eyes appeared between the slot. "I know what it is," she said, her tone soothing.

"He won't say anything." Hana's fingers writhed together like churning water. "He doesn't tell people."

The officer's eyes curved upwards like almonds and the creases became more defined in the corners. "It's okay," she appeased. "We won't beat him until morning."

A metallic click ricocheted around the cell and the slot disappeared. Hana seized on the jovial tone in the woman's voice and held onto it. The association with New Zealand meant they shared the same currency and the same laws. Hana's son refuted every claim of police brutality in the media and she prayed the same applied on the tiny island. But it didn't stop her wishing they'd stayed home.

She slumped onto the plastic mattress cover, settling herself between the rips which dotted its surface. The blanket held a worn appearance and despite its neat folds, sweat mingled with alcohol ingrained into its scratchy fabric. No amount of laundering could ever make it smell fresh. So Hana ignored it and wrapped her arms around herself. She bent at the waist, curling herself into an arc around her thighs.

A gangly male officer had booked her and Logan into the prison. Hana had sat on a low bench and watched her husband remove his cowboy boots and relinquish his leather belt, watch, wallet, phone, and the St. Christopher necklace she'd given him years earlier. He'd glanced back at her once and offered a reassuring smile. She imagined him wishing he'd just accepted the dud twenty and destroyed it back at the villa. But it wasn't in his nature to endure injustice and so here they would spend their first evening in Rarotonga.

Hana closed her eyes and focussed on the blossoming ache, which began at her liver and wended its merry way through her thighs to mirror its journey along her ribs. And she figured it was a good thing that Christians didn't curse other people. Otherwise, the lying girl at the supermarket checkout would most definitely drop dead. Like a chunk of Rarotongan stone.

9

Accuse - ‘akapari

The police officer lifted Logan’s wallet from a tray and flipped it open like a mouth. A pile of hundreds slid free, clean and straight and new. The twenty-dollar note appeared rumpled and valueless next to them, its edges bent and a rip along the centre fold. “Contact my bank,” Logan growled. His tone held more reasonableness than his stiff body language. “They’ll tell you the numbers of the notes I drew from the cash-point yesterday. I bought coffee at Auckland airport which will show I used my card. We arrived in the middle of the night and this is the first time we’ve left the resort.” He cocked his head and stared at the police officer, engaging in the silent war of wills between them. “There’s a security camera over the checkout line. Look at the footage.”

Hana blew out an exasperated breath and bent double, folding herself so her vision encompassed her knees. Hairy knees. She groaned, ruing her failure with the razor after a month of poor self care. Her lips tightened as she hauled her skirt hem over her legs and straightened.

Shadows lined the corners of the interview room, the dim bulb dangling naked from its centre and unable to banish the night. The sergeant had interviewed them separately and then together, getting the same answers to his barrage of questions. He fingered the crisp hundred dollar notes, and Hana frowned, wondering if the action hinted at a bribe. She pursed her lips and took more interest. Surely not.

A knock on the door halted the proceedings and the female officer left her sentry position to answer it. Whispering echoed from the corridor outside and the sergeant scraped his chair back and added his bowed head to the discussion.

"Cameras broke a while ago," he announced, the first inkling of genuine regret in his voice. He thudded into his plastic bucket seat. "And there's confusion about what happened."

Logan's chin rose, and he treated the sergeant to one of his most chilling glares. "What confusion?" Sarcasm oozed from the short sentence.

The officer's wrist bones protruded through his skin as though he lacked a nutritious diet. He slumped against the back of his seat, gratified by a resounding creak. The pallor of the delicate bags beneath his brown eyes reminded her of the jaundice she'd fought following her surgery. She cringed at the memory of Phoenix asking her if she'd like Marge Simpson's blue hair to go with her yellow face. The man sighed with tiredness, and Hana spared him a split second of sympathy. He looked young enough to be Bodie's age and her son had already spent more than a decade married to the New Zealand Police Force. She flexed her fingers and forced herself to relax. The sergeant touched the hundred dollar notes again, as though enjoying the contact with the shiny paper. His fingernail tapped the forehead of Lord Rutherford of Nelson. "The witnesses provided different statements," he said with a sigh. "The cashier claims you gave her the counterfeit twenty-dollar note, but a tourist in the queue behind you says you handed over a hundred and objected immediately to the twenty."

"So?" Logan shrugged. "Charge me or release me. My wife has nothing to do with this, so whatever happens to me, please escort her back to our villa. I've requested legal assistance and yet seen no lawyer. I've asked for a phone call and no one let me make one. The Cook Islands Police follow the same legislation as New Zealand, so we're exercising our right to leave your custody now." Logan rose, his head almost touching the low ceiling. He tucked his tee shirt into his sagging jeans, and Hana noticed the whiteness of his knuckles. Her knees wobbled as she pushed herself to a standing position, using the edge of the table to force herself upright.

"Wait," the sergeant said, his exhaustion creating fine lines along his jutting jaw. "Please, just wait."

Logan turned sideways and observed Hana through his intense grey eyes. Her world narrowed to just the two of them. The tired police décor and the officer's confusion distorted to vague smudges in her peripheral vision. She focussed on her husband.

"Are you okay?" he asked her. His right hand rose in an instinctive motion to cup her chin. Scarred fingers with work coarsened pads stroked her face with exaggerated softness. "What do you need?"

Hana sighed, her shoulders drooping. She lowered her voice. "I hate to admit it, but a phone call to the judge might help." She rolled her eyes in an exaggerated wince. "And if you ever tell anyone I asked for Judge Eliza Du Rose's help, I'll deny it."

Creases appeared in the corners of Logan's eyes, but he dipped his head to increase the sense of seriousness. "Do you mean The Right Honourable Eliza Miriam Kaiora Du Rose? You need to use her full title if you're invoking her terrible spirit." His lips quirked upwards to match the humour in his eyes. "I suspect the police station will combust under her rage."

"Maybe." Hana lifted her fingers and clasped Logan's hand. As long as they remained in the same room, she knew she'd cope. His unshakable confidence infused her with assurance. This day would end.

The police sergeant rose and held up his hand, palm outward, in a universal sign of peace. "No need to call judges," he said, his voice jerky. He shot a glance at the officer still standing sentry by the unlocked door. "Maybe coffee, instead." He cocked his head at her and Hana gritted her teeth at the inference that the only female authority in the room assumed waitress duty. She practised funnelling the irritated breaths through her nose, though she hadn't done yoga for months. The door clicked shut, though the woman left without taking coffee orders. The sergeant shuffled pages in front of him. He slipped them into a brown cardboard folder and rested his hands on top of it. Then he studied them in turn, as though needing to regain his superiority as it slipped away in the glare of Logan's natural mana.

"Call the bank. ASB in Auckland. I have the emergency number in my phone, but you'll need to use your land-line to speak to them." Logan jerked his head towards the tray containing his confiscated mobile.

The sergeant's shoulders sank lower, and he switched his gaze to Hana. She imagined him labelling her as the weak link in the team. Right then, it made for a correct diagnosis. Her side ached, her scar prickled and hunger set up a cacophony of sounds in her digestive system. She fought an inappropriate smirk. If he didn't release them soon, she'd pee herself, or worse. She focussed on the officer's name tag, which hung at a jaunty angle over his left shirt pocket.

Sergeant Wally George tutted. "New Zealand is twenty-three hours ahead of us," he announced. He flipped over his left wrist and examined his watch. "The bank is closed, but I'll email them tonight. Please, sit down."

Island time, Hana thought. They'd arrive at Auckland Airport before the bank replied and the sergeant galvanised himself to respond. Rapid blinking blurred her vision. Unless he forced them to remain behind after their flight left for home. What then? Her mind ran amok at the litany of problems their delay threatened. She catastrophised in her own head and missed the sergeant's next sentence.

"Counterfeit currency is a disaster for our island economy," he said. Hana picked up the gist of the conversation, taking her cue from Logan, who listened with a blank expression. "If our cash becomes worthless, so does our reputation. It's an ongoing battle."

Logan exhaled but he accepted the order to lower himself into the chair. Hana followed his lead. "Why are you labouring this to us? We didn't bring the cash to the island. We're victims of your local traders trying to pass fake notes to us." He shrugged. "I'll tell you what, search our villa. Turn it inside out. You'll find nothing in our belongings. Do that, email the bank, and release us." He turned to smile at Hana, his lips flat in a silent concession. She slipped her fingers through his in response as he protested on her behalf. The plastic seat didn't help the ache in her side. She squirmed in discomfort.

Then Logan rose for the second time, dragging Hana alongside him. "We're leaving," he stated, a menacing edge in his tone. "If this is how you treat visitors, we'll catch the next flight out of here. This holiday sucks." Logan placed his giant hand on Hana's shoulder and edged her ahead of him. He leaned across to snatch his belongings from the tray in front of Sergeant Wally George. The notes crinkled as he stuffed them into his jeans pocket, the villa key and his phone clanking against one another in his hand. His belt whipped the air as he collected it with his sunglasses, the crack of the leather both deliberate and menacing.

Hana padded to the door, her reclaimed sandals squeaking against the floorboards. The female officer had returned their footwear and Hana's handbag before leading them to the interview room. The thin strap dug into her shoulder as she clutched the bag to her stomach. It contained prescription medication and an unopened packet of tissues. She'd seen no point carrying her empty wallet or useless phone. Logan followed her to the door, his fingers against her spine, guiding her through the gap and into the corridor. He took her hand in the narrow hallway, tracking the yellow glare of the reception's light bulb. She jogged to keep up with his angry strides, puffing as they passed the surprised desk officer and burst out onto the front steps.

The fading light cast a rippled effect over the concrete pavement at the bottom of the steps. It took a moment for Hana to register the corrugated detail and the shadowy stains from wear and tear. The potted palms in the irregular planters appeared thirsty and sick, their leaves yellowing with neglect. "What should we do now?" Her voice held a nervous catch, which came from the back of her throat.

Logan blew out an aggravated snort. "I don't know about you," he breathed, "but I need a stiff drink."

10

Liquor - kava papa 'a

A walk along the seafront revealed a blinding array of sparkles on the water. The light caught the ridged waves and put on a stunning show. Hana stumbled next to Logan, her fingers clamped around his forearm. "Where are we going?" she puffed.

"There," Logan replied. The gentle lapping of the sea against the low harbour faded beneath a roar of laughter. The voices carried on the quickening breeze and Logan steered Hana towards them as though following a beacon. She tensed as they entered the sprawling bar via low steps, noise and light folding them into its beer scented embrace.

Not a single person showed an interest in their presence. Logan gripped Hana's right hand and towed her through the crowd to the bar. He shouted over another roar of hearty laughter and a woman behind the counter nodded and reached for a glass tumbler.

Hana protected her side with her opposite arm, wrapping it around her and snagging a handful of her dress to maintain her grip. Logan didn't release her other hand, not even when he dug in his pocket for his wallet. Hana held her breath.

But he didn't use cash to pay for the neat whiskey or the foaming glass of ice cold soda. Logan tugged a plastic card from within the folds of his wallet and the server handed him a digital terminal. He tapped the screen with his card and the machine trilled a successful payment. Hana forced the rigidity from her spine and shoulders and blinked around her at the sea of bodies.

People stood with their drinks or rested them on raised tables. The jovial mood acted as a balm for her rattled soul. Logan jerked his head through the open frontage to the outside and released Hana's hand so she could pick her way towards it. She recognised faces from their flight to the island but saw no empty seats at the wooden tables. A group of heavyset men bunched around a high table, elbows propped on the wooden surface. They sipped foaming pints of amber liquid. Hana had noticed one of them at Auckland airport and allowed her gaze to linger on his uniform of a shaved head and brawny arms. She'd also seen him eating breakfast at Paradise Villas and absentmindedly decided he was a nightclub bouncer. The group laughed as a collective like bachelors enjoying a last hurrah before enclosing their ring fingers into bands of gold. Shooting her an upward jerk of his chin in recognition, the man ruined the effect by winking at her. Hana glanced away, feeling embarrassed for staring.

Logan spun and leaned his spine against a metal railing, a boat bobbing in the shallow harbour behind him. "Hope this is okay," he said, handing the soda to Hana. When she glanced back at the bachelors, the man had spotted Logan and turned back to his mates as though bowing out to a recognisable alpha.

"Thank you," she replied, taking the soda from her husband. Condensation trickled over her fingers as she gripped the glass and sipped the welcome contents. The thirst hit her and the sips turned to gulps. Carbonated soda exploded in her mouth and the back of her throat and took her breath away. She paused and wiped her lips with the back of her hand.

A woman at a nearby table noticed Logan, and her interest grazed him from head to toe and back again. Hana recoiled against the greedy sparkle in her eyes. She'd seen it before a million times. It never got easier to bear, the cost of marriage to a man so oblivious to his devastating beauty. Her fingers tightened around her glass and she reached out with her other hand and hooked her index finger over his waistband. The action seemed both ridiculous and important at the same time. The woman glanced away, and Hana exhaled.

"Sorry," Logan said. He downed the whiskey in two short swigs and stared into the empty tumbler. "About the compulsory police station visit."

Hana shrugged. "Not a novel experience," she admitted. "For you."

Creases appeared at the outer edges of his smiling eyes. "This is true. But I can't blame a brush with the law here on my skin colour."

Hana stared around them at the merry drinkers. A decent mixture of patrons laughed or chatted. Most tourists, but some islanders. The scent of hot chips wafted from the bar's interior and Logan groaned. "Why didn't we stay at the villa and eat sandwiches? Wait here a second." He strode across a momentarily clear area of the veranda and vanished inside the low slung building. Hana turned to lean her back against the rail, watching his dark head as he weaved towards the bar.

"Hana?" She heard her name and cast around for the speaker, unable to pick out any familiar face from the crowd. An arm rose, and a hand waved, beckoning fingers at its apex. A group at a table in the corner turned to stare at Hana as one.

"Oh. Hi." Jared's greeting didn't contain the same level of enthusiasm as his wife's. He leaned sideways on the bench seat and stared at a point near Hana's feet. "Where's your shopping?"

An audible groan escaped Hana's throat. With Logan's wallet ninety-five dollars lighter, they had nothing to show for the expense. Well, if she didn't count the wasted two hours in custody, and a worrying stickiness at the back of her skirt from the vinyl mattress in the cell. Hana forced a smile onto her lips and leaned sideways, desperate for Logan's assistance in fabricating the lie they must surely tell. He glanced at her from his place in a queue for the bar, caught her eye, and frowned.

"Sit with us," Hallie trilled. She shuffled sideways on the bench and extracted her right leg to straddle the awkward table struts. She yanked on Jared's sleeve and with a visible reluctance, he slid along next to her. Hana edged towards them, shooting anxious glances at the side of Logan's face as he spoke to the girl behind the bar. He looked up, and she jerked her head in the harbour's direction. She hoped he'd assume she'd found a seat and not been kidnapped when he emerged to find her gone. Hana dumped her glass in the free space on the table and pressed her skirt between her thighs, hoping to preserve her dignity as she clambered over the sloped leg of the table. She thudded onto the bench next to Jared with a hiss of pain.

"Hi." The resort owner observed her from the other side of the table. His lips parted as though he wished to say something more, but then he clamped them shut again. A woman beside him elbowed him in the ribs. Hana recognised the receptionist from the resort.

"Introduce us then, Craig," she said, her tone harsh. She eyed Hana with curiosity and veiled suspicion. The narrowing of her eyes invited an understanding which caused Hana to bridle inwardly. The woman had identified her as some kind of threat. Hana forced a fake smile onto her lips and tamped down the rising shudder. If Craig played away with tourists, he could scrub Hana willingly from his wife's hit list.

Skill with foundation and eye-liner disguised the woman's age. As Hana reached across and shook the offered hand, she noted the fine lines and creases over her knuckles and the papery texture of her skin. Hana's porcelain tones jarred with the sun damage and uneven tan lines on the other woman's wrists and arms. "Nice to meet you, Sally," Hana responded as Craig made the introductions.

Sally Henderson's voice held a screechy quality, which set Hana's teeth on edge. Her combative air jarred with Hallie's jovial innocence from the other end of the table. Hana exhaled with relief as Logan's head appeared above the crowd. But if she'd hoped for rescue and escape, he disappointed her. "I ordered food," he said, squatting next to her. He placed a metal spindle bearing a number on the table next to her soda. Hana eyed the cursive font and her shoulders slumped. The group next to them had number twelve, but Logan's order had fifty-eight. They'd need to remain in the crowded bar for ages.

"Sit with us," Sally gushed. Her voice lowered to a seductive huskiness and her blue eyes flashed. She didn't wait for Craig to introduce her to Logan. She half rose and jabbed her hip into her companion's arm. Craig grunted and shifted sideways. He moved just enough to comply, but not creating room to give Logan a comfortable perch for his backside. Logan twisted his lips at Hana and slipped only one leg between the table and the bench. The other straddled the sloping leg and created a gap next to Sally's bare thigh. A crease lined her forehead as the move scuppered her obvious game plan. Blonde curls covered her head in orderly waves, the roots showing through red as though attempting an escape. Sally's halter dress fitted where it touched, leaving most of her torso exposed to the warm evening air. Goosebumps caused the tiny hairs on her arms to rise, and Hana wasn't sure if they responded to the breeze, or to the proximity of Logan's magnetic testosterone. She wished they'd just gone back to the villa.

Logan's grey irises glittered, betraying his discomfort to Hana. He loathed the uninvited touch of strangers, especially women who liked to prod his chest, squeeze his biceps, and contort themselves during inane conversation to not-so-innocently stroke any exposed skin. Logan pinned his elbows to his sides and avoided Sally's adoring glances as she stroked his chiselled jawline with her covetous gaze.

"Sorry," Logan mouthed again to Hana. His lips flattened into a line of displeasure. "They don't serve takeaway food. We'll need to eat it here."

As though conjured by a genie, a waitress navigated the crowd of standing patrons bearing three plates loaded with burgers and fries. Hana blinked in surprise as she dumped them in the centre of the table. Before she could comment on Logan's raging hunger, Jared snatched up the nearest platter and passed it to Hallie. Hana groaned and dipped forward to catch Hallie's attention. "Sorry," she called. "We've gate crashed your dinner."

"All good," Hallie trilled. She waved the fork in her left hand and the prongs caught in the fabric of Jared's blue shirt. She extracted it without embarrassment and jabbed it towards Hana's non-alcoholic glass. "Oh, goody!" she cried. "Sober driver! You're it!"

The evening went further downhill from that moment. Having made Hana their designated driver, the resort manager, his wife, and their two guests went on a mission to get absolutely trollied. The alcohol flowed from the bar like a river, Craig in possession of a tab as a local business owner. Logan finished his whiskey after satiating his hunger with hoki and chips. He extracted himself from Sally's groping fingers and returned to the bar. Hallie followed him, weaving towards the bathroom. Hana picked at her plate of chips and sifted through a mental list of sins as Jared and Craig argued over a horse race. She figured she'd inadvertently committed a doozy to have earned such a punishment. After a few minutes, she rose too and navigated her way to the women's bathroom.

Hana picked the stall nearest to the door. She'd once asked Logan, which was statistically the cleaner, unsurprised when he'd known the answer. Despite her inclination to head as far away from other bathroom users as possible, she'd restrained herself. The other two remained occupied as she flushed and washed her hands with soap and water. A woman in her twenties staggered from the middle stall and left without using the sink. Hana wrinkled her nose and turned back to her own stall to snag a wad of toilet paper to assist her exit using the door handle. As she wound a sufficient amount around her fingers to protect them, she heard sniffing from the toilet nearest the wall.

"Are you okay in there?" The tissue muffled the sound of her fingers knocking against the wooden door. "Do you need some help?"

"Nope." Hallie gave a hiccough of distress. "I'm okay."

"Shall I wait for you?"

A disgusting sniff filtered through the door. "I'm coming out now. Tell me something funny. I need to take my mind off it." She didn't elaborate, and Hana stared at her perplexed reflection in the mirror.

"Erm," she began, not finding anything to laugh about in her recent history. "We just got arrested in the supermarket."

"What?" The door swung open and Hallie faced her. She'd cried her makeup into a series of dark lines and smudges across her face. She walked to the sink and ran cool water into her hand before dabbing it over her cheeks. "Who arrested you?" The question seemed odd. She hadn't asked the most obvious one first. Why?

"A Sergeant Wally George," Hana answered. She wished she hadn't mentioned it, shame burning up her chest and into her neck. It flared across her cheeks. "Misunderstanding. Forget I mentioned it."

Hallie glared at Hana's reflection in the mirror. "I know him," she admitted. "They all seem so sincere, don't they? When you're giving them what they want?" She turned her attention to her face, dabbing at her eyelids with a scratchy paper towel.

"Who, cops?" Hana put her weight into her right hip and leaned against the vanity.

"No." Hallie shook her head. "Men." She held out her hand for Hana's ball of tissue and took it without thanks. She blew her nose into it before ditching it in the dustbin. Waggling her head as though giving herself a mental shake, she yanked the main door open.

Hana followed her back to the table and slipped into her seat. A heaviness had descended over her and she yearned to go back to the villa and enjoy the silence.

Logan returned with a glass of cola for himself and another soda for her. He raised an eyebrow, telling her without words that the clock ticked towards their exit. In less than ten minutes, he'd downed his drink and wiped his mouth on the back of his hand. Hallie went to the bar for another glass of wine and weaved back to the table, appearing uncoordinated and giggly. More damp streaks on her cheeks caused her foundation to spread outward in orange lines. Hana eyed her with concern, wondering if she'd argued with Jared again, though he hadn't yet left the table.

With each fresh glass of gin poured from a pitcher on a tray in the centre of the table, Sally grew more handsy. Her largesse movements groped every part of Logan she could reach. At one point, she waved her right hand in a dramatic arc before placing it on his thigh without apparent shame. He used the cuff of her flouncy sleeve to lift her wrist and place her dangling hand on the table, an action not dissimilar to a crane depositing a hod of bricks on a building site. Even the double whiskey hadn't spoiled his reactions. His lips pulled back from his teeth in a snarl, and Hana rose at speed. She caught her stomach against the sharp table edge. "We're leaving now," she said, her tone decisive. She slipped her bag strap over her head and one shoulder, freeing her hands for the awkward climb from the bench. "If you want me to drive, you can come with us now."

Jared had made the mistake of leaving the car keys on the table beside his wallet. Hana snatched them into her palm and looped the ring around her index finger. None of the drunks had considered the difficulty of squeezing six people into a five-seater vehicle.

"I'm coming!" Sally declared. She released a raucous hyena imitation as she fumbled standing and slipped backwards from the bench. Hana observed her thrashing between the railing and the seat, holding out her arms to Logan. Despite the volume of alcohol she'd imbibed, her eyes lacked the haziness of Hallie's blown pupils. Hana pursed her lips and her glare at Logan warned him not to get sucked into the ruse.

"We'll stay," Jared slurred. "Craig brought his car."

The resort owner listed to one side and hiccoughed, his head nodding as though he intended to loosen it from his stalk of a neck. Hana sent a silent arrow of grateful prayer zinging to heaven that they didn't need to rely on Craig for a ride back to the villas. But she caught the nasty glare he sent in Sally's direction and doubted the extent of his intoxication. His lips pursed into a line at Sally's shrill laughter and a flash of realisation told Hana his wife embarrassed him. She glanced at Logan and her confidence sank a little lower as she wondered if he ever viewed her with the same critical eye. A moment of sympathy extended towards Sally as a fine tendril as the mask fell away. She saw a vulnerable woman who sensed she rated poorly in her husband's eyes and over corrected to compensate.

"I'm leaving now too," Hallie declared. She extracted herself from the bench, sending cutlery clattering to the deck from the towering pile of plates beside her. "I feel sick."

Hana heard Logan's throaty groan. He reached for her hand and they turned in unison. "Don't let either of them sit behind me," she hissed.

Logan lowered his head to reply. "I'm not sitting in the back seat with Sally. You can't make me. I've spent the last hour defending my crotch under the table."

Hana's lips pursed tighter, and she shook her head. A glance behind them revealed Hallie using the railing to steer herself towards the steps and Sally tilting her head to get an eyeful of Logan's backside. She sighed and asked, "When's the next flight out of here?"

11

Revelry - kariei

Hana drove with exaggerated care, heading anticlockwise on the main road. She followed a wobbling snake of yellow scooters past the airport and the hospital, keeping away from their weaving back wheels. Two of them carried passengers, only one rider in the group wearing a helmet. A warm breeze blew her hair back from her face and she relaxed, enjoying the sense of freedom.

Then the convertible's engine burped and performed bunny hops as Hana changed down to second gear. "Fantastic!" she groaned. The red and blue strobing lights of an emergency vehicle lit the darkness ahead of them like a misplaced disco.

Logan turned to face Hallie. "Is this car roadworthy?" he demanded. The question seemed a little late after having already driven most of the way back to the villas.

Hana pulled the vehicle over to the left and stopped. She killed the lights and the engine. Turning in her seat, she found Hallie lolling sideways, a line of dribble speckling her chin and her mouth open. Light snores issued from between her lips. Sally smirked and spoke to Logan, ignoring Hana as though she didn't exist. "Jared picked this up from a mate on the island," she purred. "He's not renowned for taking care of his stuff."

Hana leaned forward and peered at the sticker clinging to the top right-hand corner of the windscreen. Scuffed and faded, it refused to divulge the date of the vehicle's last Warrant of Fitness.

"Oh." Logan peered at the registration sticker he'd peeled from the holder on his side. He flapped it at Hana before stuffing it back into place. "This is out of date."

"How out of date?" She winced and considered their dwindling options. "The owner has twenty-eight days to pay it."

Logan's right eyebrow rose high enough to vanish beneath his fringe. "2016," he growled. "This car is illegal."

"I'm not losing my licence for this!" Hana snapped. She glared at Hallie, noticing the snores grow heavier. "Let's walk back to the villa. How do I lift the hood in case it rains?"

The answer gave more difficulty than she'd imagined. A button on the dashboard activated a metallic grating sound, and the hood rose to half way before stalling. Only brute force by Logan hauled it creaking the rest of the way and hooked the relevant catches into place. The central locking didn't work. Hana secured the vehicle by walking around it and turning the key in each individual lock. She dropped the keyring into her handbag and closed the flap.

Out on the street, Hallie clasped Sally's right arm, her head lolling against her shoulder. Without warning, she jerked forwards from the waist and vomited between her sandals. Neat alcohol splashed in a wide arc around the women's feet and Sally released a piercing shriek of annoyance. Hana pressed her fingers over her mouth and turned away, willing herself not to join in the puke festival. Sally heaved as she peeled Hallie's fingers from around her arm and used a stray tissue to dab at her bare legs and expensive heels. "Stupid bitch! These are Jimmy Choos!" she complained, her volume rising.

Logan wrinkled his nose and pointed to a half-digested chip clinging to the pointy toe of her right foot. "Well," he offered, "I don't think he'll want them back now." He dodged sideways as Hallie made an uncoordinated lurch for his arm, her glistening fingers grabbing at the air. "You two can help each other," he suggested, striding towards Hana and clasping her hand.

Together, they walked towards the police checkpoint, maintaining a reasonable distance between themselves and the two women. Sally kept up a constant diatribe of complaint as Hallie clung to her and weaved a circuitous route along the street. The drunk woman lurched to a stop twice more to vomit into hedges belonging to unsuspecting locals.

Hana kept a careful eye on them, not wanting to abandon them in the darkness. She forced Logan to walk slower as they grew within twenty metres of the busy police officers. Four yellow scooters occupied the hard shoulder, parked at jaunty angles. Two of the drivers sat in the back of the police truck staring at their feet while their passengers milled around, seeming lost. "We need to wait for those two," Hana whispered. She turned to watch Sally administer an unkind shove to Hallie as the other woman attempted to lean against her. "I feel responsible for making sure they get home safely."

Logan snorted, a derisive sound which echoed off nearby houses. "They're not our problem," he growled. "Their husbands should take responsibility for them, not us! They couldn't wait to offload them. Nice guys."

Hana pursed her lips and released Logan's forearm. She walked back to retrieve Hallie from another hedge. Seeing Logan standing at the side of the road with his hands on his hips, Sally picked up speed and latched onto him. She glared back at Hana, her lips turned up in a coquettish smile, back-lit by a hint of victory. The renegade fry no longer occupied her pointed shoe, but it had left a greasy streak along the fabric. She clung to Logan and rose on tiptoes to whisper into his ear. He jerked away from her as though stung.

Hallie crawled from the hedge on her hands and knees, and Hana gave up trying to get her to her feet. The woman's ponytail hung at a sorry angle, the pretty floral scrunchie having slipped half way along it. The petals of a daffodil peeked from within as though trapped. Hallie had accidentally caught her skirt in her knickers, revealing too much thigh. Hana's side ached, and the scar complained each time she hauled on Hallie's arm. "What now?" she hissed to Logan.

He shrugged. Tiredness, jet lag, and a heady sense of disappointment at the awfulness of the holiday so far seemed to influence his reaction. "I don't really care," he announced. He shook off Sally's grip and raised his arms above his head to avoid her grappling fingers. "We're almost at the villas. Let them find their own way home."

Mortified, Hana gave Hallie's arm another valiant tug. She dropped it at speed and dodged sideways to avoid a stream of projectile vomit. "What's with this?" she demanded. "This is more than just alcohol. What did she eat?"

"Not the cop!" Hallie burbled. "Please not the cop! I'm okay. I promise, I'm okay."

Logan heaved out an exaggerated sigh. He spun in a circle to avoid Sally's pawing, and Hana sensed his last nerve snap. "You go back to the villa, but I'm not leaving her!" she hissed. "It's not right!"

"Fine!" he growled. Three strides carried him to her side. "I'm not leaving you either."

"Is everything okay here?" Sergeant Wally George stepped from the knot of flashing lights. His female offsider stopped writing a ticket for the scooter driver and looked in his direction. She shielded her eyes against the strobing glare and frowned at the sight of Logan and Hana. Her arms dropped to her sides, and she turned her body to follow her sergeant, distracted when the scooter driver clambered back onto his machine.

"No!" she shouted at him. An alcoholic haze shrouded his head. "You're way over the limit! Park the bike away from the traffic and hand over the keys. Find another way back to your resort." His voice rose in argument, ensuring she remained distracted and unable to join Sergeant Wally George in his enquiries.

"Why does she keep falling over?" He pointed towards Hallie and his dark brows drew into a concerned frown.

"I don't know." Hana took a step towards her but wrinkled her nose when Hallie released another stream of vomit onto the scrubby verge beside the bobbing purple heads of a hydrangea.

"Go away!" Hallie snarled, her throat constricting in another agonising retch. "It was a mistake. You're a mistake. I'm a mistake. My whole bloody life is a mistake. Don't touch me! You all had your chance. I'm done with it. Done!"

"Drunk?" he asked, his tone sad.

Hana switched her pity from Hallie to him. Rarotonga survived on the equity raised from the tourist trade, but it must gall him to spend his life cleaning up the results. His concerned frown slipped for long enough for Hana to glimpse the resignation beneath. "I don't think she's drunk," she replied, ignoring Logan's raised eyebrow in her peripheral vision. "She drank far less than the other people at her table."

"Mussels." Sally shadowed Logan, dogging his steps like a devoted spaniel. "We came across a man selling them near the harbour." A crease appeared in her nose as she conveyed her disgust. "I told her not to bother. You can't eat anything from inside the reef. And the locals didn't buy from him. That's a clue."

Sergeant Wally George's shoulders slumped. "What did he look like?" he demanded of Sally. He tugged a fat notebook from his shirt pocket. "Give me a description."

Sally's lips tightened, and she became mute. She slipped her arm through Logan's and tugged hard enough to unbalance him. "Can't remember," she mumbled. "Heaps of tourists bought from him. The low prices were a dead give-away." Something about her calculating smirk revealed the lie. There was no man selling seafood.

"Get off me!" Logan raised his voice, and the police officer blinked in surprise. Hana winced as her husband stepped away from Sally's grasping hands, smoothing his fingers along his forearms as though disengaging cobwebs. He bent at the waist and seized Hallie by the arms, hauling her upright. With an elegant dip of his torso, he absorbed her weight and flipped her over his shoulder like a hay bale. Sally sighed with delight and Hallie released an unladylike grunt. "Don't you dare puke on me," Logan warned and strode towards the entrance to Paradise Villas.

12

Cajole - vare

Logan dispatched Sally to fetch a spare key to Hallie's villa as he deposited her in a chair on her porch. Hana wrestled the woman onto her side in a semblance of the recovery position, unable to prevent her left arm hanging through the gap in the seat like a collapsed puppy. She rose to admire her handiwork and pressed a hand to her aching side. "Do you think she'll be okay?" she whispered.

Logan grunted and stepped off the porch. "First plane home," he growled.

"You go back to the villa and I'll wait for Sally." Hana settled into the chair opposite Hallie.

Logan grumbled and shook his head. He dug his fingers into his back pockets and turned away from her, taking up a sentry position at the bottom of the steps.

"I'm fine." Hallie roused herself and released a giant hiccough which rocked her body. She giggled at her own base humour. "You can go." She flapped a hand towards Hana. For the first time Hana noticed a red pinprick in the crook of her elbow, a bruise eking through the skin. "Why are we waiting?" Hallie snorted at the familiar sentence and broke into song, warbling the childish ditty resonant of bus rides, queues, and intense boredom. "Oh, why oh why are we wai-ai-ting?"

"Yes, lovely," Hana commented. She closed her eyes and avoided reading the irritation in Logan's rigid spine. She tuned in to the night noises, the chirp of crickets adding their percussion to the cluck and peck of the rogue chickens. A car engine rumbled nearby, and she strained her hearing enough to pick up the gentle hiss of the swimming pool filter sifting the day's dust and insects from the crystal blue water.

"Just go." Hallie rallied. She sat up straighter and placed her fingers in her lap. "No one is coming for me."

"What?" Hana cocked her head. "Do you mean Sally? She's fetching a spare key from the office."

Hallie snorted, the sound devoid of humour. "Stupid Sally. I know all about it. Craig hasn't got a clue." She cackled then, an eerie sound as though she'd called the devil from the earth.

Logan turned at the waist, his attention piqued. His cowboy boots still faced outwards, but his gaze raked Hana. "What's she talking about?"

Hana shrugged. She leaned forward in the wicker sofa which matched the one outside their villa, wincing against the dry creaking of the wood beneath her. "What do you know?" she asked, her tone light. She wondered why she cared, but the statement seemed oddly loaded for a drunk, late night revelation.

"Nothing." Hallie lifted her finger and thumb in a pincer action. "Nothing." Her voice trailed off. She cleared her throat and pulled herself together, straightening her shoulders and tugging her skirt over her knees. "Just go," she urged again. Her tone held sadness which plucked at the worn strings of Hana's heart.

"We can't leave you here alone," Hana replied. She glanced across at Logan and saw resignation in the set of his shoulders. "Leave no sister behind." She voiced the unofficial code which had dominated female thinking for generations. The words held an intimation; anything could happen.

"Just go, Miss Perfect." Hallie's features curved into an ugly snarl, a million miles away from her former affable visage. "Go to bed with your dreamy husband and don't give the rest of us another thought. People like you make me sick!" She dipped her torso as she administered the jibe, her breasts attempting to escape her low-cut bodice as her hands pressed against her stomach as though she might projectile vomit again. "Just bugger off!"

Hana jerked backwards as though slapped, aware of Logan making a full turn to face them. "Hey!" he rebuked. "That's enough!"

"Go away!" Hallie demanded. She tipped sideways on the narrow couch and rested her cheek against an upturned pillow. Her stilettos rose beneath her full skirt like a cat drawing up its paws.

A door banged somewhere close, and Hana imagined the patter of footsteps as Sally's. Logan held his hand out to her, bouncing his wrist once and flexing his fingers. "Come on, Hana," he said with determination. His upper lip curled from his teeth in distaste. He'd grown up surrounded by nasty drunks, and she sensed him reaching the outer limits of his patience. She rose and her sandals clicked against the boards of the porch.

"Night Hallie," she whispered, just in case the woman could still hear her. No reply, but that wasn't unexpected. She followed her angry husband to their villa and waited as he fitted the key into the lock on their front door. He swore, struggling as it failed to twist.

Then Hana remembered something, a flush rising from her chest to her neck as her error stressed her foolishness. "Oops," she said, slipping her hand into her bag. "I've still got their car keys." She lifted the loop and dangled the bunch for Logan to see. "I bet their villa key is on here, too. We made Sally run to the office to fetch a spare, and I had it all the time." She turned to run back to Hallie, her shoulder bumping Logan's forearm.

"No. Let the idiots take care of each other." Logan grunted and pushed their door open, holding the screen for Hana to slip through first.

"Oh," she said, her tone aghast.

Their room bore the hallmarks of a careless search. The clothing which Hana placed on hangars and in drawers just hours earlier lay strewn across the double bed. She side stepped their open suitcase, the zipper which housed the metal structure of the wheels and supports gaping. It reminded Hana too much of the stab wound in her side, the whitish-grey bulge of an intestine trying to escape through her fingers.

Logan stepped through the doorway and lifted a rumpled shirt from the floor at his feet. "Without a warrant," he hissed. "I expect our friendly neighbourhood resort manager oversaw the search."

A dull knocking caused Logan to spin around. His steps thudded back to Hana as a vibration. She heard

Craig's raised voice as though Logan's assumption had conjured his presence in reality. "Hello?" he called, his voice over-loud in the hush of the sleeping resort.

Logan wrenched the door open and glared at him. "What?" he snarled.

Craig's blond brows furrowed into a severe line. He pushed between Logan and the door, snagging his shirt on the handle when Logan stood his ground. "What are you doing?" He spread his arms and glared at the wrecked villa. "Why are you trashing it?"

Logan exhaled. He raised an eyebrow at Hana and sighed. "Well, that answers that," he concluded. He lifted a hand to halt Hana's tidying. "Leave it babe." His tone sounded dull. "The cops didn't do this."

Hana squeezed the bridge of her nose between thumb and finger. The tiredness, held at bay by stress, activity and sheer willpower, flooded through her veins like a chemical rush. It left her ragged and without energy. She sank onto the mattress, her sandal catching in the rumpled bedding strewn on the floor. "Burgled?" Her mind resisted acceptance, leaving her in a limbo between devastation and fear.

Logan rested his hand on the door handle, preparing to yank it open. But his gaze moved between Craig and Hana as he debated leaving her alone with him. She gave a feckless flap of her hand. "Go," she said with a sigh. "I'm okay."

"Two minutes." Logan held up the fingers as though to reinforce his promise. "Hopefully the cops are still at the entrance. Did you see Sergeant Wally George on your way in?" He watched Craig for a reply and the resort owner frowned.

"I left my car on the road," he admitted. "I had too much to drink. Yeah, they're there."

The door closed and the click of the screen followed it. Hana sensed the vibration of Logan's quick footsteps as he navigated the villas in the darkness. They lay like Jenga pieces in the silence.

"Why is he bothering with the cops?" Craig rested his hands on his hips and pirouetted on the tiles. His rubber soled beach shoes emitted a static squeak with each jerky turn. He stood in the dead centre of the villa, like the pin of a compass placed on a square page. "They're useless. Anyway, how do you know Sergeant Wally George?" he demanded. His tone held an unexpected harshness devoid of drunkenness. Hana blinked up at him.

"We just do," she replied, reluctant to serve up their evening of incarceration for his and Sally's amusement. She shrugged. "You should probably wait here for the police to arrive, but touch nothing."

Craig spun again, the squeak from his shoes cutting through Hana's brain like a cleaver. She covered her ears with her hands. "Can you take off your shoes? Or maybe just sit down for a minute?"

He glared at her before stalking towards the two-seater sofa. The contents of Hana's wash-bag covered the cushions, and he changed his mind and returned to the centre of the room. "How do you know Sergeant Wally George?" he demanded again.

"Why are you here?" Hana ran a tentative hand over her side before rising. Craig's caged tiger routine increased her sense of vulnerability.

"What?" He frowned. "Oh. Sal said you had Hallie with you."

Hana shook her head. She blinked at the sight of a lone bra strewn over the armchair. The left strap looped around a cushion as though hugging it. She pursed her lips, hoping Craig hadn't noticed the slinky black number which Leslie forced her to pack. It mocked her, the underwire in the cups forming twin smiles against the cream sofa. She pushed aside the sense of violation at a stranger handling her most intimate clothing. The emotion seemed wasted when Sergeant Wally George and Co would soon see it, too. Craig's words filtered through the tired mechanisms of her brain late. She stared at him in confusion. "No," she said with a definitive shake of her head. "Hallie's at her villa. Sally ran to fetch a spare key."

Craig's head jerked back on his neck as though his chin operated on a track. He resembled a mullet as his lips formed an inverted smile. "She isn't." Lines creased along his forehead. "Sally has the key, but can't find Hallie."

Hana blinked at him. Her mind ran through scenarios involving a wandering drunk woman. The recent pinprick in her elbow suggested either a medical issue or a foray into drugs. Not wanting to condemn Hallie without information, Hana pursed her lips and kept that gem to herself. "We left her literally three minutes ago," she said, her tone defensive. "We walked across the grass, let ourselves in here and found this mess." She spread her hands in disbelief. "And then you arrived." She dipped to peer into the bag hung across her body. Digging into its folds, she retrieved Jared's keys. "Here." She held them out towards Craig. "I forgot I had them. We left his car parked up the street when we noticed the police check. Logan pulled up the hood, and it's locked. He can fetch it in the morning."

Hana realised her mistake as Craig advanced to collect the keys. She should have stepped towards him and then at least she could retreat again. But he towered over her, his gaze speculative as he examined her from head to toe. He poked the end of a pink tongue through the seam between his lips and brushed her palm with his fingers as he lifted the keys from her hand. "Ah, Hana," he said, his tone soft and filled with hidden meaning.

She squirmed away from the narrow space he'd left her. Her right shoulder clattered against his chest and caused a bolt of pain to bloom in her side. He lifted his arms to enfold her, but missed his chance. Hana navigated the single armchair and skirted the coffee table, catching her shin on its wooden corner. But she'd achieved her aim and stood with her back to the front door. "Touch me again and I'll kill you," she stated, her words flat. "And if I'm not up to the task, my husband will finish it."

Craig snorted and lifted a corner of his lip into a sneer. "Whatever," he jibed. He clicked his thumb against his middle finger. "You'll keep," he stated.

Hana clamped her teeth hard enough to feel her molars grating. Rage bloomed in her chest at the injustice. She'd run over the question too many times to count and found no answer. Why did all lecherous men see her as fair game? She'd kept their attentions from Logan over the years, suffering the indignities, the inappropriate comments and the lewd suggestions without involving him. Perhaps she'd always feared he'd take their punishment too far. Like his grandfather had. But she found herself triggered by the arrogant tilt of Craig's chin and the cocky air he still exuded, despite the knock-back. She realised she'd enjoy watching Logan defend her honour against this man. She'd even help him hide the body.

13

Trouble - pekapeka

Logan arrived with the female officer in tow. He jogged up the steps and onto the porch, the loud clatter from his boots causing Craig to tense. The woman heaved herself through the door behind him, pausing to take in Hana, Craig, and the belongings strewn around the villa. Her hands settled over her hips and a deep vertical furrow dented her brow. "We didn't do this," she stated, her tone filled with defensiveness. She moved around the room, dispelling any hope of gathering forensic evidence. "Did you find the door unlocked when you returned?" she asked.

"Yeah." Logan nodded and settled beside Hana. He smoothed his fingers over her rigid shoulders. If he noticed the stiffness of her stance, he didn't mention it. She forced her muscles to relax. Logan's shrug vibrated through her body like an electrical connection. "I assumed you'd searched it."

"Why would the police search your villa?" Craig took a step towards Logan, his brown irises sparkling in the artificial light of the overhead bulb. "What did you do?" A note of panic lifted his voice as Sergeant Wally George stepped through the open doorway and winced.

"A misunderstanding," he stated, his tone even and calming. "Nothing for you to worry about."

Craig's lips flapped as though he wished to say more, and his gaze darted from Logan to Hana. "We don't need trouble here," he growled. "This industry is hard enough without having criminals on our site!"

"Calm yourself!" Sergeant Wally George spat the command as though unimpressed with Craig's hysteria. Hana pursed her lips and wondered at the resort owner's hypocrisy. He and Sally had sanctioned Jared's drunk driving and his illegal vehicle without a second thought. But his fear of Logan's potential criminality appeared genuine. She watched his colour alter from a heady puce flush to a ghoulish white. His fingers remained in perpetual motion, blond hairs sprouting from his knuckles. He'd thought nothing of forcing his attentions on her and her stomach did a threatening flip. She decided she would tell Logan and damn the consequences. Perhaps she could persuade him to switch to another resort instead of going home and ruining Mark's thoughtful and expensive gift.

But a glance at the underside of his jaw betrayed his determination. She wished she hadn't unpacked.

"Fingerprints?" Logan spoke to the police officer. "How often does this happen?"

Sergeant Wally George's lower lip curved upwards to obscure its mate. But the female officer provided the reply. "Not often." She sounded bemused, and it backed up her statement. "We have petty thefts and road traffic violations. The tourists bring most of the crime, to be honest." She smoothed soft fingers over the frizz escaping from her ponytail in the night air. "But I'll take some prints and see what we have on file. I'll share it with the mainland, which could yield a match." Her gaze drifted to Craig. "Do you have another villa for this family? Even just for tonight."

"No!" His head shook from side to side. "We're full."

Hana blinked in surprise. She'd seen the housekeeper servicing the empty villa next to Hallie's as she'd walked to the beach that morning. The sign on the road advertised six vacancies.

"Well, they can't stay here." Sergeant Wally George pulled open the door and inspected the handle. "Whoever came in here either picked the lock or they had a key. I'll call round some of the other resorts and let the owners know what's happened. Someone will have a vacant room."

"No, please don't do that!" Craig took a lurching step forward, his hands flapping in the air. Hana noticed the flash of victory in Sergeant Wally George's eyes. It lasted a millisecond before morphing into his habitual calm disinterest. A new respect for him took root in her chest. "Let me move some things around," Craig urged. "I'll check the office and come back to you." He strode across the floor with jerky steps, resembling the chickens which clucked to themselves in the darkness outside.

Sergeant Wally George stood aside to let him leave, but he opened the screen door with his foot and held out a hand to prevent Craig defacing the potential fingerprints. He jerked his head towards his female officer. "Go with him, Carrie," he advised, widening his eyes at her. "Radio when he finds something else. I don't want him traipsing all over this mess."

Her face creased into a sweet smile, and she bounced after Craig with a nod of acceptance. Hana found it difficult not to like the uniformed duo. Sergeant Wally George stared at the wall for a moment until Carrie's soft, padding footsteps crunched onto the gravel path. Then he let the door close behind him and faced Logan and Hana. He switched into business mode, holding his arm wide to encompass their scattered belongings. "Please, can you check what's missing?" he asked. "Try to do it without disturbing anything.

I'll take some photographs." He drew a phone from his trouser pocket and clicked about on the screen. "Don't get your hopes up, though. I don't expect to find a culprit."

Hana slipped away from Logan and moved around the room. She stepped over boxer shorts and tee shirts, embarrassed to find the matching slinky black knickers poking from beneath a loaf of bread on the kitchen floor. She jumped as Logan spoke into the silence. "Use this," he said, holding out his phone to her. Hana navigated her way back to him, frowning in confusion.

"What is it?" she asked, taking the device in her palm. His fingers brushed hers in the momentary contact before he released it. A photograph shone from the screen, a sheet of white paper covered with her handwriting. She smirked. "You're amazing." Despite the awfulness of their circumstances, Logan's precision and planning amused her. He'd snapped a photograph of the paper list she'd made when packing. It served as an itemised register of everything they'd brought with them. Her smile faded at the sight of what she'd written on the first line. "Passports." She gave a slow, agonised blink. "I bet they took our passports."

Sergeant Wally George raised an eyebrow at her and cocked his head. "Where did you keep them?"

"Here," Logan replied. He dug his fingers into his back pocket and held them up. "I brought a bag with me to wear around my waist but forgot to use it this afternoon after diving."

"Well done." Sergeant Wally George appeared impressed. "Rookie tourist mistake number one." He glossed over the fact Logan hadn't relinquished them in the police station.

Logan shrugged. He didn't justify his caution by listing his experience travelling Europe or living in the UK. He just stuffed the thin wallets back into his pocket and winked at Hana.

She forced herself to relax. Logan had the passports and the cash. All they'd left in the villa amounted to clothing and food. She moved around the villa with Logan's phone, checking off the items without disturbing them. Sergeant Wally George went ahead of her, snapping photographs and grunting to himself. Once satisfied with his work, he instructed Hana to collect up the fabric items, but leave anything which might have attracted fingerprints.

Logan watched their activity, standing like a sentry by the front door. His eyes held a glazed expression, as though his mind had entered another realm. When Sergeant Wally George approached him, he turned all his formidable Du Rose perception onto the officer. "What's really going on here?" he demanded.

14

Hard labour - ngatā

Sergeant Wally George paused for a moment and considered his answer. He pursed his lips and scrubbed at his eyes with the backs of his knuckles. Hana recognised the moment he levelled with them as his shoulders lost their tension. "We have a problem with counterfeit cash which pre-dates your visit." He glanced at the sofa as though he'd like to take the weight off his tired legs. Hana cringed at her sprawled underwear masquerading as seat covers. She stepped through the detritus and snatched up the clothing, bundling it into her arms and then dumping it onto the mattress.

"Tea anyone?" she asked with a sigh. "I only have long-life milk, though. We seem to have paid eighty dollars for groceries and come away empty-handed."

Sergeant Wally George nodded and sank onto the sofa cushions with a grunt. "Yes," he replied. "I'm sorry about that. I'll speak to the supermarket owner tomorrow and ask him to refund your money. It's not how we usually treat visitors to Rarotonga."

"So, what's the story?" Logan demanded. He turned a dining chair around and straddled the seat, leaning his forearms along the uppermost wooden spindle. "Is someone bringing the cash onto the island, or are they manufacturing it here?"

The police officer gaped at him. "We assumed someone brought it here." He scratched at his cheek, budding bristles creating a rough sound beneath his fingernails. "It's not possible to manufacture it on the island."

"Why not?" Logan cocked his head and observed him with interest. "Is that what the data tells you?"

Sergeant Wally George cleared his throat. "We ship all raw materials from the mainland, either by sea or air. We'd hear if someone imported a printing press, ink and a lorry load of special paper."

Logan shrugged. "Why would you? Someone is successfully transporting the finished product without you knowing, so how can you assume they aren't importing the individual components right under your nose?"

Sergeant Wally George groaned and dropped his gaze to his shiny black boots. He stared at them for a moment, as though they might hold the answers to Logan's question. Unable to oblige, he avoided it. "It's decimating our economy. We can't get to the root." He continued speaking, his voice a low rumble as Hana filled the kettle with water and set it on to boil. "Someone heard we had you in custody and came straight here." He lifted his arm in an expansive gesture to include the mess. "There's no doubt they wanted possession of any other cash you'd brought onto the island."

Hana shrugged. "I guess it's clear profit if they can find it, isn't it? They can swap worthless paper for goods. It's a win for them as long as they don't get caught." She turned and leaned her hip against the counter.

Sergeant Wally George shook his head. "It's not that simple. Everyone is aware of the fake problem. Last month, we had an issue with hundred dollar notes. The month before we found the fake fifties. It appears this month it's twenties. There's no recompense for traders who accept the counterfeits through error. They turn them over to us, but the goods and services are gone. It affects their profit margins. No one is happy about it. The Commissioner of Police in the Cook Islands is pressuring us to solve it." He spread his arms in defeat. "But how can we? Fourteen thousand residents live on Rarotonga, but last year we saw over one hundred and seventy thousand visitors. The population changes every seven days. It's like chasing fog."

"What are you thinking?" Logan stared at Hana, his expression sharp and perceptive.

Hana looked around her at their devastated belongings. "I'm thinking this burglary isn't connected to the actual counterfeiters or their suppliers."

"Why?" Sergeant Wally George's head jerked back on his neck and he spread his hands in question.

Hana shrugged. "Because they know we're not involved. The people behind this will have a tight net over their supply and distribution chains. Whoever searched our villa did so, hoping to find free cash. They're either a vigilante or a chancer."

"How did they know the police arrested us?" Logan asked her. He closed his eyes as though sifting through every face he'd seen at the police station.

"Heaps of people saw us led away," she said, a scoff of irritation in her voice. "It's a tiny island." She jerked her head at Sergeant Wally George. "I bet the cashier made her statement in the middle of the supermarket for everyone to hear, didn't she? We're unknown faces. I bet no one will serve us tomorrow from one end of the island to the other."

Sergeant Wally George had the decency to wince. "I'll put that right," he promised. "I'm sorry."

Hana sidled next to Logan, her shoulder bumping his biceps as she lined up her feet next to his. She cocked her head at the police sergeant. "Are you saying you believe us?" she demanded. "You know we didn't import hooky cash?"

Sergeant Wally George shrugged. "Yeah. I spoke to a friend in Auckland CID. He told me about your latest troubles and I took a wild guess why you're here." He jerked his head towards Hana's side. "Not much of a recuperation for you so far, though, is it?" His tone held sadness, as though the besmirching of Rarotonga's reputation caused him personal pain.

Heavy footsteps plodded up the porch steps and Craig barrelled through the front door, holding a key aloft in his fingers. The squareness of his jaw betrayed his displeasure. "You can move to the villa behind you," he growled. "But only for tonight."

15

Rough seas - ngaru

Hana slept deep and late, her red hair sprawled across her pillow. She woke as though drugged, her lids heavy and her muscles reluctant to engage. She stretched her hand across to Logan's side of the bed, finding cool sheets and a dented pillow beneath her groping fingers. "Logan?" Her voice sounded scratchy. Fear seized her chest and squeezed. She pushed herself onto her elbows, a gnawing ache spreading across her stomach. "Logan?"

Her feet hit the cool tiles with a thud, her thin nightdress pulling taut across her thighs as she turned sideways on the mattress and sat there for a moment. Light flooded the villa, but the orientation confused her. She blinked at the unfamiliar room with the bed on the right and the kitchen on the left of the rectangular space. Her mind struggled with the mirror image, as though her brain had somehow reversed her reality.

She rose and padded around the villa, logic promising she'd find the bathroom behind the kitchen. But the room contained none of her things, the towels hanging white and sterile on the rail. Hana used the toilet and washed her hands, letting the warm water soothe her fingers.

Logan had left no trace of his existence in the villa, apart from the dent in the pillow where his head had rested. Hana remembered him folding his clothes and laying them on the armchair when they'd crawled into bed after two in the morning. Their absence, along with his cowboy boots, meant he'd dressed and left before she woke. Hana circled the villa once more, feeling feckless and cast adrift. The sensation held a soulful note of familiarity, like the well-worn groove of hopelessness she'd occupied of late. Her watch gave the time as just after nine, and she steeled her spine and opted to take back control.

Hana kept her lips pursed during her shower to avoid swallowing the water by accident. She used the courtesy products on her hair and body, emerging slick and pink from the cubicle. The previous day's sun had kissed her skin and the scar along her side looked less raised and angry. The clean towels had a thinness to them as though they'd experienced the washing machine one time too many. She used the last of the cheap conditioner as a gel on her curls, raking her fingers through the knots and smoothing out the frizz. It galled Hana to step into yesterday's clothes, but she promised herself she'd change as soon as she gained access to her suitcase.

She tidied the bed and strung the towels over the heated rail to dry. Her sandals clicked against the tiled floor as she tried the front door handle. Someone had locked it from the outside and it resisted the downward pressure of her fingers. Hana noticed the internal catch and gave it a definitive twist. It clicked, and the handle depressed, allowing the door to swing inward towards her. The screen door opened outward and Hana stepped onto the porch. The villa now contained nothing belonging to her or Logan, and she left without looking back at its yawning entrance.

Sergeant Wally George's voice carried through the silence, backed by jovial laughter. Hana paused on the steps and cocked her head, her muscles giving an involuntary twist of warning. His voice triggered a fear reaction. Her fleeting connection with him had involved two horrible incidents, an arrest and a burglary. "Mark said we should enjoy Paradise," she whispered with a sigh of regret. Her brother and his husband had loved Rarotonga, but no one had passed them fake money or locked them inside a police cell.

Hana edged towards the back of the villa they'd vacated after midnight. She rested her palm against the warm siding on the left-hand corner. The heady scent of hydrangeas filled her nostrils, coupled with the earthiness of freshly mowed grass. Sergeant Wally George spoke again, and Hana tilted her head back, tracking the sound to the narrow window above her. She recognised it as the one above the double bed, the one from which she'd watched Craig arguing with Jared just the day before.

She spread her fingers against the wood, her thumb smoothing the raised splinters. The early warmth blurred everything in sight with a haze of steam as it superheated the moisture gathered overnight in the tangle of villas. Hana lifted her eyes to the sun's refracted rays and closed her eyes.

"What the hell do you think you're doing?" The voice contained enough venom to make her jump back. She clattered her elbow against the building, her eyes snapping wide and frightened. Craig loomed above her, casting her into shadow. His fingers closed around her wrist, his grip firm and his pressure blanching the colour from Hana's delicate skin.

Craig's eyes widened in the split second before his head jerked backwards, a gagging sound emitting from between his parted lips. His pincer-hold increased and then ended, his nails leaving long rakes of raised skin across the back of Hana's hand. He hit the ground at speed, a whoosh of grass clippings rising around him in a haze. A red aura of fury shrouded them, Logan's teeth bared in a growl of anger. He straddled the prone resort owner, cowboy boots planted either side of the man's waist. Then he reached down and hauled Craig upright by the front of his shirt, knuckles white and his chin set in a harsh, familiar line.

16

Running noose - mārei

"This is my place!" Spittle sprayed from Craig's mouth as foam, his throat restricted by Logan's stranglehold on his shirt collar. "She doesn't get to snoop."

Indignation bridled in Hana's confused mind and she took a step towards him. "Looking for my husband is not snooping!" she protested. But the sting of yet another accusation touched a guilty chord in her brain. "I came looking for you," she told Logan. Her tone changed to one of scandal. "He scratched me!" Blood rose to the surface of the painful gouges and she dabbed at them with the hem of her dress. "This is a nightmare!" she breathed. "We need to leave this hell-hole."

Sergeant Wally George appeared at a run, summoned by Craig's gurgle of protest and Hana's raised voice. "What's happening?" he demanded. He flattened his right hand and pushed it between Logan's squared jaw and Craig's fringe. Edging sideways as though separating warring dogs, he added an elbow and then a shoulder. "Enough!" he shouted.

With a grunt of dismissal, Logan relinquished his grip on Craig's shirt. The man fell back, staggering to one knee as he failed to right himself. He made exaggerated choking sounds as though to emphasise his role as victim. Hana's lips curled back in disgust. Sergeant Wally George put his entire body between the two men and faced Logan, his hands resting on his belt. His fingers edged towards a cannister of pepper spray tucked into a cloth pocket. "What the hell?" he demanded, without finishing the sentence.

Hana sprang to Logan's defence. She raised her hand; the welts bulging and painful, blood leeching through the broken skin. "He scratched me." She infused her tone with indignation, skewing the truth to Craig's disfavour. He'd administered the injury through a panic reaction as his weight tipped backwards. Not because he'd intended to hurt her. But his behaviour stank of an overreaction at finding her between the villas. Determination budded in Hana's brain to get to the root cause of it. But she dealt with the matter at hand. "He assaulted me," she pressed, holding her hand in front of Sergeant Wally George's nose for inspection. His eyes crossed over as he frowned at the obvious scratches. Then he stepped away from Logan.

"Nobody touches my wife!" Logan barked, taking another step towards Craig. Still playing for the sympathy vote, the resort owner remained on the ground as though preparing to propose marriage, his fingers still scrabbling at his throat.

"She's snooping!" he croaked again, the same argument he'd used for apprehending her. "This is my place!"

Hana shook her head at Sergeant Wally George. "We slept there," she said, pointing behind her at the vacant villa. "I woke and found my husband gone. When I reached the bottom of the steps, I heard your voice and followed the sound." She narrowed her eyes at Craig, his air of pathos churning in her stomach. "I got to here, and he grabbed me."

Sergeant Wally George released an exaggerated breath and raised his arms to cover his head against the baking sun. Sweat stained the pale blue uniform shirt beneath his armpits, the fabric bearing a crustiness of having dampened, dried, and dampened again. "Get up!" he snarled at Craig.

The resort owner rose and Hana blinked at the wet stain seeping down the thigh of his shorts. She gasped as a soggy peach slice slithered from the fabric and plopped into the grass. It joined another and, frowning, Hana listed sideways to see an upturned white bowl poking from the grass. A matching coffee mug sat beside it, half the contents still inside and the rest leaving a brown stain like a waterfall around its outer edge. The abandoned crockery explained Logan's absence. He'd fetched her breakfast from the communal dining room. She imagined what he'd seen as he rounded the corner, his wife in the grip of the smug resort owner. He'd done what life had programmed him to do. Logan Du Rose always struck first and asked questions later, especially in defence of his wife.

Rogue testosterone filled the air around the three men, most of it Logan's and some of it belonging to Sergeant Wally George. Hana could attribute very little of it to Craig, who adopted the role of a victim with almost no effort. His bottom lip wobbled as he acted out his exaggerated reaction to the extreme injustice.

"Assault then," Sergeant Wally George began. A quizzical black eyebrow rose into his fringe. "You assaulted his wife, and he acted in her defence." He shook his head from side to side as though the incident held nothing new for him.

"No, no!" Craig waved his hands in front of him, his head shaking as he sensed the ground shifting beyond his ability to control it. “I didn’t mean it,” he protested. “It’s a misunderstanding.”

Sensing victory, Logan’s features fixed into a smile he couldn’t hide. His lips curved upward, matching the twin arches of his almond-shaped eyes. But then he glanced sideways at Hana’s scratched hand and his grey irises darkened to the hue of soot. “We’d like to press charges, officer,” he growled, capitalising on Craig’s confusion.

Hana exhaled, the sound a faint hiss against the clucking of nearby foraging chickens. She recoiled at the expectation of another wasted day in the police station.

Craig made a sound low in his throat. He took a placatory step towards Logan but thought better of it as Sergeant Wally George stiffened. “I’m sorry.” He turned to face Hana, speaking to her instead of the wall of Logan’s chest. “A mere accident. Please forgive me.” He pressed a hand over his breast like a theatre player acting out a scene involving an expression of sincerity. She might have believed him, but for the eerie sparkle behind his hazel irises which hinted of an ulterior motive.

“Fine!” she snapped. “Just leave us alone and we’ll stay away from you. I’m sure we can both manage that for another six days!”

Sergeant Wally George stared hard at Logan and then at Craig. "Is that it?" he demanded. "Don't make me revisit this."

Craig nodded with enthusiasm. His right hand caressed the red mark where his shirt collar had bitten into his neck. With a speculative glance at Logan, he turned away and disappeared around the corner.

Sergeant Wally George relaxed. Tiredness shrouded him like a cloak. He'd worked for over twelve hours, and Hana experienced a flash of sympathy for him. It seemed unfortunate that most of his workload related to her and her husband. He shot a quizzical look at Logan. "Is it over, Mr Du Rose?" he demanded.

Hana hid her smile at his perception. Logan's temperament mimicked the fiery stallions he raised on their mountain farm. They never stopped striving, herding and protecting their mares until the last drop of blood. Driven by seasons and biogenics, they moved through the landscape like dappled white ghosts. And they never forgot a challenger.

Logan's jaw flexed, and he didn't answer. Hana rested her fingers over his forearm. "Yes," she lied. "It's over for now. Like I said, if he stays away from us until we leave, we'll enjoy our holiday. I'll post a nice review if he's lucky." She added the last sentence without believing it herself.

Sergeant Wally George tutted and his heavy steps tracked around the spilled breakfast crockery and scattered peach segments. He reached the corner of the villa and turned to stare at Hana. "You can go back to your original villa now," he said in a more official tone. "We pulled some fingerprints, but enough people have passed through this site to render them useless." He sighed. "I'll leave you to tidy everything away how you want it. Enjoy the rest of your stay on Rarotonga."

Logan turned to grin at Hana. "What's the likelihood of that?" he asked with a laugh.

17

Flying fish - maromaroā

"Are we leaving?" Hana lay on the bed after changing into clean clothes. She watched Logan feed his shirts onto hangers. Their intruder had scattered the clothing during their hurried search, leaving it creased but undamaged. She fought the urge to hand wash every item, but the tiny clothes line under the porch had only enough room for a few drying towels at a time.

"Na." Logan folded jeans into a neat square and pulled open the uppermost drawer of the tallboy at the end of the bed. He laid the clothing in the far right corner and patted the items flat. He shrugged and smiled at her. "The outbound flights are all full. I checked. Besides, I don't want to upset Mark and Dean." He glanced up at a shaft of sunlight cutting through the narrow window behind Hana's head. It bathed her in a soft glow. He smiled at her, his gaze sultry.

Hana snuffed. "Yeah, and you don't want to give Craig the satisfaction of having an empty villa which is already paid for." She narrowed her eyes and observed him through her lashes. "I bet you were that irritating kid at school, weren't you? Got away with murder, but no one quite knew how."

Logan pressed his right hand over his heart and dropped his chin in a hang-dog expression. "Oh, the injustice," he groaned. The action mirrored Craig's insincere apology earlier, but on Logan it created an effect of mock humour. He glanced at his watch and clicked his fingers. "Come on Mrs Du Rose," he urged. He held his hand out to her, waiting until she clasped his fingers. "We have a car to collect, a market to visit and some fun to have."

Her shoulders relaxed. "Sounds nice," she said, a note of hope breaking through the dark cloud of doom which shrouded her. "I guess we could start again."

"Oh, I wouldn't go that far." Logan clasped her around her waist, his fingers gentle against her injured side. He leaned down and kissed her neck. "We have a better read on this place today with thirty-six hours of lived experience, my darling. Shifty Craig is up to something and I have six more days of leisure to fill.

It's game on, baby." He bopped the end of her nose with his index finger. "The hare's a runnin'." His eyes lit with the glint of the chase, and Hana sighed at the inevitability of more drama before the week ended.

They caught the anticlockwise bus twenty minutes past its scheduled time. Hana had come prepared, a wide-brimmed hat protecting her against the glare of the sun. A knocking sound came from beneath Hana's seat as the bus rattled around the island. The driver stopped without warning for potential passengers, throwing her forward hard enough for Logan to need to grab the back of her dress. The ancient vehicle bumped and clattered from one unmarked stop to the next, brakes squealing amid a cloud of acrid, burning rubber. A heat haze lifted from the asphalt behind them, and Hana held her breath for most of the journey. Other tourists came and went, riding the bus with nods of acknowledgment, like partakers in a shared conspiracy. Hana returned their smiles of camaraderie as an elderly couple staggered into their seats mere seconds before the driver stamped on the gas pedal. The old man's stick catapulted towards the back of the bus and the tourists engaged in a silent game of footsie as sandaled toes nudged it back to beside his seat.

"This is us." Logan jerked his head towards a cluster of low buildings amid towering trees. He nudged

Hana's hip and forced her to stand. His scarred fingers pressed a buzzer on the support rail and the driver lurched the bus to the side of the road and screeched to a halt.

"Kia orana!" he sang as Hana staggered down the steps. "Have a lovely day." A floppy hat made from woven coconut leaves cast his smiling face into shadow. Hana managed a wave of thanks, holding her breath as he gunned the engine. The bus surged away as Logan's back heel left the bottom step. A cloud of exhaust fumes filled Hana's open mouth and caused her to cough.

"Terrifying!" she choked.

Logan tutted. "You have no sense of adventure, my love. How many fairground rides only cost five bucks and put you through the waltzers, the big dipper and the pirate ship? I'd call that value for money."

Hana groaned. "Why did you buy a concession ticket?"

"I only hired the car for a few days. The bus is fine for the rest of the week."

"He drives like Toby." Hana ran a hand across her mouth and gave herself a mental shake.

Logan dipped to administer a kiss to her forehead. "Yeah, but he smiled more."

Scooters occupied every parking space in front of the car rental shop. Hana touched the handlebar of the nearest one and imagined scooting around the island with Logan as her pillion passenger. She'd owned a moped at university, arriving in lectures with hair flattened by her helmet. The tiny motor had strained up Penglais Hill with extreme difficulty. Sometimes she'd half expected it to roll backwards as it ran out of steam. It had managed nothing north of sixty miles per hour, yet her father had insisted she purchase a padded leather jacket fit for a Formula One race. The happy bubble popped in front of her face, and she followed Logan into the shop.

They emerged half an hour later. Logan stood on the forecourt and shook his head in disbelief at the tiny vehicle in front of them. "I can't drive that!" he exclaimed. The desk clerk frowned and shrugged.

"Sorry, sir," he crooned, his tone lazy. "Someone piled the SUV into a power pole last week. It's still waiting on parts from the mainland." He winced at Logan's expression as they surveyed the tiny two-seater vehicle in front of them. Hana tilted her head sideways and wondered where Logan would store his long legs.

"Does the seat go back any further?" she asked, pulling open the side door.

Logan groaned. "It looks like a shopping trolley! You must have something else." His voice held a pleading note.

"Just the scooters." The gangly attendant gave another shrug. "Sorry. I emailed you but you maybe don't have service here. Few people do."

Logan released a whimper, which sounded as helpless as Hana had ever heard him. He looked at the scooter and back at the tiny Smart car. Then at Hana. "I don't know what to do," he said, a frown lining his forehead. He held his cowboy hat in his hands and twisted the brim in a constant motion.

"We could have a scooter," she suggested. "We could pretend we're Snoopy and Woodstock."

Logan shifted his weight, grit crunching beneath his heels. "But what about going around the bends?" He jerked his head towards her right side, where a surgeon spent hours repairing the damage to her liver. "Won't it hurt when you twist?"

"I could drive," Hana suggested. Her fingers twitched with muscle memory at the thought of twisting the throttle.

The attendant brightened. He withdrew his fingers from his mop of dark hair and stood up straighter. "Do you have a motorbike licence?" he asked, his tone enthusiastic.

"Not a current one." Hana's shoulders sank.

"I do." Logan raised his index finger as though answering a question in a class. He licked his lips and frowned at Hana. "You want to do this?"

"Okay." She shrugged, already losing interest. The sun warmed her shoulders and pressed through the light fabric of her dress. She closed her eyes and inhaled the scent of her sun cream, the coconut and floral mixtures creating a heady haze. Scooters buzzed along the road behind her. The locals didn't bother with helmets, rasping along the road towards their destinations without care. Knots of tourists zipped past with less certainty. They rode slower and with less purpose, buckled into helmets as they took in the sights. Hana's mind flicked to the drunks of the previous night. She'd noticed their scooters still parked at the roadside beyond the resort entrance as they'd waited for the bus. Poor Sergeant Wally George and his offsider. She imagined they'd gone home to sleep by now after a chaotic night shift.

Logan emerged with two helmets and an ignition key. He grinned with a mysterious satisfaction. The attendant loped behind him, deep in discussion about horsepower and revs. Hana followed, clopping along in her sandals. The men walked away from the road and into a small car park behind the shop. "Here she is!" the attendant exclaimed. He pulled up a roll door to expose a room filled with junk and old car parts. "You can have her all week if you like. She's roadworthy and all the tax and road charges are up to date. What do you think?"

Hana stared at the unwieldy motorbike, leaned on its stand like a loitering youth. Low slung and matte black, it had chrome handlebars which rose high above the usual riding position. Logan gave a low whistle and ran a gentle index finger over the leather seat. "Nice," he breathed under his breath. Hana's heart sank into her stomach, bashing everything on its way down. She forced her lips into an indulgent curve as Logan turned towards her, his eyes already burning with an inner thrill. "This is great, isn't it?" His voice lifted at the end like a child's with a new toy. "I've always wanted a Harley."

A mid-life crisis motorbike. She kept her groan internal, letting it ricochet around her head like a stone thrown inside a cavern. Logan loved speed and danger, a characteristic he'd passed onto Phoenix. His eyes glinted with a familiar spark and his fingers twitched over the bike key.

The attendant's enthusiasm matched his. "My boss doesn't let just anyone hire this," he crooned. "It's a Heritage Classic Cruiser. He must have liked the sound of you. You've got it all week." He leaned over the bike and snapped photographs on his phone. In between shots, he pointed out tiny existing scratches on the near pristine paintwork. Then he stepped back and lifted a black helmet from a shelf beside the bike. "Here you go, sir." He handed it to Logan with a flourish. "This baby does from zero to seventy in three seconds, but I don't recommend it. The speed limit on the island is fifty kilometres per hour and thirty in the towns. The cops are sick of finding people wrapped around trees and power poles, so they're heating the road blocks and ticketing." He patted a chrome handlebar and then used his sleeve to wipe off his fingerprints. "Don't get this impounded or the boss will make you pay."

"Understood." Logan gave a mock salute and set the helmet over his head. He lifted the lid to the side pannier and stowed his cowboy hat inside it. His long right leg cleared the bike in an experienced swooping action and he settled onto the seat. The key turned beneath his fingers and the engine roared to life.

"There's a chain and padlock in the carrier." The attendant leaned close to speak over the rumble of the engine. "Use it when you park. Don't leave helmets or personal items with the bike or someone will nick them."

"Okay." Logan's eyes sparkled as he nodded in response. He turned his head as though remembering Hana, his gaze raking the space in front of the garage. As though doused by a bucket of ice water, his expression morphed to one of regret as he read her misgivings in her rigid stance. His shoulders drooped, the solid muscles rounding towards his collar bone.

He seemed crestfallen as he beckoned her closer. "We don't have to do this." His fingers clasped the key and tensed as though to kill the purring motor. "Sorry. I got carried away."

Hana swallowed and sifted through the possible responses. Buzzkill. The word berated her with its two syllable condemnation. Logan loved his motorbike, but seldom found time to use it anymore. Quad bikes, stock horses and a heavy ute had become the tools of his trade. She licked her lips and imagined herself denying him this pleasure. The lazy island in the South Pacific Ocean suited her and not him. Her need for rest and recuperation offended Logan's constant flow of movement and activity. He'd come here for her.

She shrugged and forced a smile onto her lips, recognising the high stakes involved in the deceptively minor decision. Hana snatched the sun hat from her head and held out her hand for a helmet. *All or nothing*, she told herself.

18

Lost - ngaro

She shouldn't have worried. Logan handled the bike with skill and precision. He obeyed the speed limits and drove through the shallow bends with exaggerated care. The manufacturer had worried more about the pillion rider than the maker of Logan's current motorbike. Expensive padding cushioned Hana from the impact of the wheels against the asphalt. The heavy chassis required no dramatic leaning or twisting to exacerbate her injury. She sat higher than Logan, able to see the road ahead and anticipate turns and hazards. Foot rails assisted her stability, and she didn't grip his waist with the same sense of fatalism as usual. Instead, she rested her hands on his shoulders, connecting with him through the thin fabric of his shirt.

A warm breeze tugged at her skirt and made her glad she'd worn jogging shorts beneath it. It seemed freeing to ride without all the squeaking leather gear which Logan insisted on at home. Hana wanted to throw her arms wide and squeal with delight, but resisted for fear of alarming her husband.

They rode as far as the Saturday market at Avarua before meeting heavier traffic. Logan headed for a parking space on the main road and avoided the cluster of scooters parked in a haphazard heap near the entrance to the market. While Hana clambered off, he locked the bike and used the chain between the front and rear wheels, finding a hefty padlock in the right pannier. He secured everything possible before looping his forearm through the visors of both helmets. Then he held out his free hand to Hana.

Punanga Nui Market bustled with noise and people. Hana saw families and groups from their flight and nodded to those who recognised her. Logan chose a jade necklace for each of the children and they waited for the stall owner to engrave their names onto them. Hana tensed as he paid with cash for the souvenirs, but none of the smiling traders caused a fuss. They ate food from street vendors and drank bottled water. Vibrant fabric fluttered from beneath awnings and clothing swung from makeshift rails. Music played over a loudspeaker and tourists milled around as though time had called a temporary halt.

Hana relaxed, drawing deep breaths filled with sea air laced with salt. She took a turn at carrying her own heavy helmet as they wandered towards the outskirts of the market. Logan bent to kiss her, his lips spiced by the burger he'd eaten. "Had enough?" he said, lifting his voice over the cries of a stall owner selling fruit and vegetables.

Hana smiled up at him. "How long does it take to drive around the entire island?" she asked, her tone speculative.

Logan wrinkled his nose and blinked against the sun. "Under an hour," he replied. "Do you fancy it?"

Hana nodded. She tugged a map of the island from her pocket and unfolded it. "Let's go back the way we came. We already passed the golf course and the airfield last night."

Creases appeared in the corners of Logan's eyes as he grinned at her. Hana sensed the first soothing notes in her heart that this may actually feel like a holiday.

Then a shadow fell over her and Jared stood beside Logan. His hair stuck up all over his head and dark circles beneath his eyes gave him a haggard appearance. "Is Hallie with you?" he demanded, not bothering with preliminaries.

"No." Hana squinted up at him and shook her head. "She's at home, isn't she?"

Jared's lips pursed into a thin line. "No. I haven't seen her since you drove her home. I've found the car, but not the keys. Hallie must have them."

Hana blinked in confusion and stared at Logan. "I gave them to Craig last night," she said. She lifted the flap of the handbag slung over her body and dug inside, doubting herself in the moment. "Yes, Craig has them. We left Hallie at your place last night and sent Sally to the office for a key. I forgot I had yours after all the drama. We got back to our villa and discovered someone had burgled us."

"Really?" His eyes widened, and he dipped his head forward with enough speed to almost head butt Hana. "Someone went into your place?"

Logan put an invisible pressure on Hana's fingers and tugged her out of range of Jared. An air of unpredictability shrouded the other man as though his sanity clung to a washing line by a single peg. "Yeah," he replied, his tone guarded. "They trashed it. We still haven't worked out what they took."

Hana nodded from behind Logan's left biceps. Her cheek grazed his sleeve. "We can't find anything missing. Logan kept the cash and passports with him. They pulled everything out of drawers and cupboards and slung it around the room. The cops took fingerprints from the hard surfaces. I imagine we'll be back at home before they discover who did it."

Jared released an agonised breath and bent at the waist. "So where's my wife?" he demanded. "Why isn't she in our villa?"

Hana gaped at him. A split second of guilt made her responsible for a woman they'd taken home and left snoozing in a place of safety. She shook off her tendency to assume the blame for everything that went wrong. "I don't know," she replied. "We left her on the couch on your porch. I put her in the recovery position, but we knew Sally would arrive back in seconds. Hallie seemed very drunk. I can't imagine her going far by herself. Logan carried her from the car to your place."

"So. Where. Is. She?" Jared's tone hardened and spittle launched from between his lips. Sweat and grease stained the front of his shirt, a hint of faded aftershave doing little to mask his unwashed scent. Hana took a step backwards, her hip clattering with the stall behind her. She turned and apologised to the jewellery maker whose wares she'd caused to wobble on their stands. "She's not at the villa!" He raised his voice. "She hasn't been inside since we left for the pub last night. Sally said she unlocked the door like you asked her to, but Hallie wasn't on the porch when she got there. She left it open and went home. I've checked the whole resort. She isn't there."

Logan's jaw hardened in his cheek. "Craig arrived at our place just behind us. Why are you only looking for your wife now?" He stressed the burden of responsibility in the words, *your wife*.

Jared floundered. His thick set torso swung from side to side as he looked around him. He lowered his voice. "I joined a poker game. Craig didn't want to. He left me his car and hitched a ride with some buddies from the next resort along from his."

Hana gasped. "You played poker all night?"

Jared brushed off her horror. "There's no law against it." He bit his lower lip at the error of his statement. Resident Cook Islanders abhorred casinos and worked hard to keep them off the group of islands. He shrugged and wiped his sweating palms down the front of his shorts. "I got home an hour ago. Why is my convertible parked on the street?"

Logan snorted. "The cops set up a road block at the entrance to the resort. And your shit bucket is overdue its Warrant of Fitness and its road tax. We figured you'd rather pick it up when they'd gone instead of buying it out of the impound lot and paying the fines."

Jared groaned. He cast his frantic gaze around the market again. "I borrowed it from a mate of Craig's. He doesn't take care of things. After I saw the car, I hoped Hallie caught the bus here. No one's seen her." He grabbed the front of Logan's shirt and tried to shake him. Taller and bulkier, Logan didn't budge, not even to rock back on his heels. He took a calculating step backwards, forcing Jared to release the fabric bunched in his fingers. "You're the last people who saw her. Give me a ride to the villa!" he demanded, his voice rising above the market's habitual clatter. Other shoppers around them stopped chatting and turned to observe the action.

"How did you get here?" Hana asked. "Didn't you drive Craig's car?"

"No." Jared shook his head. Stale beer fumes and cigarettes rolled off him like a cloying fog. "Craig nipped to the supermarket. He dropped me here in case Hallie caught the bus. Give me a ride back to the resort. I need to find my wife."

"We don't have a car." Logan kept his voice a low rumble. He raised his index finger and pointed across the main street to the concrete building almost opposite the market. Not wasting his breath on platitudes or suggestions about where Hallie might have gone, he said, "Walk over there to the police station and report her missing. That's what I'd do."

Jared swung to face the direction Logan pointed in, his shoulders rounding until he resembled a boulder from behind. He stared at a fixed point to the left of a stall selling shells and the fight seemed to leave him. People jostled around them, bearing bags filled with colourful fabric and tinkling trinkets. The locals called to each other, a wave of bon homie in each interaction. "Hey, Po!" someone shouted to an acquaintance, changing course to weave across the marketplace and cause the foot traffic to bunch.

Jared heaved in an exaggerated breath as Hana watched, his expression dull. Sweat beaded across his forehead and stained his underarms. "Okay," he replied, his tone laden with heaviness.

Without saying another word, he lumbered away from them. He didn't bother navigating the milling tourists, barrelling through them like a missile. People scattered left and right as he steered a beeline for the police station. A man called an insult after him as he sent an elderly woman sprawling. He didn't check the road either before stepping onto the asphalt.

The squeal of brakes split the airwaves, rising above the cacophony of the market like a claxon of doom. Hana saw the flash of blue metal as the vehicle flew past, obscured by the fluttering awnings of the market stalls.

The screech of rubber on asphalt. A thud. And then a woman screamed, the sound loud and long. High and wavering, it filled the atmosphere with a horrible portend, before the cry turned to a wail and died.

19

Revival - ‘akaora

Hana turned to face Logan, but he’d gone. She blinked at the sight of his familiar heels as his long legs carried him across the market. By the time she’d roused herself from the shocked stupor, he’d knelt beside Jared’s prone body in the road and rested his ear over the man’s twisted mouth. A shake of his head as though hopelessness had gripped him, then he began the process of revival. He ran his capable hands over Jared’s limbs, looking for breaks. His fingers lifted at speed, jabbing at the gathering crowd.

“Ambulance,” someone called in response. “Get the ambulance.”

Hana pushed her way through the bodies, which formed a knot of protection around the scene. A man sat on the curb beside a dirty blue truck, his head wedged between his knees. The woman from a stall selling cakes patted his back as though not sure what else to do. "He just stepped out," he repeated over and over to anyone who approached him. The stained confession drove them out of range, the curious bystanders eager but reluctant to touch the incident for fear of contamination.

Hana knelt on the ground beside Logan. "What do you need?" she demanded, her tone filled with confidence she didn't possess.

"He's not breathing," Logan said. "His heart has stopped." He jerked a head towards her side. "You can't sustain compressions. Do you think you could breathe for him until help arrives?"

Hana gave a convincing nod, though doubt crept in like an inevitable tide. Logan checked Jared's mouth and tongue for obstructions, before tilting his head backwards and waiting for Hana to take the weight.

"Okay?" he said. He crossed to Jared's other side to avoid clattering her as they worked together. "I'll count to eight and then you give him a good lungful. Ready?"

Jared's hair at his nape held a dampness she forced herself not to dwell on. Just sweat, she promised herself. Not blood. Just sweat. Hana waited as Logan linked his fingers in a spooning embrace and pushed the heel of his joined hands against Jared's sternum. She listened as he counted aloud, his hissed numbers obliterating their noisy surroundings. It blocked out the voices, the whispering, and the mawkish curiosity. "Go," Logan said, ceasing the rhythmic pressure.

Hana's fingers gripped Jared's neck in her left hand, double checking the angle of his head and the width of his mouth. She aimed for his bluing lips before releasing all the air she possessed. The seal wasn't good enough, and she lost most of it through the left side of her mouth, cursing her inefficiency as Logan again compressed Jared's rigid chest. "Go," he said again as he finished counting, the intense heat and the unexpected activity already causing him to sweat.

Hana did it again, pushing aside the awkwardness of covering another man's lips in front of her husband. She gave him everything, holding nothing back. This time, his chest rose and fell.

Jared's body rocked as Logan performed eight more compressions. "Now," he said. Hana dipped forward, sweat tricking between her breasts and beneath her armpits. Voices twittered behind her, dividing her concentration. She wanted to shout at them, tell them to stop, to force them away from her. The crowd grew closer, encroaching on their diminishing circle without thinking. They blocked the sky with their curiosity and introduced a growing claustrophobia. Feet shuffled in Hana's peripheral vision and a man's dusty sandal bumped her knee. Someone behind jostled for a better view as she came up for air, shoving the man until he clattered against Jared's right knee. Logan swore at him, his words carrying enough venom for the crowd to give them more room. "Take deep breaths for yourself in between," he told Hana as he nodded at her to continue. "You'll faint if you don't."

Jared's chest rose and fell again. Someone else tripped over the motorbike helmet at Hana's side and white-hot rage turned Logan's irises to flint. "Back off!" he yelled, his voice carrying over the heads of the gathered crowd. "Just back the hell off!"

The sun beat down on Hana's neck and bare shoulders, its relentless kiss filled with delight at her vulnerability. Her hair hung in damp strands of frizz, sticking to her freckled cheeks. "Check again," she gasped to Logan, sitting up after sharing another gargantuan breath with a man she hardly knew.

Someone tapped her right shoulder, and she raised her arm and used her elbow to bat the hand aside. Irritation danced across her emerald eyes as she glared up at its owner, expecting to find another spectator taking a tasteless photo on their phone. But the crowd had filtered away to create a respectable ring around her and Logan. A uniformed police officer herded them aside and Hana recognised Sergeant Wally George's female sidekick.

Then a small-framed man wearing a forest green jumpsuit stared down at her, his lips raised in a sympathetic smile. "Paramedic," he stated, the single word an antidote to fear and hopelessness.

"Thank God," Hana breathed, and she meant it. Grit attacked her knees as she slid aside, rolling onto her bottom without dignity so the man could take over. She rose with difficulty, her legs almost boneless beneath her weight. She retrieved the heavy helmet, cringing against the thought of placing it on her overheated head. Logan's fringe plastered his forehead with long black tendrils, his shirt stained a darker colour between his pectorals. He continued to press against Jared's chest in tandem with the paramedic, only ceasing when another man in a green jumpsuit relieved him. He too rose, raking the crowd for Hana's face and relaxing when he sighted her. His legs seemed less unsteady than hers when he pushed himself upright.

The paramedics brought lifesaving equipment with them, using a defibrillator on Jared's bare chest to revive him. The crowd cheered and clapped as the paramedics nodded to one another and hoisted his limp body onto a gurney. A curious trembling began in Hana's calves as the prone man disappeared head first into the bowels of the waiting ambulance. "Urgh!" she groaned and sank to her knees. "I feel sick." The helmet clunked against the pavement, the scent of tar rising to fill her nostrils. It didn't help.

Her senses woke to the severity of the moment. She pressed her fingers to her forehead and regretted it, Jared's acrid scent leeching into her pores. The urge to vomit proved difficult to suppress.

Logan squatted beside her, supporting her back and resting his chin on the top of her head. A familiar voice spoke to them from overhead, the tone clipped and even. "Mr and Mrs Du Rose," it said with resignation. "Please, come with me."

20

Exhausted - pou

"Not the police station again!" Hana hissed as Sergeant Wally George led them back to the interview room. Her thighs objected as her muscles remembered the seat she slumped into beside Logan.

Sergeant Wally George raised his right hand as though swearing an oath. "Just a statement this time," he promised, pulling a pad of lined paper towards him. "You saved that man's life. The island doesn't forget things like that."

Hana sneaked a glance at her husband's profile. A twitch above his clenched jaw showed how he ground his teeth. Her gaze followed the strong cords along his neck to the collar of his tee shirt. She imagined smoothing her lips across his skin and almost felt the roughness of the underside of his jaw. Heat flared from her gut and embarrassed her, forcing her to look away from the source of her discomfort. She tuned back in to Sergeant Wally George's monologue.

"Victim's name?" He raised an eyebrow and the nib of his pen paused a hair's breadth above the pad.

Hana waited for Logan's reply, ploughing on with an eagerness for escape when he said nothing. "Jared," she responded. "Married to Hallie. I don't know their surname."

"The driver says he just stepped in front of him. He couldn't stop in time. Is that what you saw?"

Hana flexed her toes against the cool fibreglass of the helmet at her feet. She ached to reach across and touch Logan's bunched fingers, feeling like a spark of electricity caught adrift in a void. She wanted him to earth her, wondering if Sergeant Wally George would misinterpret the action as guilt. It occurred to her that perhaps he held them responsible, anyway. She sighed. "We didn't see the moment of impact. Or the driver." Hana shifted in her seat, the plastic fusing to the backs of her sweating thighs. "I couldn't even tell you what kind of car hit him, other than an older model utility vehicle. It ended up on the other side of the street, so I just remember the back bumper and the tyres. Jared had approached us at the market and asked if we'd seen his wife." She raised her shoulders to meet her ears. "We left her at their villa last night and Sally went to find a spare key to let her inside. Jared couldn't find her this morning, and said she hadn't been home. So Logan suggested he visit the police station and report her missing." Horrifying sounds returned to her, broadcast like a radio show inside her head. The screech of tyres on hot asphalt. The thud. A woman screaming. Hana gulped and spread her fingers across her lap, staring at the chipped red polish on her nails. She recalled Phoenix's bobbing head as she'd done her very best, smiling up at her mother and ignoring the overspill which coated everything else in sight.

The frown deepened in Sergeant Wally George's brow, creating its own shadow across his forehead. "That seems a little drastic," he observed, looking straight at Logan. "What about helping him to check the supermarket or accompanying him back to the resort and searching there? Why jump straight to calling in officials?"

Logan exhaled, exasperation and misery in the single, long breath. "It doesn't matter what we do, does it? Our fate is to end up sitting right here. We're destined to spend our entire holiday inside this concrete mausoleum. We should have just taken our chances at home."

Hana held her breath and focused on her husband's expression of futility. She reached across the gap between the two chairs and clasped his rigid fingers. "Logan," she soothed. "This isn't on you, sweetheart.

You've kept me safe for an entire month. Not everything is about her and her threats. This situation is very different."

Sergeant Wally George faded from her peripheral vision as she turned her body to face Logan. The chair legs ground and screeched against the tiled floor and her knees bumped his leg. She noticed the new flecks of grey leeching the black from his sideburns and the fresh agony in the fathomless depths of his sparkling irises. Receding shock from Jared's momentary death washed over her and left her with a bone deep emptiness. His blue, lifeless lips imprinted themselves on her inner vision and her memory caused her to dip towards them over and over, her lungs filled with life giving air but her senses recoiling.

"Let's go home," she breathed. Tears flecked her eyes as she stared up into Logan's face, attempting to infuse him with comfort and solidarity like she would one of her children after a fall. "Let's just take our chances at the farm."

Sergeant Wally George fetched tea and teased the story from the painful annals of Hana's memory. He listened in silence as she detailed the attack, which left her with a serious knife wound. Before the end of twenty minutes, he possessed the facts, knew of Mark and Dean's kind gift and the Du Rose couple's craving for rest and peace. He also understood Logan's suggestion to Jared that he seek official help when he seemed adamant that something was wrong. It no longer appeared quite so drastic in the light of their own circumstances.

Logan remained silent, his head bowed as he performed an internal audit of his careful strategy and examined the data on what went wrong. Hana kept talking, sensing her husband's mental absence and understanding his need to analyse and reformat their plans. His lips parted, and he released a breath through his nose. She understood then that he'd returned to her, regrouped and revitalised. But something would change. "We'll stay because there are no spare seats until our original flight home next week," he announced, his tone flinty. His grey eyes fixed on Hana's face. "But no more socialising. Other people are our downfall."

Hana reared back in protest. "Hallie came to me!" She lifted the thumb and index finger of her right hand in the air and performed a pecking motion. "She wanted sugar!"

Logan snorted. "Yeah? The old sugar trick. Well, that's worked out great, hasn't it? The groceries we paid for are still on the shelves of the supermarket."

His left hand moved in an anticlockwise winding action. "Every time we leave that bloody villa, something goes wrong."

"No." Hana's spine thudded against the plastic chair and she folded her arms. "No," she repeated, although the rest of her denial escaped her. She couldn't collect her thoughts enough to know what she intended to refuse. But she suspected her husband meant to confine her to the villa, and that horse had bolted. She'd seen the white beaches and aqua waves from the pillion of the motorbike. The warm water called to her bare toes, and the sun whispered to the freckles across her nose. She couldn't stay in the villa. Not now she'd seen paradise for herself.

Hana blew out a ragged breath and released her arms, pressing her right hand at the wounded space beneath her ribs. Logan relented and turned his attention to Sergeant Wally George. "How's Jared?" he asked. His dark curls wobbled as he shook his head. "We couldn't revive him, but it looked like perhaps the paramedics succeeded."

Sergeant Wally George's lips flattened into a thin line. "Never underestimate the effort taken to keep someone's organs functioning," he stated. His tone held the bitterness of previous experience. "He's critical. Broken bones, a head injury. The doctors will keep him unconscious and stable until they can fly him to Auckland." He licked his lips. "I hope he has insurance."

Hana exhaled. "His wife is a travel agent. I imagine they have the very best products." Her brow knitted into lines. "I wonder where she is." She turned to face Logan.

"Why did you leave a drunk woman unattended?" Sergeant Wally George tempered the question by holding both hands out in front of him. "No judgement. It's a reasonable question."

Hana's next breath ruffled her fringe, warm against the cooling of her sweating forehead. Her clothes stuck to her in uncomfortable ridges and she ached to collect her long curls into a ponytail. "She turned nasty," she admitted. "We tried to wait with her for Sally to return with her villa key, but she became aggressive. Told us to go away." Hana shrugged. "Perhaps we should have hung around nearby, but I heard Sally's footsteps."

"Why did Hallie return to the villa without a key?" Sergeant Wally George scratched crabbed script onto his pad. His actions resembled the pecking chickens at the resort, with their curved claws scrabbling in the mulched flowerbeds.

Hana winced. "I had it in my handbag. In all the kerfuffle of the trip home, I didn't realise I had it amid the bunch Jared gave me. By the time I remembered, we'd arrived at our villa and discovered the break in."

Sergeant Wally George made a sound low in his throat. "About that," he began. He scratched his crown with the pen's rounded point. "Whoever entered your villa had a key. They didn't force the door, but unlocked it. My colleagues are running the fingerprints through the system, but so many people have passed through the resort I'd urge you to foster low expectations."

"What about the prints you took from the suitcase?" Logan asked.

Sergeant Wally George shrugged. "Again, it's hard to distinguish anything clear between yourselves and the baggage handlers at the airport." He clicked his fingers. "We've eliminated the prints we took from you both yesterday and your burglar wiped the suitcase zippers, so we got nothing from there." His shoulders relaxed, and he leaned back in his chair. Hana's eyes widened as it tipped onto its rear legs before crunching forward onto the tiles. The officer seemed unworried as though he'd perfected the juvenile action from his schoolboy days. His words didn't falter. "At least I now know your reason for visiting Rarotonga and have no fear that you're a crime wave waiting to happen." He tapped the pad with the end of the pen. "We'll search for the victim's wife. She needs to know what's occurred. Hopefully she didn't go for a drunken swim in the ocean."

Hana shook her head. "She didn't have time. Speak to Sally. She's the resort owner. I heard the office door slam and her footsteps heading towards the villa as we left. Or Craig. He showed up at our villa moments after we did." She blinked as Logan rose beside her. He tucked his chair beneath the table as a mark of finality.

Hana clambered from her seat, wincing as her thighs stuck to the plastic surface. She smiled at Sergeant Wally George as Logan collected both their motorbike helmets and headed towards the door.

"Thank you," Sergeant Wally George called after them. "I truly hope I don't see you again."

21

Smoke - ʻauaʻi

They collected the bike from the road, not going back into the market. Logan carried both heavy helmets and Hana slouched along behind him, her mind still occupied by the thud of Jared's body hitting the bumper of the blue ute.

"Hey!" A voice cut through her thoughts and she turned.

"What now?" Logan sighed, placing his body between Hana and the middle-aged man hurrying towards them. He wore a sun visor created from woven coconut leaves, silver tendrils escaping from beneath its stiff edges in damp spikes. He carried a bulging paper packet beneath his right arm. Its fluttering edges revealed mangos bumping against one another like naughty children under a blanket. Logan set both helmets on the pavement and Hana watched his fists ball as he assessed the newest threat, which barrelled towards them at a jog.

"These are for you." The man held out the paper bag. When Logan didn't take it, he shoved it against his chest to force the hand-over.

"Why?" Bemused, Logan poked an index finger into the bag. "We didn't buy these."

"From me to you." The man touched a hand to his grizzled cheek and then to his chest. "For what you did earlier. You saved that man."

"Oh." The breeze caressed Logan's fringe to disguise the creases in his brow. He shrugged, refusing to release the platitudes clamouring for release on his tongue. "Thank you?" He lifted his chin, towering above the man by a head. "You didn't need to give us anything."

"I did," he replied. He scratched at the stubble gracing his cheeks, work-worn fingers with lined nails. "We know how to thank people on this island."

Logan nodded, holding the paper bag and the mangoes one handed. He held out the other to the man, a gesture of solidarity and peace. He took it, their brown fingers meshing in the universal handshake. "Jared had something on his mind," he assured the man. "The cops don't think it's the driver's fault. We told Sergeant George we didn't see the impact, but others did."

"We're grateful to you for saving him, anyway." The man's smile caused creases to appear in the corners of his eyes, matching the lines beside his mouth. He bobbed his chin. "And it's Sergeant Wally George. That's his name."

Logan cocked his head, staring at the man with their hands still linked. "Wally George, is his entire name?" Hana sensed him still not understanding.

The man shook his head. "No. Sergeant Wally George is his Christian name. He has a different surname, but it doesn't fit on his badge. We use all his first names when we speak about him."

"Sergeant Wally George?" Logan's voice hushed almost to a whisper. "Like, on his birth certificate?"

"Yep." The man grinned, pleased at Logan's comprehension. "Bred to be our police chief."

"He's the police chief?"

"Na." He dropped his grip on Logan's fingers and his arms swung by his sides as though boneless. "Not yet. One day, like his father and his grandfather before him."

"Right." Logan sounded unsure. He clutched the mangoes tighter, and Hana feared for their plight. "Is he even a sergeant?"

The man shrugged. "I'm not too sure. We just do what he says. Always have. Always will." He jerked his head towards the fruit and fixed a beatific smile on Hana. "Thank you again. Both of you." He turned and walked towards the bustling market, his movements smoother without his double burden of the mangoes and the gratitude.

"Wow," Hana commented, watching as Logan turned towards her. She smiled up at her husband as he cradled the delicate fruit against his chest. Her lips flattened into a line. "You look like me when I take off my bra."

He frowned and stared down at how he'd cupped the bag. The mounds settled across his giant palm. Unable to summon a smart retort, he held them out to her, twisting the paper bag at its lip. Her humour wasted, Hana waited for him to unlock the right pannier and stowed the fruit inside her sun hat. They fixed the heavy helmets over their heads. Logan removed the chain and padlock from the wheels, fired up the engine, and swung his leg over the seat. When he'd taken the weight of the heavy bike, Hana clambered on behind him, resting her hands on his strong shoulders. "Home, James," she commanded in a mock Victorian accent. "And don't spare the horses."

Logan took the route back to Paradise Villas via the car rental shop, stopping twice to park up beside stunning beaches. At Aro'a Beach, Hana stripped off her light summer dress to reveal a swimming costume beneath it. She paddled in the shallows, laughing back at her husband as he reclined in the sand beneath a coconut tree. The fringing reef surrounding Rarotonga created a safe lagoon. A few narrow passages led out to the ocean and tiny boats buzzed in and out in the distance. Surf slapped the reef, leaving the lagoon almost untouched by all but the natural tides. Hana had noticed the bigger boats using the army built harbour at Avatiu and wondered if that's where Logan had gone out on his diving tour. She paddled back through the shallows to the beach to ask him.

The warm sand enfolded her as she sank down beside him. She tried not to shower him in the fine white grit as she settled. "Did you snorkel inside the lagoon?" she asked, rolling onto her side with exaggerated care. "Or did you go out to the ocean? You didn't get to tell me about it with everything that happened."

Logan shook his head. "No. There's a shipwreck about seventy metres down just outside Avatiu. The water is crystal clear. You can see it from above. That's the Intrepid which sank in the 1990s. But we spent the most time looking at the Matai wreck. The guide told us about another ship which sank during a cyclone last summer. A live-aboard scuba diving boat. The Sail Fish. It's a triple decker, the same as the tour boat. Bit sad seeing it snapped in half with the bow smashed on the bottom of the ocean like that. Someone should retrieve the name plate. It's painted on beautiful teak wood and just lying fifty metres away from the wreck." He wrinkled his nose. "But I also swam with turtles." He crossed one ankle over the other and rested his head on his linked fingers. "Pretty spectacular. Not something I'll forget in a hurry."

"Hallie told me Jared went on that tour." Hana rested her head against her hand, her bent elbow creating a triangle against her body. She tilted her head to watch Logan's reaction. But he'd closed his eyes against the glare of the sun on the white sand. His chest rose and fell in a steady motion. Hana picked through her next words with care. Logan's comment as the stall holder approached them with his gift told her he'd tired of intrigue and drama. *'What now?'* he'd asked. She flicked sand from her fingers, sifting through the roughness and examining the integral sparkles in its structure. The unanswered question hung in the air between them. She couldn't leave it there. Lifting her voice like a racquet, she batted it back into Logan's court. "Did you speak to Jared on the boat?"

She glanced up to find her husband studying her features. A smirk tugged at one side of his lip. He rolled his long body to rest with one arm propping up his head. "Oh, sorry," he remarked, his tone teasing. "I didn't realise the first part held a question and wasn't just an observation."

Hana sighed. She dug her fingers into the sand until only her wrist showed, her arm appearing disembodied and strange. "You know very well it was a question," she grumbled, pushing out her lower lip. "Hallie said Jared went on the trip. I want to know if you met him then."

"No, you don't." Logan narrowed his eyes. "You're asking if Jared went on the boat at all? That's a strange question, and I want to know why you're asking."

Hana pursed her lips. She turned her gaze to the ocean, its powerful surf washing the reef in rhythmic splashes of white foam. The flecks carried into the lagoon, lying like debris on the flat surface until the bubbles popped. "I saw Jared arguing with Craig behind our villa while you were on the trip," she said. "Until we met Jared last night at the bar, I didn't realise that's who I'd seen." She wrinkled her nose at Logan. "Why did Hallie think he went snorkelling with you?"

Logan reached out to her. He ran his index finger over the space beneath her swimsuit, where the scar from her surgery lurked. The tender action caused her no pain, and she contemplated the restraint of a man filled with such power. She'd seen what his scarred knuckles could do to a man's face. Yet such love governed every interaction with her, their children, and his horses. "Haven't you had enough intrigue for one lifetime, Mrs Du Rose?" he whispered, his tone tight and questing.

Hana stared back at him, noting the sharp contour of his nose and the way his fringe bounced against his eyelashes. His hair hid a scar across his forehead where the child-Logan had walked into an open window. His clothes covered a multitude of bone-deep ridges and wounds poorly served by a lifetime of living with the haemophilia once known as the Du Rose Curse.

Hana knew she loved the very bones of her husband, but she replied with a question of her own. "Have you?"

Logan shifted in the sand as he dug into his jeans pocket. The gritty spray vented from underneath him as his wriggling action disgorged his wallet. His scarred fingers dug inside, tugging out a weathered twenty dollar note. He held it out for Hana's inspection.

She took it, sand cascading from her palm like a waterfall. "What?" she demanded. "What am I looking at?"

"A fake." Logan brushed the white sparkles from the fold of his leather wallet. "I picked it up last night at the bar."

Hana cocked her head in confusion. "You used your Visa card. I watched you."

"Not for the second drink." His irises lost their glitter, turning to flint in the shade of the coconut tree.

"I saw a woman at the bar holding it. She stood behind us in the queue for customs when we arrived on the island. Either she brought it with her or acquired it here. I'm a reasonable judge of character and I'm picking she got it here. Busyness made the bar staff sloppy, so I handed over a fifty, forcing them to give me the change of coins and a twenty. I got served fast enough to get that note." He took it back from her outstretched fingers and stuffed it into a pocket on his wallet, zipping it in and keeping it separate from his other cash. "It's obviously a problem on the island, and I kinda like it here." He leaned forward, drawing up his knees and hugging them against his chest. "I have no data or phone signal. There's no way to access my emails or do anything that isn't already on my laptop." He shrugged and turned his face, resting his cheek against his knee. "And the devil makes work for idle hands."

Hana chewed on her lower lip and dipped her face towards his, planting a kiss on the end of his nose. They conspired together in the shadow of his knees, heads bowed and excitement prickling at the edges of their peace. Unity and togetherness lulled them further into the intrigue. They'd pull together instead of against each other. A first.

This couldn't get them stabbed or killed. Five days remained of their holiday and then they'd return to reality. Bodie would catch Hana's attacker and lock her up before they reached home. The mystery stretched before them like an unwritten novel, the characters still needing flesh and features. No danger threatened their holiday smitten minds.

And the devil would for sure make work for idle hands. But the hands weren't theirs. And the devil already had a face. And a name.

22

Riddle - piri

They meandered around the island on the Harley, exploring the streets which led off the main orbital highway. With an easy pace, they stared at each low slung dwelling and deserted store front for something they couldn't yet fathom. Perhaps a hungover, wandering Hallie, or a man carrying a pile of currency still warm from the printing press.

Hana grew tired and her side set up a blossoming ache, so Logan headed for home just before lunchtime. Her discarded breakfast on the grass between the villas seemed a lifetime ago, as she slipped from the pillion. Logan unlocked the front door and checked the bathroom and main area before allowing her access. He peeked in the fridge and wrinkled his nose at the bread they'd brought with them. "You rest here," he suggested, quirking an eyebrow at Hana. "I'll drive back to the supermarket and fetch supplies." He watched as Hana removed her sandals by the front door and lifted a fabric band from the bedside table. She scooped her damp curls into a ponytail and folded it into the scrunchie before patting the back of her neck with her palm.

"Okay," she agreed without a fight. Her limbs had gained a familiar heaviness. She touched light fingers to her forearm and winced. "I'm still covered in sand. Think I'll take a shower."

Logan cocked his head, concern furrowing his brow. "Want me to wait until you've finished?" Hana sensed his protectiveness reach for her across the room. She exhaled, banishing the memory of fainting twice in the shower after her surgery. The nausea and light-headedness had dominated that first week at home. She cleared her throat and straightened her shoulders.

"I'm fine," she asserted, putting effort into convincing him. "Please, can you pick up some decent conditioner while you're there? It's the one thing I forgot to pack."

Logan nodded and crossed the room to her side. He wrapped his arms around her and kissed the top of her head. "Shouldn't take long," he promised.

Hana laughed. "Liar. You want to race around the island on the Harley without me looking over your shoulder?"

Logan stood up and pressed a hand over his heart. He affected an expression of mock sincerity. "You have me all wrong, Mrs Du Rose. Two visits to the police station are more than enough for me."

"Whatever," she jibed. She snapped her fingers. "Oh, don't forget to retrieve our stuff from the panniers or you won't fit any shopping in them. It'll ruin the effect of the Harley if you ride with shopping bags dangling off the handlebars."

Logan made a gagging sound and went outside to the bike. He reappeared with Hana's sun hat, his cowboy hat and the souvenirs. He balanced the paper bag containing the mangoes in his hand. "I think these need to go in the fridge," he said, his tone even. Then he waved and stepped back over the threshold. "I'll lock you in and take the key. Then I can let myself in again without disturbing you if you're sleeping. You can get out by using the button on the back of the door handle." He flicked the locking mechanism with his finger. "Is that okay? Or would you rather go to the swimming pool?"

"I'll stay here. I won't sleep," Hana replied, but a yawn cut through her words. A flash of anger at her attacker consumed her vision for a moment. She'd stolen more than just a section of her liver and exacted her revenge. Hana had lost a month of her life. For what? "I'm okay." She waved Logan away with a smile.

He collected his helmet and then left, his steps quick as he moved onto the porch. The key clicked in the lock, Logan's fingers precise and accurate. Hana imagined him dashing to the supermarket and back, his actions devoid of holiday spirit or enjoyment. He worried about her. The suggestion he ride around the island as though he had all the time in the world fell to the tiled floor like the smokescreen it represented. She'd kidded herself.

The bike fired up outside, a throaty roar followed by a steady purr. She stroked her helmet, still on the kitchen counter where she'd left it. Her lips curved upward in a reluctant smile. She would relish every second of having Logan to herself. No farm, no stock, no children. No demands on their time except for each other.

"Shower," she told herself and clicked her fingers.

The housekeeper had refilled the bottles of toiletries, and Hana washed her hair and banished the sand from her limbs. She watched the foamy water trickle down the plughole and recounted her conversation with Logan. Only then she realised he hadn't answered the question about seeing Jared on the boat. "He couldn't have," she whispered to herself. "Because I saw him here." She drew a smiley face in the condensation on the glass and depressed the lever to halt the water flow.

Humid air shrouded her, robbing her of breath and energy.

It took all her effort to clamber from the shower cubicle and wrap herself in warm towels. She lowered the toilet seat lid and sat on it, waiting for her blood pressure to fall and the nausea to dispel. The silence of the villa swaddled her, creating space and time for her to unwind and collect her thoughts. Hana relaxed into it, listening to the chickens clucking in their throats as they pecked around the building. She closed her eyes and waited.

A click reached her, causing a dull echo through the building. She recognised it as the screen door opening and gave herself a mental shake. Logan must have sped to the supermarket and run around it, smashing and grabbing their groceries to return in such a short time. She patted the skin on each cheek to revive her colour and leaned forward to retrieve the hair band from the vanity. Her lack of balance reared itself as she scooped her hair into a wet ponytail and dragged another towel from the rail to pat it dry. Water leaked down both sides of her face as she performed the actions in the wrong order. She always squeezed the water from her curls before she tried to style it. Again, exhaustion bit at the space beneath her sternum and she focused more hate on the blade wielder. "Bitch!" she mouthed beneath her breath. "You'll get yours."

Keys jangled against the front door lock and it creaked as it opened, but Logan didn't call out to her. Perhaps he hadn't yet checked the bed and assumed she'd fallen asleep. Hana pictured him returning to the bike to retrieve groceries from the panniers. She rose and tested her equilibrium. Wobbly but passable.

She hadn't closed the bathroom door, so she tugged it open while fixing a smile onto her lips. But the breath locked in her chest at the sight of Craig closing the front door with exacting care.

Hana cast around her in panic. With one door in and out of the villa, it left her nowhere to run. And Craig stood in the only other room, which served as a bedroom, lounge and kitchen. She had nowhere to hide and no route to escape. And only a towel covered her nakedness.

Craig's footsteps moved around the villa. His flip-flops created a tiny squeak as he stepped from tile to tile. Hana withdrew her head and stared around the bathroom, her options diminishing with each passing second. His lecherous grin, his veiled threats and suggestions, added up to a monumental threat.

Hana scurried to her wash bag, withdrawing a pair of tiny nail scissors without disturbing the other noisy contents. She folded the second towel and pressed it over the rail, gripping the other one at a knot between her breasts. A drawer opened and closed and Craig grunted as he sifted through Logan's jeans and tee shirts. He took care over his search, his time lengthening as his fingers dipped into the drawer containing Hana's clothing and underwear.

She gritted her teeth, fighting the urge to burst like a banshee from the bathroom and stab him with her tiny scissors. Her mind sent telepathic messages across the distance to Logan, urging him to return. She imagined the bloodshed when it happened. His relentless rage would send Craig to the hospital or to his grave. She longed for her husband's imposing frame and bunched fists. But the only weapon she possessed created lines in her palm from the strength of her grip.

Hana slipped behind the bathroom door and held her breath, the scissors clasped in her left fist. She imagined herself slamming her hand downwards, digging the sharp points into whichever part of Craig's body presented itself first. Her bare feet made no sound on the tiles and her slender body only just fitted into the gap. The wardrobe door opened, and the hangers slid across the rail with muted squeals of metal on metal.

Logan always told her that an apology often proved more effective than a request. She readied herself on that principle, to stab Creepy Craig and then apologise. The squelch of her blood filled her hearing as it pumped through her eardrums. And she waited.

23

Peril - mate

Craig grunted to himself as he hauled the empty suitcase from the wardrobe. The wheels clunked and skittered against the tiles as he released it. Hana recognised the thud of it falling onto its long side and then the chirrup of the zipper. They'd contemplated locking it after the break in but Logan dismissed the notion. It contained nothing.

Unaware of her presence, Craig made the kind of noises in his throat and chest which he might keep contained in the company of others. He breathed through his nose and burped twice without ceasing his activity.

Hana controlled her breathing until her vision filled with bright spots and haziness, desperate to avoid him hearing her panic from the next room. Her mind presented images and scenarios on a film reel behind her eyes; Craig entering the bathroom and discovering her wearing only a towel. Craig, with the twin blades of nail scissors protruding from his chest, or his forehead, or his right eyeball.

He moved around the villa without stealth, crashing and banging as he opened and closed the cupboard doors in the kitchen. The fridge hummed as he checked each shelf, every drawer, his hairy fingers rustling the bag containing bread. Hana had run out of options and prepared herself for Craig to enter the bathroom. Sweat coated her fingers, making it difficult to maintain a grip on the scissors. She leaned her head against the wall, the towel rail heating her left arm as she pressed herself into the narrow gap. The mirror beside the shower reflected a reverse image of Craig's activity as he searched the villa with precision. He even gazed up at the vaulted ceiling with its fake beams, perhaps considering Logan's height in his estimation of their ability to hide contraband. Hana's brain whirred with possibilities, still no wiser about what he thought they'd brought to the island.

Cash, perhaps? Fake cash. The idea whooshed into her brain as he fixed his gaze on the bathroom and took a step towards it. The island already seemed small and the gossip insular. He could have learned of their dramatic exit from the supermarket in the police's company. It seemed reasonable he might want to eject them. But this search seemed more than just an evidence hunt. He knew they'd suffered an intruder and that the police had both searched and fingerprinted the villa. Why did he think he could locate something which they'd already failed to secure?

His rubber soled flip-flops squeaked as his momentum increased, set on a course for the open bathroom door. Hana turned her face sideways and away from his mirrored reflection with its odd refraction, aware that if she could see him, he could also see her. He stepped through the opening, his knuckles brushing against the door. It drifted back further, bumping her bare toes with the underside. Hana squelched a hiss of pain as the surface grazed the knuckles of the highest toes, jagged chips of compressed wood digging into the soft skin. Her heart pounded in her ears and chest, creating a rhythm which rocked her body in time to a silent tune.

The back of Craig's head appeared in her eye line, blond, tousled hair rising in disordered crests. His rounded shoulders held the definition of one who'd worked out in a gym once, but lost impetus and descended into a shadow of muscle. But the mirror still painted an image of the bodybuilder to the man who peered in to it, a man who drank too much and ate whatever he wanted.

Hana peeked through the corner of her left eye, seeing a reflection of Craig sifting through Logan's wash bag. He tapped a fingernail against a deodorant nestled beside an electric razor. A bottle of aftershave clunked as it slipped onto the shelf.

A dilemma rose in Hana's mind. Her hushed internal voice urged her just to stab him in the back and run screaming from the villa in her towel. She'd attract attention, and raising a commotion might offer safety from Craig's wandering hands. Someone would call the police and she could throw the spotlight on his creepiness. But Logan would kill him. She knew that in her heart, sickened by how her mind egged him on to produce the inevitable bloody pulp from Craig's cocky features. The jail cell in the bowels of the police station had left enough of a residue on her soul for her to wish otherwise for Logan. And so she waited, the scissors still raised in her left hand and sweat running from her palms to her armpit.

Craig's fingers switched to her wash bag, lingering over her deodorant and lifting a mascara wand from the bag's folds. Hana's stomach recoiled as he sniffed it, her healing liver producing a stab of protest at the stress consuming her body. She inhaled, preparing to burst from behind the door, embed the scissors into his left shoulder and run. Run. Run.

It echoed in her mind as she rolled the plan through her brain, strategising and estimating the steps to the front door and her ability to make them. He would turn towards her, shock rising across his expression, and she would dash to the front door. The door he'd left unlocked.

A throaty roar echoed in the distance, sneaking through the vented bathroom window and bouncing off the walls. Craig's fingers stiffened, and he dropped the mascara wand. It bounced against the sink and as he scrabbled to retrieve it; the rumble grew nearer.

Hana recognised the Harley's welcome cry as Logan slid the bike along the narrow entrance road. The steady rumble reverberated off the glass windows of the reception and he made the first turn towards home. He'd slip beside Jared and Hallie's villa, making a sharp right and then a left before drifting to a standstill. Hana estimated the seconds before he arrived at her rescue. Six more until he parked in the grassy space beside the bedroom wall. Perhaps another five while he stood the bike up and removed his helmet. Another five before he crested the steps of the porch to the front door and found it open. One more while he processed Hana's apparent disobedience by unlocking it and leaving herself vulnerable. Then the explosion of his fury at finding Craig handling their intimate possessions.

Hana tensed, sending a shaky command to the fingers which clutched the scissors. To hell with it. She'd stab him anyway and cry self defence. She'd tired of wearing the victim's hat of shame. Her fingers tightened around the scissors and she shifted their position, swinging them in an arc in her damp palm and pressing the blades between her index and middle fingers. Not a downward action now, but a sharp jab, punching forward to do the most damage. Craig turned as though in slow motion, and Hana pictured herself digging the scissors into the space between his ribs. One hit and while he reeled from the shock, she'd run. To safety, to Logan, and then inevitably to a police cell.

24

Praise - ʻakapaʻapaʻa

But Craig fled. Hana blinked, and he'd gone. Pounding footsteps carried him through the open bathroom door and across the villa. The front door handle dented the wall at the force of his push. Hana lost track of him, not knowing if he'd turned left or right at the bottom of the porch. Logan's voice carried through the building as he crested the steps and discovered the front door still swinging on its hinges in the light breeze.

"Hana?" Plastic bags rustled as he set them on the kitchen floor. She heard him swear and his cowboy boots clicked across the tiles. "Hana? I thought I told you to keep the door locked."

Hana breathed through pursed lips, her husband's protests drowned out by the blood pulsing through her eardrums. The scissors glinted in her trembling hand. She registered Logan's sudden panic as he stepped into the bathroom and cast around him, not seeing her behind the door. “Hana!” he shouted, a ragged edge to his voice. “Hana!”

The door of the shower cubicle creaked, and she visualised him touching its damp surface, estimating the temperature of the droplets gathered on the glass. She whimpered deep in her chest and the door flew away from her face, exposing her towel-clad body and the scissors raised in threat. Logan caught her in his arms, lifting her until her numb feet left the tiled floor. The scissors’ sharp blades caught in his tee shirt sleeve, but he disregarded the painful scratch against his biceps. He carried her to the bedroom, setting her down on the mattress before squatting before her. The scissors moved from her hand to his in a reflexive snatch. “What happened?” he demanded, his tone severe.

“Craig.” She managed the single word as her body convulsed with delayed shock. “I almost stabbed him.” The realisation rocked her psyche, the logic of moments ago highlighted by the return of rational thought. “Oh, gosh!” She pressed a hand over her mouth. “I almost stabbed him. With those.” Her head jerked towards the nail scissors clamped in Logan’s left hand. “That makes me like her.” The realisation drew a bloom of pain from her healing liver. She pressed shaking fingers over the scar, the fluffiness of the towel muffling the connection. Hana covered her eyes with her hands, recriminations already beginning.

"What did he do?" Logan drew her back to Craig, and she released a shuddering breath.

"He let himself in with a key." Her words seemed to shimmer in the air between them. The rising humidity stole the oxygen and left her sweating and breathless. "He searched our stuff. I hid behind the bathroom door, but I could only find the scissors to defend myself."

"Good girl!" Logan's approval whooshed over the negative narrative coursing through her brain. "Well done." He grinned, rising from his squat to sit beside her on the mattress. It dipped beneath his weight and caused her to pitch against his shoulder. He spun the scissors in his large palm and peered at them. "Geez, Hana! I'm sorry you went through that alone."

His praise dumbfounded her. She'd expected him to rush to the front office and pound the resort owner into a pulp. She acknowledged a flash of irrational disappointment which vied with the relief. His arm slipped around her shoulders and she inhaled his familiar scent of pine and summer. Her heart returned to something close to its normal rate, and the shaking lessened. "I thought you'd kill him." The sentence held an unintentional criticism.

Logan pressed a tender kiss to her temple. “I want to,” he admitted. “If he’d laid a finger on you, I’d already be on my way over there with blood in my nostrils.” His body jerked as he fought the animal instinct for revenge. He dropped the scissors onto the mattress beside him. “But you had it covered, babe. I’m proud of you.”

Hana let her weight slump against his side. She wanted to argue, to disprove his faith in her abilities. A mere three centimetres of sharpened steel might deter a determined attacker, but they wouldn’t permanently halt his progress. But Logan seemed thrilled at her adaptability. He crushed her to his side and rained kisses on her damp hair.

“You’re so resourceful,” he whispered. His torso twisted as he used both arms to enfold her. “Nail scissors. I love it. Enough to defend yourself, but not unreasonable force if he called the cops.” His appreciation filtered through her brain as the adrenaline withdrew. Her desperation appeared as bravery and cunning through his eyes. Hana forced her muscles to relax, keen not to destroy his rose-tinted illusion of her.

“He won’t stop.” Her voice held more steel than she expected. She pushed herself up straighter. “He’s creepy. I keep running into him and there’s something off about his behaviour.”

Logan nodded. "I know. He's also connected to this counterfeiting racket somehow. I feel it in my bones." He nudged the nail scissors with a careless brush of his hand. "You need something better than this to defend yourself." He licked his lips and forced her to meet his gaze. "We should find something else."

"A weapon?" Hana mouthed the words, and no sound emerged. She reared back, and the towel slipped to reveal a delicate slice of breast. "Are you for real?" Her voice sounded stronger as horror took root. "Where do you get something like that without Sergeant Wally George finding out?"

"Sergeant Wally George." Logan's right eyebrow quirked in a familiar arch. "Oh, and Hana?" His clenched jaw created a hard line through his cheek. "Craig's on my shit list. I won't forget this."

Hana nodded. She stared at her bunched fingers and released the digits one by one, forcing mindfulness into each bent knuckle. "I don't need anything like a gun," she said, forcing confidence into her tone. "I have you. You're my secret weapon."

"True." Logan withdrew his arm and pointed to the sagging bags on the kitchen floor. "But I met this guy today." Logan cocked his head. "He seemed a little off kilter, if you know what I mean? The sort I might go to if I wanted an illegal means of defending myself."

25

Assistance - tauturu

Of course, he knew a guy. Logan always found someone who responded to his alpha qualities.

"But we're on holiday." Her reply held an unattractive note of self pity, which jarred against Logan's kick-ass view of her. Hana sighed and drew her towel up to cover her escaping breast. Logan's irises flickered, and he clamped his teeth over his lower lip. He'd fancy her even in a sack, or better still, nothing at all. "Let me get dressed," she urged, exhaustion lacing her tone. It didn't seem possible that the day had progressed only as far as lunchtime. Much as she'd enjoy spending the rest of it rolling around in bed, they needed to talk. "Then we'll eat and you can tell me what's new and how you met this dodgy sounding guy."

A bag rustled in the centre of the kitchen floor, resisting the mournful sliding action of a milk carton as the tension in the thin plastic gave way. Logan nodded in assent and rose to put the shopping into the fridge and cupboards. Hana tugged on underwear and shrugged a light tee shirt over her head. She added shorts in case Logan intended to ride the bike again. His jerky movements suggested an antsy mood had settled on him. He used his busyness to cover it but didn't fool her practised eye. It took all his resolve not to seek out Craig and exact his revenge. But he'd praised her adroitness and didn't wish to undermine her. Hana suspected he'd do it later. Quiet, deadly and with enough violence to emphasise his irritation.

Hana wrestled her long curls into a low ponytail, which wouldn't impede the motorbike helmet's effectiveness. Her vision of a holiday involved lazy days beside the pool, her novel clutched in her fingers beneath the shade of a wide umbrella. She could taste the rum and coke in her imagination and hear the steady buzz of foraging bees. Her shoulders drooped at the prospect of the reality. She'd spend the next five days buzzing around the island on the back of the Harley while Logan chewed over the mystery of the counterfeit cash. His strong shoulders moved into her peripheral vision as he bent to retrieve a saucepan from a low cupboard. At least they'd spend time together without the constant push and pull of life.

Hana smiled at Logan's bowed head as he fought a rusty tin opener. His scarred fingers wrestled it around the circumference of the tin, the knuckles showing white as he twisted the awkward steel wheel. He pursed his lips into a determined line and his tongue poked through the tender seam of his lips. She sighed and love swelled in her breast at the realisation she still had him all to herself for a miniature snapshot in time. That hadn't changed. All hers. She no longer cared how they used the week, as long as they did it together.

She joined him at the counter, inspecting the empty soup can Logan set in front of her. He retrieved a wooden spoon from a drawer and set the saucepan on the reddening ring of the hob. Hana gave an appreciative nod. "You remembered," she said, lifting the empty tomato soup can and rinsing it beneath the cool stream of water from the tap. She cast her eye over the loaf of bread and tub of butter on the counter. "I guess that's one benefit of a photographic memory. Did you replicate our shopping from last night?"

Logan shook his head. He didn't remove his gaze from the saucepan as he stirred the blood red mixture with the spoon. Bubbles formed on the surface, turning their lunch into volcanic lava. Hana seized the crinkly bread packet and unfastened it at the neck. She withdrew slices and used a nearby knife to spread them with butter. "I still had the receipt," Logan said.

"Found it in my jeans pocket. I asked for the manager and made them replace what we'd paid for."

"Ohhhh." Hana nodded at her husband's logic. "How did he treat you?"

"She," Logan corrected her. "Fine. Apologised for what happened. She reprimanded the cashier, who lied about the note. Says they're all scared. Until now, the company has recouped its losses through docking staff wages. She's promised to rethink that as it's causing distinct problems."

"Right." Hana sensed herself bristling at her husband's productive interaction with another woman. She imagined the supermarket manager fainting at his feet like so many others before her. Some had fancied their chances at knocking Hana out of the pole position, but they'd all failed. Yet the anxiety never left the fringes of her security. Her voice held a flatness as she asked, "So, did she offer you a gun, then?" She raised her pitch and volume to an irritating whine. "Sorry and all that, Mr Du Rose. Here, take this gun with our compliments. Make sure you shoot Creepy Craig right between the eyes and call me to dispose of the body." She slapped a glob of butter onto a slice of bread and smeared it without care. When Logan snorted, she turned to find him studying her movements, one eyebrow raised in understanding. "What?" she demanded, her tone huffy.

He smiled and turned back to his stirring. "You're beautiful when you're jealous."

"I'm not jealous," she muttered under her breath. But a flush rose from her chest, coursing along her jawline and into her cheeks. It flustered her, and she focused on her activity to avoid looking at him.

They ate at the small dining table designed to seat four. Logan opened the front door wide, but kept the metal screen across it. He introduced a cross draught by unlatching the bathroom window. Hana served herself a small portion of the rich tomato soup and tugged a slice of the doughy bread from the board in the centre of the table. It balanced on the lip of her soup bowl, its situation mirroring the precariousness of her mood. She jumped as Logan laid a hand over hers, causing her spoon to pause in mid-air. "Are we good?" he demanded, his voice a low rumble in her chest.

Hana nodded and sighed. "Sorry," she admitted. "I feel vulnerable and touchy. I hated seeing Sally pawing at you last night. You think I'd get used to women lusting after you, but sometimes it just catches me on the raw."

Logan squeezed her fingers. "I get it," he soothed, and Hana relaxed her shoulders. He didn't add the obvious rebuttal that he hated it too, leaving her emotions loose in the airwaves and free to disperse without adding his own to weigh them back to earth. "It sucks," he agreed. "If a guy grabbed a woman with the same sense of entitlement, he'd end up in a police cell." He shook his head as though bemused. "She stroked my crotch right in front of her husband. How could he just ignore it?"

Hana swallowed. A heady mixture of rage and shame prickled her skin like sunburn. She chewed the hunk of bread in her mouth but found herself still unable to swallow its clogging remains. Her memory replayed an image of Logan lifting Sally's arm by her flouncy sleeve and laying her hand on the table. "I didn't know," she whispered, but shook her head against the immediate lie. She'd sensed Logan's discomfort but chosen to bypass his sense of violation to concentrate on her own. "Bitch!" She let her spoon drop into her bowl, where it caused a scarlet tsunami in sympathy.

Logan reached for his second slice of bread, peering at the lavish smearing of butter slapped over its surface as evidence of Hana's frustration. "She'll get hers," he advised, his tone sombre.

Hana resumed eating, working her frayed bread around the bowl to clean up the splotches on the white surface. "Did the supermarket manager offer you a gun, then?" The question sounded casual enough to jolt her senses. When did such things become commonplace for her?

"Nope." Logan licked his lips before speaking. He stared at a greasy line of butter on his index finger before pushing it into his mouth. "A guy waited by the bike when I came outside. I saw him in the distance, but he'd picked a public venue, so I figured he meant me no physical harm. Perhaps a threat or a warning."

"What did he want?" Hana leaned forward, eager for speed in his retelling. "Who is he?"

Logan placed his spoon in his empty bowl. He spun to survey the kitchen cupboards as though considering raiding them for dessert. As he turned back to the table, his gaze rested on Hana's avid expression. His shoulders dropped, and he glanced at the open front door. He lowered his voice and leaned forward, his fringe mingling with hers. Black and red. "Remember the guy who ran over Jared in his ute?" He waited for her nod before continuing. "Him. Gantry Hosking. He's also the guy who owns the diving tour boat I went on. I saw very little of him. He drove the boat and his assistant did all the safety stuff with the divers. But Sergeant Wally George has indicated he won't charge him with any road traffic offences because enough witnesses saw Jared step into the street. But there's a massive psychological difference between an accident and an accidental death. He thanked us for trying to help Jared. He asked if we needed anything and I said a man at the market gave us a couple of mangoes."

Logan lifted his index finger. “But we got talking, and he seemed amenable, so I asked him about the fake money.” He blew out a whistle between his teeth. “And that’s when it got really interesting.”

26

Gossip - puka

Hana fidgeted as Logan rose to set his empty plate in the dishwasher. She ached to drag the story from his lips like a magician tugging scarves from his assistant's sleeve. But experience had taught her the art of waiting. No one rushed Logan Du Rose and as he closed the door of the dishwasher and rinsed his fingers under the tap, she sensed him ordering his thoughts. He leaned against the counter and pursed his lips; the moments passing with agonising slowness.

Hana sighed and released her spoon against the side of her bowl. The chair spindles dug into her spine as she slumped in her seat. She jerked like a sleeper as Logan spoke. "The fake cash turned up a few months ago. At first, the local traders figured it came from one hooky tourist who'd spent their way around the island. The bank confiscated the notes as they circulated back to them, but it meant someone had enjoyed free goods and services. The unfortunate guy who banked his day's takings lost out."

Hana blew out a frustrated breath. "I understand all that," she remarked, her tone piqued. "The banks have counting machines which detect fake notes. That's not a new thing."

Logan clicked his fingers, as though irritated. "It's data, babe. Part of the backstory." If he heard Hana's grumbling, he ignored it. "It gives us a starting point. The first notes turned up roughly three months ago. The traders searched for triggers."

"Such as?" Hana spun in her seat, her brow wrinkling.

Logan shrugged his muscular shoulders. "New folks on the island, either business owners or residents. Someone bringing their bad habits with them. They figured anyone manufacturing counterfeit cash would need a secret warehouse, heavy equipment, and employees willing to stay quiet. Between them, they watched the spending habits of everyone they knew, looking for a sudden and unexpected influx of disposable income or someone purchasing a flashy car or new stuff for their house. Nothing."

"What about power and resources?" Hana nudged a breadcrumb around the surface of the table. She narrowed her eyes in concentration.

Logan joined her back at the table, his chair legs scraping against the tiles as he sat. "One of them called in a favour on the mainland and obtained electricity readings for all residences and businesses on the island. The hospital uses more power than the airport and the rest of the island put together. More even than the supermarket. But that makes sense, doesn't it?" He leaned forward, forcing Hana's gaze to meet his. "It's the only building which functions for twenty-four hours a day and seven days a week. There's nothing unusual about those findings."

Hana nodded. "I guess so. But it's also a marvellous place to hide a power greedy industry."

"Na." Logan shook his head, and the chair spindles creaked as he sat back hard. "I've researched counterfeiting operations before and they're big business. It requires a massive outlay at the start, professional equipment and expensive graphics. And even if you sourced all of that without issue, you'd still need access to the correct paper to print the money onto it."

"Where could you get that?" Hana's voice sounded tiny in the silence, like the squeak of a mouse before it bolted from a cat. She side stepped her curiosity about why her husband might have researched such an operation, hoping he hadn't considered a sideline. "Australia? That's not far away."

"Canada, now. Ottawa, if you want a precise location. They make the Series 7 banknotes from polymer, ship them to the Reserve Bank in New Zealand and they distribute them through the banks."

"Right." Hana dropped her chin. "Checks and balances, then. The banks will run the incoming notes through their machines and pick up any fakes at the source. Is it possible for a counterfeiting organisation to access the special paper?"

"Doubtful." Logan's head shook from side to side. "And Sergeant Wally George already decided they weren't manufacturing here. Which means the island has its very own distributor."

Hana tutted. "Anyone on this island could fit that role."

"Not anyone. Remember what he told us? The static population of Rarotonga is under fourteen thousand people."

"So, he needs to identify one person out of that fourteen thousand who either joined the island as a resident or changed their behaviour in the last three months."

Logan shrugged. "That takes us back to the traders and the fact they've already looked at that. Nobody stood out. Gantry Hosking told me that himself."

Hana cocked her head like a little bird. "Gantry Hosking? The man who ran Jared over offered to help us?"

"Yeah."

"So why did he tell you all this?" Hana collected up her bowl and spoon, walking into the kitchen to add them to Logan's in the dishwasher. "It's an odd thing to do, isn't it? Do you usually spill your guts to tourists in the supermarket car park?"

"Yeah." Logan watched her while running a hand through his hair. "Maybe because I asked him a direct question, and he felt obligated. I said we found ourselves arrested on our first day here because the supermarket cashier tried to pass us a dirty twenty. He said he'd heard about it and someone pointed us out at the Trading Post last night."

"Is there any news on Jarad?" Hana closed the dishwasher door and twisted her lips in concern. She pushed away the humiliating notion of everyone at the bar, pointing and whispering about them. "Or Hallie? What if she's still missing and doesn't know he's in hospital?"

Logan heaved out a sigh. "We told the sergeant," he replied. "It's up to him, isn't it?"

Hana tapped a gentle beat on the counter and let her mind sift through the many issues. Her eyes brightened as she turned to Logan. "The counterfeit cash thing is too hard for us. We only have a week to solve something the police haven't got a clue about. They've had three months and turned up nothing. Let's look for Hallie instead."

Logan gave a slow nod. "Okay," he agreed, although he seemed less committed to the new task. "Where do you suggest we start?"

27

Malicious - uruto'e

Logan shielded his eyes from the sun's glare and peered through the front window of Hallie's villa. He squinted at the rust-coloured sofa which twinned the one in their lounge. "All the furniture is identical," he remarked, his voice muffled against the glass. "I guess it makes sense. It's not exactly bespoke, more like the stuff from a cheap end motel in south Auckland."

"Ooh la-de-dah," Hana commented. "Says the posh hotel owner."

"Hey, all our suites had purpose-built furniture. They named each one after an ancestor." He blinked and his fringe bounced against his lashes. "The events company stripped it all out and bulk ordered this crap." Pique entered his tone. He'd sold off the individual pieces before the lease began, but it had pained him.

Hana lifted her knuckles and rapped again on Hallie's front door. She shook her head even before the sound completed its last echo from inside the villa. A deadness surrounded the building and her instinct told her no one breathing remained inside. She pursed her lips. "Do you think housekeeping has already visited this morning?"

Logan tipped his head to study the door handle. No sign hung from the knob to ask the maid service to stay away. "Yeah, they arrive before ten o'clock. Did they come to our place?"

Hana nodded. "Yes, while we visited the market. The ladies refilled the toiletries and left us fresh towels." She dropped her hand and tried the knob. It turned beneath her fingers before halting. The door didn't budge. "Locked," she concluded and took a step backwards, her arms swinging by her sides.

They both jumped as a sharp voice lifted to bark at them. "What the hell are you doing?"

Hana blinked and turned to stare at Sally. Her eyes narrowed as she caught the distinctive English accent forming a base to her speech. She wondered why she hadn't noticed before, but dismissed the notion of the image of a drunken, lascivious Sally draped across Logan. She couldn't have noticed much. Hana's lips curled back in a silent snarl of injustice. But Logan spoke first. "Looking for Hallie. We left her here last night, but Jared said she's missing." The soles of Logan's cowboy boots ground against beach sand caught in the ridges of the deck. He faced Sally and raised his eyebrow. "Jared's in hospital. She needs to know."

"Oh." Sally frowned and her stance relaxed. She'd pulled her bleached curls into a tight bun at the back of her head, and she wore loose cotton trousers which matched a plain v-necked shirt. The colour seemed important as Hana surveyed her, the shade of cornflower blue familiar and inducing a wave of anxiety in her chest.

"Are you a nurse?" Hana frowned and stepped to the edge of the deck. She gripped the hand rail and forced her view of the drunken Sally to crystallise into something more responsible.

Sally shrugged. "I work a few shifts at the hospital each week. They phone me when they're short staffed in between."

Hana nodded and forced a smile onto her lips. "Do you know where Hallie is? Is she aware of Jared's accident?"

"No idea." Sally's gaze roved over Logan like a carnivore sizing up a swollen steak. "Haven't seen her since last night." She spun to face Hana and levelled her accusation without inflection. "What possessed you to just abandon her like that?"

Hana glanced up at Logan, regretting the covert action which drew instant suspicion on them. She swallowed, picking through a choice of words to form a reasonable reply. It seemed uncharitable in the light of Jared's accident to focus on Hallie's behaviour. Logan answered for her. "She sent us away," he replied, his tone even. "Didn't want us to stay with her. We left her here to wait for you." He pointed to the outdoor seating, still bearing the dent in the cushions from a prone, drunken body.

Sally's dyed brows drew into a continuous dark line, which appeared stark against her blonde hair with its escaping red genetics. "I didn't find her," she said, her tone acquiring a civility previously missing. Concern added itself, making Hana's worry metre climb. "I unlocked her front door and searched around but didn't find her. She didn't walk to the pool or back to the road. Craig arrived home, so I sent him to ask you. I knew I had this afternoon shift and I can't cope if I'm too tired. He told me this morning about your break-in." Deep crevices formed over her brow and she pressed her fingers together. "I'm sorry about that. We're usually quite safe out here." She took a step towards the deck as though only just registering part of Logan's statement. "What's happened to Jared?"

"He stepped into the road and got mowed down by a ute."

Hana winced at the starkness of Logan's reply. He didn't couch it in a better description, but gave her the skinny right on the nose. Sally blew out a breath and swore. "Stupid idiot!" she snarled. "Did he fall off the curb or something? Craig didn't mention it last night." Her features screwed into lines and creases, betraying her true mileage as older than she at first appeared. Hana had mistaken her age as mid-fifties, the same as her. But in the harshness of the afternoon sunshine, the bleached hair and tan lines put Sally in her early sixties. It took a moment for her to notice Sally's wrong assumption.

"It happened this morning." She curved her right hand around the banister rail and gripped, wincing at the sharp pinch of a splinter entering the delicate pad of her index finger. "At the Saturday market. He'd searched for Hallie and seemed worried. We said we hadn't seen her and he walked into the road." The explanation sounded ludicrous, and Hana licked her lips as she stated the truth. In her peripheral vision, Logan frowned as though something had just occurred to him, a light flicking on behind his grey irises like the beacon from a lighthouse.

Sally's snort jarred with the peaceful chirp of birds in the coconut trees and the gentle buzz of a foraging bee. "Bloody idiots!" she remarked. "I don't know why Craig bothers with them." An ugly smile transformed her expression into something more sinister, and her fingers twitched. "I'll check on Jared during my break," she stated. Her tone of voice suggested he wouldn't enjoy the experience.

They watched as Sally retraced her steps across the shared lawn and strode towards the reception. The wide girths of several trees caused a strobe effect as she moved between them. She unlocked a silver hatchback with a key fob and slid into the driver's seat. The brake lights flashed red as she reversed onto the narrow road, the motor obscuring little of the background noise with its tinny purr.

"Hmmmn." Logan turned to face Hana with his eyebrow raised. "Weird, or what?"

28

Lean on - ʻirinaki

Hana considered the odd conversation without finding a decent thread to pull. She frowned up at her husband. "Which part did you find weird?" she demanded.

His lips curved upward in a smile before his nose wrinkled. The conclusion both amused him and created discomfort. He paused a moment before voicing it. "Swingers," he stated, waiting for Hana to catch up with his thoughts.

"What?" She jerked her head back in disbelief. "You believe Sally is sleeping with Jared? I didn't think she much liked him."

"They're all sleeping with each other," he confirmed. "Put the facts together."

The notion disturbed Hana, pushing her over the edge into denial. "What facts?" Her voice rose.

"It doesn't matter. Forget it." He slipped an arm around her shoulder and led her towards the steps, sighing as she locked her knees and resisted his embrace.

"What facts?" she demanded again. "That's one hell of a leap. You've met them a couple of times less than me. I didn't pick that up at all!"

Logan turned to face her. His lips pulled back from his teeth as though he'd sucked a lemon. "Did any of them proposition you?" He set his hands on his hips and his body stiffened. "Did they, Hana?"

"No." The word tailed off in a whimper. She lowered her voice and stepped up to her husband, pressing her palms against his broad chest. His heartbeat pulsed through her palms, strong and steady. The plate of muscle encasing his major organs offered reassurance and grounded her in a cocoon of certainty. She smoothed her sore finger across the pale grey fabric of his tee shirt. Resignation entered her tone. "Maybe. You think that's why Craig let himself into our villa this morning? And why he keeps trying to get close to me?"

"I don't know." Logan tucked a stray red curl behind Hana's ear. Another escaped from her ponytail to flutter against her cheek. He blew out a ragged breath. "While you pulled Hallie from that bush last night, Sally gave me a quick run down on what's on offer. She made it sound like a bordello menu and believe me, anything goes! Do you want to know the special offer for last night?"

"I'm not sure I do." Hana eyed him sideways.

"Tough! You wanted facts, babe. Well, the special offer for last night was just me and her. Swingers. What else can it be? Those four are all over each other like rabbits. There's no other explanation."

Hana gasped and covered her mouth with her hand. "I feel sick," she breathed. "But also furious and upset. You'd just met her. It's hardly appropriate small talk."

"Are you upset on my account? Or at the thought of not getting to watch?"

Hana sank into Hallie's vacated seat. She ignored Logan's sarcasm. "This makes no sense," she said with a weak sigh. "What did Hallie say last night? It sounded odd if they're partner swapping all over the place."

"She said, '*Poor Sally. She has no idea.*' Or something of that ilk."

Logan snorted. "Poor Sally has plenty of ideas and most of them relate to me naked in her bed." He gave a visible shiver. "I'm not sure what Hallie meant. It seemed an odd thing to say, regardless."

"Do you think Craig and Hallie are having an affair and they're not, you know, cross pollinating?"

Logan closed his eyes and shivered. “Can we not continue this discussion, please? It’s definitely all four of them at it together, in pairs or…” He sighed. “As a group.”

Hana pursed her lips and let her gaze rove over his sturdy frame honed by farm labour and the hotel gym. “Do you feel you’re missing out?” she whispered.

Logan’s eyes widened, and a fleeting expression of horror caused him to flinch. “What? Oh shit! Do you?”

“No.” Hana shook her head. “But I worry I’m not enough for you. I mean, you’re, you know. Buff. And I’m weak and wimpy and it seems I’m always injured.”

“Oh, Hana.” Logan tracked heavy steps back to her and, dipping his torso, scooped her into his arms. He carried her back to their villa, his expression grim and his intentions scored through the laugh lines at the corners of his eyes. She squeaked and slipped sideways as he balanced her weight over one leg and stabbed the key into the lock. The screen door swung back and bashed her elbow.

Logan carried her inside the villa and slammed the door behind them. He laid Hana on the mattress as though depositing fine china on a display stand. Seconds later, he’d kicked off his boots, drawn the curtains and dragged the two-seater sofa in front of the door.

And then he showed her how he felt about monogamy.

Just the two of them.

Without a twisted audience.

29

Comforted - pūma 'ana

"We didn't get far searching for Hallie, did we?" Hana yawned and rolled onto her side. "We should at least visit Jared in hospital."

"Should we?" Logan leaned up on one elbow and rested his temple against his knuckles. He used the fingers of his other hand to draw patterns on Hana's bare skin. She sighed and pressed her cheek into the pillow, enjoying the ticklish sensation along her spine. Logan wrote something almost discernible as a word, rubbed it out and scribed something else. Hana closed her eyes and concentrated. He'd written *'I love you'* using the space between her shoulder blades. Rubbing it out, he drew a heart. Hana smirked into her soft pillow. Logan Du Rose portrayed an image devoid of sentimentality. She knew the other side of him, the tender giant with the unwavering loyalty.

And then she went and ruined it. "Where do you think Hallie went?" she asked, her voice a low drawl in the silence.

Logan sighed and disconnected from her. He rolled onto his back and stared at the ceiling. "Don't know. Don't care. I wouldn't spit on any of them if they caught fire." He grunted and used his stomach muscles to sit upright. His St. Christopher necklace tinkled as the silver links moved against his skin.

Hana raised herself up and leaned against the headboard, tugging the sheet until it covered her breasts and the livid red scar at her side. "Why don't we shift to a different resort?" she asked, her tone even. "Start again. Craig didn't want us gossiping about the break-in to other tourists. I'm sure we could find an empty room on another part of the island if we searched for ourselves."

Logan sighed. He turned his head and squinted at her. "I don't have the energy, Hana. We could waste a whole day mucking around and end up somewhere we hate. It's five and a half days. I'm sure we can survive."

"Okay." Hana stretched out her hand and laid her palm on his pectoral. Relief formed her primary emotion. She didn't have the energy to waste either. Logan's skin reflected the healthy glow of copper, contrasting with the silver necklace, which cascaded like a waterfall to one side. But when Logan rose from the mattress, his back, sides, and stomach presented an alternate view. Only Hana and his children ever saw the scarring he'd collected over a lifetime of accident and injury. Some had darkened to brown lines and others showed as white. The worst one wrapped around his torso from beneath his right armpit before diving towards his hip. It had healed with exaggerated slowness, hypertrophy raising it to a winding ridge which always appeared swollen and red. Ugly perpendicular lines bisected it, emergency surgery giving each stitch the illusion of a millipede's legs crawling around his body. Hana wrapped her arms around his waist as he sat on the edge of the bed, pressing her lips against the ridge. Her acceptance of all his fault lines had drawn them together. His appreciation of hers turned them into a powerful team.

"Hungry?" Logan asked. He reached back and ruffled her hair with his capable fingers.

Hana sighed. "Not bothered," she replied. "Why don't we ride around the island? Let's go anticlockwise again. We might find somewhere serving food."

Logan nodded his acceptance, perhaps keen to avoid Craig, Sally, and their alternative relationship style. Hana didn't mention Hallie again, not wanting to trigger a disagreement. But she figured a ride around the perimeter road would at least confirm Hallie's absence from the outer edges of the island. She didn't have a plan beyond that.

They showered and dressed. Logan caused another delay by joining Hana beneath the warm spray, his ministrations making her squeak and press a hand over her mouth. He laughed at her, turning his body to take the brunt of the water pressure as he kissed her in the confines of the cubicle. She escaped after water from the shower head filled her mouth for the second time. She spat it onto the tray beneath her feet and prayed she didn't suffer a bellyache from the impurities for the next five days. Paradise viewed from the toilet seat.

Logan locked up, snagging long, fine strands of Hana's red hair to set traps for Craig if he searched the villa again in their absence. Hana waited by the motorbike, wondering what they'd do if they returned to find themselves victims of another intruder. Sergeant Wally George seemed sincere, but also hamstrung by the island's archaic systems and the constant population churn. Hana sighed, wishing Logan hadn't set the traps at all. Perhaps it would be better not to know.

They circled the island in the balmy air, visors open and a breeze from their motion banishing the day's relentless heat. Logan dismissed Hana's request to drive anticlockwise, instead turning right at the resort's entrance and taking her to the Shipwreck Hut just below Sunset Quay. He ordered them each a burger and a soft drink before settling on a wooden bench just a few metres from the waterline. They watched the glowing ball of flame sink towards the horizon in amicable silence. It splashed its dying light across the ocean until only silhouettes remained.

Hana sighed with satisfaction. "Amazing," she breathed. "I could watch that every night." She couldn't see Logan's features in the instant darkness as the sun died, but she heard the rustle of his tee shirt as he nodded.

"It's beautiful," he agreed with a deep sigh. "Paradise."

Hana nodded and picked at the salad which had slid from between the burger and its bun. Peace shrouded her for the first time in months. The fibrous, earthy scent of coconut trees surrounded them, mingling with the tang of salt water and fast food. Her cares slid from her shoulders for long enough to refresh her, before thoughts of her children crowded into the vacant space. "Have you heard from Mark?" she asked. Despite her casual tone, a maternal yearning ached from beneath the request.

"Yeah." Logan shifted on the seat, tugging his phone from his pocket. A blue glow flickered in the darkness like a jellyfish beneath the tide as he unlocked the screen. He pushed it towards her across the table's slatted surface. "The roaming kicked in for about a minute while we showered. He's sent photos of their visit to the zoo in Hamilton. It rained yesterday, so he got them painting Dean's office."

"Wow. Brave man." Hana lifted the screen and its reflection revealed the naked hunger in her eyes. Mark had lined up the children in height order, each clasping a paint brush in their fist. Phoenix sported a streak of white paint in her hair and Wiremu wore only his boxer shorts. Hana gnawed at her lower lip, forcing herself not to worry about what happened to the rest of his clothing. Mac grinned for the camera, but Hana spotted his iPad peeking out from behind his back. Not a single speck of paint stained his person or his brush, indicating he'd opted out of the activity. Edin waved her brush in her left hand, a wicked smile on her upturned lips. It explained Wiri's nakedness, anyway. She'd painted him instead of the wall.

Hana flicked through the glittering images to find the zoo pictures. Dean carried Mac on his hip, hoisting him to see into the monkey enclosure. An unnatural pink stain encircled the child's lips to create a clownish grin, the effect eerie and unnerving. She shook her head, grateful she didn't need to face the inevitable sugar rush and hyperactivity which resulted afterwards. A glance at Logan found him smirking.

"They're fine," he soothed. "Scroll to the end of the album. Mark and Dean drove them to the beach today. They're still alive."

"Who's still alive?" Hana quipped. "Mark and Dean, or the kids?"

Logan grinned. "I'm hoping they all are. Dean looks a bit ragged in that last picture. The kids are fine, but your brother might have divorced by the end of the week." He leaned across and jabbed a finger at the screen. "Look at Dean's hair in that picture from the zoo. It's sticking up on end. Mark said in the email, a gorilla spat at him."

"Oh, nice!" Hana turned her lower lip down in disgust. "They look happy. Well, the children do, anyway. Not sure about Mark and Dean. Are there more?"

"One of Leslie with her skirt caught in her knickers. The kids are laughing, and Dean looks horrified. I deleted it." Logan shook his head before taking back his phone. He leaned back and returned it to his pocket. "I had internet for long enough to download these pictures from an email to my phone. Then it crapped out again."

Hana wrinkled her nose and leaned forward to hug her knees. Guilt and responsibility settled after their short hiatus. She'd pushed all mental images of Jared's accident from her immediate vision, praying their efforts weren't wasted but dreading confirmation. "What time do you think visiting hour finishes at the hospital?"

Logan raised an eyebrow at her, but he didn't reply. The mood dampened, but then his irises lit with a curious glow. Suspicion budded in Hana's chest. "Yeah," he replied with a smile. "Let's do it. Let's visit Jared."

30

Nurse - nēti

Darkness enfolded the island in a Pashmina shawl of Payne's grey and Ivory black. Without the light pollution of the mainland, stars spilled overhead like water tipped from an ethereal bucket. Venus rose beneath the crescent moon, bright and confident in her placement within the broad highway of galactic activity. Hana tilted her head back as Logan indicated and turned onto the road leading to the hospital. A pang of longing tugged at her heart. This same sky covered her babies. She reached out her right hand as though able to straighten the wrinkled sheet of time and tug it hard enough for her children to notice. The twenty-three hour time difference seemed like a lifetime, though the journey to Rarotonga took only four hours.

The bike tilted as Logan drove into a space between a slew of abandoned scooters. Lined up beside a white single storey building, they sat quietly in shadow awaiting their riders. Logan engaged the stand and killed the engine. Hana hopped down first, tugging the heavy helmet from her head. She ran a hand through her hair and spun on the spot, already seeking a direction. Logan locked the bike and joined her, taking the weight of the helmet from her. "I wish we could leave them with the bike," Hana commented. "Can't we lock them to it?"

Logan shrugged and nudged her towards a low slung porch lit by a yellow glow. "The guy asked us not to. He has his reasons."

Hana traipsed behind him, her mind whirring with possibilities for the request. Intrigue irked her, muddying her vision with its spidery stain. She fought the desire to know everything, aware of the trouble it had caused in her relationship with Bodie. They reached the covered porch and Hana stared up at two overhead signs. A blue outpatients banner butted up to a red emergency label. It seemed clear enough until she realised both culminated in only one set of doors.

Logan turned to his right and tugged open the door. It creaked on tired hinges. He waited for Hana to pass through first, and then followed. A uniformed receptionist greeted them with a smile, appearing fresh and jovial. "How can I help you?" he asked in accented English. The wide gap between his upper incisors gave him a sparkly grin, which Hana returned with ease. Blue scrubs similar to Sally's fit his plump body like a comfortable shroud. Logan cleared his throat, bobbing his head to draw the man's interest from Hana. "Please, can you tell us what time visiting hours finish?"

The receptionist shrugged and beamed at Hana again. Jet black hair sprouted from his scalp like new grass. He replied to her as though she'd asked the question. "You can come anytime," he said with sincerity. Hana pursed her lips, wondering if he meant she could visit anytime or everyone. Logan huffed next to her, even his bent elbow sharper and more pointy from his irritation.

"Thank you," Hana replied. "Our friend had an accident this morning at the market. We'd like to see him."

"His name?" The receptionist's fingers poised over the keyboard as though he prepared to serenade her with a piano concerto.

Hana floundered. Having got thus far, she realised she only knew Jared and Hallie's first names. "Jared," she said, earnestness entering her tone. She leaned forward, bumping Logan's knotty elbow against her upper arm. "He's staying at Paradise Villas. We just met him yesterday."

The receptionist's fingers sprung to life, eager to please despite the scant information. He seemed elated when his search returned the location for Jared Clarke on the high dependency unit. He offered directions and handed a leaflet to Hana. Bemused, she accepted it with thanks and turned her feet toward the double doors leading into the bowels of the hospital. The receptionist turned to the couple behind them, betraying a latent distrust for all males by behaving in exactly the same way. Hana shrugged at her husband, but he still appeared annoyed by the obvious slight.

A wheeled trolley beside the first set of doors on their journey contained hand sanitiser, paper masks, and disposable gloves. The tatty, handwritten sign on the wall urged them not to enter if they felt unwell. With frustration as their only symptom, they cleaned their hands, fixed a mask over their noses and mouths and took a set of gloves each for good measure. The door clanged behind them.

Dense bush surrounded the hospital site, the chatter of insects adding background noise to every conversation. Open windows fed the buildings with a light breeze, which distributed the chemical scents. The hospital's construction comprised buildings grouped into a huddle like gossiping schoolchildren. Paths joined each satellite to the main section. Paint flaked in the corridors although someone had taken pains to make economical repairs. But the shade they'd used didn't match the original, creating jarring blobs of light or shadow which drew more attention than the damage they sought to cover. A bulb flickered, casting an eerie, strobing effect along the scarred walls of the corridor.

They found the high dependency unit near the surgical theatres, barred by the only locked door they'd so far discovered. Another trolley bearing more protective and sanitary items sat outside. To the left of the unit ran a perpendicular corridor, the double doors marked with a sign which said, 'Danger. Asbestos.' Hammering and the whir of a drill sounded from beyond them. The left door swung in the breeze just enough to create whirling dust motes in a stray shaft of light. Scaffolding poles winked from inside.

A smiling nurse saw them through the glass of the HDU and walked to meet them. It seemed to Hana that despite the lack of funds and resources, everyone she encountered within the island facility greeted them with a smile and the intention of giving their best efforts. Logan let Hana take the lead, still perplexed by the receptionist's behaviour towards him. "Kia orana," she began. "Please, may we see Jared Clarke?" As the nurse's smile faded, Hana panicked, dreading the worst possible news. She jabbed a finger from Logan to herself in a feckless flapping motion. "We tried to help him at the market this morning. He didn't look good." She stopped and pursed her lips. "Could we at least know how he's doing?"

To her surprise, the door swung open, and the nurse waved them through the gap. A magnetic tag affixed to her shirt hung at an angle, the hospital logo beside her name in a serif font. Karla. She lowered her voice to a whisper in keeping with the dim lighting and mausoleum atmosphere. "He's very sick," she said through her mask. "Are you the couple who resuscitated him?"

Hana swallowed, and her gaze slid to Logan. The details felt more important than she realised. She nodded before changing the action to a shake. "We tried. The paramedics saved him, really."

"Would you like to see him?" The question surprised Hana after the woman's initial resistance. A blockage formed in her mind. She wanted to know how Jared fared after his ute versus man disagreement, but she wasn't sure she wanted to view the aftermath with her own eyes. Not again.

"Yes, please." Logan answered for her, edging his body across hers as though protecting her from an unknown threat. He turned to speak to her. "You can wait here if you'd, rather. I'll visit with him." He raised an eyebrow in question, but his sudden eagerness heightened that niggling sense of suspicion.

Hana shook her head. Her eyes narrowed. "No, I'll come in with you."

31

Likeness - taipe

Jared slept in a bed cranked up to waist height. Rails along each side prevented him from waking and tipping onto the floor. Wires fed from his right hand to a monitor which stood over him like a guard. It ticked and chirped to itself as though participating in a one-way conversation.

An empty bed flanked Jared's, but the one opposite contained a man who groaned often. The woman with him wore a sarong, which barely covered her swimsuit. Dark shadows lurked beneath her dull eyes, evidence of a holiday gone horribly wrong on day three. Hana recognised her from Auckland airport and shot her an encouraging smile. The woman didn't register it and arched her body in despair, pressing her forehead to the mattress beside her partner's hand.

Hana edged nearer to Jared's bed and released a sigh of relief from behind her mask. She turned to the nurse who'd accompanied them. "He looks much better," she whispered.

A cast encased his left arm from wrist to elbow, its sibling wrapped around his leg. Hairy brown toes protruded from the end of the fibreglass. Apart from a deep scrape on his left cheek and an engorged eye socket, his head appeared less damaged than the paramedic first declared. Hana surveyed the wires running from his chest like a pile of dropped spaghetti. Recognition caused lines to appear across her forehead. Cardio monitors.

"His heart stopped." The nurse leaned closer to Hana, her breath puffing out the fabric mask as she spoke. "The doctor thinks he suffered a cardiac arrest because of the shock of the impact. He has breaks and contusions, but we believe he'll make a full recovery."

Logan remained motionless, his fingers gripping the motorbike helmets and flexing over the bars beneath the visors. His knuckles showed white through his tawny skin, and Hana frowned. He wore what Wiri called 'his thinking face.' So Hana took responsibility for making small talk with the attentive nurse. "Did his wife visit?" she asked, keeping her tone light.

A pebble of worry lodged in her chest as Karla shook her head. "Wife?" Her lips flattened into a line and she turned her body to mirrored Hana's posture. "No.

Could you ask her to visit? We need her to make an insurance claim for Mr Clarkes' medical bills."

"Right." Hana frowned. She imagined the dilemma of a surgeon faced with a life-threatening injury. Did they treat the patient or wait for the ink to dry on the cheque first? She nodded, grateful the staff had allowed necessity to trump reimbursement. She sought to reassure the nurse. "His wife is a travel agent in New Zealand. They'll have a great insurance policy."

Karla smiled, brown tendrils escaping from her bun like waving antennae. "Good," she said. "Ask her to visit soon. Our receptionist has her paperwork at the front desk."

Hana nodded and changed tack. "Did Sally visit?" she asked. Logan's head tilted in her peripheral vision as he tuned in to the conversation.

"Sorry?" The nurse dipped forward as though seeking more information before she could reply.

"Sally," Hana whispered. "She works here on a casual basis. Her husband manages the resort we stay at with Jared. And his wife." She swallowed, the disjointed sentences trailing off as a flurry of thoughts ambushed her. If Sally altered sexual partners as Logan suspected, swinging between Craig and Jared and anyone else who seemed interested, she would have visited. Wouldn't she?

"Excuse me?" The woman in the sarong lifted a hand to get the nurse's attention. She pointed to the groaning man in the bed. "Is he due any pain relief?" she asked, her tone tight as though forcing the words from behind her tongue. "Because he's bloody killing me."

Hana darted her attention to Logan and met his amused gaze. He angled his body alongside the foot of Jared's bed and while the woman distracted the nurse with her litany of tired complaints, he bent and lifted Jared's medical chart from where it hung. His keen eyes speed read the slanted script, soaking up the information and replacing the chart before Hana finished reading Jared's full name. Someone had ticked the check box beside an authentication question, scrawling *'passport sighted'* beside it in red ink.

Jared didn't stir.

Satisfied, Logan turned to Hana, indicating the door with a jerk of his head. It seemed strange to just walk away, adding nothing to Jared's plight. Hana felt honour bound to kiss his cheek or stroke his static fingers, but recoiled at the notion. Instead, she caught the nurse's eye, waiting until the woman finished soothing the groaning patient's partner. "Hey," Hana whispered as she drew close. "We'll keep looking for his wife. Sergeant Wally George knows she's missing. He can find us if Jared needs anything. Clothes, toiletries or something from the store." She nodded her head to emphasise her offer. Karla repeated Sergeant Wally George's name as though praying to a deity.

Logan cleared his throat behind Hana. He directed his question to the nurse. "Jared had alcohol in his system, but no drugs?"

She blinked, confused by his directness and his obvious knowledge of Jared's medical details. But Hana's mention of the revered police officer placed them in an unknown category. A millisecond of conflict crossed the woman's tired face, the mask shielding lips, which perhaps pursed in disapproval. Then she relented, wrongly giving the police connection too much weight. "Alcohol, yes," she whispered. Her gaze turned to Jared's prone body, the chest rising and falling like a gentle, rolling earthquake. "But no drugs. And not much alcohol. Perhaps left over from the night before. Not enough to impair his reactions."

"Right. Thanks." Logan gave a definitive nod of his head, his analytical mind already sifting the next set of facts into a neat order. "When do you expect he'll wake?"

"Tomorrow." She dropped her chin, her brown eyes jerking towards the ceiling as she fought the automatic eye roll. Another groan issued from the other occupied bed, and Hana experienced a moment of sympathy. The groaner and his complaining partner would occupy all her shifts without Jared making demands, too. Hana offered her an encouraging smile, and they left the high dependency unit faster than they had entered it.

Outside in the balmy air, Hana gave a frustrated shrug. "We're no better off," she stated, taking her helmet from Logan. "Still no Hallie, and no reason for Jared to step into traffic."

"Hmmn." Logan sounded unsure, and Hana pulled off the mask and jabbed it into her shorts pocket with the gloves.

"What does that mean?" she demanded. "Why did you snoop in Jared's medical chart? What's with the question about the drugs?" She proceeded first through the next set of doors, not giving him a chance to behave as a gentleman.

Logan popped off his mask with a sigh and ran his free hand over his face. He dropped the fabric into the nearest dustbin. A smug expression bloomed across his handsome features. The overhead lights caused long shadows from his eyelashes to create a slatted effect across his cheeks. He slipped his arm around Hana's shoulders as they retraced their steps through the hospital. His body tilted as he leaned sideways to whisper to her. Hana lifted her chin, straining to catch every gruff word. Logan's shoulder bumped her left ear.

"First up, Jared wasn't drunk or drugged when he stepped in front of that ute."

"He stank of fags and beer!" Hana protested.

Logan's head bobbed in a silent acknowledgement. "Yeah, but he spent the night gambling. The nurse confirmed his blood results showed little remaining in his system. He'd have passed a breathaliser when he returned Craig's car. And do you remember noticing him with a cigarette?"

"No," Hana admitted. "So what? He spent the night losing money to other people who drank beer and smoked. What difference does that make?"

"Because he stepped into the road."

Hana shot a smile at the receptionist as they navigated the wide waiting room. A queue snaked from his desk to the doors, a bleeding multitude in varying states of undress. A cut to a forehead, a weeping toe and the inevitable child complaining about the pea wedged up his nose.

The clang of the outer door halted the hum of muted chatter, and Hana savoured the fresh balmy air. The sleeping sun had taken its warmth to bed with it, leaving behind a subtle chill. "We'd just told Jared to report Hallie as a missing person," Hana stated, peering into the darkness for the Harley's location. "Of course, he seemed shocked."

But Logan didn't move. He stood beneath the porch and shook his head at her. "No, Hana. When he approached us, the only thing he displayed was anger. He demanded we take him back to the resort. Then something changed."

"What?" Hana lifted her arms and dropped them to her sides, the motorbike helmet clattering against her thigh. Tiredness snaked around her calves, feeding her self-pity with promises of cool water from the fridge and a well deserved lie down. She turned away from Logan, her footsteps sending gravel skittering into the darkness beyond reach of the dim lighting.

"He saw something." Logan lifted his voice, and Hana halted. She half turned to face him, her brows drawing into a line. "Remember? I told him to go to the police station, and he stared at that stall selling shells or pebbles." He flapped his hand in irritation. "Jangly things made of beach crap."

Hana's lips parted. She'd wanted one of those mobiles. "Not beach crap," she muttered. Undeterred, Logan continued working through a list of details she'd failed to notice.

"What if he didn't stare at something, but at someone?"

"You think someone pushed him? Or forced him to step into the traffic?" Hana tilted her head to the side and replayed the scene through her mind. She hadn't seen the moment of impact, stalls and meandering knots of people blocking her view.

"I don't know." Logan heaved out a heavy sigh, plagued by a lack of conclusiveness. "Let's go back to the villa."

Hana nodded, her mind whirring with the horror of Jared's accident replayed on a loop in her inner vision. Gaps marred the view, her mind already striving to make up suitable scenarios. She felt glad she'd given Sergeant Wally George her statement straight away. The whirling images wove a fantasy to overlay the blank spaces, making her memory unreliable. Her calves locked as Logan urged her forward, and she tipped her face to his with something else she'd missed. "Hey," she said, her tone thoughtful. "The nurse looking after Jared didn't know Sally. Isn't that weird for such a small community?" She spread her hands and Logan reclaimed her helmet. "Everyone is related or friends. If Sally works a couple of shifts a week at the tiniest hospital I've ever visited, why would that one nurse not know her name? I watched her eyes, Logan. No recognition there at all."

Logan tilted his head back to observe the stars. It offered a depth perception for him, one he relied upon often on the mountain when life got hard. Hana watched him find his place in the universe, relying on the navigational expertise of his forebears, who journeyed to New Zealand using the aerial roadmap. He located Venus, Jupiter and Saturn, peering through tufty clouds which softened their location. The cleft in his chin deepened as he flattened his lips into a line. "I think you're right," he agreed. "But there's another possibility." He tugged the Harley key from his jeans pocket and waited for Hana to fall into step beside him.

"Jared's nurse could have just started at the hospital, I guess," Hana mused.

Logan shook his head. "Nope. She wore really scuffed shoes. New job, new shoes. Especially if you're in a role where you're on your feet for nine hours at the very minimum. Someone with the calibre to work in HDU doesn't transfer from the local medical centre. She's come from the mainland or Australia and knew to bring brand new work shoes with her. Did you notice any footwear shops on the island because I didn't? And the magnet hung off her name tag like she'd clipped it to her scrubs for long enough to need a new one." His irises reflected the weak light from the porch as he turned to face Hana. She caught the faint scent of his aftershave, overlaid with bush greenery and sea air.

"So, she's not new. What about Sally? What if she only just returned to nursing?"

"Maybe." Logan offered her a watery smile. "But someone's not telling the truth here, babe. I can sense it. And it's in the small stuff that doesn't seem to matter." He jammed the helmet onto his head and swung his long leg across the Harley's saddle.

Hana groaned aloud as she pressed the restrictive foam and fibreglass over her hair, resenting the weight and the way it made her neck feel like a flimsy stalk. "I look like a dandelion," she grumbled.

Logan started the engine, and it purred with the lasciviousness of a satisfied cat. Hana settled onto the pillion and the inconvenience of the helmet faded into insignificance against the powerful vibration coursing along her thighs. She leaned forward and tapped Logan's shoulder, her visor bumping his helmet as she underestimated its size. "Let's go right round the island again," she pleaded. "Anticlockwise."

32

Mend - ma'ani

The full circuit of the island took over an hour. Hana pursed her lips together, the raised visor allowing a cool sea breeze to whistle through her helmet. It pried at her mouth as though wanting to release the scream which had built since the awful moments following the stabbing. Hana dipped her chin to relieve the pressure and the banshee shriek remained captive behind her sternum.

Logan drove with exaggerated slowness, his head turning left and right as he studied the houses, the deserted townships, and the empty beaches. Hana gripped his shoulders with white-knuckled fingers, disconnected from the journey and wrestling with her inner demons. Hallie's disappearance had shaken the tenuous safety which Rarotonga had offered. It seemed incredible that even paradise couldn't guarantee her safety. Bad people doing bad things flanked the world from end to end. Her attacker could reach her and finish the job, even here.

Logan took a gentle bend and swerved across the road to avoid a knot of tourists exiting a vehicle on the left. Taken by surprise, Hana's hands slipped from Logan's shoulders and she scrabbled for purchase against his smooth tee shirt. She snagged a fistful of the fabric beneath his right armpit and lolled to the side. The weight of her helmet turned into a bowling ball and dragged her forward until it clattered against Logan's. Hana inhaled in fright, and the whoosh of air locked into her chest. The bike tipped perilously to the right until the slow speed and Logan's skill brought it to a gentle stop a hundred metres beyond the oblivious pedestrians. His right arm shot out, rock steady enough for Hana to right herself and regain her seat. Her chest hurt against the pressure of the scream lodged in her throat.

Logan extracted himself from the seat after securing the bike on its stand. He tugged his helmet free and sat it on the verge, moonlight splaying its possessive fingers along his body as he dipped to place it on its base. Hana blinked at its resemblance to a head poking from the grass as though its owner stood vertical and buried from the neck down. She wanted to laugh, hysteria bubbling behind the locked breath. She raised a hand to her mouth, desperate to prevent her fear, anxiety and the spectre of her own mortality from vomiting out of her core and staining her reality. Once escaped, it would deny her permission to imprison it within her box of insurmountable terrors. How would she manage the fall-out? But her hand caught against the helmet and she released a pitiful wail of misery.

Logan released the chin strap of her helmet with expert fingers, tugging it free without catching Hana's ears or bumping her nose. He set it on the road and wrapped his arms around her shoulders. He said nothing. His strong biceps and veined forearms encompassed her, blotting out paradise and the frightening world beyond and within its borders.

Hana finished soaking the shoulder of his tee shirt with her snot and tears. Satisfied she'd calmed enough to walk, Logan pushed the bike and carried both helmets across the road to the beach. She trailed behind him, her sandals dragging in the white sand glinting beneath the shadowy half moon. Logan parked the bike and set the helmets on the beach. Then he held out his hand to Hana. She took it, his fingers a lifeline in her tsunami of doubt. "Tamatea-whakapau," he said, his voice wistful.

Hana blinked and stared at him, the words familiar but their definition unassailable. "Pardon," she managed, her voice wavering. The words tumbled free as though a barrier lifted and they cascaded over one another. "I'm sorry, Logan. Why do I always fold at the worst possible moment? I could have caused you to lose control when I leaned the wrong way. How much is the excess on the bike insurance, anyway? Two thousand dollars? Three?" She released his hand, their fingers sliding apart as she crouched in the sand and covered her head with her arms. "What are we doing? Our health insurance doesn't even cover us for riding motorbikes on the island. We have children, Logan! What was I thinking?" She hovered over her centre of gravity before tipping back onto her bottom. The sand deadened her impact. Her scar set up a nagging ache as though a hidden hand dragged a rusty nail across its delicate surface.

Logan sighed and sank down next to her, stretching out his legs like black rail tracks against the dull grey of the sand.

"Also, what the hell is Tamatea-whakapau?" Hana demanded.

Logan braced his arms behind him and tilted his torso so his splayed fingers took his weight. The sugary substance swallowed them to the third knuckle, blotting out the glittering hue of his wedding band. He stared up at the moon. Its grey light danced across the chiselled contours of his face, highlighting his sharp features. He sighed. "It's the name of tonight's cycle of the moon," he replied. "Great for planting food, but not so good for fishing. Tangata whenua Māori didn't name the days of the week. They operated on the moon's cycles to make the most of their time and measured from sunset to sunset. Maramataka is the calendar." He turned to face her, his grey irises sparkling like twins of the silver dappled water. "What's really wrong?" he demanded.

Hana gulped and shook her head. A glance at his sleeve revealed the darker patch where she'd sobbed until the knot relaxed its hold on her lungs. "I didn't cry," she admitted. "I lay on the bathroom floor watching my blood pool on the tiles and I didn't cry."

"Okay?" His reply held an unspoken question.

"I just got mad," Hana admitted. "Really bloody mad. Ropeable mad like never before. How dare she do that to me? My children need me. You need me. How dare she rob me of this?" Her right hand flapped towards the rolling waves as they cast wriggling, foamy lines over the reef. She cussed like a bushman then. If her diatribe shocked him, Logan didn't show it. "Stuff happens to me." Hana's words held an uncharacteristic brittleness. "I attract trouble. And I'm sick of it."

"Yeah." Logan's head bobbed once, and he turned to face her. "I get that." He shrugged and sat up, releasing his hands from the sand's embrace. Gentle movements of his long fingers banished the dusting from his palms. "So, what are you gonna do about it?"

Temper flared in Hana's breast, red hot and desperate for an outlet. She gritted her teeth and viewed paradise through the lens of fury. "I'm not wearing a helmet anymore," she stated, her tone flat.

Logan threw his head back and laughed, the sound carrying over the expanse of water and bouncing off the coconut tree trunks edging along the beach behind them like a rearguard. "Deal," he whispered, his voice low. "But if we're taking risks, I have some ideas." He leaned across and kissed her, his lips soft and his chin scratchy against hers. His fingers lifted Hana's tee shirt, his fingers gritty against her soft skin. He kissed her until the anger in her chest subsided, retreating into its box. For the moment.

They removed enough of their clothing to make love on the beach, the half moon watching from above like a disapproving parent. It wasn't quite the stuff of romantic movies, but it was fast and exciting and filled with the risk of discovery. Sand entered their clothes and most intimate places. And Hana didn't care.

33

Search - ranga

"Let's search the hospital grounds for Sally's car," Hana suggested. She winced as the sand in her underwear chafed against the seat.

"Okay." Logan handed her the cumbersome helmet. "Let's drop these at the villa first."

Hana flattened her lips into a line. "Yeah," she said, lengthening the word. "About that. Is it illegal to ride without a helmet here?"

Logan chuckled, his chest vibrating with the force of it. "No, Hana," he replied. "It's not illegal."

"Good, then." She fitted it over her head, trying not to resent its bulky awkwardness. "Villa first, then let's go a-hunting."

The night air grew chilly as Hana deposited the helmets and used the bathroom. Logan waited by the deserted reception area with the engine switched off. Hana jogged back to the bike, a sense of freedom prickling her skin at finding herself unencumbered by the helmet. She added a skip to her final steps and peered at the phone in Logan's left hand. "Is it the children?" she demanded, excitement in her tone. Her fingers curled around Logan's, his skin warm. The dark hairs dusted across his wrist tickled her palm as she cupped her hands beneath his. A dart of pleasure ploughed south from her navel at the contact.

The phone's blue glow lit up her face as she tilted it towards her. Leslie glared from the image, her hair screwed into a hundred mini ponytails which stuck up like tufts all over her round head. Phoenix and Edin posed on either side of her with raised hairbrushes. Hana released an undignified snort and covered her face with her left hand. "Priceless," she whispered with a laugh. "Dean and Mark both shave their heads. That must have thwarted their fun. Poor Leslie." Her mood brightened, and she climbed onto the pillion and settled. Logan started the motor, the throaty gurgle echoing off the windows of the darkened reception. Hana leaned forward and placed a gentle kiss against his left cheek. "I love you, Logan Du Rose," she whispered, and stretched her arms around his neck.

He dipped his chin and kissed her wrist. "I don't suppose you checked the traps?" he asked.

"Oh." Hana shot upright, withdrawing her arms. "I forgot. Do you want me to go back and set more?"

She winced behind him, not sure she'd know where to start. But Logan shook his head.

"What does it matter in the grand scheme of things?" He patted the bag affixed around his waist. It contained their passports and boarding passes for the return flight. Logan slipped his phone into it and fastened the zipper. When he dropped his tee shirt, it became invisible.

Hana settled onto the pillion and ran her hands over Logan's shoulders. She'd relied on him to sort out their money, flights, and related documents. Her mind ran a mental check of the belongings remaining in the villa. Apart from a hand drawn card given to her by the children, everything else was replaceable. Logan turned right at the resort's entrance and headed towards the hospital. Hana noticed little of the ten-minute journey, consumed by thoughts of Craig's meticulous search and the need to know what exactly he thought they'd brought to the island with them.

Logan made a right turn before the golf club and then a left onto Ara Metua. Another right turn took them back onto Sanatorium Road. They cruised the hospital site at a walking pace, searching the lines of cars and scooters for Sally's vehicle. Logan weaved the bike from left to right on the narrow roads to maintain control at the slow speed. Hana forced her stomach muscles to loosen, persuading herself to trust him and leaning into the bike's changing energy.

"Stop!" Her fingers gripped his shoulders as she spotted the glint of metal in the moonlight. He hissed and his muscles clenched beneath her. Too late, Hana realised she'd pinched both his tee shirt and skin in her excitement. "There." She lowered her voice and pointed into the darkness. Logan set his heels on the pavement as their momentum ceased. He peered into the shadows, saying nothing for a moment.

"Ah, I see it," he whispered after an age. The bike rumbled beneath them and Hana craned her neck to look around. Her eagerness dissipated as the sense of danger drove it out with a stiff broom. Hana rested her chin on Logan's left shoulder and spoke into his ear. "At least she told the truth," she hissed. "She does work at the hospital."

Logan turned his head towards her and his nose brushed Hana's cheek. "Let's park the bike and do some snooping," he suggested. Hana winced in the darkness, but his determined tone offered no room for protest. He drove the Harley around a corner and parked it behind the nearest building. Deep shadows absorbed the matte surfaces and muted the chrome details. Logan offered his hand, and Hana clambered down, clinging to his fingers even as he dismounted. Sweat stained her clammy skin, and she blinked as

Logan shook his hand free and wiped his palm on his jeans.

"Sorry," she mouthed. Then, "What now?" She spun on the spot, staring up at the wide soffit overhanging the gravel path.

"No cameras." Logan answered her unasked question. "I already checked. There are a couple inside random corridors of the hospital, and one at the reception. Nothing here."

"Okay." Hana wiped her palms on her shirt and linked her hand through Logan's. First, they examined the silver hatchback. Parked alone on a narrow patch of grass, bushes obscured its presence from the road. A blue light flashed on the dashboard, but Logan dismissed it.

"Fake alarm LED," he whispered. His breath slid across Hana's exposed neck like melting butter, and she clamped her lips shut. She reached for his hand and slipped her fingers into the hollow of his palm. Her waning libido had returned without warning or propriety, taking her by surprise like a flash flood. All it had required was Sally's lascivious gaze drinking in Logan's powerful aura. Jealousy had banished Hana's feebleness, which had beset her following the attack. It consumed her with the need for possession and domination, as though Logan represented a flag to fight over to the death. She gave herself a mental shake, surprised at the competitive streak she didn't know she owned.

A sense of devilment rose from behind a knot of excitement, reminding her of the smooth contours of his muscular chest and the way his waist narrowed before the band of his boxer shorts. "Eesh!" she hissed under her breath, alerted to Logan's confusion when he stared at her and squeezed her hand.

"Okay?" he asked. His lips curved upward into the briefest smile.

Hana nodded and remained silent as a warm flush crawled from her chest cavity and prickled her neck and cheeks. She drew closer to her husband, lifting her free hand and smoothing it across his chest. "You're hot," she whispered, working her voice into something sultry.

Logan shook his head. "No, I'm good," he replied. "The temperature is dropping. Can't you feel it?"

Hana whimpered. "I can feel something," she stammered, the heady lust consuming her good sense. He blinked and his black fringe cast his eyes into shadow. Hana cleared her throat and waved away his concern, keen to hide her embarrassment.

Together they circled the building nearest to Sally's parked vehicle, taking tiny, calculated steps to avoid disturbing the gravel. Hana half expected Logan to use the torch on his phone, but he didn't. He'd spent most of his life navigating the bush in the darkness and moved with confidence. She blinked in rapid succession and wished she'd listened to her mother and eaten more carrots. Instead, she'd believed Mark, who'd told her the carotene would make her hair more orange.

A faint glow spilled onto the gravel from a long window half way along the building beyond Sally's vehicle. Logan lifted their joined hands and pressed his index finger over his lips. Hana nodded, and they crept closer. An unknown occupant had raised the sash window from the bottom, allowing light along with a fluttery voile curtain to escape. The milky fabric fluttered like bunting in the breeze. Logan released her hand, dropped to his haunches and peered inside, lifting the curtain to peer underneath it. His lips formed a circle of realisation and he winced, his fingers releasing the filmy fabric in the same motion.

He stood and edged back towards Hana, but his soles grated against the gravel beneath them and, in his haste, he stepped on her toes. Sharp needles shot through the slender bones and into her instep like an electric shock. And Hana opened her mouth to cry out, a natural, understandable, instinctive wail filled with indignation and pain.

34

Sneak - kōtaka

The breath caught in Hana's chest as Logan's heavy hand clamped over her mouth. The wail died on her tongue and she tasted the dustiness of the sand still lingering on his palm. He pressed her against the slatted wood of the building, the rough surface snagging the fibres of her tee shirt as though conspiring to pin her in place. He kept his free hand splayed across her chest.

Logan didn't release his hold until certain the calamity hadn't drawn attention. He lifted an index finger in the air before withdrawing his hand. The breath whooshed from Hana's lungs and she dropped to her haunches, pressing knotted fingers over her sore toes.

"Sorry." Logan crouched beside her, his voice a low hiss. "I didn't expect to find you right behind me."

"Really?" she raged in an aggravated whisper. "Where did you think I'd be?"

"Fair enough." He leaned close enough for his fringe to brush her forehead. "Are they broken?"

"No," she grumbled. "Just squished by a seven-foot elephant wearing cowboy boots."

"Right. Sorry." Contrition entered his tone, and he pressed his fingers over hers as though desperate to smooth away the pain in her toes.

Hana forced her shoulders to relax and peered at her foot through the gloom. "Help me up," she demanded. He rose, the veins in his forearms prominent in the light from the half moon as he offered his hands as support. Hana stood and leaned against the rough wall. She wiggled her toes and winced. "Just bruised, I think," she guessed. "Serves me right for not wearing my plimsolls."

Logan didn't contradict her, already moving forward with their ridiculous sleuthing mission. Hana wondered at that moment why they'd thought this was a good idea. Who cared if someone brought fake cash to the island? They could use the credit card for all purchases, stay out of trouble and spend every day on the beach. Thwarting the threat from Craig and Sally involved carting their important documents around, and not letting Logan out of her sight. If Sally saw him in his shorts or worse, naked, all bets were off and their joint future included a bitch fight. Hana released a ragged breath. Her toes hurt, her side ached, and she still needed to wash the gritty sand from her underwear.

But the glint in Logan's flashing irises doomed her to yet more time crawling around in the darkness. "It's a bathroom," he whispered as explanation. He pointed towards the lighted window. "There's an old lady getting into her pyjamas."

It kind of explained his shock reaction and his natural instinct to behave like a gentleman. He would never peep on a kuia's nakedness. The aunties and nannies owned a sacred position in his cultural structure. She loved him for it, but her toes still complained. Her body turned back towards the darkness, to where the bike waited out of sight. "Okay," she replied, her tone dull. "I'm done now."

"But we need to find Sally! Don't you think it's weird how Hallie went missing in the two minutes between us leaving her on the porch and Sally arriving?" Indignation crept into Logan's voice, his sense of intrigue and adventure refusing the sudden dousing of cold water which Hana wielded. His breath ruffled her fringe as he leaned close. She rose onto the balls of her feet and covered his lips with hers. Promise filled her kiss and his mouth curved upwards. Hana's hands pushed under his tee shirt until his soft skin ran like warm silk beneath her fingers. She stroked his nipples with her thumbs, and his mouth opened with a gasp of surprise. But then his strong fingers clamped round her wrists, and he tugged her hands away from their mischief. "Not yet," he protested, his voice husky.

The rejection stung, and Hana disconnected from the moment. Her features drew into a pout and her limbs stiffened. She straightened her spine and leaned against the wall, no longer interested in Sally's whereabouts. Her folded arms communicated her dissent as she resigned from Logan's pitiful team of two.

"One minute," he whispered, lifting his index finger again. It irritated her this time, reminding her of the way he placated Edin. She wanted to remind him she wasn't five years old, but the argument died in her throat. Her toes throbbed and her liver set up a rhythmic answer, as though her body had formed its own band and launched into a concert beyond her control.

"Whatever!" she sniped under her breath.

Logan pretended he'd gained her permission and slipped beyond the lighted window and into the darkness. In seconds, he'd become invisible, swallowed by the inky night.

Hana fought the irrational urge to stamp and scream like a toddler throwing a tantrum. The idea seemed more fulfilling in her head. The reality promised more pain accompanied by a sense of powerlessness and resulting anger. So, she edged back the way they'd come, the temperature dropping as Logan had noticed.

Hana reached the corner of the building and jumped as light bloomed from overhead. She froze, imagining a torch licking her outline and revealing her stupidity. But as her vision adjusted, she realised the glow came from a half sized window near the apex of the structure. Open to admit an airflow, it allowed a woman's voice to drift into the night. It still sounded shrill and irritating, but Sally attempted to infuse it with kindness as she dealt with the person inside the room. "Here we go," she said, as though speaking to a child. "Let's get you all tucked up in bed for the night. I'm due back on the ward in ten minutes." Her vocal moderation produced the effect of nails on a blackboard smothered with a soft cloth.

The fire of curiosity and natural nosiness drove Hana around the side of the building and out into the open. This time, she paid more attention to where she put her feet, avoiding the sparse gravel and stepping on the stubby tufts of sun-scorched grass. She found the large sash window which corresponded to the room abutting the gable wall and flattened herself against the building. Then she twisted her torso and peered through the glass, keeping her movements gentle to avoid drawing the occupant's eye.

She shouldn't have worried. Her keen gaze met the back of faded curtain material, made patchy in vertical lines by the sun's rays. She sighed at her wasted effort and placed her feet in front of the glass. Light spilled from a narrow sliver where the right curtain didn't meet its mate in the centre of the aperture. But she needed a better view.

With the sash window raised, it provided enough room for Hana to slip her fingers through the gap and touch the curtain. She edged the fabric sideways, grateful when it remained open as she removed her hand. Her nose hovered just centimetres from the glass as she stared at a clinical bedroom. Peeling patterned paper marred the moldings at ceiling height, swathes arching backwards in a gymnast's somersault. Hospital beds lined the far wall, shrouded in clinical paraphernalia.

Sally assisted an elderly woman into the high bed opposite the window. Her gentle hands offered a supportive frame while her body formed a protective cradle. A long white nightdress gave the patient a ghostlike appearance. Hana's shoulders slumped and guilt burgeoned in her heart. She'd misjudged the resort owner.

Sally smoothed the bedsheets over the woman's torso as the old lady wilted back against the pillows like a failed bud. A collapsed mouth betrayed an absence of teeth, and her porcelain complexion appeared waxy and sallow. Hana held her breath as Sally dipped forward and kissed the plate of bone beneath the woman's grey-speckled hairline. "Night, night," she soothed. She rose and lifted the rail to form a barrier between her and the patient. She traversed the bed to repeat the action on the other side, trapping the woman in a metal prison designed to prevent her from falling out of bed. The rail clanged into place.

"Baby." The voice wavered, the undertone a pitiful wail. "I want to see his baby."

Sally's posture altered. Her rounded edges became diamond hard and her jaw showed through her cheek. "What baby?" Hana saw her flounder, the simple question striking at a wound deep in her soul.

"Baby," the woman said again, her voice strangled by the kind of disconnection induced by sedatives. "My boy's baby."

Sally shook her head. She took a moment to compose herself, fiddling with the medical notes at the foot of the bed. Her fingers slid along the page as though she comprehended the doctor's recommendations for a woman teetering on the edge of life. She replaced the clipboard and a metallic clank sounded as she fumbled the hook into place. "See you tomorrow," she said, her voice too bright for the situation. But the woman in the bed yawned and didn't respond. Her head lolled to the left, her lips hanging open as though falling unconscious in mid-horror.

Hana glanced down at her feet, eager to leave before Sally emerged. She'd said she needed to return to whichever ward she worked at. Taking a careful step away from the window, Hana took note of where she put her steps. She didn't want a repeat of Logan's mishap on the sparse gravel. When she glanced up again, the crack in the curtain revealed Sally standing over the old lady, a bulky pillow in her raised arms.

35

Pain - mamae

Hana inhaled, a squeak bursting from her throat as she pitched backwards. She fell, her brain unable to comprehend the vision of her feet passing over her face. The back of her head contacted something hard and unforgiving. Stars burst into pinpricks of white and yellow behind her eyelids.

A soft surface grabbed her, sucking her into its damp folds. Nothing made sense, and when she stopped rolling, Hana lay still and waited. She tried to call for Logan, but her thoracic spine's impact with the ground had winded her. Focussing on tiny, inconsequential breaths, she managed to suck enough oxygen into her lungs to banish the stars. And in the back of her mind, the image of Sally clutching the pillow over the defenceless old lady's face played like a movie scene.

Heavy footsteps landed beside her left ear and she tried to speak. Only a faint squawk emerged. An exterior door clattered shut in the distance, followed by footsteps scrunching along the path. A pop of ricocheting beads of gravel echoed in the darkness like shots from a toy gun. The moon disappeared from Hana's vision as something covered it. A wide palm slipped over her mouth and a low hiss in her ear said, "Shush."

She realised she couldn't speak, anyway. With her body arranged carelessly on the ground as though she'd dropped from space, she used her energy to concentrate on breathing. Her mind ran routine checks to her limbs, searching for irrevocable damage. She wriggled her toes first and the ones Logan had stamped sent a returning signal of pain. First one foot, then the other. Left hand. Right hand. Make a fist.

An engine sputtered to life and Hana registered more grit, scrunching beneath car tyres. Headlights seared the sky, and she ceased worrying about the hand covering her mouth or the face next to hers. The twin beams had revealed Logan's tousled hair, highlighting the strands like candles. As Hana's panic exited, it left his familiar deodorant behind to comfort her. Silence returned, settling over her like a warm blanket. Logan swore. He removed his other hand from her neck, his index finger ceasing its tracking of her racing pulse. He sat up. Swore again.

Hana groaned. She forced her knees to bend and clasped her hands over her stomach.

Logan crouched beside her. The half-moon turned his irises to a glittering silver. "What happened?" he demanded. "I came around the corner and saw you staring through a window. You stepped back and went ass over tit. Didn't you see the concrete planter behind you?"

Evidently not. Her temporary muteness kept the biting rebuke fixed inside her head. Logan's thumb stroked her cheek. "Where does it hurt, babe?" he asked. Concern caused him to stammer the question. She imagined the horrid images of the bathroom scene returning to haunt him. She groaned again, unable to reassure him. "I'll get help." He spun around on his knees, his gaze fixing on the light distortion rising from the hospital's main building.

"No," Hana managed, the word punched from her tight chest. "I'm fine."

"You don't look fine." Logan's breath mussed her fringe. "You did a complete flic flac."

Hana groaned. The technical term conjured an inappropriately timed mental image of her daughter's foray into gymnastics. Phoenix could command the most difficult horses on their mountain property, but her body didn't bend like the other girls. She rolled like a square wheel, never ending up where she intended. And her floor routines resembled an ostrich fleeing a wildebeest stampede. Head pushed forward, arms flailing behind her and the same mania in her eyes. She'd already lost two front teeth through a dust-up with the parallel bars. Yet Phoenix believed with all her heart she'd carry the New Zealand flag at the Olympics. "That good," Hana murmured. She strengthened her voice and raised a trembling hand. "Sally killed an old lady. I saw it."

Logan inhaled and stared at her for a moment. "For real?" But the words didn't have the correct intonation for a question. He hadn't doubted her since those first tumultuous years of their marriage. A tear slipped from Hana's left eye, leaving a cool trail along her cheek and into her ear. She nodded, and it didn't hurt like she'd expected.

"Yeah. Smothered her." She cursed and planted her palms on either side of her. "Help me up," she grunted. "Then we'll find Sergeant Wally George."

Her lungs relaxed, the initial trauma already fading. Her spine ached between her shoulder blades as Logan leaned her against him, but she sensed no grinding joints or broken bones. Just the cloying aroma of wounded pride. And humiliation. Logan's description returned to taunt her. He'd said he watched her fall ass over tit. Why did he not just say she fell backwards?

Hana blew out through pursed lips and stared at the cliff edge she'd flown over. She'd convinced herself of its vastness, an illusion destroyed by the metre high retaining wall and concrete planter beyond it. The darkness hid her flushed cheeks as she urged Logan to look through the window to check on the murder victim. He went with great reluctance, and Hana used his absence to stretch out her muscles and examine the burgeoning egg on the back of her head. Wiremu had formulated an interesting measurement for lumps and bumps based on his favourite food. Hana's fingers informed her she'd created a sizeable chicken nugget.

Logan vaulted the planter and thudded into the soil beside her. It disturbed the rotting scent of compost which had stayed too long in a plastic bag. The toe of his left cowboy boot bent the bobbing head of a lonely primrose into the fresh loam. "She's fine." He sounded surprised.

"I saw her." Anger flared in Hana's chest. No one had gaslighted her for such a long time, yet the familiar rage remained on a hair trigger in her heart. "Sally smothered her with a pillow." Antagonism entered her tone, and she sensed herself spoiling for a fight.

Logan didn't contradict her. He knew better than to argue. Instead, he helped her into a standing position and led her back to the gravel path. Together, they returned to the scene.

Somewhere between that moment and Hana's swan dive, someone had closed the window. But their efforts had pushed the curtain aside even more. With the bush canopy driven back only far enough to provide a narrow driveway and no other buildings nearby, the need for privacy remained low. Logan kept an arm around Hana as they peered through the dirt speckled glass. The increased aperture had exposed two more beds on either side of the one Hana saw earlier. A male nurse assisted another elderly woman into the left one, tugging the sheet up to her chin before lifting and securing the railings on either side of her. Hana held her breath as he moved to the next bed and lifted the hand of the woman she'd seen murdered.

She grunted and turned over, a screeched curse escaping from her lips. They watched through the window as the nurse persisted, taking her pulse, temperature and blood pressure. He marked the results on the clipboard Sally examined with such interest. Hana gaped at Logan and raised her shoulders in a bemused shrug. He jerked his head towards the darkness of the bush line and edged her away from the window.

36

Baby - pēpe

"What did you see?" he demanded. He leaned against the Harley, his arms folded across his chest. His chin dipped as he studied Hana, and she bristled beneath his scrutiny. "Did you watch Sally put the pillow over her face?"

"No." Hana bent her knees and tested her thigh muscles. The lump on the back of her head swelled more towards a potato fritter. "The old lady said something about her son's baby and Sally seemed angry. She picked up the pillow and stood over the bed. That's when I took a step back and fell out with the planter. I tried so hard not to disturb the gravel I missed a bloody great concrete block and a ledge right behind me." Disgust oozed from her voice.

Logan tapped the pillion seat, his gaze misted. Then he drew the bike key from his front pocket and inserted it into the ignition. "Let's go back to the villa," he said, his tone decisive. "We'll have a kōrero about it all."

He used the Māori word for discussion, and Hana's chest tightened with the futility of it all. She knew what she'd seen and although Logan didn't challenge it, only the woman's death would prove her right. It seemed like a painful kind of victory.

Logan drove the Harley through the resort at a slow speed. Sally's car hadn't reappeared in her space by the reception and Hallie's villa sat engulfed in darkness. Once inside, Hana waited for Logan to close the curtains before stripping to her underwear. He whistled at the vibrant blue of her toes, the throbbing red patch on the fine bones of her spine and the beef burger sized lump on the back of her head. Hana sulked on the double bed while he scraped ice from inside the tiny freezer compartment and tossed it into bags to soothe her injuries.

"My scar feels better," she mused. She lowered the waistband of her belly-hugging knickers and examined the red welt.

Logan fixed a fake smile on his lips, which didn't involve the rest of his face. He handed her another weeping bag of ice chips. "I guess it's best to look on the bright side," he retorted. "You've gained another set of injuries, but hey, the severed liver is healing well."

Hana glared at him. "I know what I saw," she growled.

"I don't doubt it." Logan lay on the bed just beyond her feet. He stretched out on his back and rested his head on his crossed forearms. He sighed. "Sally is a nurse, just like she told us. I admire her. Aged care for Alzheimer's patients isn't for everyone."

"Dementia?" Hana closed her eyes and pressed the ice against the beef burger. "Did you see a sign somewhere?" She continued at Logan's nod. "Anyway, Sally doesn't work in that building."

"How do you know?"

"She told the old lady she needed to get back to her ward. I think she just visited in her break."

"Right." Logan turned his lower lip downward and stared at the ceiling. The window and door screens kept out most insects, but a few brave flies had left brown dots of excrement on the white paintwork. He sighed. "I don't know then, Hana. This is a non-starter. Hallie is still missing and Jared saw something which made him walk into a stream of traffic. Sally works at the hospital and runs the resort. She also visits an elderly kuia on the dementia ward."

"There's a baby." Hana shifted forward and cold water from the ice pack slithered along her spine and soaked into the bedspread. "The lady said it belongs to her son. She actually said, 'My boy', so it could be a grandson or nephew, I guess. We need to find out his name and the link to Sally." She rolled her eyes. "Because mention of that baby made her furious."

"What about the fake money?" Logan turned his head towards her and his gaze raked her underwear. His irises receded beneath his blooming pupils.

"Dunno." Hana shrugged. "But in the spirit of risk taking, I might get my belly button pierced while I'm here." Her lips quirked upwards at the corners as her humour made a valiant return.

Logan's gaze softened. "Are you turning into a rebel, Mrs Du Rose?" His voice held a gravelly quality which vibrated through the mattress and into her core. He edged onto his side, bending his elbow and supporting his jaw against his palm.

Hana grinned. "Maybe a tattoo instead. The only way a belly button piercing would work is if they go right through and put a matching hook at the back."

Logan sat up and removed his tee shirt. His hair stuck up like the plume of a cockerel with the static. "You just described upholstery," he remarked. He rose to his feet and unbuttoned his jeans, exposing the gentle V which sloped towards his groin. "Either way, I think I should inspect the relevant areas first."

Hana giggled and sank back against the pillows. "Yeah, forget the piercing idea. I'll get a tattoo."

"What will it say?" Logan collected a fallen bag of melted ice from the tiled floor and walked across the room to empty it into the kitchen sink. The white flakes clattered against the chrome surface.

Hana paused for a beat, waiting until he'd got eye contact with her. "I'd like it to read, 'This way up'," she replied.

37

Secret - muna

Hana woke as though she hadn't slept. Her numerous bruises made it painful for her to sleep anywhere but on her left side. Turning over during her lighter sleep phases ended in cursing and agony.

Logan sprang from the bed with his usual exuberance and an irritating cheer, which made her fingers itch to throttle him. "Sunday today," he announced, as though assuming she'd forgotten. "I can drop you at church, but don't forget to wear white." He plonked a mug of ginger tea on the cabinet beside her before locking himself in the bathroom. Shower spray hissed like heavy rain against the partition wall and Hana stared at the ceiling.

A clank vibrated through the building, shaking the iron bedstead until it rattled. Hana sat up fast, causing her vision to fade for a split second. "Earthquake!" she breathed. But no other signs followed it. No steady rumble or the clatter of crockery. Just silence and the clucking of the annoying chickens. Then a male throat cleared, the ominous sound like the pretext to a disgusting hawking of phlegm.

Hana tipped herself onto her knees, her feet entangled in the thin sheet. She scrambled to her feet and rested her fingers on the windowsill behind the headboard. The glass presented a view of the villa behind theirs, the one they'd stayed at after the burglary. Hana stretched out her right foot and hooked Logan's pillow, dragging it towards her with urgency. The jerky action caused her almost to pitch sideways off the bouncy mattress. She edged backwards, nudged it into position over her pillow, and clambered on top.

At first, she saw nothing unusual. Then the building shook with another echoing clunk. Logan whistled in the shower, creating a cheerful echo, and Hana held her breath as a blond head popped into her eye line without warning. He paused on the grass beneath the window, and Hana held her breath, fearing he might glance up and see her. The face tilted so its owner could glare at the adjacent bathroom window instead. He cocked his head and registered Logan's whistling before his lips pulled back in a spiteful snarl.

The venom in his expression held more than a casual dislike.

Hana's vantage point revealed a bald spot on the crown of Craig's head. He'd combed his glossy yellow curls in a whorl to hide it from anyone smaller and facing him. It created an element of vulnerability, and Hana frowned. She'd guessed right at his vanity but failed to detect the inadequacy which drove his arrogance with relentless reins and whip.

Craig stared down at something in his left hand. He lifted the other and his fingers took care to assess the curls and draw them over the patch with exaggerated pecking motions. Hana almost pitied him. Almost, but not quite. His expression at the sound of Logan had put her on notice.

She listed sideways, eager to see the thing in his left hand. Her mind whirred with questions, providing its own answers and then dismissing them. What did he have? And why did he keep it hidden beneath their villa?

Craig lifted the back of his polo shirt, revealing his tanned spine and the rolls of flesh like an escaped cake mix piling over a muffin case. He stuffed the thing from his left hand into the tight waistband of his shorts and dropped his shirt to cover it.

Hana gripped the wooden sill with her fingertips, her nose pressed to the glass. Craig sauntered away, heading for the gap between Hallie's empty villa and the vacant one behind the Du Roses. She stared at the item lodged in his waistband, impatience demanding she identify its rectangular shape before Craig disappeared. But he turned the corner and moved out of sight at the same moment the pillows slid apart beneath Hana. And dumped her onto the hard tiles with another squeak of pain.

"Hana?" The bathroom door whipped open with a whoosh, steam shrouding Logan as though he'd stepped from a geyser. Hana couldn't appreciate his impressive nakedness with her head wedged between the bed frame and the side table. "What happened?" he demanded, scooping her into his damp arms and placing her on the mattress. His large palms coasted at speed over her limbs in search of more injuries. His fingers stalled over the lump at the back of her head. "That's an egg, babe," he said, his tone oozing rare sympathy. "Good job we dispensed with the bike helmets. Yours wouldn't fit."

Hana examined a new scratch on her left arm and waved away his concern. "I'm fine," she gushed. "But Craig is keeping something under our villa." She registered his immediate surprise, but the view distracted her. Despite the livid scarring to his torso, Logan had honed his body into a machine capable of lifting two heavy hay bales at a time without breaking into a sweat. Hana stared at the muscle definition across his chest and lost her important thread. Water droplets cascaded from his wet hair and ran in rivulets, snaking sideways across his right pectoral and glistening against the distinctive black tattoo marking his upper arm and shoulder. Hana's name threaded through the design, leading a troupe of their own children and those grafted onto the Du Rose vine. She sighed, understanding Sally's yearning and frustration for something she'd never enjoy and couldn't steal. Hana forgot about her scratch, and pursed her lips into a bow.

Oblivious, Logan stepped with care across the slippery trail of water he'd left in his haste. He returned to the bathroom for a towel and reappeared with his intimate regions covered. He dipped and used a spare flannel to mop up the wake of footprints and drips. "Explain what you mean about Craig?" he asked, lifting his chin to peer at Hana from beneath his fringe.

Hana rose and tested her limbs for further damage. An ache bloomed from her elbow and the scratch on her arm, but nothing major. She pointed towards the window above the bed. "The villa vibrated like it did a few days ago. I climbed onto the pillows and watched him take something from beneath it." She clicked her fingers. "I saw him and Jared standing out there on

Friday. They talked about this being as good a place as any. I didn't realise they meant as a hiding place. Oh." She gnawed her lower lip and raised her index finger as though drawing on an invisible blackboard. "That also explains why Craig lost his mind when he found me standing right there the other morning. Maybe he thought he'd caught me snooping at his mysterious stash."

Logan threw the soaked flannel into the mouth of the bathroom door. He set his hands on his lips and his pensiveness scored lines into his brow. "I might drop you at church and do some poking around," he said, a light sparking from within his irises.

"No way!" Hana exclaimed, rising to her feet. "You'll need a look out!"

38

Spy - 'ai 'ai

Hana's white dress fluttered around her knees as she strode towards the reception office. She'd volunteered to locate Craig before Logan searched the underneath of the villa. Excitement whipped up her heart rate and her movements appeared jerky. She pulled open the office door and stepped inside, disappointed to find Sally seated behind the counter. "Hi," she said, forcing brightness into her tone. "Is Craig around?"

"Why?" Sally dipped her chin and displayed the auburn roots emerging from beneath the bleached blonde. Her defensive tone caused Hana's smile to falter, but she hoisted it with a valiant recovery.

"The bulb over the porch fell out," she stated, setting the glass orb on the counter. The element tinkled inside, the result of the hearty shake Logan gave it after extracting it from the socket. "Does Craig fix these things?"

"No." Sally growled her reply. "We have maintenance staff."

"Oh. Okay." Hana produced a passable shrug of nonchalance. "It's just that he mentioned I should come to him if I needed anything." Her coquettish smile produced an expression of rage flashing in Sally's blue eyes. They mirrored the hue of a thunderous sky.

"When did he say that?" she demanded, her tone guarded.

"Oh. On the beach." Hana spun towards the brochure rack and fingered a leaflet on sea fishing. As she turned, she sensed movement from the office behind Sally's desk. A calf shrouded in blonde hair shifted back from view. Hana imagined Craig sitting at the computer she'd spotted in the back room during her first visit with Hallie. Tension crackled in the atmosphere and she pictured him attempting to remain quiet and still. She wondered why. A glance at Sally's livid expression provided the answer. It seemed unfair to drive the knife harder into the other woman's heart. "Ask him to pop round when he gets a free moment," she said. "We're going into town now. Tell Craig I'm sorry I missed him." Her voluminous skirt swished as she headed for the door, the bodice form fitting and highlighting her lithe shape. Sally glared holes in the side of Hana's head and blinked as she spun to face her. "Any sign of your good friend Hallie yet?" Hana stressed the cordiality of their relationship as Hallie had painted it. Sally's lips tightened hard enough to disappear as she shook her head. "Pity. We visited Jared last night," Hana added. "We'd hoped to catch you there, but the nurse said she hadn't seen you."

A hint of fear crossed Sally's expression as a fleeting darkness. Had Hana blinked, she'd have missed it. "Didn't have time," she replied, the words projecting like missiles. She shuffled pages on her desk and severed her connection with Hana.

Logan had coached her on what to say, urging her not to mention they'd seen her at the dementia unit. While she trusted her husband's instincts, Hana couldn't resist poking the bear. The trait caused much conflict in her marriage, but the itch required scratching. "Which ward do you work on?" Hana paused with her hand on the doorknob. A creak from the back office suggested Craig leaning on his chair to better hear the conversation.

"I move around," Sally growled. "I go where they need me."

"Do you know Karla?" Hana narrowed her eyes and studied Sally's reaction. A flush crawled from the neck of her blouse and edged beneath her jaw line.

"No!" she snapped. "Is there anything else?"

"I'm good." Hana hauled open the heavy door and flounced onto the pavement. She let it slam shut behind her. Her plimsolls tapped against the loose flagstones as she circumnavigated Hallie's villa and arrived on the porch where Logan waited for her.

"All good?" He quirked a black brow upward to emphasise his question. His muscles tensed, his body ready for action.

"Yeah." Hana nodded. "I believe to the best of my ability that Craig is in the back office. Sally's at the counter. I mentioned our intention to go out this morning."

Logan headed to the porch steps, moving past her at a steady pace. He descended to ground level in one easy bound. "Why did you say that?" he demanded.

Hana jogged to catch up to him. "I thought you could drop me at church and come back here."

"Why?" Logan reached the rear of the building and looked up at the long window above their bed. He studied it, shading his eyes with his right hand.

Hana arrived beside him. She surveyed the grass between their villa and the one behind it. "Because you're not interested in church and he's developed a habit of letting himself in when he thinks we're not home. You could hide under the bed and see what he's looking for."

Logan snorted and waved a hand at the corner of Hallie's villa. "Watch the reception like we discussed. If you see him walk in this direction, run back and tell me." He narrowed his eyes at her. "Give me time to crawl out from underneath."

Hana frowned and shook her head. "You don't need to go under the villa," she stated, her tone sure. "He didn't have any dust on him and no grass stains." She jerked her head towards a horizontal groove below a wooden panel. It appeared wider than the one above it. "Check that out." She tapped the groove with a painted fingernail. "I reckon that's a door."

"What?" Logan drew back and glared at the section of slatted wood in front of him. His shoulders dropped as though to dismiss her, but by the time he'd turned, Hana had reached the corner of Hallie's villa.

She gathered her skirt into a ball and thrust it between her thighs, out of reach of the grasping breeze. A quick twist of her auburn hair created a rope-like tress which she slipped beneath her collar. Then she peeked around the corner and fixed her gaze on the door into the reception.

An elderly man helped his wife up the high step, removing his tweed cap as he held open the door. His waddling wife bustled into the reception ahead of him, a pile of used towels clasped in her outstretched arms like a lahar overflowing a volcano. Hana watched through the tinted glass as Sally exchanged the dirty linen for clean.

"You wanted me?"

Hana inhaled in an exaggerated gulp as Craig spoke to her. His voice held a suggestive edge reminiscent of a fish flailing beneath a sharp knife. Hana blew out the breath, angry at herself for failing thirty seconds after her mission started. He'd approached from the opposite direction, coming not from the office but from the swimming pool. "What's that?" Hana managed, pointing at the bag tucked beneath his arm.

"A ball of hair from the filter in the pool," Craig replied. His fingers didn't have the wrinkled appearance of someone who'd spent hours with their hands in the water. Hana glanced down at his bare legs and flip flops, certain she'd seen him in the office just moments ago.

"Yuk," she replied. "Did you fish it out of there?" Her nose wrinkled as Craig withdrew the bag and she spotted the gag-worthy bundle of hair wrapped into a wad within the plastic.

"No." He shook his head. "I met the maintenance guy. He asked me to put it in the commercial skip behind the cafeteria."

"Right." Hana eyed the bag sideways. A chicken feather pressed against the translucent plastic, the shaft creating a protruding bump like a green stick bone fracture. Any attempt to distract Craig dried on her tongue.

"Are you waiting for me?" His jaw appeared even squarer when he grinned. Teeth with white veneers glinted at her from the cavern of his mouth. He glanced across to the office. "Why are you watching the reception?"

"I'm not!" Hana infused her tone with indignation. "Logan's fetching the Harley. We're going to church."

"Oh." His chin retracted in a pecking motion. "Fair enough." He took a step backwards, confusion in his eyes. "So, you didn't want me specifically?"

Hana suffered a moment's indecision. Not because she burned a noxious torch for Craig made from beef dripping, but because she couldn't warn Logan about his proximity. She'd had one job. Just one. And she'd muffed even that simple task. She inhaled a deep breath and tugged her hair from her collar. It eased across her left shoulder like an uncoiling snake. "Just someone to replace the bulb. But not you in particular. I'm afraid of you." She offered the admission, hoping it shocked him and knocked him off kilter, and bought Logan more time. No man filled with as much arrogance as Craig expected a woman to openly fear him. Hana smoothed her dress across her thighs as she spoke, allowing the bunched material to right itself. "You seem angry all the time," she stated without getting eye contact with him. She raised her voice enough to carry and prayed the narrow channel between the villas amplified the sound. "And you grabbed me without warning and hurt me."

She sent a telepathic message to Logan, begging him to hurry. He'd seemed to reject her suggestion of there being a door in the back of the villa. She hoped he'd abandoned his quest in the dust beneath the building until they had more time for a thorough search.

Her words had the desired effect and Craig took a step back as though buffeted by a gale force wind. "Oh." His blue eyes widened behind successive blinking. "I didn't mean it," he gushed. He edged closer before correcting himself, though the effort required to respect Hana's personal space grooved a deep furrow in his brow. His fingers shook as he ran them through his blond hair. But he used the hand holding the sagging bag. Hana spotted the outline of a used condom as the sun smiled through the plastic and turned it semi-transparent. The bag's contents shifted as Craig lowered his hand. The condom disappeared. She shuddered and rejected any notion of a swim in the cool swimming pool.

"It's fine." She raised a hand as though in surrender as the Harley choked to life in the distance. She fixed a fake smile onto her lips and stepped out from behind the corner of Hallie's villa. The bike rumbled towards her, still screened by the buildings planted in a haphazard pattern, only discernible from an aerial viewpoint. The mechanical grumble sighed and altered as Logan changed into a higher gear. Hana tapped her fingers against the wooden slats beside her as she turned towards the road. "Any news on Hallie?" she asked, tilting her gaze to observe Craig's expression.

He still appeared shocked at her revelation and shook his head in a slow arc, which reflected his momentary mental absence. "No." His voice held a hushed quality. A light flicked on behind his eyes, his irises seeming to glow from within his tanned features. He took a faltering step towards Hana, but didn't touch her. "I'm worried about her," he whispered. "Sergeant Wally George won't let me file a missing person's report because I'm not her next of kin." He pursed his lips and angst stripped the melanin from his complexion. "Sally said you'd seen Jared." He cleared his throat, a horrid, hawking action. "I keep meaning to pop by, but I'm so busy here." He glanced around him at the neat resort, as though single-handedly responsible for its upkeep.

A woman Hana recognised as a local from the Trading Post pushed a heavy cart between two villas. She navigated the wet swimsuits dangling from a washing line beneath the nearest porch. Her pale pink uniform accentuated her gentle curves, and she wore her salt and pepper hair in a tight bun on top of her head. A frangipani blossom poked from behind her right ear, the white and turquoise of the petals stark against her hair. The maintenance man jogged across the road and behind the reception office, a long pole held outstretched in his arms. More detritus bowed the net at the end of it, filled with leaves and things Hana didn't want to ponder. A piece of fabric caught her eye, its floral pink pattern stained and torn. Craig rustled his bag as though impatient to leave and Hana's gaze turned back to him.

She glanced at his bunched fingers around the bag's neck and pursed her lips. He'd taken it from the maintenance man before he'd even finished cleaning the pool. The action smacked of a manager who inserted himself into his employees' roles to fill the time. Hana had suffered under his kind of micromanagement before, and it hadn't ended well.

The bike appeared with enough suddenness to make Craig jump, though the purring echo of the heavy engine had promised Logan's arrival seconds earlier. Hana tamped down a sigh of relief and offered a feckless wave to the resort owner. Then she hopped on the Harley with more speed than care and clasped Logan's shoulders.

Her husband ignored Craig. The action clanged like a gong, saying far more than words.

39

Hiding place - pininga

"I'm sorry!" Hana dipped forward to shout in Logan's left ear as he turned the bike onto the main road. "I messed it up as usual." A breeze whipped Hana's hair into a frenzy and she regretted not returning to the villa to retrieve a hair tie. It streamed like a flag behind her, dragging at her neck muscles.

Logan slowed the bike and tilted his head to speak to her. "It's fine," he replied. "You did great. I heard you talking and figured out what happened."

"What did you find?" Hana rested her chin on his shoulder and he bumped her nose with his cheek.

"Tell you when we stop," he promised.

Hana sat back and enjoyed the ride. The white fabric of her dress tapped against her thighs in the breeze and sea air filled her lungs to bursting. Life felt good for the first time in ages. She closed her eyes and raised her chin, allowing the wind to buffet her in the slipstream from Logan's head. The urge to throw her arms wide on either side of her and lean back caught her by surprise. Her hands retook their position on Logan's shoulders and a low rumble met the soft pads of her fingers. She tilted her head, embarrassed to realise he'd watched her antics through the chrome side mirrors. He avoided her gaze, but his lips quirked upward in a barely contained laugh. A giggle bubbled from her chest, cascading over her like tinkling raindrops.

Logan used the indicator and pulled over to the side of the road opposite the church. A scraggly brown chicken crossed in front of him before changing its mind several times. It darted sideways in numerous directions before resuming its original trajectory towards the grass verge.

"Thank you." Hana clambered from the bike, struggling to maintain her modesty as the billowing fabric of her skirt tangled itself around the rear mudguard. "I'm wearing shorts," she puffed at Logan's expression of alarm. He supported the bike between his thighs and reached out an arm to provide her with support.

"I'm more concerned about your dress getting caught in moving parts," he growled. "Important things, like the spokes or the exhaust."

Hana pulled her skirt down and flattened it against her thighs with her palms. "That happened once!" she protested. "I mistook the exhaust pipe for the foot-rest and melted my favourite wellies."

Logan raised his left eyebrow, but remained silent.

"What did you find under the villa?" Organ music destroyed the muted strains of paradise. It sounded like someone falling from a great height and landing on every one of the eighty-eight ivories. Logan jerked his head towards the ruckus and grinned with the satisfaction of someone not about to subject themselves to it. The white stucco church shone in the sun's rays as though God smiled on his faithful. Linear shadows denoted the corrugated iron of the shamrock-coloured metal roof.

"You guessed right about a door in the rear section of the villa," Logan said. "The hinges are underneath and the panel falls out and down like the overhead locker on an airline."

Hana drew closer, her eyes wide and sparkling with wild excitement. She lifted her left hand and brushed Logan's fringe from his eyes. "Say that again," she whispered, her tone light. "I don't care about the door. I want to hear you admit I was right after scorning me with such disdain."

Logan's lips parted with a protest but he closed them in defeat. Hana tilted her chin back, exposing the gentle arc of her neck, and she smiled in victory at the sky. "How unexpected," she simpered, her movements exaggerated in her self-congratulation. "And what did you find in there?"

"Nothing." Logan shrugged. "Ten empty plastic wrappers, and a lot of sand. I think there's a leak in there though. The floor was soaked."

Hana's jaw dropped open, and she gaped at him in disbelief. "Empty? But I saw Craig go in there and take something." Her shoulders drooped with the loss of her short-lived victory. She pushed out her bottom lip. "He shoved it down the back of his shorts and covered it with his shirt." The awful clanging hiccoughed before dissolving into silence. Then the organist began again and the beautiful strains of an old hymn piped through the open front doors. Hana wrinkled her nose. "Did you take the plastic? We might find something important on it."

"No." The reply held more than a vigorous denial. A warning crept through the single syllable like a slap. "Because I don't want my fingerprints on his dirty dealings." Logan jerked his head towards the church. "You should go inside." He lifted an index finger as she opened her mouth to speak. "And no, I'm not spending the morning hiding under the bed in case he searches our place again. I'd rather smack him in the face and finish it once and for all."

"But I told him we were going out. To encourage him. Oh my goodness!" She clapped a hand over her mouth. "What if he didn't let himself into our villa to search for anything but to touch my stuff?"

"Then I'll kill him." Logan's jaw fixed into sharp, angular lines. The rest of his body showed little of the turmoil which seized him, but Hana sensed the aura of violence flutter over their heads like silken threads of pure fury.

"Don't," she urged, wishing she'd kept the thought to herself. "I probably got it wrong."

But she'd said it now. And the more it took hold in her mind, she sensed the truth in the notion. That's why he'd fingered through her underwear. And her wash bag. What other reason could he have for searching in such a tiny bag containing female paraphernalia? A shudder of dread ran through her. She hoped nailing Craig with the truth had deterred more of the same creepy behaviour.

Logan watched her walk across the street. Hana glanced back several times, wondering if she should flag the service altogether, or force her unwilling husband to accompany her. She decided on the latter and turned, but he must have sensed her changed energy because the bike set off with a roar. The wave Logan gave her said, *'You snooze, you lose.'*

40

Church - ‘iero

Hana didn’t think she’d relax in the service, but the Good Lord proved her wrong. Generous female arms enfolded her at the door and welcomed her. A woman who introduced herself as the pastor’s wife strung a garland of live flowers around her neck. A sense of safety enveloped her, along with the perfume of frangipani and fern.

The singing proved raucous and spirit filled. Hana sighed beneath the familiarity of the cry of her forebears’ hearts. The liturgy and beliefs of the Christian faith crossed oceans with the same integrity as air, arriving with the identical chemical components as when its journey began. Hana knew the words of the prayers and the tune of the hymns. For an hour of peace, she pushed aside the sight of Craig’s hairy hands sifting through her belongings, and the disappearance of a woman she’d met only three times in her life.

The ache of her children's absence and the bottled rage at her attacker paused for long enough that she remembered how contentment felt.

At the end of the service, the women ushered her into a community room and pressed a China cup into her hands. Tea sloshed over the floral pattern and a biscuit appeared on the saucer. These were wise disciples. They knew a plane would carry her away in five days' time and didn't care. Their mission field stretched from beach to beach, recognising that prodigals might arrive with sun dresses and a suitcase.

Hana blew out a breath and wished Logan had stayed. Marriage to her hadn't lessened his suspicion of anyone with a pulse. But she would have liked him to meet these people and witness their goodness.

"You arrived last Thursday?" The pastor's wife hung out next to Hana, shielding her from the busyness of coffee time and chatter as she introduced herself. Her white muumuu masked a body which might have looked skeletal or overweight. The fabric made it impossible to tell. Dark curls cropped close to her head revealed hints of grey, but she wore her advancing age with class and dignity. An enviable straight bearing gave her the poise of a dancer.

"Yes." Hana nodded. She pursed her lips, the woman's cordiality bringing on a painful bout of verbal diarrhoea, which Logan would have hated. "My brother paid for our trip. I had surgery a month ago, and he thought the peace and sunshine might help me recover. He and his husband visited a travel show a few weeks before my surgery. They picked up a discount and decided to use it for me." The cup tittered against the saucer as though laughing as Hana's right hand touched her side. But it stalled her brain enough to stem the nervous burbling. The woman's gaze followed the unconscious motion but she didn't comment. Instead, she smoothed Hana's cheek with her thumb before squeezing her shoulder in a gesture of solidarity.

"Are you enjoying it here?" She cocked her head and her unconditional attention seemed alien and intense, stripping Hana bare to the bone with the brush strokes of kindness. The sense of nakedness turned her blood to ice in her veins despite the humidity of the room.

Hana pursed her lips, wanting the verbal purge to stop, but knowing instinctively it wouldn't. "No," she heard herself reply. "The police arrested us on suspicion of passing fake cash the first time I left the resort. Someone burgled our villa the same night. Our neighbour went missing, and people are lying to us."

A deep frown marred the woman's brown forehead and concern radiated from her hazel irises. "That's not usual," she said, like someone watching a cyclone approaching from the wrong direction and wreaking unexpected havoc. “We pride ourselves on our aro’a, our love.”

The word held the familiarity of its Māori cousin, aroha. Hana struggled to swallow the tea in her mouth. A lump filled her chest, its ache blossoming outward to lock her lungs on an inward breath. The sense of alienation which their experience of Rarotonga had heightened contained a bite she’d forgotten. If such behaviour wasn’t habitual, then the island and its inhabitants had selected her and Logan for their unusual hostility.

Her hand shook, and the cup rattled against the saucer. The tea dregs sloshed against the crisp China. The pastor’s wife leaned closer, coffee and floral perfume washing over Hana. “I was at the market when you saved that poor man’s life,” she said. “You have my admiration.”

“You were there?” Hana’s eyes widened. The revelation had pricked a balloon filled with tears in her heart. Her dreams still carried an image of Logan pumping Jared’s chest and her lungs aching with the strain of sharing breaths.

“Yes. I always buy my veggies there.” She smiled, calm radiating from her demeanour. Her fingers didn’t writhe like Hana’s. She glanced across the room towards where a group of school-aged children picked through a plate of biscuits. “I’d just said goodbye to

Sergeant Wally George. He bought a bag of coffee beans and we joked about him hefting them across to the police station."

Hana nodded. "That makes sense. I guess he called the paramedics."

"Would you like to share lunch with us?" the woman asked, the question coming from left field.

The denial stalled in Hana's throat. She wanted to, more than anything. She ached to plug into the source of this woman's power and surety. But she felt as though angry wasps had pursued her from that first moment in the supermarket. Yet this woman had showed her the closest thing to friendship since she'd arrived in paradise.

But Logan wouldn't play. She knew that even without asking him. The pastor's wife smiled as Hana faltered. "I'm sorry," she began. "My husband arranged to pick me up here after the service." The bubble of safety burst and she clung to its remnants despite their fading influence. "Thank you for inviting me," she whispered.

"My name is Mary." The woman pushed a slip of paper into her palm. The neat, left-handed cursive spelled out her full name, a phone number and an address. "Most people know me. Ask for Mary or the pastor's wife. I'm here if you need anything," she said. She stood a head taller than Hana, her shoulders wider beneath the voluptuous fabric of her muumuu. But she bent and kissed Hana's cheek, the lightest touch and yet filled with genuine human compassion.

A sense of extreme loss flooded over Hana, as though she'd been offered something precious and rejected it. She nodded and turned away, finding a nearby table on which to discard her mug and uneaten cookie. The door to the community room stood open, the breeze causing the heavy wooden structure to sway on its hinges. Outside, the sky appeared massive enough to gobble up the island in one bite. A single threatening rain cloud hovered over the foothills of the mountain.

She almost reached freedom unhindered, but not quite. A light touch on her arm caused her to spin around, Mary's slip of paper still clutched in her fingers. The cashier from the supermarket faced her, lower lip trembling in an unconscious revelation of discomfort. She swallowed and spoke, her voice wavering. "Māmā rū'au said I should apologise," she whispered. Her shoulders shimmied as she spun to detect eavesdroppers.

Hana forced her toes to face the girl, reluctance in the slowness of the movement. The rubber of her plimsolls bit against the quarry tiles as though adding their silent protest. "The pastor's wife is your grandmother?" She sent her gaze past the girl, but the astute woman had gone. Hana had told her they'd been arrested for passing fake notes. She'd discerned their innocence from Hana's presence in the church instead of the police cells. Island gossip had allowed her to complete the puzzle at speed and attempt a resolution. Hana frowned at the frightened girl before her. "Why did you do it?" Her eyes narrowed as she asked the question. "Why pretend my husband gave the note to you when he didn't?"

The girl blinked. She appeared younger than she had in the supermarket's uniform of pale green and white. With her hair released from its restrictive tie, it hung around her shoulders in glossy black tresses. Thin shoulders sloped in gentle arcs above the budding breasts of a schoolgirl. Hana's stance lost the stiffness of injustice and righteous indignation. She shrugged. "It doesn't matter. What's done is done."

She released a sigh of hopelessness. This wasn't their paradise. It belonged to others. The island's damaging secrets would close over its residents like the sand spreading its continual blanket over the dunes. They were welcome to them, so long as no more trouble attached itself to her. Hana turned to leave, and the girl reached out and touched her bare forearm. "He isn't nice," she said, keeping her voice low.

Hana blinked in surprise and the fingers of her right hand lifted to touch her left collar bone. The pacemaker waited beneath, the ambulance at the top of the cliff. Hana pressed her fingers together and dismissed the stress-tell. "Who?" she demanded, assuming the girl meant Logan. Perhaps this formed the basis of her excuse. She'd blamed the new tourist for the counterfeit because she didn't like the look of him. A rational voice dismissed the notion before it could land and take root. Women and girls loved Logan. The north of his male compass magnetised females as though sucking them into a vortex. Who then, if not Logan?

The girl edged closer, the breeze from outside sneaking through the open doorway and mussing her hair. "The man who gave me the fake twenty," she whispered. "He isn't nice. The local girls avoid him."

"You know him?" Hana kept her voice low, though the desire to shout the words formed a knot in her throat.

The girl nodded. "He wanted me to clean at his business premises. It's better money than the supermarket, but I don't want to be alone with him." She glanced back into the room, her eye muscles twitching as she took stock of her community. Her need to offer something to Hana in return for her forgiveness drove her into the realm of gossip. The pinching of her smooth, teenage features into lines and shadows showed it pained her. She displayed more reluctance in that moment than she had while lying about Logan handing her the counterfeit twenty. Hana reasoned it was easier for her to lie in a supermarket than gossip in church.

"He owns a business on the island?" Hana's heart rate ticked up, sending the blood pounding through her ears. Like a junkie facing a hit, she sensed the presence of important knowledge.

The girl nodded. "Yes," she breathed. "And he's done it before. Once more to me and a few times to the other cashiers. Fifties and now twenties. Maybe hundreds a couple of months back. We can't tell anyone because he's not nice. We're scared." Tears caused her eyes to speckle and shine, the salt water refracting the line between her tawny irises and pupils. "I'm sorry," she said. The apology brought a catharsis and heralded tears of relief. "I panicked." She hiccoughed and placed a hand over her mouth. Wariness shrouded her again as though sensing her open emotion would attract those nearby like wasps to sugar. "I'm saving for college," she confided. "The supermarket manager threatened to dock my wages if it happened again. She showed us what to look for, so I checked all the fifties, but the twenty took me by surprise." Her body deflated like an air mattress springing a leak. She dropped her chin and stared at the tiled floor, her fingers a writhing ball against her white skirt. "I'm sorry," she said again, as though the first time didn't count. "But please don't tell anyone. You're leaving soon, so it won't matter."

Hana picked her words with care, sensing the tenuousness of the moment. She would forgive the girl, but she wanted more from her still. The girl's upper arm exuded warmth as Hana's cool fingers closed around it. "Who gave you the fake money?" she demanded, her voice a hoarse whisper.

She didn't expect the reluctant answer. Not in a million years.

41

Lizard fish - karaea

Hana stamped across the church car park, pausing to allow a weaving group of scooters to pass. The tourists rode four abreast, ignoring the road rules as though such things didn't apply to them. The anticlockwise bus honked its horn in warning and they wobbled into a wonky line like toddlers needing training wheels. Hana let them pass and stamped across the road to where Logan waited.

He'd propped the Harley on its stand on the verge. He laid on the grass beside it, his long legs stretched out before him and his elbows supporting his torso. His casual air filled Hana with regret at the knowledge which burned in her chest. She possessed the necessary ingredients to ruin his day.

"Bloody Craig!" she snapped, throwing herself down on the ground beside him. Her scar gave a twinge of pain and she ignored it. "That bloody man!"

Logan lifted his sunglasses onto his head and squinted at her. "He goes to church?" Surprise and incredulity stripped away the soft edges from his tone.

"No!" Hana flapped her hands in exasperation. "He's passing the fake cash!"

"In church?" Logan used his stomach muscles to sit upright. He brushed dust and flecks of scrubby grass from his palms.

"Noooo!" Hana's voice rose, and he lifted an eyebrow in warning. The look infuriated her further as she recognised it as the one he bestowed on his youngest son. In moments of frustration, when Mac shouted and stamped, Logan would lift his eyebrow and encourage him to use his words to explain. It worked on the five-year-old, but sent Hana's temper a notch higher. She swallowed and took a moment to collect herself. Right then, she needed her husband's solidarity more than his irritation.

She lowered her chin and her voice. "I met the cashier who swore to the cops that you gave her a fake twenty. She admitted Craig used it to pay for some groceries about ten minutes before we showed up at her till. It's like the guy in the car park told you. The businesses are docking staff wages when they allow the fakes through their registers. Remember, Sergeant Wally George told us they'd had fake hundreds and fifties? That's what she told me. It was the first fake twenty she'd seen, and she panicked because she'd let it through without noticing. She apologised and cried a bit." Hana pursed her lips, hating how uncaring the sentence sounded. She shook her head. "Her description matched Craig. The young girls on the island refuse to work for him because he's so handsy. His reputation precedes him, apparently."

"So, why not come clean now?" His tone held a peculiar hardness. "She can tell Sergeant Wally George that Craig used it to pay. Her statement will clear me."

Hana cocked her head and shifted onto her left hip. She folded her legs to the side and stared at Logan. "But the police didn't charge us," she said. "Sergeant Wally George believed you. He let us go." She tilted her head as though needing to peer beyond the stormy grey irises and into his swirling thoughts.

Logan ran his tongue over his bottom lip before turning to face her. "I have some news too," he said, forming the words with exaggerated care.

Hana sat up with the interest of a meerkat, her back straight and her gaze intense. "About Craig?" she breathed. "Did you hide under the bed? Did he let himself into the villa and sniff my underwear?"

"No!" Logan's face twisted into an expression of distaste. "I tried to buy some flowers for you."

"Oh." Hana infused her tone with brightness. It didn't seem like big news, though it cheered her.

But Logan didn't appear happy, and he hadn't yet handed her any flowers. She fingered the wilting wreath around her neck and prepared her best smile.

He fixed his gaze on her face and paused long enough for worry to blossom from its hiding place behind her sternum. "No one will sell to us, Hana. Sergeant Wally George failed to squash rumours of us passing counterfeit cash. Every business is now displaying a poster created from security camera footage of us entering the bar the other night." He lifted an index finger to stall Hana's immediate outrage. "Not flattering images, either. It shows our names, where we're staying, and tells the trader to refuse us entry." He shrugged, a jerky, antagonistic movement. "We're screwed, babe. I can't buy food or water on the island. I got chucked out of three shops, including that tiny dairy in one of the villages."

"But we didn't use fake cash at the bar," Hana whispered. "They can't do that." The remaining five days in paradise stretched before her. No food. No access to anything behind a pay wall. What if they couldn't refuel the bike? What if the Harley owner reclaimed their only mode of transport? Her fingers closed around Logan's forearm, the slender digits not covering even half of the muscle. "What if Craig throws us out of the villa?" Her voice sank to little more than the movement of her lips. “What will we do?”

“I don’t know.” For the first time in their shared history, Logan Du Rose appeared clueless. It rocked Hana more than the threat of starving for the next five days. The casual air he’d evoked when she crossed the road to meet him fell away like a smokescreen blown on the wind. He’d constructed it with care to spare her more stress, but he had no plan beyond it. The ruse collapsed like a rock fall.

42

Sister - ‘akatua ’ine

They sat in silence on the grass verge, the shade of a coconut tree sheltering them from the sunshine. Clouds increased in number, dashing across the azure blue like passengers on the London underground. Hana’s skin still prickled with the rays which sought her white arms and seared them until they turned red. The mood of devastation lay heavy on their shoulders, the sense of entrapment overwhelming.

Hana spoke first. “Mark paid for the villa already. Craig can’t evict us without offering a refund.” She sighed. “And you paid for the bike, too.”

Logan’s shoulders twitched, the muscles moving as though he lacked the energy for a definitive shrug. “They’ll find some term or condition we’ve breached. No one seems to care that it’s an unfounded accusation.”

"Well, I care!" Hana's temper flared. She hadn't seen her husband so defeated for a long while. He stared at the ground, his body still and only his Adam's apple bobbing as he swallowed. His fingers sifted the grey dust beneath the scrubby grass as though operating on autopilot. It pained her because Logan always knew what to do. He planned and strategised and led his family through one disaster after another. It seemed an impossibility that he'd finally met his Waterloo, the battle he couldn't win.

Hana tossed her head and aligned her body with his. An eerie chill rippled down her spine when he didn't reach out and enfold her. His mother's suicide had floored him, the truth of his parentage following hot on its heels. Yet he'd recovered. "It's just a holiday." She reached out and laid her left hand over his. His index finger continued to bore a divot in the baked soil. "It's gone badly wrong from the start, but it's just a holiday. We'll work it out." Her tone held too much cajoling, and she knew how he hated it. She withdrew her hand when he still didn't react. "Phone," she demanded, holding out her hand, the white palm glowing in the sun's glare.

Logan dug in his jeans pocket, laying back to stretch out his right leg. He retrieved it and dumped it into her palm. But he didn't look up at her.

"This will be expensive," Hana declared. She rose and walked closer beneath the tree's canopy to sift through Logan's list of contacts until she found what she wanted. Her thumb called up a name which threaded fine tendrils of dread through her heart. She took a deep breath.

"You almost died." Logan's voice held an uncharacteristic dullness.

"What?" Hana glanced back at the church and then at her husband. A tight band encased her head and spread out across her body. Her healing liver chose that moment to remind her of its delicate state. She swallowed. "Right."

Logan's head shook from side to side in a swaying motion. "So much blood, Hana." He ran a shaking hand over his face, bristles scratching against his palms. "We should never have come here," he said with a deep sigh which seemed to originate from the soles of his feet. "I'm sorry." His lips twisted as though struggling to contain a sound which would crack the earth in two splintered halves. "I should have gone looking for you earlier. Bodie and I got talking. And I should have refused the holiday. It's too soon."

Hana squatted beside him. She wrapped her free arm around his neck and pressed a kiss to his temple. "Oh, Logan," she breathed. "You have such big shoulders, but you pile way too much onto them. None of this is your fault. Unless you have a crystal ball, none of this was foreseeable." She peppered kisses on his temple and the part of his forehead she could reach. "We'll fix it," she promised. She rose, gripping the phone in her right hand and dialling the dreaded number.

But while she might alleviate their current difficulties, she sensed the psychological trauma of the stabbing would take more than a phone call.

Judge Eliza Du Rose picked up after the third ring. Hana didn't kid herself. Liza always picked up for her little brother. Everyone else got her voicemail. Hana opened her mouth to speak, still formulating the question in her mind. But Liza beat her to the punch. "Hey bro, please tell me you've left Ginger Barbie and want legal counsel for the divorce."

Hana gulped, swallowing the polite greeting she'd planned. "Er, hi Liza," she stammered. "It's Ginger Barbie here. We have a spot of bother and wanted some advice."

Liza didn't bother to disguise her snort of mirth. Only once in their shared existence had she ever shown a sliver of emotion over a lost love. Hana often wondered if it happened in her imagination, because no trace of it lurked behind their subsequent, fraught interactions. Liza sighed and released a blasphemous inhalation assured to make Hana wince. "What now?"

she snapped. "Did you break a nail and want to sue someone?"

Hana tilted her head back and stared at the sky from between the rustling fronds of the coconut tree. The cloud cover had swelled to create pockets of greyish-white bobbles like mothers in puffer jackets gossiping in the playground after school. She closed her eyes and dispelled the image of Logan's phone credit gurgling down a plughole. "The police arrested us two days ago," she stated. Stick to the facts, she urged herself.

"When? Why am I only hearing about this now?" Liza's tone sharpened. It lost the snide after-taste and became clipped and business-like. Paper rustled and a pen nib scratched on a pad as though she tested the ink and readied herself to write an essay. Hana envisaged the subject decrying stupid brothers who marry auburn-haired widows and get them pregnant. Twice.

Hana cleared her throat. She straightened her spine and squirmed against the familiar sense of intimidation. "The cops released us without charge. The investigating officer acknowledged we didn't use a fake twenty dollar note. A witness backed up our story."

"So, what's the problem?" Liza barked.

"We can't buy food or supplies on the island. Logan says someone distributed our photos around all the businesses and told them not to let us onto their premises." She exhaled through her nose. "It's humiliating. We have five more days here. And there are no spare seats on any of the flights back to New Zealand before our scheduled leaving date."

"Put Logan on the phone," Liza snapped. "Let me talk to the organ grinder instead of the monkey."

Hana formed an O with her lips and released a slow breath filled with anger and recrimination. Her tone held a curious lightness, like someone who'd stepped off the cliff and took their mortal enemy with them. "He's unavailable at the moment."

"They've put up pictures of you in their shops despite the police releasing you without charge?" Scribble, scribble, scribble.

Hana wondered if Liza's pen recorded the details or inked rude pictures of a redheaded Barbie with pins protruding from every available space. A ginger Barbie hedgehog version of her. She practiced yoga breaths while Liza shouted at someone in the background. A scripture sprang to mind, one she'd heard not half an hour earlier in the sanctity of the white church with the shamrock green roof. *'It is a fearful and terrifying thing to fall into the hands of the living God.' Hebrews 10:31*. Despite the warning at the end of the bible,

Hana changed the scripture, adding *'and Liza Du Rose'* as a PostScript. "Suck on that, princess," she whispered out loud.

"What?" Liza snarled through the phone. The unexpectedness of her reappearance shocked Hana, and she jerked and released a squeak of surprise.

"Nothing," she replied, a croak in her voice. She wanted to gaslight Liza, to think of another sentence which sounded similar to the original and extracted her from blame. But her mind wouldn't bend to the semantic gymnastics, not with Logan still sitting so silent and defeated on the ground. She forced herself back to the immediate problem. "What can we do to defend ourselves?" she asked.

"Drive somewhere safe," Liza advised. "I'll call you on this number." A sharp click echoed in Hana's ear and the scratch of a pen nib on high quality notepaper ceased.

43

Minute detail - rikiriki

The church car park had emptied by the time Hana glanced up. She hadn't connected well enough with the community to seek help, but their absence quenched a silent hope deep in her soul. "Right then," she said, surveying her situation through the uncomfortable lens of reality. A sleight of hand shoved the phone and Mary's note into her bra. She jiggled to ensure both sank to a place of safety. She squatted beside Logan, dismayed at how he'd drawn his knees to his chest and wrapped his arms around them. Her innate instinct recognised the pain it signified.

Over two decades earlier, when Hana's first husband died, she'd faced a new life as both a single-handed counsellor and prison warden. Her sweet daughter Izzie presented very few problems, and the counsellor role sufficed. Bodie proved a whole unique brand of teenager. Hana had wrestled him into adulthood alone, her nerves frayed and her self-respect in tatters. He'd pushed her to her limit. But during one pivotal moment after Hana caught him smoking with his risk addicted mates, he'd sat on the floor of Hamilton's busy bus station and refused to move another centimetre.

Hana had cajoled and begged, bribed and encouraged, to no avail. He'd sat on the dirty floor where the 18a bus to Ngaruawahia should have parked and broke his seventeen-year-old heart. Commuters and school children watched with interest through an endless parade of swerving windows as Bodie fell to pieces. Buses drove around him, puffing out noxious exhaust fumes which took days to leave his clothes. But still he sat there, oblivious to Hana's own devastation. A mere shell. A boy's empty body with the lights extinguished in vibrant eyes the colour of a walnut.

She hadn't known then that he'd met Vik's mistress by accident, or that he'd carried the burden of guilt and hatred on his thin shoulders ever since. But the police had arrived, summoned by an irritated bus driver who'd said Bodie had a weapon just to hurry them along.

And hurry, they did. The Armed Response Unit closed the bus station and its surrounds and Hana found herself lying face down on the oil stained tarmac in her smart work suit.

From the knot of black clad officers crouching behind a strobing police vehicle, one brave man approached the confused woman and the stricken boy. "Get up, son," he said to Bodie, holding out his hand. "You can do this."

Hana reached out for Logan, waiting until he stared up at her. "Get up, Logan," she said, her tone containing the same authority she'd heard in the brave police officer's voice. "You can do this."

Hana couldn't drive the Harley even without a tender scar covering her ribs. But she couldn't support Logan on the long walk back to the villa, either. He rallied enough to ride the bike with her as pillion, his body remembering the familiar actions by rote.

An eerie blackness had descended over him, robbing him of the effort required to form complete sentences. Hana kept up an irritating commentary intended to cajole and encourage him, sick of the sound of her own voice by the end of the journey.

"I want to ride." Logan stopped the Harley on the grass beside the porch. He didn't elaborate on whether he wanted to ride a horse or the bike. She imagined he'd turned to normalcy in his desperate state. A gallop on a horse or a blast up the expressway on his bike at home to clear his head. The engine rumbled, its throaty call reverberating off Hallie's empty villa and echoing around the wooden structures like a crooning song. Hana slipped from the pillion, keeping her hand on Logan's arm as she dashed forward and turned the ignition key. She snatched it free and stuffed it into her bra with the phone and the note. Logan blinked at her as though she'd experienced the momentary breakdown and not him.

"Inside!" she ordered, raising her eyebrow at him in a rare role reversal. "I'm hungry and it's lunchtime." She snapped her fingers at him, pushing him to react with irritation or anger at her treating him like a pet dog. She realised she'd accept either. "Come on!" she complained. "You have the villa key."

Logan engaged the Harley's stand and rose, his long legs splayed on either side of the listing machine. When he didn't move, panic seized Hana like an icy slap. She shoved his arm, instinct screaming at her to get him inside and to safety. Before what? The silent reply sent the ice coursing through her blood stream to grip her organs. Before he snapped like a twig and collapsed, catatonic, empty and too heavy for her to carry up the steps alone. She acknowledged the selfish need to protect his dignity.

"Logan!" She raised her voice. "Get inside. Now!"

He moved then, his actions laboured as though his cowboy boots contained wet concrete. He flung his leg over the back of the bike, a natural reflex action, a familiar groove in a well-worn rut. Heavy steps carried him onto the porch, an automaton following a set of pre-coded programs. Hana tugged the villa key from the front pocket of his jeans, lifting the hem of his tee shirt and encountering the bag containing their valuable documents. The backs of her knuckles brushed against the smooth fabric. She plucked out the key and fitted it into the lock.

The villa looked untouched, the bed made and the room tidy. Fresh towels sat in a pile on the sideboard, a pair of white face cloths shaped into teddy bears. Hana's chest locked, the simple gesture of kindness cutting through her fake bravado and threatening to unleash her fear.

"My phone." Logan patted his pockets and half-turned, as though expecting to see it trailing behind him.

"I have it." Hana lifted it, but his glazed eyes didn't register the device she pulled from her bra and gripped in her left hand. "Take off your shoes," she instructed, hiding her trembling fingers behind her back. Logan kicked off his cowboy boots but took a crazy amount of time, squaring them in line with the skirting board.

"Food," Hana muttered to herself, reaching for the oldest remedy she knew. A cup of tea and a sugary biscuit. She spun in a circle to face the kitchen before circumstance pressed down on her head until she felt her spine might snap. The cupboards and fridge didn't contain enough to sustain two adults for five days. She fought a hysterical cackle at the notion of rationing their supplies. It didn't matter. She'd give him every morsel if it helped to soothe his ragged nerves.

"Blood everywhere," he said again. He slumped onto the bed and listed on his side. His eyes still contained that mirrored appearance, as though the real Logan Du Rose had stepped out for a moment.

Nausea rose into Hana's throat, the urge to vomit overwhelming and raw. Her stomach always absorbed a crisis first, quelling any need for food and purging her body of everything else without warning. She ran to the front door and turned the lock. The legs of the dining chair screeched across the floor as she dragged it towards the entrance and jammed it beneath the handle. Logan lay on the mattress fully clothed, his lips moving as though he chewed something bitter and distasteful. But he could still exit the villa without her stopping him. If that's what he wanted.

Hana dragged two more chairs in front of the door, figuring if he left while she used the bathroom, at least she'd hear him declutter the tiny lobby. She piled one on top of the other with her last flakes of energy. "I need the bathroom," she told Logan. "Back in two minutes."

She took his phone with her in case Liza called, setting it on the vanity beside her wash bag. The earlier nausea dissipated with the passing minutes, and her stomach lost its painful tension. "We're good," she told herself. The chrome tap squeaked as she ran cold water into the sink, using her cupped hands to douse her face. The sense of panic lost its grip and the silence of the villa gave her time to think and to plan. Hana glanced at the phone with its dark, lifeless screen. And Liza would call. The judge wouldn't abandon her favourite brother.

Hana slipped from the bathroom and removed her sandals. Logan had discarded all his clothing onto the armchair and climbed into the wide double bed. His back faced her, the knotty ridges of his spine like a mountain range to the junction with his neck. Despite the mugginess which heralded a coming weather change, he'd covered himself in a thin sheet. Hana watched him, studying the angles of his muscular frame through the translucent fabric. He appeared so still, and the sight jarred her nerves again. She recalled so few moments in their marriage when he'd looked motionless, no part of him jiggling or tapping. He moved even while sleeping. It was as though someone had stilled the ocean and forced it into a flat, foreboding calm.

Hana stepped to the other side of the bed and gazed down at him. His lashes fluttered and his eyes opened. She held her breath. His irises sparkled from within his tanned complexion, like headlights sweeping her in their full beam. "Sorry," he said, his voice cracking. "I've messed up everything." He rolled onto his back and lifted his right arm, stretching it behind his head. "We're trapped here now."

Hana released a sigh and observed his struggle. Her natural empathy caused an ache in her soul for his futile internal wrangling. "None of this is your fault," she asserted. She laid the phone on the bedside cabinet and sank onto the mattress. "Do you want company, or should I give you space?"

Logan shook his head and shuffled into the centre of the mattress. He stretched out his free arm in a welcoming motion. Hana shrugged out of her dress and wriggled beneath the sheet. She turned onto her side and pressed her body alongside his, stretching her left leg over both of his in an act of possession. The softness of her calf moulded against his hard shins. "It's about more than finding ourselves trapped in paradise with no supplies, isn't it?" Hana asked, keeping her tone light. "You play your cards so close to your chest, it's impossible to tell what's really going on in your head."

Logan swallowed. Hana watched his Adam's apple rise and fall in his throat. He'd shaved that morning, but missed a single hair beneath his jawline. She raised a hand and stroked his rugged cheek. Logan's lips parted twice before he spoke, as though the effort of formulating an explanation cost him all his energy. His voice held a gravelly quality. "I know one of us will die first." Hana frowned. She hadn't expected him to lead with such a statement. Logan cleared his throat, and his voice strengthened. "I understand one of us will continue without the other. But I don't want to exist without you."

She clamped her teeth closed. So many possible replies sprang onto her tongue, but she recognised most of them as worthless cliches. Vik's death had rocked her world. It seemed possible Logan believed because she'd visited the rock bottom of the pit, she could go there again. Hana closed her eyes, her lashes fluttering against Logan's side like butterfly wings. His words held a powerlessness she didn't want to consider. Only God dictated a person's time line. No amount of strategising could anticipate or thwart the end. But she kept her counsel in a rare moment of wisdom as Logan revealed the hidden cry of his heart.

"I thought I'd lost you when you collapsed at the pa," he said. He licked his lips and forced himself onward in his uncustomary candidness. "I said every prayer I've ever uttered that day. I've never felt such relief and gratitude when you survived. But you won't remember the blood left on the bathroom floor after Bodie stuffed you into his car. It looked like a slaughterhouse. The ambulance didn't come, so we rushed you to the emergency room. I sat in the back with you until you lost consciousness, using my shirt pressed against your stomach to stem the bleeding."

Hana quailed against the retelling of a story she'd forced herself to forget. Blurred images scrolled across her inner vision, memories of horror movie proportion. A blood bath. The tiles slick beneath the men's shoes. The fear, then the pain, and a blissful nothingness which smudged the chaos to a hazy grey. Hana's jaw ached from clenching it hard enough to break her molars, but she couldn't deny him the outpouring of sadness and fear. She'd craved hearing his honesty without expecting to receive it. It seemed churlish to stunt the confession pouring from his heart. She owed it to him. And so she forced herself to listen and to understand.

44

The lawyer - rōia

Logan spoke about his fears for their future. The stabbing of his wife had once again forced him to face the stark reality of living without her. The words tumbled from his lips like Jenga bricks knocked from their perilous tower, dripping with a terror she couldn't comprehend. Couldn't, because she refused to absorb the impact of the stain on his security. "I can't change anything about our future," he confessed. "I have less control than I believed. These last few days prove it."

His honesty seemed addictive in its rarity. So Hana hung onto every word as though the utterance might be his last. He spoke about his mother's death, her treachery, and his forever fractured relationship with Alfred. His fears for Phoenix and Mac trumped all else but his terror of losing her. Eventually, his last sentence ran aground and exhausted, he slept. But Hana's mind sifted and sorted through the debris until nothing made sense.

She wrapped her arms around Logan's powerful torso and clung to him, aware of the cataclysmic shift in their marriage. The newness caused a cleft to yawn in the pit of her stomach, summoning the stress-nausea again and making her shiver. Logan slept beneath her embrace as though drugged.

A car engine rumbled nearby, the vibrations moving through the villa and adding a soporific shaking which rippled through the mattress like an electrical hum. The metallic slam of a car door echoed through the wall behind her head.

Hana detached herself from Logan's sleeping body. His chest rose and fell in the gentle rhythm of peace. She slipped from the bed backwards, snatching up her dress and feeding her arms and head through the holes. The fabric shimmied over her to create a static haze, which made her hair crackle as though on fire. She grabbed the phone and activated the screen, disappointed to see no message from Liza. The last bud of hope in her heart bobbed beneath the weight of an unexpected snowfall.

Voices sounded outside, the chickens clucking and shifting around in protest at the disturbance. Hana ran to the front door, her bare feet pattering against the tiles. She moved the chairs aside, cringing as the legs squeaked against her clumsy dragging. A glance at Logan showed him still lying on his back, trapped in that strange, dreamless place between light and deep sleep.

Hana unlocked the door and tugged it open. The muggy air hit her like a wall of damp heat as she pushed through the screen and closed both doors behind her. By the time she'd walked down the porch steps to the grass, her visitors had finished their discussion and rounded the side of the building.

"Mrs Du Rose." Sergeant Wally George gave a curt nod. He didn't offer his hand, his reluctance stark against the effusiveness of the man who'd arrived at the same time.

"Mrs Du Rose?" The stranger's words held a note of question as he stepped forward and seized her hand in paws the size of boxing mitts. "Charlie Clay. Clay and Rocco are the law firm near the airport. I'm here to provide you with legal assistance."

Sergeant Wally George's upper lip peeled back from his teeth in a snarl. The air between the men crackled. Charlie Clay's physical appearance formed an antithesis of the police officer's. Where one looked skinny and malnourished for his thirty-odd years, overworked with a complexion the hue of used grey plasticine, the other oozed good health and indulgence. Charlie Clay hadn't just taken a bite of paradise, he'd eaten the whole thing bones as well. Six decades of life in the sunshine had tanned his skin like a wrinkled okra. When he chuckled, his belly stretched against the tenuous barricade of a wide tan belt. It acted as a cliff, protecting his baggy brown suit trousers from a landslide of flesh and generous living. He beamed at Hana, his blue eyes like tiny slits from within mountainous cheeks. She smiled back, liking him already for the confidence and authority he brought with him. "Nice to meet you," she replied. A heavy sigh escaped her lungs. "But I don't understand why you're both here." Dread snaked along her spine like a python, its grip tightening. She shivered despite the balmy air. Her gaze switched to Sergeant Wally George, an eyebrow rising in question. "Are you here to arrest us?"

Her mind flicked to her husband, still sleeping just metres away from her. She tensed her thigh muscles, preparing to dash up the steps and barricade the door. In his stricken state, Logan altered position within the family dynamic like a chess piece shifting on a board. He ranked with Hana's children and she would die for them. Hana backed up the first step, giving her a nominal height advantage over the two men. She stretched her hands to either side of her and gripped the twin banister rails, using her body to form a gate.

The lawyer frowned, but the police officer missed the implied resistance.

"My Lady Judge Eliza Du Rose contacted me." Clay tilted his head as though expelling water from his right ear. Folds of skin piled over his shirt collar like expanding dough. His eyes glinted with a peculiar light, as though her phone call formed the stuff of career-daydreams.

"And me." Sergeant Wally George seemed less thrilled about the once in a lifetime experience.

"Right." Hana pursed her lips and imagined the brief conversations. A demand, a clear exposition of the consequences, followed by a threat. Liza's trademark. For once, Hana admitted a flicker of gratitude. She kept her arms braced across the narrow gap. "So, what do you suggest?"

Sergeant Wally George made a clicking sound with his tongue. "I'm sorry for the notices. I plan to travel around the island and insist the shop keepers remove them."

Charlie Clay released a snort with all the force of a bull. "That's the least of their worries. I've taken photographs of all those displayed between my office and this location." He turned his giant frame to face Sergeant Wally George, the effect containing all the fascination of a cruise liner manoeuvring. "My office is drawing up defamation lawsuits as we speak.

For libel, misrepresentation, hurt and humiliation. My Lady Judge recommended a litany of potential infringements against my clients' excellent character." His shiny shoes twitched against the grass as though tapping the introduction to a jazz dance. He oozed pure glee and professional pride. His enjoyment communicated itself to Hana, and her lips parted in an unexpected smile. This man would fix it. For a fee as big as himself.

Sergeant Wally George cleared his throat. A dark shadow passed across his hazel irises, surprising Hana with its intensity. He took a step towards her, his right hand raised as though making an oath. "Just give me time to sort this out," he asked. His gaze rested on her face, ignoring the vibrant lawyer less than a metre away. "Please?"

Hana swallowed and glanced at Charlie Clay. Liza's actions had given the man autonomy. The relief made Hana's knees tremble. A faint musky scent reached her as he clapped his fleshy paws together, his deodorant working overtime in the heat. "Is your husband available, Mrs Du Rose?" He turned his effusive gaze on Hana. "I think we should talk."

45

The High Secret - Nui Ngaro

Hana gnawed at her lower lip and put her weight into her right hip. Her fingers clutched the banister rails in a death grip.

"I'll get on then." Sergeant Wally George turned in a lazy circle and trudged away, offering a feckless wave over his shoulder.

Charlie Clay smiled at Hana, an air of expectation in his expression. His body dipped from the waist as though about to broach the steps.

"My husband isn't well." Hana licked her lips. "He's taking a nap. Is it possible to go for a walk?"

Clay blinked as though she'd slapped him, his head jerking back on his neck. "A walk?" he said, the word foreign and unwelcome. "No, no." He lifted a set of car keys from his trouser pocket. A sweat stain spread from beneath his right armpit to engulf the fabric of his smart shirt. "Let's go for a drive."

Hana released a groan low in her throat. She glanced down at her bare feet and then back at the front door. The first thought which burst into her mind reminded her of the danger of getting into a stranger's vehicle. The second admonished the first. Liza sent him. If the lawyer had nefarious intentions, he wouldn't risk the judge's ire. "Okay," she agreed, praying she didn't regret her hasty decision. She jogged up the steps and drew back the screen, balancing it against her elbow as she opened the front door.

Logan hadn't moved. He lay with his back to the door, a long, muscular leg pinning the sheet beneath his knee. Her gaze roved across his contoured buttocks and the sensual dip at the base of his spine. She padded around, finding a notepad and pen provided by the resort and jotting a message for him so he wouldn't worry. Then she flicked the catch on the locking mechanism after snatching up the key, and pulled the door closed behind her. A satisfying click told her she'd secured it. If Craig went snooping in her absence, he'd get more than he bargained for. Logan didn't rouse nicely like a normal person. He'd have buried the body before she returned. She stepped onto the deck, only then realising she'd forgotten to grab any shoes.

Clay eyed her bare feet as she padded across the grass, but he said nothing disparaging. Hana rounded the side of the villa to discover a smart Audi convertible parked in the space between her building and Hallie's. Clay left dents in the springy grass as he bounded towards his expensive silver vehicle. He'd left mere centimetres between the front bumper and the Harley's mudguard. "Let me back up a bit," he called, slumping into the driver's seat. The suspension groaned and the tyres on his side flattened against the hard ground.

Clay reversed out of the narrow space until the driver's side lined up with the rear of Hana's villa. She glanced sideways at the door Logan had found, squinting to catch sight of the hinges set at the bottom edge. A flower border obscured them, the planting of agapanthus with its bobbing purple heads perhaps intentional.

"Get in," Clay called over the hum of the engine.

Hana lifted the door handle and slid onto the buttery leather seat. She jammed the villa key into her bra as she turned away to grab the slippery fabric of the seatbelt.

Clay said nothing more until they reached the main road through the resort. He blasted past the reception office in a haze of exhaust fumes. Craig leaned against the door frame and watched them leave. Despite the frequent signs deterring smoking, he clasped a cigarette between his index and middle finger, the ash forming a coiled spring. His brow furrowed as though in irritation. Hana craned her neck to peer through the tinted window running along one wall of the office. Sally beetled across the carpet to the door and tapped Craig's shoulder. He turned in a lazy arc, the cigarette ash plunging to the paving slabs between his flip flops. Sally followed his gaze and spied Hana watching her. Some monstrous emotion burned behind the other woman's irises. It reeked of spite and jealousy beneath a heady coating of venom. Hana gulped and turned her attention back to Charlie Clay's erratic driving. She held onto the door handle as he careened left at the resort's entrance and followed the anticlockwise bus for a few kilometres. He turned left at Matavera and joined an inland road before heading into the bush. Hana released a curse in her head. She'd made a terrible mistake. If Charlie Clay didn't murder her and dump her body, Logan would.

Grit crunched and spat from beneath the tyres as the convertible lumbered deeper into the bush canopy. A stern sign declared the area out of bounds, a typo in the threat of persecution instead of prosecution. Ferns waved overhead, shrouding Hana in the clean scent of healthy green fauna. Her knuckles whitened as she gripped the door handle, fearing for her bare soles if she needed to make a run for it. Charlie Clay drove with concentration, his heavy grey brows drawn into a bushy line rising half way up his forehead. A tufty mop sprung like hedgehog spines skyward, fine tendrils of electrified hair. The expensive vehicle listed and the steering wheel fought Clay's hands as he navigated the pot holes and sections of washed out road.

"Here we are," he announced as the car rounded a final, death defying bend. He parked in front of a low slung wooden building and secured the handbrake with a series of teeth grinding ratchets. Charlie Clay released the steering wheel and wiped his sweating hands on his trousers. The dampness did little to dull the sharp creases in the fabric. "This is Raro's best kept secret," he declared, clapping his meaty palms together like an excited toddler. His eyebrows waggled in a comical dance as he faced Hana. "And it has air conditioning."

A wall of freezing air hit them as they stepped across the threshold. Hana paused at a sign which read, *'Shoes must be worn inside.'* She stared down at her bare feet and winced. "Oh," she whispered. "I'm not allowed in."

Clay waved his hand behind him as though distributing foul air after a fart. "You're with me," he stated, his confidence in his ability to circumnavigate written rules paramount.

Hana ventured further into the room, the wooden boards cool beneath her soles. A bar occupied the far wall, optics and twinkling lights creating an illusion of decadence. Comfy armchairs grouped around low coffee tables, cardboard beer mats protecting the polished wood. A framed picture of the English queen commanded the far wall, no other decoration deemed regal enough to hang near it. The remaining two walls bowed beneath the weight of a taxidermist's handiwork. A wild hog's head grinned to reveal fanged tusks and sharp teeth. Small birds froze mid stride or flight on shelves pivoted on decorative iron buttresses. Hana gave a visible shiver and avoided the glare of an indignant tui, appalled at its undignified fate. Rifles and decommissioned muskets hung in between the creatures, as though forcing them to spend eternity alongside their killers. No windows.

Hana refused an alcoholic drink and Clay appeared disappointed. "I can't," she said, infusing determination into her voice. "I had emergency surgery a few weeks ago. My liver needs time to recover." Her right hand rested across her side, her fingers aware of the delicate scar beneath her dress. *'Get some sunshine on it,'* the surgeon had said. *'Avoid stress.'* The notion made her want to explode with hysterical laughter at the irony. She'd managed neither so far.

Clay carried two drinks to a group of armchairs below the hog's head. Hana frowned, noticing the man behind the bar took no payment. A tall glass containing cola sweated onto the cardboard mat, and Hana seated herself in front of it. If she darted her eyes to the left at speed, it appeared the pig glowered at her. She turned her body and reached for her glass, not sure of her liver's reaction to a drink almost as corrosive as vodka.

Clay sipped the tan liquid from a crystal tumbler with relish. Then he set the glass on the table where it sparkled beneath the light from skylights overhead. He folded his chubby fingers across the ample belly straining from behind his belt. "My Lady Judge Du Rose gave me strict instructions," he began. He lifted his voice and glanced around the empty bar as though disappointed to have no audience. The barman ran a dry towel over glasses steaming from the dishwasher and showed no interest.

Hana cleared her throat and relaxed her shoulders. "Can we just call her Liza?" she asked. "She's my sister-in-law."

Clay's eyes glinted and his lips turned downward. "Oh." His body seemed to melt into the seat. "I realise you share a surname. There are only three law firms on the island and I might have answered the phone as the judge's first choice or her last." He leaned forward, his neck spilling over the sides of his shirt collar. "But I'm here for you and your husband. There's little mileage in challenging your arrest, but the posters are ammunition for a gross misrepresentation lawsuit."

"But the police sergeant is taking them down." Hana took the soaked glass in careful fingers. The condensation bled over her knuckles and made it slippery to hold. She sipped the cola, enjoying the sugar hit and anticipating trouble later from her damaged organ.

Clay made a sucking sound through his teeth, as though enduring the bitterness of a lemon. "Don't get your hopes up regarding Sergeant Wally George." The slightest sneer lifted his lips, but professionalism overruled, and he returned to business. "I have photographic evidence of the posters displayed in enough shops to take legal action. My assistant trawled the island in the other direction and took photos of the rest. You have a solid case against each of the traders. We'll sort it out ourselves."

Hana set her glass back on the mat. She aimed for the dark ring it had already created but missed. "We just want the posters down," she replied. "Otherwise we can't buy food or use the amenities. I don't know how far this thing goes. Are we banned from the medical centre or the hospital? That's the issue for now." Her eyes narrowed to create flashing emerald slits. "And I want to know who started it." Clenching her teeth sent a blossoming headache pulsing in her temples. "They need to answer for their actions."

"You don't want court injunctions and solicitor's letters?" Clay cocked his head. His tufty blond spikes rippled in the breeze from an air conditioner above the bar. Disappointment shrouded him like a heavy winter coat.

"I don't think so." Hana wrinkled her nose. "Not yet. But Liza picked you for a reason. I want you to investigate where this mess started. Bring me a name. If I'm suing anyone for slander or libel, it's that person."

46

Surprise - pō'itirere

Hana told him everything. She detailed their unfortunate trip to the supermarket, the mystery of Hallie's disappearance, Logan's theory that they'd stumbled on a private group of swingers, and their confusion about Sally's occupation. She finished her cola, discomfited by the trapped air bubbles which rumbled through her digestive system. Clay drank another whiskey before getting to his feet. He asked for time to think about the deluge of facts she'd dropped in his lap.

"We're all aware of the counterfeit cash," he concluded as he opened the passenger door of the convertible for Hana. She noticed he hadn't bothered locking it. His bottom lip protruded as he set his sunglasses on his nose. "I haven't heard of a swingers' club, though. That's a new one on me." He scurried around to the driver's side, the suspension groaning as he sank into the seat. The engine fired without complaint and Clay executed a gravel spitting arc of the car park to face the vehicle downhill.

"What do I owe you?" Hana leaned her head against the seat and enjoyed the sensation of the wind through her hair. Clay had rolled down the hood of the convertible. Flies and a bumble bee splatted against the windscreen, and he used the wipers to dislodge them.

"Nothing yet." He glanced across at her, massive sunglasses obscuring most of the top half of his face. "My Lady Judge." He paused and gave a visible shudder, which Hana attributed to an inner thrill. "Liza." His fingers tapped a rapid beat on the leather steering wheel cover. "She gave me access to a limited account." He beamed with something like adoration. "She said she'd scrutinize any charges and make my life not worth living if I diddled her."

Hana frowned, imagining Liza using the word 'diddled' as a verb. But it didn't deserve the mental energy, and she turned in her seat to face the lawyer. "Mr Clay, why didn't you pay for drinks at the bar?"

Clay tutted. "Call me Charlie," he said. The tyres crunched as he navigated past a washout, which appeared as though a giant took a bite from the mountainside. "You mustn't mention Nui Ngaro to anyone."

"Nui Ngaro." Hana turned the word over on her tongue. "What does it mean?"

"High Secret," Charlie replied. "And it's the best kept secret on the island. Our grandfathers started it as a gentlemen's club. It's for business owners and prominent locals. We each pay a stipend for membership. It's a closed clientele. Membership gets handed down through the families."

"Like the Masons?" Hana raised an eyebrow in fascination.

Charlie turned his gaze on her and his lips quirked upward in amusement. "Yes, and no. It's private and there are rules. But we don't conduct strange ceremonies or run it like a cartel. It's a quiet bar devoid of tourists." He jabbed his head towards her. "No offence. The bar manager monitors stock and consumption and provides a report at the end of each month. Anyone taking advantage is liable for sanctions, and no one wants that. It's a safe place where we can discuss business without fear."

"And no women." Hana pushed out her lower lip. "But you let me in. And without shoes." She wiggled her toes against the rough carpet.

"I made an exception." The vehicle bounced down through the bush towards the sealed road. "And I knew none of the members would be there this afternoon."

"Is Craig a member?" Hana studied his face as he checked for other vehicles before leaving the overgrown entrance and pulling onto the street.

"Craig who?"

"He owns the Paradise Villas, where we're staying. He's a local business owner."

Charlie snorted. "He's not from here. Fathers hand the membership to their eldest son. Or daughter." He blinked as though the revelation brought him discomfort. "We have one female patron, and she sometimes graces us with her presence."

"Who?" Hana's eyes sparkled with interest. She leaned forward until her seatbelt tightened across her breasts.

A grin broke out across Charlie's wide face. "I shan't tell you," he said with a laugh. He waited for the clockwise bus to pass before turning onto the outer road and heading towards Titikaveka. Then he frowned and his manner became serious. "I'm trusting you," he said, his tone tense. "Nui Ngaro is a secret and it must remain so."

"Okay," she agreed, turning to face him. "But why the typo on the sign leading to the bar? I'm sure you know the difference between prosecution and persecution."

Charlie threw his head back and laughed. "I do. But can you imagine a better deterrent than the image of a deranged bush dweller defending his property? We spread rumours of a man named Ngaro who lives up there. No one can testify to seeing him. If anyone stopped to consider it, they'd realise he's over two hundred years old." He giggled at the ruse, the notion amusing him all the way to the resort.

Charlie dropped Hana at the entrance. He roared off along the road, travelling clockwise towards his office. Hana pictured the poor legal assistant whose ruined weekend involved trawling around the island, taking photos in shop doorways. She wondered if they'd taken covert shots or halted foot traffic to capture the perfect angle. Bowed by the humidity which gripped the island in a damp, sweating heat, Hana turned her feet on the hot asphalt lane snaking through the resort. It burned against her bare soles and she took giant steps until able to reach the warm grass verge. She paused a moment for the painful tingling to cease in her feet. A pat to her left breast located the villa key, and she wrinkled her nose. It had slipped sideways in her bra and come to rest against her underwire.

Hana caught herself as her fingers dug into her dress. Despite the silence backed only by birdsong and the ever present chickens, she wasn't alone. Just because she saw no other person in her eye line didn't mean they weren't there. The hotchpotch placement of the villas caused many lounge windows to face the narrow street. The tree lined entrance created a deceptively public setting. Hana withdrew her hand and dried her damp palms against her shorts. A sense of insignificance shrouded her as she paused beneath the vibrant blue sky. Black clouds circled each other in the distance, promising rain but reneging at the last moment even as land locked buds opened their colourful mouths and waited for relief.

A police motor scooter leaned against its stand in a parking space next to the reception. Hana frowned and wondered if Sergeant Wally George had come with any news. She held her breath and bounded across the molten surface, using tufts of grass in crumbling cracks to deaden the heat. The curb edging offered some comfort, its lighter shade repelling more of the sun's glare. Hana navigated along it like a tightrope walker, dismayed at her lack of balance and feeling ridiculous as she teetered. A bright yellow kayak leaned against the wall beneath the main window, a strand of seaweed adorning its pointed front end. The paddles lay next to it, crossed in the centre in an X as though discouraging entry. Two seats, two yawning black mouths punctuated the sleek yellow body, the tangled thread of a fishing line swirling against the grass. The front end of the kayak showed significant gouging of the surface, strands of polyethylene creating an illusion of yellow hair. Hana shivered despite the heat. She wasn't a fan of messing around in vast bodies of water and hoped Logan didn't suggest such a pastime.

Hana followed a damp set of footprints to the steps and pushed open the heavy reception door.

Craig dropped his arms at speed and took a giant step backwards. It lacked coordination and his torso tilted in a dangerous arc before his flailing hands caught hold of the brochure rack. He steadied himself and the leaflets rustled at the disturbance. Sergeant Wally George's sidekick cleared her throat and wiped a hurried hand across her mouth.

"Hi." Craig recovered well, fixing a smile onto his tanned face and turning towards Hana. "How can I help you?" he asked.

47

Shift - 'iki'iki

Hana had to hand it to him. The guy had class. The thought crossed her mind that perhaps he enjoyed the risk of getting caught. She eyed him from the doorway, giving Carrie a moment to collect herself. Her reactions proved slower as she straightened her uniform shirt and tucked it into the waistband of her navy trousers.

"I didn't hear your vehicle." Craig moved behind the reception desk to hide the protruding bulge in his shorts. He reached for a folded towel from the fluffy stack behind it. Lifting it, he clutched it to his bare chest. "I thought I saw housekeeping refreshing your place this morning."

"They did." Hana stepped over the threshold, breathing in the frigid breeze pumped out by the air conditioner. She turned her feet towards Carrie and raised an eyebrow. "I saw the bike and wondered if Sergeant Wally George brought news for me."

"About what?" Craig dumped the towel and braced his forearms on the desk behind the reception counter. It created the impression of a head bobbing like a balloon above the melamine shelf. He appeared uncomfortable, lust and adrenaline retreating to leave a pit of numbness behind his eyes.

Hana pursed her lips and ticked off items from a list in her head. "Our burglary. Hallie's disappearance. The posters displayed all over the island with our faces on them."

Craig frowned and his eyes narrowed. He released the fake casual pose and stood. Hana saw genuine confusion in his muddy irises. "Posters?" He cocked his head to one side and his gaze flicked to Carrie. "Posters?" he repeated.

Carrie avoided Hana's gaze, choosing instead to focus on Craig as he pushed his damp fringe away from his eyes. "Yeah. Someone told the trade association about them passing fake twenties at the supermarket." Her hand flapped in Hana's direction.

"We didn't!" Hana asserted. "I met the cashier in church this morning and she apologised for accusing us. We didn't do it. It's a fact!"

Carrie shrugged and kept her attention on Craig. A line of sweat trickled from her temple to her jaw.

Hana saw her frustration and embarrassment turning her into a perspiring mess. The tinted windows might have protected their risky sex act, but leaving the front door unlocked smacked of stupidity for a business owner and a cop. "The shopkeepers put up posters showing them at the Trading Post the other night and denying them entry. He's sorting it." Carrie didn't use Sergeant Wally George's incredible full name, and Hana didn't blame her. It took an inordinate amount of effort to say all the various parts and not shorten it. It beggared the question of what they could shorten it to. Wally, George or just Sergeant, even though he apparently wasn't a legitimate police sergeant.

"I have a lawyer," Hana stated, staring at the side of Carrie's face. The sweaty drip darkened her shirt collar like the start of polka dots. "Charlie Clay is acting for us." She turned to Craig. "Are you part of this association? Did someone notify you to put up a poster or ban us from your resort?"

For a long moment, he appeared nonplussed. "Sally deals with all that," he concluded. His head bobbed as he bent to peer at the computer monitor in front of him. "I went fishing in the kayak." He glanced up at Hana, holding her gaze for an inappropriate beat. His irises twinkled. "I caught nothing." The hidden jibe seemed to amuse him. They both knew she'd stopped him from catching Carrie with his disgusting lure.

Carrie shifted on her sensible soles, seeming lost. Hana realised she didn't know whether to stay or leave. She fiddled with a radio attached to her belt, creating intermittent bursts of static in the silent room. Craig bobbed up again, his fringe already covering his left eye in a damp curtain. "I can't find an email from them," he announced. "Maybe Sal deleted it." He twisted his lips and stared around him as though his wife might materialise like a genie. "She's around here somewhere. I'll ask her when she comes back." He clicked his tongue and grinned at Hana, his earlier awkwardness shucked from his shoulders like an unwanted blanket. "Anything else?"

Hana exhaled and narrowed her eyes at him. "Yes. Hallie. Any news?"

He shook his head and flattened his lips. "Na. Maybe when Jared comes around, he'll know where she is." His lack of concern jarred Hana's nerves compared to his earlier anxiety.

"Aren't you good friends?" she asked. "Hallie talked about you like you were besties. We sat with you at the bar. You said you'd asked the police to declare her a missing person."

Craig gave a shrug of dismissal and his nose wrinkled on one side. "You know what it's like. People visit your hotel or resort and you're nice to them. They think you're their best mate because of how you treat them." Hana studied his expression, confused by the lack of guile in his eyes. "They're just people who visit often. Jared's wife is a travel agent. She recommends our resort on the mainland. It's good to keep these people on your side, isn't it?" He asked, as though seeking affirmation. Thousands of guests moved through Logan's hotel each year, but the Du Roses adopted none in particular. She wondered if the tiny size of the island had fostered a false sense of camaraderie. Her heart ached for Hallie's naivety. It smashed Logan's theory of their partner-swapping in an elabourate swinging scheme.

She studied Craig with intense dislike flashing in her green irises. He offered no account for his dramatic change of direction concerning a customer's disappearance. It occurred to her that the ruse had been for her benefit. But Craig didn't need to swing with other couples to get his kicks. The guy whored from one side of the island to the other, making his own fun in the process. Hana experienced a wave of pity for Sally. It explained her fixation with Logan. She'd selected him as the alpha with which to spite her husband. "So, nothing on Hallie then?" Hana clenched her jaw and her angry gaze bore holes through the side of Carrie's face.

The police officer shrugged. "No one reported her missing."

Hana's lips parted in disbelief. "Perhaps that's because her husband is in a coma!" She raised her voice and stared from one to the other. "Unbelievable!" she snarled. "Absolutely unbelievable!" She whirled from the room, her temper stoked. Her soles hit the baking pavement without registering the pain until she'd crossed the road and dashed for the grass verge.

Sympathy for Sally's disastrous marriage occupied Hana's thoughts as she traversed the shared lawn between the buildings. She touched the banister of Hallie's deserted villa as she passed, wondering where the effervescent woman had gone. No one seemed bothered about her disappearance, with Jared unable to advocate for her. Hana swallowed a knot of discomfort and imagined Logan's disinterest if she vanished without warning. Though she often sniped at her family that no one would notice she'd died unless she collapsed in front of the fridge, she didn't believe the criticism held any actual truth.

Hana skipped up the steps to the front door, her fingers already digging in her bra for the key. She contorted herself as she retrieved it, the jagged edges scratching her skin. A smile of triumph crossed her lips as she pulled open the screen and dug it into the lock. The front door swung inward.

All compassion for Sally died as Hana stepped over the threshold.

A low vibration pulsed through her feet as the motor for the water pump thrummed beneath the floor. Water sloshed in the shower cubicle behind the closed bathroom door. A familiar whistled tune offered comfort alongside the dismay which engulfed Hana.

48

Shock - ʻakamaitu

"Oops!" Sally's tone held indifference as she sprawled in the wide double bed. The sheet which had creased beneath Logan's sleeping body shrouded her like a veil. Pink toenails peeked from underneath the rumpled fabric as Hana froze in place on the mat. The heavy door slammed behind her hard enough to toss her hair in the sudden breeze. Logan whistled a new tune, sad and doleful, unaware of the catastrophe occurring just metres away. Water cascaded as a backing track, its flow into the shower tray distorted by the presence of his slick body in its way. It slapped an irregular beat against the melamine surface at his feet.

Hana forced herself to study the woman in her bed. Raised bumps in the light fabric pinpointed Sally's nipples, betraying her nakedness beneath the sheet. The hard edges of her jaw appeared dulled by thick foundation, the determination in her eyes giving her a rock steadiness she perhaps didn't feel. Sally turned onto her side, showing no sign of leaving. Hana pushed her hands behind her back to hide her shaking fingers from view. Showing weakness wouldn't help her now.

Sally waited for Hana to react, flicking at a strand of cotton escaping from the seam of Logan's pillow. Hana's continued silence seemed unexpected, and worry drew a faint line on Sally's brow. Her blue irises sparkled beneath black eyeliner and tufted fake lashes as though she recognised she'd bitten off more than she could ever chew. She pushed herself up on one arm, the sheet falling away to reveal bulbous breasts with an unnatural bounce and a stomach unblemished by the rigors of childbirth. "He's so gorgeous, I couldn't resist. I figured you wouldn't mind sharing." Sally's tone held a curious sense of entitlement, as though she'd borrowed the cup of sugar which Hallie had forgotten. If Hallie had ever wanted sugar more than she needed an excuse to invade Hana's sanctuary.

"Did you?" Hana cocked her head to the side, answering the rhetorical question through a voice which held a brittle quality. Surely the woman hadn't expected her to share her husband without protest. Sally frowned and glanced down at the pillowcase, and the action allowed Hana to disconnect from her.

A cursory glance around the bedroom and lounge area revealed a discarded floral dress with spaghetti straps slung over the single armchair. The sheer fabric allowed the pattern of the chair to peek through it. High heeled electric blue sandals lay on the floor where Sally had sat in the chair to remove them. One had fallen on its side while its mate stood to attention, the toes pointing towards the bed and the scene of her planned fornication. No bra, but a skimpy thong hung over the chair arm at an artful angle as though she'd taken care of its placement. Sickness roiled in Hana's stomach, eking its return journey into her chest and pricking the back of her throat with its destructive acid.

The white noise which had entered her brain made it impossible to think. She'd been here before and her passive aggressive stance hadn't done her any favours against the other woman who'd conspired to take her husband. Hana had run from trouble and needed more than her own two hands to put the mess back together again afterwards. It had taken her wider family's help restore order.

"Not this time," Hana whispered.

"What?" Sally peered across the room at her, jerking and drawing her chin downward at the fury she saw in Hana's flashing green eyes. She sat up and swung her legs around, planting her feet on the tiled floor. Her right hip brushed against Logan's pillow and Hana's imagination went wild, conjuring pornographic scenarios she couldn't stem.

Hana's heels rapped against the tiles as she strode across the room. Sally winced and rose to standing, the sheet dribbling sideways to expose a woman unashamed of her nakedness. Her breasts lost a little of their perkiness against gravity. Daylight cast the dents and shadows of cellulite onto her thighs. In other circumstances, Hana might have complimented her on the lusciousness of her mature body, but not here, and not now. Not with the woman's rounded, tanned ass and the neat V of her dark pubic hair on display for Hana's husband.

The overwhelming urge to get Sally out of the villa increased the buzz in Hana's brain. She acknowledged the rise of a murderous spirit in her chest, shocking her with its dark malevolence. Unable to trust herself near Sally's naked person without hurting her, Hana dodged right and snatched up the woman's clothes from the chair. The lace from the thong had an unexpected roughness against her clenched fingers, and the pooling fabric of the expensive dress seemed to faint across her wrist. Before Sally could react, Hana swept up the sandals and spun, furious, stamping feet carrying her to the front door.

She opened it with such force it clattered the back of the kitchen counter, rebounding after her and catching her heel and her right elbow as she propelled herself onto the porch. It didn't seem enough to discard Sally's clothing on the grass between the villas, and Hana's feet continued marching.

A straight trajectory carried her as far as the swimming pool just metres beyond Hallie's empty villa. The pool maintenance man wearing a vest and shorts glanced up at her, a long handled net clasped in both hands. He paused in the process of dragging it through the water, his attention drawn by the buzz of Hana's chaotic energy. He stared open mouthed as Hana sent Sally's clothes and sandals into the crystal water with a wonky overarm throw.

The dress and thong floated atop the water, but the sandals sank with satisfying speed. They gave twin bumps against the bottom before shuffling together in the gentle current from the filter vent. They resembled synchronised swimmers, pausing before the performance of their lives.

With her face a grim mask, Hana spun and stamped back to her villa, her steps a dull thud on the baked earth. Chickens scattered away from her in alarm, and she fought the burgeoning cry threatening to break her chest open and reveal her misery to the world.

49

Temper - ririririri

Hana stalked into the villa and slammed the front door behind her. It rocked the entire building on its pilings and the bathroom door open. Sally hadn't moved. It astonished Hana to find her still standing where she left her half a minute earlier. A reversal of roles would have found Hana skittering across the grass, wearing whatever she could find. Either Sally wasn't quick enough, or she truly didn't care.

Logan emerged from a steam haze with a frown, a fresh towel clinging to his hips. The haunted expression of earlier had gone, banished by a wide-eyed look of surprise. "Babe?" The single word held an unspoken question as his gaze tracked from Hana to Sally. "Erm, well, this is awkward." Logan checked the knotted towel at his hip and edged towards Hana. He folded his brawny arms across his chest and she ached at his futile attempt to cover his scars. He didn't have enough hands to mask the pink ridges crisscrossing his torso and marring the refined plates of muscle.

"Awkward. You think?" Hana's words dripped like stalactites from her lips, cool enough to leave a damp puddle on the floor.

Logan straightened his shoulders and his legs shifted into their usual stance of feet apart and knees locked. Sally's eyes widened, catching sight of a muscular, hairy inner thigh as the towel gaped.

"I'm not into this," Logan stated, his tone bland. He searched Sally's expression with his astute grey eyes. "Thanks and all that, but no. My brother is the one who's into threesomes. You might wanna call him." His nose wrinkled, and he emphasised the rejection with a shake of his head. The hair he'd combed back from his forehead released tumbling strands into his right eye.

Hana stood her ground, her teeth locked into a painful grinding action. "How did you get in?" she demanded, keeping her focus on Sally despite the urge to look away. She owed the woman nothing and refused to offer her anything to protect her dwindled modesty.

"Master key." Sally's gaze grazed Hana before settling on Logan. Her eyes devoured him with a gnawing hunger, which made Logan take a step backwards as though bowled over by the force of it.

Hana whirled on the spot, her bare toes squeaking against the shiny tiles. She saw the bunch of keys sitting on the kitchen counter, bulky enough to satisfy a jailer. “You ransacked our stuff the other night,” she stated. “Why?”

“Not me.” Sally’s brow puckered into lines clogged with makeup. “Craig and I met up with Hallie and Jared at the Trading Post. You were there. I came home with you.” The accusation rocked her, though the others hadn’t touched her warped sense of justice. While she appeared unapologetic about settling into a married man’s bed wearing nothing but a seductive smile, she didn’t like the burglary accusation.

“You disgust me.” Hana’s voice shook as she delivered the insult. “It’s one thing to enjoy swinging and open marriages, but keep it to yourselves! I just discovered your husband getting hot and heavy with the local police officer at the reception. Can’t you control yourselves?”

Logan’s chin jerked backwards and his lips parted. “Wow!” he breathed. “Police officer? Sergeant Wally George definitely gets around on his scooter.” Hana didn’t correct him. He cocked his head and addressed Sally. “I’m not interested, love. Please leave and don’t come back, dressed or otherwise.”

Sally's teeth ground in her jaw and she snatched up the sheet, which she'd abandoned on the mattress. The light duvet over it put up a reasonable fight, and it forced her to turn and begin a tug of war. Her buttocks jiggled as all traces of the seductress abandoned her. Logan closed his eyes and turned sideways, fixing his gaze on Hana's feet. He studied his irate wife's toes as though assessing how much of her fury might land on him next. An eyebrow crept towards his hairline at the sight of the painful bruising he'd caused.

Hana ignored him, watching Sally fight the bed sheet, her arms folded across her chest in a far more aggressive stance than Logan's. She huffed with impatience as a blanket slid onto the floor and a tearing sound issued from the end of the mattress. "Just leave," she snarled, taking a calculating step towards the other woman. "Go before I throw you out."

"You stole my clothes!" Sally turned to her, breasts following as though surprised to find themselves left behind. "I'll invoice you for them."

Hana twisted her mouth into an unattractive grimace. "Well, you tried to steal my husband." Her sardonic smile and the eerie intensity of her irises made Sally cease her wrangling. "I'll leave a Google review, which will attract the international media."

Sally crossed one arm over her chest as though her nakedness only just caused her discomfort. Her other hand splayed over her pubis.

Hana continued, "I wonder what tourists you'll attract, then." She tapped her lower lip with her finger as though thinking of the repercussions. "You're disgusting!"

Hana regretted the word the second it left her lips. Not because she absolved Sally of her behaviour, but because of the effect it had on her. The woman took a physical step backwards, her breasts bouncing in response to the tremor which ran through her body. Her lips turned downward as though she might cry. Someone else had once bestowed that label on her and caused a bone-deep wound. Anger born of guilt sent warmth into Hana's cheeks. Unable to trust herself not to let fly more insults or resort to physical violence, Hana ground her teeth and stepped sideways to leave Sally a clear buck naked run towards the front door. "Bye!" She jabbed her chin in Sally's direction, the action containing enough venom to spear her. She wanted to dig her nails into the tanned shoulders and haul her towards the door, but wouldn't trust herself to let go, even after Sally exited. Her body vibrated with a latent fury.

Another realisation flooded her like a tidal wave as Sally eyed the fresh bundle of towels on the credenza outside the bathroom door. She took a step towards it, her eyes glinting with the possibility of coverage for her awkward journey home.

"Oh my goodness!" Hana exclaimed. "You did it!"

Sally's gaze darted around the villa, fear radiating from her in waves as she found herself cornered. "Just let me take a towel," she begged. "Please."

Hana knotted her fingers behind her back in an effort to stop them from closing around Sally's throat. "You told the trade association to ban us from every store on the island." Her chin trembled as she spoke, molten lava bubbling deep in her gut. "What is wrong with you?" she shouted into Sally's face. Her spittle landed on the woman's cheek and Hana envisaged herself wiping it off with her fist. She sensed Logan's presence before his hand enclosed her left shoulder, the action stalling her murderous spirit.

"Let her go." His baritone seemed to rumble through Hana's body. He edged her out of Sally's personal space and, reaching down, gave the sheet a valiant tug. Hana stared at his scarred knuckles as he held out the sheet to the other woman, turning aside to preserve the remnants of her dignity as she wrapped it around herself. Logan's arm seemed heavy on Hana's rigid shoulders as he drew her against him. "Leave her a little self-respect," he said, his tone soft.

Sally's fingers stalled in Hana's peripheral vision. Logan's kindness stung more than any of Hana's furious accusations. Hana saw the sense of it. Even so, she yearned to push Sally into the pool after her clothes and then hold her underneath the water.

Sally reached the door, the sheet trailing behind her like a stage princess' wedding train. She hauled it open and wrestled with the screen door. Her shoulders lifted and fell. "We're not swingers," she stated, her tone without emotion. "I just liked you."

"Hey." Logan's raised voice caused her to halt, but she didn't turn around. "Stay away from us," he said. "You've had your fun."

Hana brimmed with anger as Sally stepped over the threshold. She wondered at Logan's strange idea of fun as her venomous thoughts spooled like an uncoiled spring. As the screen door banged against its metallic frame, she yanked herself away from her husband's grasp and rounded on him, a familiar caged monster breaking free through her ribcage.

50

Caught - mou

"What the hell?" she began.

Logan's wide hand clamped over her mouth and he jerked his head towards the open front door. Only the screen covered it, but it wouldn't prevent sound carrying after Sally. "Let's not give her any satisfaction," he growled in Hana's ear. "I know her sort. She's a mischief maker. I don't think she believed I'd sleep with her, but she didn't seem too upset by you walking in on her."

Hana jerked away from him and he busied himself closing the front door before turning to face her. He set his hands over his hips. "I hope you realise nothing happened?" he stated, one eyebrow raised. "She wasn't there when I walked into the bathroom."

Hana ground her teeth in her jaw. "No," she conceded. "I don't think you'd roll over and mistake her envious body for your scarred, twig-like wife's."

Her tone held bitterness. She wiped her mouth with the back of her hand before dropping her arm with a groan. “Sorry, that sounded less self-deprecating in my head.”

Logan leaned against the kitchen counter and rolled his eyes. “Don’t make me put the hard word on you, Mrs Du Rose.” He dipped his chin and narrowed his eyes. Long lashes swept across his mahogany cheeks. “I own the monopoly on scars, thank you. And don’t you forget it.”

Hana turned and sank onto the bed. Her thighs locked in midair and she pinged upright, staring at the mattress with an expression of disgust. “I’m not sleeping in that bed now,” she stated. Every muscle in her body cringed at the thought of laying on sheets which had touched the other woman’s most intimate parts.

Logan exhaled. “Me neither. I’ll get dressed and we can walk to the reception and grab clean sheets.” He stepped towards the tallboy containing his clothes and then halted. “Well, that’s if you think Craig and Sergeant Wally George have finished their loving.”

Hana barked out a laugh, which seemed pulled from her core by an invisible string. She shook her head and pressed a hand against her prickling scar. “No! Officer Carrie and Craig.”

"Oh." Logan cocked his head. "You caught the resident weirdo and the local cop in flagrante delicto?" His chin bobbed as he considered the idea.

Hana groaned. "Trust the English teacher to understand Medieval Latin," she said with a sigh. "And no, not quite. They'd just progressed from snogging to dirty touching as I blasted through the door."

Logan snorted and shook his head as though he had water in his ears. "Okay, I'll get dressed while you explain your weird note. Tell me where you went with a lawyer I didn't know we had. Then we'll hunt up some fresh sheets and how about a ride on the Harley? I need to feel the wind on my face."

Hana waggled her eyebrows, her sense of humour returning. "If you'd still been in bed when Sally arrived, you could have enjoyed that lying down." She studied the loose thread on Logan's pillow, which had interested Sally so much.

"No." Logan raised his hand and gave a visible shudder. "Just no." He released the knot at his hip and the towel shivered from its tentative hold over his buttocks. It slid over his dark thighs, seeming to ripple at the backs of his knees. It puddled onto the floor at his feet, and Hana sensed the fire burgeoning in her belly scream at her to join it. Her gaze tracked from the towel to the bed, knowing that's where they'd inevitably end up.

An image of Sally reclining against the same sheets and pillows scored itself onto her eyeballs and she sighed and turned away. Her temper flared in her breast. The beast had awoken after its enforced sojourn. Recriminations flowed that she'd actually felt sorry for the woman. She'd even sympathised with another sister subjected to the wandering eye of a self-satisfied smug git like Craig. "She's messed with the wrong woman this time," she hissed through her clenched teeth. "We have four and a half days to find out exactly what's going on with her. I'm going to shake up her life if it's the last thing I do."

51

Ginger - ke'u

Hana filled in the blanks for Logan as he pulled on jeans and used an electric razor to banish the shadow from his lower jaw. His upbeat mood had returned, though the shadow of his former despair still hung over him. He splashed aftershave over his cheeks and chin, the familiar musky fragrance comforting Hana as she sat on the edge of the bath and drank in his movements. She ached to clasp his fingers in hers, to press them beneath her rumpled tee shirt until his work coarsened pads rasped against the soft skin over her ribs. But she knew what happened when she squeezed the hair trigger on their attraction and couldn't face the bed in its soiled state. So she sighed instead and stared at her fingers, her daughter's favourite nail polish chipped and dull. And her heart led her home to the mountain and her children, wishing they were together and wondering why she'd agreed to this insane holiday. "Did you hear from Mark again?" she asked, her tone tight.

Logan inspected his reflection in the mirror and ran a hand through his fringe, pushing it back from his forehead. "Take my phone." He lifted it from the night stand and held it out to her. The tanned leather belt threaded through the loops of his jeans matched the brown of his ribs. As he lifted his arms, his biceps bulged as though readying for a hay bale instead of a light threading of his fingers through his hair.

Hana activated the screen using Logan's pass code and searched his emails for news of her children. An alert slid in as an incoming message, warning she'd incurred a roaming charge from their telecommunications provider. A single unread email popped into the inbox before a red line appeared. Hana's shoulders slumped. "Connection lost," she read aloud and sighed. She lifted the phone up and spun the screen to face Logan. "You have an email from your sister."

Logan closed his eyes and moved into the bathroom. He braced his hands on either side of the sink. "You read it," he said, his voice low. The shadow engulfed his head and bare shoulders. His earlier fears drove away any indignation at Sally's sexual presumption or his attempts to rally in the face of myriad dangers to his and Hana's wellbeing.

Hana tutted and opened the email. She skim read the message which came from Liza's personal address and included impressive insults to Hana's physical attributes and nature. She'd detailed her verbal contract with Charlie Clay and added an attachment PDF of the signed original. *'Don't get banged up and don't run over budget,'* she warned. *'Let Ginger Barbie take the fall and cut your losses.'*

"Nice," Hana said with a sigh. "The love and support of your family means the world to me."

"Sorry." Logan winced. "You can swap nicknames with me if you want."

"What are you?" Hana scrolled the text and saved the PDF to the files on Logan's phone as the connection flickered to life before dying again seconds later.

"I used to be Baby Bro, but since Mum and Reuben died, she's openly called me the Bastard Son." He shrugged a light shirt over his shoulders and fastened the buttons with slowness born of perfection. The pocket over the left pectoral irritated him, the buttoned flap refusing to lie flat. He tutted, the sound loud in the silence of the villa. "It got crushed in the suitcase," he complained. His fingers fluttered over the button nearest his St. Christopher and then stalled. "It doesn't matter," he persuaded himself.

Hana inhaled and closed her eyes, letting the cruelty of Liza's mouth sink deep into her gut. She jerked them open as Logan cupped her cheek. "It doesn't hurt anymore," he said, his tone soothing. "She's the only person who says it like it is."

"Yeah. Ginger Barbie." Her nose wrinkled with disgust. She handed the phone back to him and slapped her thighs as though the action might infuse her with bravado. She ached for news of her children and lifted her useless phone from her night stand. The screen glowed to life at her touch, showing her a cute picture on her lock screen. All four Du Roses gathered together at Phoenix's last birthday party. She'd insisted they all wear pink. Mac had rocked it despite his orange curls and freckled face. Wiri had detested every second, and Edin ripped her dress at the first opportunity. Hana sighed. "The weather is worsening. I'll change my clothes." She went about the task without enthusiasm, swapping her white dress for jeans and a tee shirt. As a final nod to her thwarted maternalism, she pushed the useless phone into her back pocket. It seemed important to keep her family with her. "Right Du Rose," she said with a sigh. "What's first?"

"Sheets." Logan glanced at his watch. "Before the reception office closes."

They skirted Hallie and Jared's villa in silence. Logan steered towards the through-road before realising Hana had halted. He turned to locate her, his brow furrowed into lines and shadows at the sight of her staring at their deserted porch. "What?" His cowboy boots carried him to her side.

"Hallie told me on our first day here that Jared went on the scuba diving cruise with you. But I saw him talking to Craig behind our villa. I heard that weird click as they closed the trap door thing you found at the back of the building. Craig is up to something and Jared is involved." She turned to face Logan, twisting her lips to one side. "I asked you before if you met Jared on the trip, but I don't remember your answer."

"No." Logan shook his head, and more of his glossy black fringe plunged into his eyes. He shrugged. "I'd never met the guy until his wife called your name at the Trading Post and invited us to sit with them. I knew Craig from seeing him outside the reception. He chatted to the shuttle driver for a minute before we drove to the wharf."

Hana frowned at the wicker chair she'd helped Hallie slump into less than forty-eight hours earlier. "So, why the lie?" she asked. "Why would Jared let Hallie think he'd gone diving?"

"I don't know." Logan slipped his arm around her shoulders. "But there's no sign of whatever they hid in that cubby. It's empty now."

"And no sign of Hallie or anyone even caring." Hana tapped her index finger against her lips. "I reckon they're behind the fake cash." Then she clicked her fingers. "Hallie comes to this resort heaps. She told me. Jared could bring the cash in with him at regular intervals. Craig disperses it around the island. The girl from the supermarket told me he'd given her the fake twenty, about ten minutes before we showed up." She squirmed beneath the weight of Logan's arm. "I need to ask him about that."

"No." Logan rested his forearm on her left collarbone and his other arm joined it by pinning her right shoulder as he spun her to face him. He created a cage around her, and his stern expression heralded a rebuke. He leaned close enough for his minty-toothpaste breath to stir her fringe. "You're not doing anything, Hana."

She reared back, readying her argument in her mind before releasing it for his scrutiny. But her protest died on her lips. He smiled at her, no humour in his expression. It didn't reach his eyes or invoke the creases in their corners. "We'll do this together," he asserted.

"Like a SWAT team?" she whispered, fire crackers flaring behind her irises.

Logan's Adam's apple bobbed in his throat as her enthusiasm side-stepped his natural caution and warned of stupid risks and hair brained schemes guaranteed to end in disaster. He kissed her forehead, the motion chaste and reminiscent of a father more than a lover. “I’m the leader,” he whispered against her temple. “You do as you’re told or the whole thing’s off.”

They walked to the resort entrance, holding hands as they navigated the villas between theirs and the reception office. Hana checked through the tinted window before sending Logan inside to demand fresh bed linen. Only Craig manned the front desk, making no comment as he fetched everything Logan requested. The encounter took less than two minutes, and Hana leaned against the weather-board wall and stared at the patch of flattened grass where the kayak had rested earlier. She pushed herself upright as Logan emerged. “Did you say anything to him?” she demanded, her tone filled with righteous injustice.

Logan frowned at her. “What’s the point?” He paused so she could collect the pillowcases threatening to slide from the top of the pile. “You’re avoiding Craig. We’re both avoiding Sally. I got clean sheets. Job done. I have no interest in who they’re screwing or if they’re swingers or just promiscuous. We have five more days here and then we’re gone.”

“Four and a half,” Hana corrected, as though the extra few hours represented a massive chunk of a lengthy prison sentence. She skittered along next to him, matching each of his long strides with two of her own. “There are two mysteries,” she said, lowering her voice and smiling at the maintenance worker still walking around the swimming pool with his net. He shot her a nervous glance in return and scuttled away, holding his pole aloft with the net fluttering in the breeze. She paused, finding his reaction a little rude until she remembered how he'd last viewed her. It amused her to imagine Sally diving for her clothes and sandals. Then she realised she'd probably just order the young man to retrieve them instead. She waved at him in a silent apology and the pillowcase flapped in her hand.

Logan stared at her as though he suspected she might be losing her mind. "What are you doing?" he demanded. He followed the direction of her gaze, but the man and the net had disappeared into an adjacent shed, out of sight.

"Nothing." Hana hugged the linen to her chest. "So, two mysteries. Where is Hallie, and what do we know about the fake cash? And are those things connected?"

It took mere minutes to strip and remake the bed. Hana folded the dirty sheets into neat squares and fitted them into a refuse bag from beneath the kitchen sink. She left the bundle by the front door, ready for the housekeeper's visit the next morning. "Are you feeling any better?" She turned to face Logan as he lifted the Harley's keys in his left hand. He stared at them, his face a mask of concentration.

"Just a wobble." He forced a smile for her sake, which Hana sensed cost him. She imagined the coffers in his soul running low. "I trust your brother and David Allen with the children's safety." He tilted his head to one side. "I don't trust Leslie, but I couldn't stop her from going with them." His gaze tracked to Hana's emerald irises. "And barring hell or high water, I hope I can keep you safe on an island only sixty-three kilometres squared." He narrowed his eyes and lowered his chin to glare at her. "As long as you do as you're told."

"Come hell or high water," Hana whispered to herself. She grinned up at him. "What are the odds of either of those things happening?"

What odds indeed? She would live to regret asking that question.

52

Missing - ngarongaro

The Harley purred around the island at a steady pace, its riders revelling in the sense of freedom. The bike represented their last element of control, but even that would end once the petrol gauge shifted to empty. Hana wanted to try filling it at the garage on the other side of the island, but Logan refused. "No," he said, his chin flattening into a determined expression. "Let's leave it as long as we can. By the time we're desperate, the lawyer will have removed all the posters and the traders might let us buy stuff again."

Hana clamped her tongue between her teeth. Neither of them seemed willing to state the obvious. The posters might disappear, but the shop owners operated at their own discretion. They might still deny them basic goods.

Logan pulled the bike into a car park beyond the harbour. He pointed to a boat sitting outside the reef.

"That's the Ellie Marie," he called to Hana. The growl of the bike's engine dulled his words. "It's crazy how many shipwrecks are just under the surface. The island gets periodically hit by monster cyclones. I enjoyed the diving." His arm swung in a wide arc. "The Sail Fish sank just over there. She almost made it into the harbour."

"Did anyone die?" Hana leaned forward and rested her cheek against Logan's spine. She closed her eyes, imagining the horror of a tossing sea and the terror of a total lack of control. Only God ruled the elements. Her mind strayed back into dangerous territory, providing a bird's-eye view of her body prone on the bathroom floor. Blood pooled like a lake beneath her as her vision stuttered and her consciousness winked out. She shivered and wrapped her arms around her husband's muscular torso, grounding herself in the present and banishing the image of her helplessness.

"Yes. All hands lost." Logan's muscles moved beneath her cheek as he craned his neck to drop a kiss on the top of her head. "The boat smashed against the reef and sank. Only one body washed up after the cyclone moved away from the island. Two men and a woman crewed it before it wrecked. The couple had chartered the boat with the captain included. Someone said they were New Zealanders." He tilted his head back, trapping Hana into an unspoken embrace as she nestled against him. "They travelled from the Philippines, called into a port in Western Australia and headed for Fiji. But the cyclone blew up without warning and sent them off course. They made it as far as here and then wrecked." He sighed, the motion rocking his whole body. "Sad really. To get almost to safety and then die." He lifted his right hand and clicked his fingers. "Just like that."

Just like she'd almost done more than once. Logan didn't say the words, but Hana sensed them behind his tale. She sighed against him and closed her eyes. "I wouldn't like to look at someone's wrecked boat," she murmured. "It doesn't seem right. Like picking a dead person's pocket."

"There's nothing there." Logan shifted position and revved the bike's engine. Hana sat upright, understanding his unspoken request for release. She gave a hiss of pain as the corner of her phone dug into her buttock. She shifted position and listened to Logan's one-sided conversation. "The local skippers salvaged everything worthwhile. The boat itself had no identification, so it made it difficult to track the other occupants. The authorities matched dental records on the mainland for the captain and shipped his body back to his family. But nobody reported the couple missing, so the cops are just waiting for that to identify them."

"And they know it's the Sail Fish because you saw the lovely plaque on the ocean bottom?"

"Yeah." Logan nodded. "I did. There are two massive holes on either side of the bow and a gash in the stern. But there's only one name plate. I thought commercial vessels needed signs on both sides of the hull and a hailing port."

Hana gave herself a shake, not wanting to hear any more of someone else's world-ending misery. "Let's go to the hospital," she said. "We should check on Jared, seeing as Sally and Craig don't consider him a friend."

Logan drove to the hospital, avoiding the reception and parking the bike outside the intensive care unit at the northern end of the site. A young woman emerged, a battered teddy bear clutched to her chest. Her male companion held the front door open for them. Hana's blood seemed to freeze and stutter in her veins, her mind drawing conclusions she couldn't bear to contemplate. She kept her gaze fixed on the sterile tiled floor and her right hand encased in Logan's huge palm.

A different nurse greeted them at the doorway. Blonde hair escaped from a ponytail, a haze of wiry curls softening the outline of her face. She had brown eyes and wore a uniform two sizes too big for her. Logan gave their names, and she wrote them onto a sheet before spinning the clipboard and jabbing at the page where he needed to sign. "Good news," she said, her irises sparkling like gems. "Jared woke up this morning. He's tired and sore, but there's no need for him to move to the mainland just yet. A surgeon from Middlemore Hospital did a Zoom call with our doctors. Everyone's very pleased with his progress. Oh." She pushed the clipboard back across the desk to Logan. "You need to state your relationship with him. It's family only."

Logan frowned and retrieved the pen. He scrawled something which looked like 'brother', but its illegibility cast doubt over the claim.

Hana cleared her throat and attempted to distract the nurse from checking the form. "His wife is missing," she said, lowering her voice. "We 'tried to report her disappearance at the police station, but they won't accept our word that she's gone." She gulped and glanced at Logan. "Has anyone asked Jared about it yet?"

The nurse winced. "No. There's also the issue of his health insurance."

Hana remembered the master keys which Sally abandoned on the kitchen counter and an idea formed in her mind. "We'll check their villa as soon as we get back to the resort," she promised. "They must have brought their documents with them."

Hana couldn't tell whether the thought of financial restitution or the prospect of a visitor for Jared spoke louder. But the nurse led them to a hand washing station and provided aprons from a cabinet. She didn't wear a name badge, creating an impersonal effect. Hana didn't like it. As she fumbled with the flimsy plastic ties of her apron, she addressed the woman in a cordial tone. "We saw Karla last time," she remarked. "She must be new because she didn't know Jared's friend, Sally. She's also a nurse here."

The woman blinked and patted the space over her left breast where her name badge should have clung. Not finding it, she glanced down and sighed. "Damn," she breathed. "It's fallen off again." She shook her head as though to clear it and stepped behind Hana to sort out the mess she'd made with the lengths of fluttering tie. Logan had already finished garbing himself and watched Hana with the curiosity of a cat. "Karla started here a year before me." She looped a bow and stood back, giving Hana room to turn. "But I don't know a Sally who works here either. Look, you've knotted the ties by accident. You'll need to rip it when you're finished and drop it into the dustbin near the front doors." A buzzer sounded from somewhere nearby and her attention switched to it. "Just wait there," she urged. "Let me deal with this and I'll come back and escort you to see Jared."

Hana plastered a smile onto her lips, but it faded as the nurse disappeared around the first corner. "You were right," she concluded. "Karla's worked here a while. The hospital community is tiny. She'd know Sally even if she'd met her at the staff Christmas party." She wrinkled her nose. "What do you suggest?"

Logan's mouth quirked up on one side to create a quizzical expression. "Wow, Mrs Du Rose," he breathed. "I'll remember not to get on the wrong side of you. Anyone would think you had it in for poor Sally."

Hana dipped her chin and narrowed her eyes before snatching a surgical mask from a waiting container. She looped it over her ears and covered the lower half of her face. Her voice held a muffled quality. "I learned from the master," she said. And Logan smiled.

53

Miscarry - ma 'emo

The nurse returned after a long five minutes, rubbing hand sanitiser into her fingers. She led them to a bay containing a single hospital bed, a man sized lump occupying the centre. Hana held her breath as the nurse peered down at the static figure. "Mr Clarke," she whispered. "Jared? You have visitors."

A croak issued from the mattress. The sheets flailed as though covering a falling object.

"Press the button," the nurse urged. "Sitting will feel painful for a while. You can't use your stomach muscles yet. The physiotherapist is due to visit this evening. She'll help you." She snatched up a remote control bar attached to a white cable. A whirring signified the motor lifting the head of the mattress. Hana gulped as Jared's pale face appeared by slow degrees. He looked like he'd lost a race against stampeding elephants. Yellow and green splotches covered one side of his face and his left eye appeared swollen shut. She pursed her lips and clamped her teeth over her tongue.

The nurse turned to Logan and lifted another set of buttons. "This is to call for help," she said, pointing to a large red dome. "Don't hesitate to press it. This is still early days for Jared."

Logan nodded. As the nurse stepped away from the bed, he indicated the visitor's chair and jerked his head towards Hana. She froze in the doorway, not yet ready to sit. The nurse edged past her and lowered her voice. "Don't tire him, please," she urged. "And maybe don't mention the other thing."

Hana blinked, the action confirming neither acceptance nor denial. She couldn't guarantee it wouldn't come up in the conversation's winding course. It seemed likely that Jared's first question would demand Hallie's whereabouts. The nurse left, and the door hissed closed behind her.

Hana surveyed the room. Life experience had given her an acute familiarity with high dependency units, both for herself and for Logan. The Rarotongan hospital functioned on second hand equipment, cast offs donated by the mainland's surgical units. Nothing looked new. Every piece of furniture had a tired appearance, as though it hovered just one step away from retirement on a junk pile. And yet they'd saved

Jared's life with it. She released a heavy sigh and sank into the visitor's chair.

"Hallie?" Jared's first question seemed spurred by his recognition of Hana, despite the mask covering half her face. His hazel irises sparkled with thirst for information. "Where is she?" His voice rasped and growled as though a hidden hand dragged every word across a rough surface. "They said she didn't visit." His chest heaved and tears spurted from the corners of his eyes. Hana glanced up at Logan, seeing the flash of discomfort in his grey irises. Du Rose's didn't show weakness, but his earlier meltdown in the comfort of their villa had opened up the genuine possibility that other men broke at times, too. Especially after open heart surgery.

A garish scar slithered along the length of Jared's brown torso. It disappeared beneath the sheets like a tributary seeking the ocean. The nurse's reference to his ineffective stomach muscles suggested a surgeon had cracked him open from throat to groin to save his life. Jared caught Hana's furtive glance and touched his left pectoral with a hand encased in wires and sticking plaster. "A visiting cardiac surgeon saved me," he said, his tone laden with awe and regret. More tears leaked from his eyes. A stubbly black beard flecked with grey covered his cheeks, chin and neck. The saline coursed through it in a slalom action. "Hallie sold him the holiday." The hand snaked from his chest to his right eye and smashed at the tears sliding down his cheek and into his ear. The wires strained against the bed rail.

When his hand thudded onto the mattress, the fingers balled into a fist. Hana laid her cool palm over it. "You're very lucky," she soothed. "I had a heart attack a few years ago. Your life really flashes before your eyes."

He nodded and took a hiccoughing breath. "Bloody mess," he choked. His chest heaved, and he winced. "I remember nothing after I spoke to you at the market. It's all gone." He gulped and coughed, the sharp movements causing him to groan.

Hana reached sideways to a night stand and lifted a glass of water. A straw balanced in it, not quite reaching the bottom and tilting at an angle. She held it between her finger and thumb and lifted it to Jared's lips. He sucked on the straw, turning his face aside like a rebellious child when he'd had enough. "Thanks," he rasped. He pressed his dark head against the pillow and stared at the ceiling through glazed eyes, which struggled to embrace the truth. Hallie hadn't visited him in his time of crisis. "Where is she?" he whispered. "I need to tell her I'm sorry."

Logan's body tensed, and he edged closer to the bed. Perhaps realising his height and bulk created an intimidating wall, he dragged the other visitor's chair closer and folded into it. "Why are you sorry?" he asked.

Jared turned his head, the protective liner beneath the pillowcase crinkling and crunching. He fixed his gaze on Logan. "Because of the baby," he whispered.

A silence stretched between them as Jared closed his eyes. Unable to cope with the hiss of static and the whir of the machines, Hana spoke into it. "An IVF baby?" she asked. "Hallie told me you'd run out of options."

Jared's head shifted on the pillow. "No. A natural baby. Just not mine. I can't have kids. We were using sperm donors through an Auckland clinic, but nothing worked."

Hana closed her eyes as a thread loosened somewhere at the back of the pressing issues. Mention of a baby.

"Craig's baby?" Logan said it, his voice a low growl.

Hana gave him a definitive nod. It fitted with her overheard conversation between Sally and the dementia patient. It had angered Sally enough for her to hold a pillow aloft above a powerless woman's face. Though she hadn't followed through, Hana sensed she'd considered it.

"Craig?" Jared jerked his chin down and his lips peeled back from his teeth in a snarl. "No! Not Craig! Hallie doesn't even like him. She sends him customers because of my friendship with him. I've known him for years. She thinks he's a jerk."

Hana released a breath of exasperation and bit back her agreement with Hallie. "So, you're not swingers?" She glared at Logan. He glanced down at his hands for long enough to hide his smile. A bud of anger blossomed in Hana's chest and worked its way up to her throat. He'd tossed the comment into the air and she'd dived for it like a hungry starling seeking an insect. A joke. On her.

"I don't know what that is." Jared's eyelashes flickered. "Will you find Hallie for me? I meant nothing that I said. She started drinking that night and I should have stopped her. Instead, I went to a stupid poker game and lost a shed load of cash." He exhaled, his lungs deflating his chest like a leaky air bed. So much weight had dropped from his torso, the skin covering his neck hung like puddled fabric before the start of his collar bone. He fixed his better eye on Hana. "Find her. Tell her I don't mind. We'll keep the baby and raise it together. We used sperm donors for goodness' sake! It would always be someone else's biological child." He pursed his lips together. "I lost my job. We had to stop the IVF. I think she got desperate and shagged some random tourist when she visited the island for work three months ago. Just tell her it doesn't matter anymore. I'll make it right for her and the baby."

The nurse reappeared and shooed them away as Jared's heart rate spiked under duress. They disposed of their aprons and masks in the rubbish bin as directed. Hana needed Logan to snap the ties of her apron. She waited with enforced patience, her mind whirring.

"Why are you shaking your head?" he asked, dumping the fluttering plastic apron on top of his.

"It just doesn't sit right," Hana mused. "Women who go to extreme lengths to conceive don't just drown themselves in alcohol because their partner doesn't approve of how they went about it. Jared believes Hallie was pregnant."

"And you don't?"

Hana blew out an exasperated breath. The breeze from outside hit them like a wall of humid, oxygen poor air. "I don't know," she admitted. "But that woman couldn't stand up without assistance. Doesn't that show scant regard for an unborn child she'd craved more than anything? Even a one-off binge can damage the development of a foetus at a crucial stage."

"Maybe." Logan shrugged. "Liza said my ma drank gin and smoked forty cigarettes a day while pregnant with me. They thought I'd come out with a tumbler in one hand and a ciggie tucked between each finger of the other."

Hana pushed her lips upwards towards her nose. Not her most attractive expression, but the children called it her 'thinking face.' She resisted a debate about Miriam's pregnancy behaviour. She'd carried her brother-in-law's child after a lengthy affair. Perhaps she'd already marked her life as ruined and worthless. She'd hurt all her children, and her husband most of all in the forty-year ruse.

"I'm just not buying it," Hana breathed. "And I'm annoyed we didn't get to ask him about the counterfeit cash. I know he brought it onto the island because I overheard him and Craig talking about it."

Logan mounted the Harley and started the engine. He frowned at Hana as she paused beside him. "Are you coming?" he asked.

"Only if you promise to drop me at the police station," she replied. She waited a beat until Logan agreed before clambering onto the pillion. Once there, she dragged her phone from her back pocket and handed it to him. "Is there anywhere to keep this?" she asked. Her fingers rubbed at the spot where a bruise bloomed.

"You have no data or signal. Why did you bring it?" Logan's veiled exasperation finished with a shake of his head. He dumped the phone in the top pocket of his shirt and buttoned it. The fabric sagged, giving his left pectoral a mismatched appearance. Hana twisted her lips and chose not to mention it as Logan kicked the stand away and the bike wheels turned beneath her.

54

Stretch - ʻakaenaena

Logan pulled up in front of the police station, and Hana slipped from the seat before he'd killed the engine. "Let's divide and conquer," she suggested, her plimsolls already pointing to the steps leading to the front door. "Charlie Clay's office is a two-minute ride in that direction." She pointed with her index finger. "Introduce yourself to him, seeing as Liza did you the favour." Her teeth ground in her jaw at the fact his sister couldn't care less about Hana. "Find out the status of these damn warning posters. He might have got them all taken down by now."

Logan shrugged. He cocked his head to one side and studied Hana for the information she'd kept hidden. "No. Let's go together." He pushed her for an explanation and she dropped her shoulders. His earlier revelation of panic at her mortality set an unhealthy dollop of guilt roiling in her gut. But she wanted to do this alone. She craved his approval and his special smile when she uncovered the key to everything. In that moment, her success seemed more important than his misgivings. The sensible part of her brain told her it was ill advised and selfish. She ignored its plaintive voice.

"Look," she conceded. "I want to ask Sergeant Wally George a question. If I'm wrong, I'll feel stupid." She raised a hand at Logan's instant head shake. "No. You ask me to trust you all the time. Now I'm asking the same from you. I don't think he'll answer my question with you there. See if Charlie Clay is at his office. He might have taken down the posters, but that doesn't mean the traders will sell to us. It might change nothing." She turned away from her husband but clicked her fingers. "Oh, don't let him take you to his secret gentleman's club in the hills. He enjoys showing off, and I'll only take half an hour. You have the villa key and the bus has already left on its last run. Don't leave me stranded."

Logan's chest rose as he drew in a breath. He ticked off his instructions on his fingers like a child, but Hana sensed the bite of sarcasm beneath the action. "Trust you. Meet Charlie Clay. Don't get drunk with him. Don't leave you stranded. Got it. Anything else?"

Hana wrinkled her nose and skipped up the steps. She didn't dignify him with an answer. Her hand rose in a two-fingered salute and she heard his burst of laughter as she pushed open the front door to the police station.

The desk officer made her wait to see Sergeant Wally George. She perched on a bench with a ripped red plastic cover and shivered beneath the icy blast from an air conditioning unit. It dribbled liquid down the wall and the yellow stain on the plaster suggested its weeping had gone untended.

"Mrs Du Rose." Sergeant Wally George appeared through the creaking fire door adjacent to the reception desk. He held it open with his foot. Hana rose and preceded him through the doorway, turning to wait for him as he caught her up and led the way along a dark corridor.

He used a different office this time. The desk contained more personal effects. A picture of a brown skinned woman stood in pride of place on a bookshelf to his right. Her long straight hair held a flyaway quality, the edges fluttering against the waistband of her floral skirt. The bare chested toddler in her arms wore cotton shorts. He had Sergeant Wally George's brown eyes with the shape of two almonds. Hana gnawed on her cheek as she stepped towards the shelf and ran an index finger down the frame. "Your wife?" she asked.

He cleared his throat and the energy in the room hummed with his unease. "How can I help you, Mrs Du Rose?" he asked, his tone clipped. "If it's about the posters, I've spoken to each of the shop keepers and they've taken them down." He pursed his lips. "Charlie Clay's involvement hasn't helped your cause."

"How so?" Hana left the picture and sank into the nearest chair, even though the police officer hadn't offered it. She frowned as it occurred to her that the lawyer might also get himself banned from all the local shops. His formidable size and infectious enthusiasm conjured him up in front of her, and she smiled to herself. He belonged to Nui Ngaro, the High Secret club for prominent island residents. Her unexpected visit there had a particular purpose. He'd wanted her to witness his status within the exclusive band of upper society island members. Despite his awe over Judge Liza Du Rose, Hana sensed with hindsight that much of his effusive praise had formed part of an act. Charlie Clay was a showman, hence her instruction for Logan to meet him. Her husband would see right through Charlie's role playing much better than her.

Sergeant Wally George's hair stuck up at the front where he'd run his fingers through it. Hana studied him as he sat in front of her. She cocked her head.

"Does your wife call you Sergeant Wally George too?" she asked. "Someone told us it's your Christian name."

The police officer sat back in his creaking office chair and folded his arms. Unseen, his feet moved beneath the desk and caused his chair to adopt a side-to-side rocking motion. A stress tell, Hana guessed. "What do you want, Mrs Du Rose?"

"Call me Hana." She leaned forward and rested her forearms on the desk. The motion rocked the flimsy surface and papers cascaded from a pile to her right. "I want to report a missing person."

Sergeant Wally George groaned. "Not that again."

"Yes, that again." Hana sat up and matched his stance, straightening her back and folding her arms across her breasts. "Hallie Clarke." She frowned at him. "I'm surprised at your reticence, especially as you know her."

His brown eyes grew wary. Their almond shapes narrowed into slits. "She's a tourist," he growled. "If she's visited more than once, it increases the odds of me recognising her, doesn't it?"

Hana tutted and inhaled. She bobbed her chin and adopted an expression of sympathy. "I didn't say she'd visited more than once."

Sergeant Wally George's Adam's apple bobbed in his throat. It seemed to stick for a millisecond before bouncing and then settling. "Someone did." He faltered and gave himself a visible shake. "It doesn't matter, anyway. We filled in the paperwork. We're looking for her as resources allow."

"But you're not, are you?" Hana's green irises bored through his black pupils and into his soul. "I've seen no posters for Hallie. Is the coastguard searching beyond the reef? Have you organised kayakers to investigate the shallow waters surrounding the island? Road blocks? House to house enquiries? How are you looking for her, exactly?"

Sergeant Wally George rolled his eyes. The effect of his insolence jarred with the officialdom of his police uniform. Hana observed his acute discomfort as he glanced at everything in the room to avoid meeting her eye. When his gaze fell on the smiling woman in the photograph, beads of sweat trickled from his temple to bury themselves in his thick sideburns.

Hana saw him gulp and her heart sank. The long shot had paid off, and she discovered too late that she hadn't expected it to at all. She leaned forward in her chair and dropped her arms. The scarred plastic groaned even beneath her slightness. "She knew you." Her voice sounded soft, creating a gentleness she didn't feel. "On the night Hallie went missing, she didn't want to walk past your checkpoint. I put it down to her drunken state, but she hadn't had enough alcohol to produce that level of intoxication. Sally made up some story about a man selling mussels, but it had no substance. I've put a lot of thought into that night on the ride here and I've realised something. Hallie didn't want to avoid the cops, she wanted to avoid one particular cop. You." She leaned back in her seat. "She also said, *'Go away! It was a mistake. You're a mistake. I'm a mistake. My whole bloody life is a mistake.'* I remember thinking at the time what an odd thing to say. I also witnessed her react with distress to the sight of a police scooter at the resort earlier. It seems clear you'd had an unfortunate interaction. You seemed surprised to find her drunk that night too, didn't you? Because pregnant women shouldn't drink."

A flush crept up the police officer's neck and into his cheeks. It created a mahogany stain which enriched his tanned skin. It reached as far as his ears before he cleared his throat. "That's enough surmising, Mrs Du Rose." His tone held ice, which seemed to drip down the back of Hana's warm neck. "Take your accusations and leave. We're searching for your friend. That's all you need to know. Keep out of trouble for the rest of your stay. I don't wish to meet you again."

"Does your wife know?" Hana pushed herself to her feet, speeding up the movement to disguise the tremor in her knees. "Was it a regular affair or just a one off?" She twisted her lips and watched him squirm. "You wouldn't be the first to enjoy a fling with a tourist you never expected to see again. But as an agent for a holiday company, she visited often. Didn't she tell you that?" She cocked her head, sadness filling her heart at Hallie's desperation. "She really wanted a baby. But her husband couldn't accept her pregnancy. Did she visit you that afternoon and demand that you fulfil more than a sperm donor role?"

"Just go." The officer's tone held a brittle quality. In that moment, Hana regretted her foolhardiness. If he'd killed Hallie with such consummate ease, Hana's weakened state presented him with even less of an obstacle. The road block had put him at the entrance to the resort. He could have followed them back to Hallie's villa, but what did he do with her body?

Hana fumbled with the door handle and exited the stuffy room. She jogged along the corridor to the main office. The desk attendant glanced at her before pressing a button to let her out into the icy reception. She ran then and didn't stop until she reached the main road.

55

Fishing - tā 'iti

Logan performed a graceful turn on the street and drew alongside Hana. He reached out a hand to halt her frightened jog. "Hold up," he called over the sound of the bike. "Where's the fire?"

Hana scrambled onto the bike behind him as though chased by a rampaging mob. "Just drive," she urged. "Back to the Paradise Villas for now." She pressed her forehead against his shoulder and considered her awful mistake. So many things became evident in hindsight. She should have taken Logan with her, instead of sending him to parley with Charlie on a ridiculous pretext. Her mind ran through the inevitable confession to her husband that she'd overplayed her hand and unleashed a potential hazard, which would backfire. The laboured thought process occupied the entirety of the ride back to their villa. She ran through various scenarios, which always ended in Logan's open disbelief, followed by his disappointment.

Her nerves still hadn't settled as Logan drove the Harley through the resort and parked it at the foot of the porch steps. "I've messed up," Hana blurted. She didn't even wait for him to kill the engine. "I asked you to trust me, but I don't deserve it. I dropped a bomb at the police station and the shrapnel reached further than I expected."

To her surprise, Logan leaned the bike against its stand and slid off, pushing at his jeans until the hems met his cowboy boots. Then he wrapped his arms around Hana and lifted her from the Harley, waiting until she crossed her ankles behind him and linked her fingers around his neck. She pressed her nose beneath his jaw and inhaled his comforting scent. The curls at the back of his head tickled her cheek. But he offered no condemnation. He didn't pick through the reasons for her failure or rebuke her for the verbal diarrhoea which beset her once in Sergeant Wally George's office. Instead, he carried her up the steps. He eased the fly screen back with the toe of his boot and unlocked the front door one handed.

Hana remained glued to him like a rogue koala bear clinging to a fire scorched tree trunk. She realised the position denied Logan the ability to study her face as she considered her tale of disaster. That worked in her favour. She didn't want him to see the signs of her embarrassment. Her cheeks flushed to the colour of ripened tomatoes and dread locked her lungs with a clenched fist forced through her chest wall.

Logan leaned his hips against the kitchen counter and held her, his endless patience another tool in his extensive armoury. He could out-wait everyone she knew and most of the people she didn't. As she snuggled against him and a cramp bit at her thighs, she recognised the futility of the silent protest.

He grunted as she slithered down his body, saying nothing as she turned her back on him and stalked across to the bed. Sitting on the mattress, she dug her flattened hands between her thighs and dropped her chin. "I messed up real bad," she said, her voice little more than a whisper. "I felt certain Hallie knew Sergeant Wally George." She closed her eyes at the effort of speaking his full first name. The urge to smash it into pieces and truncate the remaining parts caused an ache at the tip of her tongue. Names were special, sacred to Māori. She didn't wish to offer another thing for Logan's disapproval. Sighing, she ploughed on through the scant information which she'd added to her gut instinct to produce a void conclusion.

"He got her pregnant and when Jared reacted to her news, she went to the police station or met him somewhere else, and asked him to step up for the child. So, he killed her."

Logan cleared his throat, but didn't interrupt. Hana glanced up to find him frowning and gnawing his lower lip. Her shoulders slumped, and she folded back onto the bed. "Go on, say it."

"Say what?" His tone held amusement.

Hana sighed and closed her eyes. "I performed a fantastical leap into empty air and then made a right royal mess of everything from that point." The mattress shifted beside her as Logan sat down.

"I wouldn't say that because it's not what I'm thinking," he said, his tone thoughtful as he pored over every word. He flopped back next to her and the bed rocked. "Let's work through the points one at a time. We'll examine each one on merit and lock it in. That's how we'll find the pattern."

Hana turned her head to face him, her hair spreading across the bedspread as though caught by a hurricane force wind. It crackled with static electricity against the woollen surface as the electrons positively charged the fabric. "You don't think it's a bust?" Her eyes widened in surprise.

"Not at all," he replied. "Walk me through the evidence."

Hana repeated her conversation with Sergeant Wally George. She turned onto her side and fingered the sleeve of Logan's white tee shirt as she unravelled her thoughts. "If Hallie and Jared argued that afternoon, why did they offer us a ride to the Avarua District? Why did they leave the villa at all? I'd want to hash everything out until we reached a resolution."

"Not everyone is like you," Logan offered. "You favour certainty and clear direction. Other people need to put a pin in things and come back to them."

"I picked up an atmosphere between them," Hana mused. "Hallie looked tearful when they offered us the ride. And I caught her crying in the bathroom at the bar. But if they'd just had a potentially marriage-ending conversation, why did Jared spend the night at a poker game?"

"Why didn't you mention all of that before now?"

Hana shrugged. "I had no evidence other than my intuition. It's difficult to explain how I see a cloud of destructive energy hanging over someone. I always know when Leslie and Alfie have just finished having a barney. You can cut the atmosphere with a knife."

Logan growled low in his throat. "Leslie and Alfred argue all the time. They thrive on terrible energy. They never make any good stuff."

"So, what's your theory, then?" Hana demanded. "Jared believes Hallie arrived on the island pregnant. The things he said suggest she'd told him about it as recently as that afternoon."

"But he didn't confirm that." Logan ran a hand over his chin. "What if she told him before they flew out of New Zealand?"

"No." Hana exhaled. "Hallie seemed at ease when she visited me here. She sat in that armchair and blurted everything about their lives. Except her pregnancy. She couldn't risk it in case I congratulated Jared. That tells me he didn't yet know."

"Then why offer us a ride?" Logan tapped his front teeth with his fingernail. "Unless they needed someone to act as a buffer. They'd talked themselves into a corner and wanted time and space before coming back to it."

"Only Jared didn't come back to it. Instead, he stayed with Craig. Perhaps Craig and Sally were also buffers. We were all placed there to prevent the need for talking or arguing."

"But you think Hallie panicked and visited Sergeant Wally George?"

"Perhaps." Hana stared up at the ceiling. "But I can't prove it, can I?"

"What do we need?" Logan rested his left arm on Hana's shoulder and kissed the end of her nose. "What will make this stick?"

"Evidence," Hana whispered. Her green irises sparkled like emeralds. "We need to know where Hallie went after leaving here, what she did, and how she got there. By the time we climbed into that awful convertible, she'd broken the news to Jared, argued with him, and potentially visited SWG."

Logan snorted. "Name shortening without permission. That's poor form Mrs Du Rose."

"I don't care," she replied, her tone haughty. "We need to get into that villa next door. I think all the answers are in there."

"How do you propose we do that?" Logan asked, his tone husky. His fingers strayed beneath the hem of Hana's tee shirt as his mind shifted to more immediate needs.

"Sally's keys." Hana batted his hand away and sat up. She surveyed the empty kitchen counter with a groan. "Damn, she came back while we were out and took them."

A tinkle of metal on metal drew her attention to Logan. His fingers dug into his jeans pocket and Sally's keys emerged with a flourish. "I thought she might," Logan said. "With management and housekeeping and grounds staff, there seems little point locking the doors. But I thought we could use a bit of help."

"You're a genius!" Hana leaned down and kissed his upturned lips. And her mind went temporarily sideways, connecting with Logan's lustful thoughts and finding herself in agreement.

56

A mess - tāotaota

Hana giggled as Logan held onto her. His arms snaked around her as he prevented her from leaving the bed. "Enough!" she rebuked. She pried his fingers from her hips, only to feel them clasp her waist. "It's getting late!" she whined. "We can't turn on lights if we're checking out Hallie's place. We need to do it before it gets dark."

"Okay, but then we eat." Logan released her and rolled onto his back. He scrubbed at his eyes with the knuckles of his left hand. "If anyone will serve us."

Hana blew out a breath and used a tie from her wrist to wrestle her hair into a semblance of a ponytail. Knotty spirals stuck out at different angles, and she admitted defeat and dropped her hands. "We have some bits in the fridge." She turned to face her husband, narrowing her eyes as his gaze traced the outline of her breasts. Her hand lifted, and she clicked her fingers to recall his attention. "We should keep hold of the bread and cheese, shouldn't we? Someone might let us eat out tonight, but then change their mind tomorrow." She frowned, disturbed by how important food became during a time of uncertainty. The urge to hoard their small reserves perplexed her. "What about the bottled water?" Anxiety flooded her brilliant green eyes, and she set her lips into a line. "We can't manage without it."

Logan sat up, using his stomach muscles, and clasped her cheek to his shoulder. "I brought emergency water purifying tablets," he said, pressing a kiss to the top of her head. Hana slipped a hand beneath his tee shirt and savoured the smoothness of his pectorals. She warred with the urge to snuggle under the clean sheets with him and distract herself. The silver St. Christopher he wore around his neck clinked against her fingers. He groaned and his nipple hardened as she continued her gentle stroking motion.

"They make the water taste horrid," she murmured. She lifted the tee shirt higher, flicking her tongue across his warm skin and savouring his saltiness.

"Stop!" Logan clasped her wrist and tilted his head to view the sky through the top window above the bed. "You're right about searching without light. We need to go now."

The temperature had dropped and Hana felt grateful for her dark jeans and black tee shirt. Logan met her by the front door, a bottle of their precious water in his left hand. "Drink," he insisted. "Otherwise we'll get sick and end up in beds on either side of Jared."

Hana stared at the bottle before taking it. "Fine, but we need a more permanent solution."

Logan shrugged and watched her tip the bottle to her lips. Her stomach gurgled, and she realised her thirst had sneaked up on her. "If they won't sell it to us, I'll steal it," he said, his tone serious. "The worst that'll happen is Sergeant Wally George will arrest us. Then we'll get free food and water at the police station." He quirked his right eyebrow in thought. "Four and a half more days to last."

Hana wiped her mouth with the back of her hand. She passed the bottle to Logan and watched him sip. It worried her he'd go without for her sake, and she pursed her lips until he'd drained the dregs from the bottom. "Most of the people on this island are good folk," she said. "But just like everywhere else, a few bad eggs are ruining their reputation. This can't be much of an advert for business."

Logan grunted and tossed the bottle into the rubbish bin. It clattered against the swinging lip and disappeared into the plastic lined mouth. A rustle signified the bin bag settling. "Let's go," he said, lifting his right hand to display Hallie's keys dangling from the ring around his middle finger.

They locked up their villa and traversed the shared lawn between the buildings. Cicadas chirruped their song in the trees, their ugly insect bodies incongruous with their comforting call. Logan strode across the grass, but Hana skittered behind him, aware of the legitimacy of their quest but the illegality of using stolen keys to achieve it.

Hana stood in Hallie's lounge and surveyed the mirror image of their own villa. She ran a nervous hand over her face. "This feels wrong," she murmured. "I only met the woman twice. We aren't friends."

Logan shrugged and turned in a slow arc. "No, but so far you're the only person who gives a damn about her. And Jared needs those medical insurance documents."

"What if we can't find them?" Belongings littered the two room dwelling as though a cyclone had ripped through it. Dresses and underwear covered the couch and armchair, two large suitcases lying open to disgorge the rest of their contents. Logan wrinkled his nose and shot Hana a glance in reply to her statement of doubt. It seemed impossible to discern the trivial from the essential amongst the detritus of someone else's chaotic life.

He pointed to the suitcases. "I'll start there," he said, his tone flat. Three reluctant strides took him to their haphazard position, with their lids resting against the wall. He shot a smile at Hana. "I tell you every day that you're beautiful," he said, squatting beside the first suitcase. "But I don't tell you often enough how grateful I am for the little things."

"Little things?" She frowned and eyed the couch shrouded in swathes of mismatched patterned fabric. Her feet stumbled against a set of discarded sandals, the heels higher than anything Hana might have dared to wear. "What little things?"

"Big, actually," Logan conceded. "I arrived back from the diving tour and you'd already tidied everything away. We could have done it together, but you did it alone. And I forgot to thank you."

"Right." Hana frowned and lifted the first of the dresses. The bodice slipped onto the seat cushion and she caught the maxi skirt between finger and thumb. She wrinkled her nose. "I can't cope with chaos. It seemed a logical thing to do."

"Well, I'm saying thank you." Logan dug through the contents of the suitcase. He hissed and withdrew his hand, a disgusted expression rounding his lips into a downward arch. "Yuk. Jared just tossed his dirty undies into the suitcase with all his clean stuff."

He gave a visible shiver. "Should have brought some gloves."

Hana folded dresses and scooped the underwear into a pile. "Hallie's is all clean," she remarked. She lifted one side of her mouth. "Well, I'm telling myself that, anyway." She created a towering pile on the armchair from everything she found until the couch stood empty. "Any luck?"

Logan shuffled papers from the bottom of the second suitcase. "Yeah, I think so." He held them up to the light and squinted. "This is a health insurance policy taken out under Jared's name with the same company we used." He dipped his left hand back into the suitcase. "Their return flight itinerary is here, too. He must have kept his passport with him because the hospital has it. Oh, that's weird. No health insurance for Hallie."

"Perhaps she keeps it with her. Jared doesn't strike me as the cautious sort. You're still keeping all our important stuff safe, aren't you?" Hana watched as he rose from the squat, his body showing no signs of stiffness or discomfort. Five minutes in that position would have deadened her legs until she couldn't walk. He tapped his spine just above his buttocks, and she noticed the outline of the bag strapped around his waist. "The staff must be honest, anyway," Hana commented. "They could have stolen anything. Who's to know?" She pushed a pile of dollar coins on the night stand, regretting it when they toppled and clattered onto the wooden surface. Her hand froze. "Gloves! Oh, crap!"

"What?" Logan rose with the paperwork clutched in his left hand. He'd included the passports in the pile.

"Gloves." Hana shook her head. "Imagine if Hallie stays missing and Sergeant Wally George finally pulls his finger out. Our prints will be all over their villa. It'll look dodgy."

Logan shook his head. He placed his other hand on her shoulder in a gesture of reassurance. "Show me what you've touched so far and I'll wipe it."

Her lips opened and closed, but she stifled the remark. It shouldn't surprise her that her husband would bury bodies for her, but it also offered relief. She indicated the coins and the clothing. Logan pulled a tissue from a nearby box and wiped the coins before stacking them upright again. He jerked his head towards the pile of documents he'd placed at his feet. "Kinda daft though, isn't it? Especially as I'm holding their paperwork." He squinted at her. "But if it makes you feel better, I'll remove any trace of you."

Hana dug her hands into her pockets to prevent any more unconscious fiddling. She noticed a slip of paper poking out from beneath the rumpled bedspread.

Mimicking Logan, she snagged a tissue from the box and bent to retrieve it.

"What's that?" Logan peered at it over her shoulder.

"A discharge notice from the hospital on the island." Hana speed read the document as a lead weight slipped from her chest to her stomach. She blew out a ragged breath, and the paper bounced in her fingers. Of poor quality, it had repelled the ink from a printer which required a cartridge change. Some words lacked clarity, but she'd understood enough. *Miscarriage at six week's gestation*. At the top of the document, she made out the date. Last Friday, although the printer had scuffed the final digit, signifying the year. The time stamp showed Hallie attended the emergency room an hour after she left Hana.

Her shoulders slumped, and she released the paper. It fluttered onto the unmade bed. "Well, that explains how she got so drunk on only a few glasses of wine. Painkillers. And now we know why." She pursed her lips and stared around the room. "I also made an ass of myself with Sergeant Wally George. She last visited the island three months ago but was pregnant for only six weeks. She had a problem with him, but that's not the reason."

Logan gave a sombre nod. "But at least we know where her health insurance documents went. She already presented them to the hospital." He stared around him at the room where a mother's heart suffered its worst of blows and her body betrayed her once more. "Now I also understand why you're worried," he admitted.

57

Threaten - ta¯mataku

They used the Harley to travel to the hospital. The burr of the engine removed the need for conversation. Karla smiled at them from behind the reception desk beneath a sign stating, *'High Dependency Unit. Wait here. Please be kind to our staff.'* "Hello again," she said, her tone bright. "Mr Clarke asked if you'd come back yet."

"We have his paperwork." Logan laid the health insurance policy document on the counter. He added the return tickets to the top of the pile. "We grabbed anything important. It's probably safer here than in an empty villa."

Karla reached out and took the papers as though sucking them into the messy vortex of her desk. Hana peeked over the counter at the sight of Logan's raised eyebrow, seeing the chaos which had triggered the ticking vein in his neck. "That'll help," Karla said with a sigh. "We do our best for people. They don't always buy insurance, though." She cast her eye over the ceiling, plaster peeling from around an original rose decoration. It seemed to highlight her point on cue.

"How is Jared?" Hana asked. She pursed her lips and stared at the nurse. "We told him his wife is still missing," she said, her tone sad. "We didn't enjoy doing it, but he asked about her straight away."

Karla smiled and bobbed her head in a silent acknowledgement. "No one's visited him. Apart from you." She rose from a creaking office chair and walked to the gap at the end of the counter. "Would you like to see him now?" She checked her watch and noticed the time. "I'll let you have a few minutes."

Hana glanced at Logan and held her breath. She'd much rather hunt up some dinner, even if it meant her husband stealing it. The choices stacked in her mind, the options weighing without an even distribution. She froze, still trying to choose; eat on a beach somewhere or break yet more awful news to a man she'd only met three times. Logan decided for her. "We're good thanks," he said, his tone determined. "Just let him know we found his paperwork, as promised."

"Right." Karla frowned but didn't challenge him. Hana sensed her muscles relax one by one. She didn't want to see Jared, to confess they still hadn't found Hallie and that no one else cared about her disappearance. She didn't want to take responsibility for issues which weren't of her making. Karla squeaked away on her sensible soles, and Hana studied her tired movements with empathy.

Her busy mind considered Jared and Hallie's messy relationship. She wondered how they continued a normal existence away from the island, working, socialising and all the time, pretending. Her gaze switched to her husband's strong profile as he turned towards the front doors and she remembered. His parents had done it. And so had hers.

Hana's silent mulling occupied her as she followed Logan into the humidity of a darkening sky. The mosquitos turned up the anti and dug into her exposed skin. Logan slipped an arm around her shoulders, hugging her to his side and digging his fingers into the back pocket of her jeans. "I can hear your brain whirring," he said, humour in his voice.

Hana nodded and smiled at his familiar rebuke. "Yeah. I'm glad you refused the offer to visit Jared," she admitted. "I feel like we've already overstepped with him." Her feet slowed as she turned to face him, her chin bumping against his chest. She stared up into his stormy grey eyes, which the lowering sun had cast into shadow. "Why did you ask the nurse to tell Jared we found his documents? You said ‘as promised’, but we didn’t talk to him about it.”

Logan shrugged. He pushed her fringe from her forehead with his free hand and dipped to kiss her freckled nose. “It doesn’t matter,” he replied. His gaze raked her face for some cue only he would recognise. “It covers us for entering his villa. We told the other nurse we’d see if we could find his health insurance documents, and now we have. I’m just laying the groundwork in case the cops get interested suddenly.”

Hana nodded and turned her feet towards the Harley. “Should we try to get dinner?” she asked, her voice fading after considering the almost insurmountable task.

“Yeah.” Logan nodded. “The Muri night market is open until eight o’clock tonight. I’ll use cash. I doubt street traders will care who we are. If we have no problems, we can eat there again for a couple of nights.”

Hana exhaled with relief. She climbed onto the pillion and settled to the steady thrum of the motor firing beneath her.

The night market on the south-eastern side of the island buzzed with life and colour. Street traders gathered in a wide oblong around tables sheltered by scruffy marquees. The cloying fried scent reminded Hana of her lack of food that day. Her stomach set up a grumble of complaint as a man walked past carrying a pizza suitable for a family of four.

They shared a cheese and ham pizza, and Logan visited a trailer selling mussel fritters. He paid using cash, and neither of the traders inspected the integrity of the notes. But nor did they show any interest in Logan or Hana, busyness driving the sense of a conveyor-belt service. The anonymity suited Hana. She allowed herself to relax, stepping back into the role of tourists and leaving behind their unwelcome notoriety. Oil from the fried food seemed to clog the air, and she took deep breaths as she waited for Logan's return. With her growling stomach satiated, a soporific calm settled over her.

"Hey." A lyrical voice spoke into the silence and a heavyset man with bulging muscles dumped a disposable plastic bowl on the table beside Hana. Curry sauce spilled over its edges and onto the wooden slats. Constructed from old pallets, the table's makeshift surface allowed the sauce to drip through the gaps and onto the gravel beneath.

Hana stiffened and scooted back on her plastic chair. The legs caught against the stony ground and she saved herself from pitching over backwards. Her gaze raked the crowd for her husband, spotting his glossy black hair above a group of people inspecting a drinks vendor's menu. She snatched up the cardboard box which had housed the pizza, the corrugated surface stained with tomato sauce smears which resembled blood. Logan turned towards her as though sensing her unease across the bowed heads of a feasting multitude. Hana watched his brows knit and his body stiffen as he strode towards her.

"You're all good. You stay," the man said, filling a white plastic spoon with onions and a bulbous mushroom. His lips parted to admit it, and he withdrew it before pointing at Hana's vacated seat. A paper cup containing hot tea landed beside her on the table, and Logan's arm slipped around Hana's waist.

"Problem here?" he demanded, his tone terse. Hana folded her shoulder beneath the safety of his arm and berated herself for the instant fear which rocked her soul at any sudden disturbance. While the cardboard box dangled from her left hand, her right strayed to the point below her ribs, where the knife blade entered her liver. She'd found herself pathetic once and hated how the stabbing put her right back there. The old Hana had risen from the ashes in her heart where she'd buried her. Because the island hadn't healed her. It had made everything so much worse.

"Sit," the man commanded. He didn't look up, but dug his spoon into his curry once more. Red drips plunged from it and joined the mixture in the stained bowl. When neither of them moved, he squinted up at Logan. "You must remember me, bro? We chatted outside of the supermarket the other day. I ran over the bloke in the road outside the Avarua Market."

"I remember." Logan remained standing. His grip tightened around Hana's shoulder. "And since then, we've gone from hero to zero. We just want to finish our dinner and *leave*." Hana wondered if he meant the heavy intonation on the word leave. He didn't just mean the night market, but the island.

The man leaned his elbows on the table and studied Logan's hard expression. He pushed out his bottom lip. A pink tongue poked through the seam and licked a curry stain from the corner of his mouth. "That's a shame," he remarked, his tone indifferent. "Because more dodgy cash showed up on one of the boat tours this morning."

"Yeah, well, it wasn't us." Logan leaned down and collected Hana's tea one handed. "Good luck with it all." He nudged Hana with his hip and headed for the exit. She craned her neck to look behind her at the man still hunched over his food.

"What's wrong?" she demanded. "I thought you liked the man who squashed Jared. That reminds me, the stall holder gave us mangoes." She cocked her head. "We still have them. At least we won't starve."

Logan groaned. "Please don't refer to road traffic accidents involving pedestrians as squashing." He tipped the cup and its liquid contents into the trash bin as they passed. “And the man who collided with Jared was okay. But that isn’t him.”

58

Sneak - mōtoro

Hana turned her whole body to stare at the man beneath the marquee. The cloth flapped overhead as the breeze increased, but he bobbed his head for another mouthful without concern. "I'm confused," she admitted. "Then who's that?"

"No idea." Logan hustled her along the street. They reached the Harley, and he dug the key into the ignition. Hana responded to his impatience by fumbling as she clambered onto the pillion, almost jettisoning herself off the other side. The bike roared as Logan climbed on and set off, the soles of his cowboy boots dragging through the grit.

They returned to the villa after taking the anticlockwise route, but Logan didn't enter the resort. He parked the bike across the road beneath a stand of coconut trees which separated the ring road from the beach.

"Are you sure about it?" Hana demanded as she slipped from her seat. She regretted the question as soon as the breeze took it and tossed it into Logan's face. He'd spent four decades living beneath his family's expert gaslighting tactics. His whole life had been a lie. She shook her head as though to dislodge cobwebs. "Scrap that." She exhaled and brushed sand from her plimsolls. "Why would he claim to remember a conversation with you, though?"

Logan shrugged. He leaned against a tree, his shirt blending into greys as the darkness closed around them. His gaze fixed on the entrance to Paradise Villas. "It's not the same guy," Logan maintained. "Gantry Hosking is heavy, but that dude had muscles upon muscles. It's not him. Hosking wore the local uniform of tee shirt, shorts, and flip-flops. Not camouflage pants and surplus army boots. I think I'd know the difference. He looked familiar but maybe from the Trading Post. Or the flight over here."

Hana blinked. She hadn't noticed the man's dress sense. A darted glance at Logan reminded her he missed nothing. "So, who is he, and why did he bother with the charade?" She ran around the tree but found the rest of the mosquito's family. She made a sound of frustration low in her throat. Logan stretched out his left arm to halt her frantic run as headlights picked out the faded sign to the resort. He tucked her against him as a ute slowed and turned onto the narrow lane. The security lights bloomed on the wall of the reception as the vehicle crept past it. "What are we looking at?" Hana coughed at the end of her sentence as a mosquito investigated her open mouth.

"Didn't you see the damage to the front of that ute?" Logan whispered. He jerked his head towards the entrance. The red tail lights bobbed along the lane, following it as it veered right past Sally and Craig's villa.

"No." Hana blinked in the glare from the security lights. White spots appeared in her vision. "Too busy getting eaten alive." She slapped at her arms, following through by patting down her entire body.

"Stop!" Logan hissed. He turned to her, his eyes alight with the thrill of danger. "Wait here. I'm going to check on something."

"Don't you dare leave me here as bug food!" Hana growled. She tensed against another crawling sensation along the neckline of her tee shirt and wound her fingers through Logan's elbow. "Lay on Macduff."

Logan's irritated grimace switched to a smirk. "Well done, Mrs Du Rose," he whispered, his lips quirking up on one side. "An often misquoted line of Macbeth."

Hana jerked her head from side to side like a nodding dog. "Well, if I wanted to annoy you, I'd have said, 'lead on Macduff' but I didn't. So where are we going?" She stressed the word *we* and gripped his bent elbow with both hands. She refused the role of guarding the Harley or listening to the blunted thuds of bone on flesh. "I'm coming too," she asserted, planting her feet.

"Or what?" Logan called her bluff, his pupils like endless pits in the centre of his stormy irises. When he turned his head, the security lights caused his nose to cast a long shadow, which obscured his full mouth.

Hana considered her options, fixing her gaze on the fluttering fronds of the coconut leaves while she conjured up a decent threat. Then she settled a calm expression over her face and set her lips into a severe line. "Or I'll push the Harley into the sea and leave it there."

The faintest flare of shock crossed Logan's sharp features. His chuckle piled humiliation onto Hana's sense of inadequacy. "You can't push it," he concluded. "It's too heavy."

Hana squeezed her fingers around his elbow hard enough to make him look down at her hands. "Watch me!" she snarled, her tone filled with bile.

Logan licked his lips. "I'm tempted just for the entertainment factor, but I'm busy here."

"Fine!" Hana released his arm and marched across the sand. She rounded the tree where he'd hidden the Harley and sensed the heavy thuds of him striding after her.

"Okay, okay!" he hissed. "You can come, but stay behind me."

Hana dropped her chin so she could enjoy her victory smirk without him noticing. Logan had already turned away and taken up his position opposite the entrance. The security lights winked out and an eerie darkness enveloped the road. The villas placed at their hotchpotch angles oozed a dim yellow glow from the solar bulbs installed beneath each porch. Cracks of light showed through drawn curtains, the residents either out drinking or already settled for the night.

Logan tapped Hana's hand, and she started, still basking in her show of one-upmanship and grateful she didn't need to push the Harley into the water. Logan had told her at some point that the bike weighed over two-hundred and seventy kilogrammes. She didn't have an impressive track record with Logan's motorbikes. It occurred to her as they scurried across the road that she might have misread his concern. Was it for the bike, or his wife? The smile faded from her lips.

“We need to avoid the security lights,” Logan hissed in her ear. She jumped and released a squeak of alarm. Though she didn’t see his frown, she felt the wave of annoyance which accompanied it.

“Sorry,” she mouthed.

They crossed the narrow ditch which bordered the resort, disturbing a gathering of roosting chickens. Hana grimaced at the sickening crunch of an egg shell beneath her plimsoll and apologised to the cockerel, who ruffled his crest at her. Unmollified, it ran at her leg and pecked her calf. “It’s not even yours!” she hissed at it, flapping her hands to distract it from her shoe laces.

Logan’s shape appeared beside her, and the cockerel retreated. Hana swore under her breath. “I didn’t need rescuing!” she hissed at him. “Even the bloody creatures do whatever you say.”

Logan’s jaw showed as hard and square in the sudden bloom of a weak moon. “You’re making a racket!” he replied, his lips close to her ear. Hana’s shoulders slumped. She didn’t have the skills for schlepping around in the darkness and fighting with the locals. But though she regretted not staying with the bike, she didn’t admit defeat. She slipped her right hand into Logan’s and took more care. His fingers closed around hers and warmth spread through her.

They skirted the resort, sticking to the perimeter fence to the north of the property and following its line to the swimming pool. The water lay flat and clear, lit from beneath by relaxing blue spotlights. A few moths held a social gathering above the surface, flicking back and forth as they bathed in the gentle glow.

Paving slabs surrounding the pool deadened their footsteps as Logan led Hana around the pump house and up the steps onto Hallie's porch. The solar glow cast highlights over Logan's hair, and Hana panicked as he pulled her to a squat between the balustrade and a heavy urn. Fronds of a palm tapped her head in a steady, lulling motion. She tugged on Logan's hand and he pressed an index finger over his lips.

An engine gave a muted splutter and stopped behind Hallie's villa. Hana's eyes widened, and she held her breath, pressing her temple against Logan's hard shoulder. A door slammed and footsteps swished through the short grass in a staccato beat. Male voices whispered in a droning baritone hum.

Two men stepped from the space between the villas and crept towards the Du Rose's porch. Hana's audible gulp locked the back of her throat.

59

Fragile - ʻōviri

The men spun on the spot as they surveyed their surroundings. "I know it's here," said the deeper voice of the two. "This is where he picks up the fakes. I've watched him. He comes around here with nothing and walks back with wads of cash stuck down the back of his shorts. I've seen him do it!" His voice rose to a hiss containing a bark of protest. He sprang up the porch steps and tapped on the front door while the other peered through the lounge window into the empty room. The second man's head resembled a bowling ball in the eerie shadows, his shape morphing into a weird, spectral creature as he raised his arm and rapped on the window. Hana recognised the man from the Muri Night Market. She darted a glance at Logan and he bobbed his head in confirmation.

"But we already checked this place!" He dropped his arm and climbed the steps to stand beside his companion. "Their room looked clean. We turned it inside out."

"We need to find the rest of it." The first man spoke again. He turned his back on the door and walked to the edge of the porch. Fabric and cushions gave a whump of protest as his weight descended onto the wicker armchair. "These people know something. Otherwise, why did they get arrested as soon as they landed? The dude in the hospital passed dirty cash all night during that poker game. I watched him do it. You know what happens to filthy players here and we don't want him drawing attention to us. You saw him drinking with the other couple at the Trading Post. These damn fakes are complicating everything. We should have sorted this out when they first appeared."

The second man possessed the bulk of a bouncer or a security guard, his head shaved to the scalp. Moonlight reflected off his pate before clouds obscured its hazy light. His companion caused her to release a gasp of shock. Logan's hand slipped around her neck and pressed over her mouth. Irritated and desperate to enlighten him, she licked his palm and he shot her a narrow-eyed glare. But he didn't let go.

The men turned their attention to Hallie's porch at the rustle of Logan's shirt. Hana closed her eyes and berated her stupidity. But the cockerel which had tracked her across the resort chose that moment to dash from beneath the porch with a ghostlike cackle. The hairs stood up on the backs of Hana's forearms. She gripped Logan's fingers with her right hand until her nails grooved ruts in his palm. But he didn't remove his other hand from her mouth. The cockerel grumbled and clucked, pecking and protesting at the bottom of the Du Rose's steps. Hana sagged against Logan, recognising vengeance when she saw it. She'd made yet another formidable enemy and could no longer guarantee the safety of her bare toes outside the villa's front door.

"Can't you get the master key for the villas again?" The heavyset man dug his hands into his jeans pockets and glared down at his companion.

"Na," he replied. "I don't need that one for my outside jobs. Craig got suspicious when the housekeeper told him I'd lifted them. I pretended I'd got them mixed up with mine and took them home by accident." Wicker creaked and the cheap foam in the cushion released a farty sound as the man shifted in position. Hana peeked through the slats of the balcony railing as the man drew his knees together and rose. He spread his hands in concession. "Look, we searched both villas. We found nothing. The cops let these guys go without charges." He waggled a hand towards the Du Rose's front door. "Gantry made nice with the husband and he seemed confused. He either put on a decent act or he told the truth."

"Gantry also said to follow them around," the other man said with a sigh. "He figured they might do some poking of their own. The woman looks harmless enough in a fragile way, but he thought the dude might make trouble. Figured he's a somebody where he comes from. A rangatira maybe."

Hana inhaled behind Logan's damp palm. Condensation from her breaths created a cloying atmosphere. She bit back her dismay at the men's assessment of her. While they'd judged her as harmless and fragile, they'd recognised Logan's natural mana. The lying, cheating Gantry Hosking had described Logan as a rangatira, a God ordained chieftain. "Geez!" she hissed behind Logan's hand. His grip tightened. The cockerel emitted a low growl in the back of its throat and dashed back towards Hallie's porch. Hana's temper flared at the injustice of her life. Her chest tightened with the urge to burst from her hiding place and nuke the bloody lot of them. Rude, arrogant men and Sally's guard chicken.

But then the other man fought her corner. "Na, the ginger chick's been quite entertaining. She threw all Sally's clothes in the pool earlier today. The old girl ran around the site wearing a sheet. It beats watching Craig shagging everything that moves. He took a tourist out to the reef in his kayak this morning. Gantry said they did it in the water. I swear there's something wrong with the guy. He's almost bankrupt and giving it away for free. Why doesn't he sell it? A package deal, board and a shag."

Both men laughed. They clattered down the porch steps, no longer attempting to hide their visit. They halted at the bottom, their bodies half turned towards each other. The muscular man spoke first. "Almost there." He sighed and lifted his left arm, turning his wrist and bobbing his head. "I need to drop Gantry's ute back at his place and pick up mine. He reckons he's fixed the brakes just for now. I'll dump it when we shoot through. It's a heap of crap, anyway. I'll meet you up at the house soon. We're almost finished and we'll each go our merry way. Not bad for a year's work."

The other man grumbled something, his voice inaudible. He aimed a kick at the agitated cockerel, drawing his foot back as the bird lunged with its sharp beak. "I won't miss this place," he said with a sigh. "Paradise is a lie."

60

Expose - mārangaranga

"The pool guy is involved in this!" Hana snarled. "And Jared might have looked like he stepped into the road, but I bet Gantry Hosking ran him over on purpose because of the fake cash. And what are they almost finished shifting?" She wiped her mouth on the back of her wrist. "Fragile, my ass! I'll give him fragile. He tossed our place on Friday night. I feel guilty now because I thought Hallie and Jared were slobs, but he tossed their place too!"

Logan nodded. He used his palms against the siding to push himself upright, pulling Hana up after him. "Looking for the counterfeit notes which Jared hid in that cubby behind our villa."

"No, it's Craig." Hana brushed her palms against the thighs of her jeans. "I saw him do exactly what the pool guy described. He shoved an object down the back of his shorts. They believe it was the hooky cash. Jared was there the first time. But I don't think Hallie knew about the stash because she genuinely believed Jared went on the tour." Hana sighed. "I bet she booked it for him, too."

Logan shrugged. "Well, the fake cash is gone now. Perhaps they've used it all."

Hana exhaled. "Do you think Jared deliberately used fake cash at the poker game? It seems logical that's how he laundered it." She wrinkled her nose. "We should just ask him."

"But then we have to tell him Hallie still hasn't turned up, and that she lost the baby."

"Yeah." Hana's shoulders slumped.

"We can't trust anyone," Logan concluded. He leaned against the wall and pulled Hana against his chest. She turned her cheek until his heartbeat vibrated through her ear. He rested his chin on the top of her head. "I wonder what the other thing is," he mused. "They're running some other scheme, which the counterfeit cash puts in jeopardy. But it started around the same time Craig began floating the dodgy notes. Everyone we've spoken to puts the date up to three months ago. The first time they used hundreds, then fifties and now twenties." He shook his head. "They aren't very intelligent, are they?"

Logan's biceps muffled Hana's voice. "Would anyone bother to counterfeit fewer than ten dollars?

I don't think so. You said the cubby under our villa is empty, which means Craig has either found a different hiding place for the fake cash, or it's run out. That indicates it's not manufactured here. It's finite. When it's gone, it's gone. And he started moving it at the same time as this other lucrative scheme kicked off." She turned her head and pressed her chin against Logan's sternum.

"No, that's not correct," he mused. "Remember the big guy said, '*it's not bad for a year's work.*' That means their scheme started way earlier. The fakes are a new thing. A bug in the ointment when they're almost finished."

"If we go back to basics, how would you get pallets of some illegal substance onto the island? And could Craig have used the same method to import his fake money?"

"Private plane?" Logan listed the options. "Not commercial. There are still port authorities here. Boat maybe? Fishing boat? Perhaps Craig intends to get more cash and he'll use the same route."

"Tour boat?" Hana sifted through the possibilities. "I read a thing recently about a drug courier who dropped product in pallets off the side of his yacht. The receiver picked it up using divers. What if someone sank a shipment off the reef? But why here? The regular population of the island is tiny."

"Don't know." Logan yawned, lifting his right hand to cover his mouth. "I'm tired of sitting still. Why don't we go for a bike ride and think about it some more?"

Hana nodded and kept hold of Logan's hand as they walked down the steps and onto the grass. "Did you recognise the other man? The one with muscles on top of muscles."

Logan squeezed her fingers. "Didn't you?"

"No." She halted and stared up at him. His elbow brushed her upper arm, and she experienced a prickle of desire. Perhaps they didn't need a bike ride, but something with more exertion. She glanced back at their darkened villa and shivered. What if the men returned? Why had they singled out her and Logan just because of a mistaken arrest? She pursed her lips and fed herself the answer. Because they'd poked the bear with their questions.

"Hana?" Logan shook her hand, and the motion ricocheted up her wrist and into her shoulder. "I said I'd seen the other guy drinking at the Trading Post. He also sat a few rows behind us on the plane ride over here. I wondered if he's either bringing the illegal shipments in or taking them out again? If he's knocking around with Craig's pool guy, he isn't a tourist."

The security lights at the entrance flashed on and Hana stiffened, mesmerised by the light pollution it caused against the darkened sky. She ducked down behind Hallie's balustrade and tugged Logan with her.

"It's just those guys leaving," Logan reassured her. His tone altered, acquiring a cajoling note aimed at placating her. "Look, why don't we go back to the villa for now? I have a couple of episodes of that series we like downloaded onto my laptop. Let's settled down for tonight and think about our next move."

Hana shook her head. She rose, feeling foolish for her overreaction. "No. I like the bike ride idea," she said, forcing determination into her shoulders and voice. "Drive me back to the hospital. There's someone I want to see."

61

Prodding - ʻakakōkō

Logan drove with care, vigilant about passing vehicles or wandering pedestrians who showed them too much interest. Tourists circled the island with abandon, wobbling on their scooters and vomiting alcohol into bushes which bordered residents' gardens.

Hana witnessed a minor ding between a passenger van and a parked car. She tapped Logan's shoulder to make him stop, mindful of the two-thousand-dollar excess on the hire vehicles if the car renter hadn't bought the expensive daily insurance waiver. The driver of the van inspected the damage but didn't appear as though she intended to leave a note. "Stop!" Hana protested as Logan waited for the bunched traffic to clear before passing. "That's not fair."

The driver overheard her despite the burble of the idling Harley engine. She strode around the van and yelled something to her passengers. Faces appeared at the windows, and a few of the women made rude gestures. Aggression leaked through the driver's expressive brown eyes as she turned towards the bike.

Logan's shoulders stiffened beneath Hana's hands, and she winced. The traffic cleared as a line of weaving scooter drivers ceased rubber necking at the minor incident and wobbled away. He revved the engine and Hana's chin lifted as he shot away from trouble, taking her with him. She screwed her eyes closed and ran helpful scenarios through her mind. In them, she justified her need to get involved in matters which didn't concern her. She'd planned a considered list of responses as Logan turned onto the road leading to the hospital, but she didn't need them. To her surprise, he parked the Harley, but didn't broach the subject of her meddling. "We're seeing Jared?" He locked the bike and stuffed the keys into his jeans pocket.

Hana clambered off the pillion and paused, pushing her jeans back down her legs from where they'd ridden above her ankles. "No," she said. She crossed her arms across her chest, partly in expectation of a heated debate and in response to the cool breeze raising the hairs on her arms. "I want to go to the dementia unit."

Logan compressed his lips into an 'o' of protest, but blew out a hissed breath instead. "Okay," he conceded.

"Do you want me to move the bike around there or leave it here?"

The question caused Hana to pause. She'd wanted more autonomy in their marriage but not responsibility for the minutiae. "I don't care." She opted for ambivalence. She stretched her fingers and gave them a shake. "Let's walk. There can't be too many bits of skin left which haven't already provided someone's dinner."

They held hands as they skirted the high dependency unit and tracked towards the rear of the hospital site. Bush sounds obscured the loud hum of the air conditioning units and the canopy muted the light pollution from the main building. Hana relaxed, linking her fingers through Logan's and crossing her other hand over her body to clasp his forearm. "I'm sorry for Hallie," she commented as they walked an uphill camber she hadn't noticed on the Harley. "She must have miscarried after walking to the reception office with me. I find it upsetting that Jared didn't accompany her to the emergency room because she believed he'd gone on the diving tour. She must have travelled to the hospital alone. Maybe on the bus." Logan squeezed her fingers, but didn't comment.

"The emergency doctor prescribed painkillers. I think Hallie took too many, which is why she got so drunk." Hana shook her head and her ponytail bounced, causing long curls to tap against her shoulders. "It makes me heart-sore that she sat with us all evening while losing her baby."

"I thought they just prescribed normal paracetamol," Logan said. His jaw clenched and Hana remembered Liza's disastrous, short-lived marriage and failed pregnancy. She pursed her lips, not knowing the answer. The discharge notice had listed pain medication. Hallie would have exchanged the prescription in the pharmacy for the pills. She'd seen nothing in Hallie's villa, which meant she'd kept them with her in the bar.

Hana spun on the spot and released a sigh. "I wondered if she'd injected drugs when she appeared so drunk. I saw a mark on the inside of her elbow and jumped to the wrong conclusion. The hospital must have taken blood."

"How do we get into the dementia unit?" Logan changed the subject. The easy segue told Hana he didn't want to wallow in Hallie's emotional quagmire of grief and sadness.

She blinked in the darkness and stepped over a tree root growing through the gravel surface of the road.

"Watch and learn, Grasshopper," she replied.

Hana ignored Logan's eye roll as they reached the low-slung building. Scratches covered her arms from a hazardous wrong turn in the darkness. Her heart burned with yet another missed opportunity to impress him.

Light glowed from behind the row of windows. Logan headed towards the front door, but Hana yanked on his hand. "No," she whispered, clinging to her fragile autonomy. She jerked her head towards the site of her earlier catastrophe. No one had yet drawn the curtains across the sash window. Muted lights showed the clinical ward with its peeling white paint. Beds with side rails lay in wait for their captive occupants. The plant pot still occupied its space to the left of the windowsill.

Logan moved with surprising stealth for such a tall, muscular man. He crouched below the ridge of the retaining wall she'd pitched over, bobbing his head down so only his eyes showed over the brick lintel. "Be careful," he whispered, releasing her to her ill-fated mission.

Hana slunk to the corner of the building and edged along the wall, flattening herself against the wooden siding. A man's rambling and plaintive complaints emitted from a window further along. Hana ducked her head around to peer through the glass opposite the old lady's bed. She didn't risk turning her body for fear of exposure. The curtains fluttered against the frame as the cool breeze increased its grip on the island. Leaves rustled in the canopy and the sturdier trunks creaked and bowed like an elderly man's bones. She peeked at the room before jerking back out of sight. The window offered a clear view of the bed opposite, the sheets pulled back ready. Hana had spotted a notice board above the row of power-points, leads and dials. She tilted sideways and her gaze zeroed in on the names scrawled there in a cursive hand.

'Mable S. Soft food only. Dr Klein.'

Hana frowned and whipped aside as footsteps carried a male nurse into the room. His Croc shod feet tapped into view on the tiled floor and he carried a water jug and glass. He laid it on the wheeled locker beside the bed and retreated.

Hana took another look through the window, focussing on the board above the bed. She memorised the words written there and dodged out of sight. She bent her body in an awkward bow as she jogged across to Logan and dropped onto the lower level beside him. "I'm going inside," she whispered. "The woman I saw with Sally is called Mable S. I'll ask for her at the reception desk and see if they'll let me visit with her." She swallowed and stared at Logan's widened eyes. His lips parted in disbelief.

"That's a ridiculous idea!" he hissed. "Why is this important?"

"I don't know!" Hana drew her shoulders to her ears as she crouched behind the low wall. The baked earth seemed cooler beneath her flattened palms. Loose soil peppered her fingers and the right knee of her jeans. "It just is."

Logan released a breath laced with exasperation. "What's your plan?" he demanded, his tone less aggravated than his expression. "What do you want from this?"

Hana stared at a point in the distance as she considered her answer. She feared he might dismiss her gut instinct as irrelevant, but realised too late it was her only justification. She sighed and twirled a ragged blade of grass between her fingers. It clung to the earth with delicate roots, fragile yet determined. Logan's mind worked like a super computer. He blinked as he watched her struggle, expecting data and reasoning. Not feelings. "It's a loose end," she admitted. Her fingers left the frayed strand alone as she braced herself against Logan's knee for balance. "It seems logical to push all the doors we come across. We're barred from everywhere but the night market. I'm certain Sally mobilised the traders against us with her poster campaign. She's spiteful, so I'm looking for anything we can use as ammunition against her."

Logan studied her for a moment. His lashes cast long shadows across his cheeks and shrouded his piercing grey irises. He exhaled through his nose like the snort of a stallion. "Fine then," he conceded, though his tone held reluctance. The stiff outline of his bunched shoulders said more than words about his misgivings. "What do you need from me?"

Noise sounded from beyond the window. A woman's voice rose in protest. "It's not bedtime!" she wailed. "I want to watch TV!"

"Let's get you settled," the male nurse soothed. "Look, it's dark outside. Definitely bedtime. I'll bring your hot milk."

"Hate hot milk!" the woman grumbled.

Hana popped her head over the lintel and peeked to the right of the planter. Excitement ticked in her chest as the woman Sally had visited wandered into view. The male nurse held onto her elbow and steered her towards the bed. The same fluttering nightdress tapped her skeletal calves.

"Where's my boy?" she demanded. "Where is he?"

"It's almost time for your friend to visit, isn't it, Mabel?" The nurse kept hold of her elbow, the bone birdlike beneath his strong fingers.

"No!" Mabel turned to face him, her beaked nose just centimetres from his cheek. "Where's my boy? I want to see the baby." She yanked her arm, but the action appeared futile. Her faded strength had no impact.

The nurse sighed and his shoulders drooped. The lowering of his chin indicated a man nearing the end of his patience and energy reserves. He led Mabel to the side of the mattress, where the lowered rail offered her access. She sat without protest as though she'd already forgotten her earlier complaint. The nurse dipped forward and made a brushing action with his left hand before gazing up at the ceiling. "There's plaster on your nice clean sheets," he said, forcing joviality into his tone. "That won't do, will it?"

Mabel's jaw tightened with a sucking action, the resulting sound both alarming and disgusting. As the nurse bobbed in front of her and rose holding two worn slippers, she hawked and spat into his upturned face. Hana gasped and clasped a hand over her mouth.

"Yuk!" Logan hissed in her ear. She turned her face in response and his nose brushed her temple. Their shared horror united them for a moment until Logan spoke again. "You're not going in there," he stated. "Not if that's your plan." He swore under his breath as he watched the poor nurse wipe his face on a handkerchief he tugged from his pocket. "No way, Hana," he growled. "No bloody way."

62

Keel - tātakere

Logan rose to leave, ignoring Hana's protests as he brushed dirt from his jeans. His firm grip around her elbow seemed reminiscent of the old woman's powerlessness against the nurse. Hana imagined herself feeling desperate enough to spit in revenge, her sympathy split equally between Mabel and her under resourced, minimum wage carer.

"Okay, okay!" She raised her other hand, palm facing Logan, in a signal of submission. An idea sprang from the back of her mind and she pivoted her loose plan. "I won't go in." Logan relaxed, and he dropped her arm, using his hand instead to run his fingers through his hair. He turned his feet to face the downward slope and the artificial yellow glow from the hospital, which hazed the night sky and obscured the stars.

"Let's go," he said. His voice held a husky quality.

Hana's fingers closed around his forearm, the fine hairs tickling the webbed purlicue between her thumb and forefinger. The ends of her longest fingers didn't reach all the way around the rigid bone and muscle. "I said I wouldn't go in," Hana whispered. "But you will." She clasped her other hand around his forearm and tugged him towards her. His body tilted and she pulled again. Enthusiasm built in her voice. "Mabel wants to see her boy." She shifted behind him and braced her palms against his spine. "So, pretend you've arrived."

"You're insane!" Logan spun towards her, but Hana dodged aside. She gave him another shove in his ribs.

"Go on!" she urged. "Her name is Mabel, and she's only allowed to eat soft food. She's cared for by Dr Klein. I want to know who Mabel thinks Sally is and why she visits her." Hana snapped her fingers as the questions tumbled through her mind. "And the baby. I want to know more about the baby she keeps asking to see. Perhaps she has a link to Hallie."

Logan released a huff of impatience. "Anything else?" he demanded, his irises sparkling like gems in the light from the window. He set his hands on his hips and stared down at her. His expression formed a series of hard lines and angles. His grinding jaw created moving shadows along his collar.

Hana pushed her weight into her left hip and placed her index finger over her lips as she adjusted her original cover story for his benefit. "Yes," she said, her tone faraway. "You've flown in from Auckland this afternoon. You're staying for a few days but couldn't wait to see your Aunty Mabel." Her eyelashes fluttered with pleasure. "Yeah, that's good."

"Fantastic." Sarcasm dripped from Logan's tone. "And what's my name?"

Hana's lips made a popping sound as she blew a slow breath through them while thinking. She raised her index finger. "Boy!" she said. A grin flickered across her mouth. "Yes. She knows you as Boy. She talks about her boy all the time. It'll add validity."

Logan growled low in his throat. "Sally must come every night, Hana. The nurse just said as much. We arrived at the Trading Post late on Friday evening. She could have been here first."

"If you think she'll come, then hurry." Hana risked shoving him one more time before figuring she'd already pushed her luck beyond its reasonable limits. Logan swore numerous times until his angry steps stomped him out of Hana's hearing. She bobbed down behind the wall again and watched him yank open the front door. Even though he couldn't see her in the darkness, she felt the glare he shot in her direction pierce her soul.

It seemed like hours before Logan appeared on the other side of the window. He bobbed his chin in reply to something the nurse said to him. The other man's black hair stuck to his crown as though he'd just run his entire head under a tap. Hana couldn't blame him. She sent silent vibes of sympathy across the distance and watched her husband's muscles bunch beneath his shirt. His jeans hung low on his hips, the gentle curve of his buttocks drawing her gaze. She pursed her lips and wondered at his unusual obedience. He detested her hair brained schemes and usually put up more resistance. She tamped down a nervous giggle.

Mabel lay in the bed beyond Logan, her clawed hands yellow against the white sheets. She squeezed her eyes closed in a pretence of sleep. When the nurse leaned over her and gave her shoulder a gentle shake, Logan put his left hand behind his back and made a rude gesture for the benefit of his watching accomplice. Hana bit down hard on her lower lip to prevent the laugh escaping. The open sash window relayed the muted conversation, though the growing breeze chopped out some of the words. Hana struggled for context as the nurse stepped back with a shrug to Logan. "She's asleep," he said, though his tone showed he didn't believe that for a second. "You should come again in the morning."

"Oh well." Logan played the game with superb skill. "That's a shame. I'm busy tomorrow."

Mabel's left eye cracked, and she peered at Logan from beneath her lashes. "I'm here," she croaked, her voice wavering. "Hello, son."

"Hey Ma."

Hana's amusement at the success of the ruse evapourated at Logan's use of the word. He'd called both Miriam and Alfred by their given names since discovering the magnitude of their lies. They'd lost the right to the titles of Ma and Pa almost a decade ago. Logan cleared his throat, and Hana pressed her hands to either side of her head and squeezed her eyes closed. She'd taken her scheme too far.

As though watching a terrible movie she couldn't escape, Hana crouched behind the wall and listened to the nurse make small-talk with Logan. He included Mabel in his inane prattle about the changing weather and the plaster cascading from the ceiling. And the digital display on Hana's watch seemed to speed up. She jumped at the honk of a horn in the car park less than half a kilometre away. It held a forlorn note, as though heralding an unavoidable doom. Because Sally would arrive any minute and discover Logan in his feigned role as devoted son.

The nurse spoke again, and Hana fought to push the clamour of misgivings from her mind. "Be nice,

Mabel," he said. He lifted his right hand to scratch at his cheek as though mindful of the spittle he'd washed from his face moments earlier. "You can have a few minutes, but I need to get the other patients from the bathroom." He gave a definitive nod. "I'll see you soon." His rubber soles squeaked against the tiles as he retreated.

Hana observed the stiffness in her husband's spine and regret lit a fire in her gut. She rose and clambered up the low wall, edging towards the open sash window. Her palms sweated, and a gnat buzzed near her right ear. She shook her head to discourage it, not wishing to add to the myriad bites already covering her exposed skin. They prickled and itched. She forced herself to ignore them as she reached the siding and pressed herself against it.

Logan spoke to the old woman in the bed. "You shouldn't spit at people," he said, his voice low. "It's unkind."

"Can we go now?" Mabel sat up, pushing the sheets away from her emaciated body. "Take me away, boy. I want to see your baby. They keep telling me I can go home, but they're liars. I've been here for months and months." Her clawed fingers rattled the metal rails, keeping her prisoner.

"Can you remember the baby's name?" Logan forced his hands into his jeans pockets. The action turned his strong shoulders into rigid lines.

"No." Mabel frowned. She scrubbed at her eyes with both hands. "I forget things. Why did you leave me here? Where's the woman who puts me to bed? I don't like that other nurse. When can I go home?"

"Where's home?" Logan asked. "Tell me about your garden."

Hana's gaze softened. She would have asked about Mabel's house and perhaps tried to locate it. Logan would get the same answers by asking about the land.

Mabel sighed. "Roses," she said. A yawn tugged at her lower jaw and revealed a white coated tongue and pink gums. "Where are my glasses? I can't see." She patted her mouth with her right hand."I need my teeth. They took them away." Her head turned towards the door, her neck a spindly stalk rising from her sloping shoulders. "I'm not ready for bed. The woman makes me tired. Where is she?"

"Tell me about your garden," Logan persisted. "Is it here on Rarotonga?"

"What?" Mabel blinked at him in surprise. "Why would I go there?" An incredible clarity entered her gentian irises. Her lips parted, and she sat up straighter. "Where's my son? What happened to our boat?"

Light flared in twin arcs behind Hana. The yellow glow lit up the side of the building and she dropped behind the concrete planter and scrunched herself into a ball. Engine sounds followed the headlight beam and tyres sent grit skittering away from their pressure. The driver drove too fast for the narrow lane and braked without care in front of the main door. The compact car slewed to a halt, the engine reduced to heated clicks as the motor ceased.

Sally spilled from the driver's seat, batting the door twice with her elbow before regaining her footing. She slammed it closed without looking, leaving it unlocked and already running towards the entrance in her nurse's uniform. A rattle sounded as something fell from her bunched fist and hit the floor. It rolled over grit and stones, a tube shaped object with a white lid. Hana watched as Sally stooped to retrieve a plastic pill bottle and shoved it into her right pocket. "What are you up to?" Hana mused as the blonde passed through the heavy front door and into the building.

And then she remembered Logan.

63

Stealthily - ʻītoro

The corner of the planter attacked Hana's right leg as she shot from behind it. Heat bloomed from her knee in protest. She tripped again just before the window. Her palms landed with a bang against the glass as she struggled to save herself from entering through it head first. Logan jumped and spun towards her, but she'd already clasped the bottom edge of the frame and started hauling it upward. The wood resisted, releasing a tell-tale creak which revealed why nobody ever closed it. "Help me!" she hissed to Logan. "Sally's here!"

He batted away her fingers, and she bunched them into a fist. Splinters from the rotten wood sent painful pinpricks through her soft skin. Voices rose in the corridor, Sally's louder than any other. "I got caught up!" she declared. Heavy breaths bisected her words. She responded to her companion with a tone of regret.

"You already put Mabel to bed. But I do it! Every morning and every night. I deal with her!"

Hana recognised the rumble of the male nurse's voice. "She spat at me." Rubber soles squeaked against the tiles. "Oh, and she has a visitor."

The window edged higher by degrees. It twisted, groaning as the right side moved with more ease. The frayed cable supporting the mechanism on the left gave a sad twang and snapped. The window sagged against Logan's palms. He swore and gave a gargantuan heave. The window rose, but without the mechanism, it represented an impossible weight for him to support while crawling underneath. Hana wedged herself, head and shoulders, in the gap, her eyes popping from her sockets. "Go!" she hissed as the window crushed her chest against the sill.

Logan wriggled out face first, forcing his bulk through the narrow gap like a lizard. He used his hands to crawl forward, his knees crashing onto the scrubby grass after him. Clambering to his feet, he returned to Hana's side and thrust his arms through the aperture. He seized the curtains, whisking them closed over the catastrophe and hiding them from the view of the room. But with Logan's body released from the gap, the worn edge of the window pinned Hana to the sill. Her lungs compressed and she couldn't breathe.

Sally's voice entered the room seconds later. "What visitor?" she demanded. Fear edged her tone with a piercing screech. "What's their name?" Her ballet flats tapped against the tiles, squawking as she whirled on the spot. "Where are they?"

"Dunno." The male nurse stifled a yawn. "Mabel knew him. Said his name was Boy. He flew in from Auckland this afternoon. She arrived a year ago, and he's the first person to show up to see her. Dr Klein wants to run more blood tests. He's not convinced she has dementia."

Sally's voice rose in protest. "He's meant to speak to me before he runs tests. I'm happy to attend all appointments with her. She doesn't need bloods. I don't consent. My husband and I pay for her care. Old ladies who spit at people aren't in their right mind!"

"But she's not from Rarotonga," the nurse persisted. "Why is she here and not on the mainland? Is her name even Mabel? She doesn't answer to it, although the man who visited asked for Mabel, so maybe it is." A long pause ensued before he spoke again. "He called her Ma when they met. I think he's her son. She knew him."

"I've talked to Dr Klein about this!" Sally growled. "She visited on holiday and stayed at our resort. We believe she came with family and they abandoned her here. We're working on finding out her identity, but until then, we're paying the bills! I need a description of the man who visited!"

Logan took the weight of the window on his palms and lifted it. Mabel's wail of fury covered the agonised creak it made as Hana slipped backwards, her ribs crushed and her breathing laboured. She landed on her bottom in the dirt.

"Where's my boy?" Mabel yelled. "Where am I? Give me back my glasses and my teeth. You can't keep me here like this!"

"Go!" Logan whispered to Hana. He jerked his head towards the bush. The heavy window frame and its ancient glass bore down on his straining arms.

She frowned at him, his jaw square and his biceps bulging. The broken cable spewed from its housing on the left side of the window, the cords frayed and blunted. A rusty screw poked from the frame where it had loosened years ago, a time bomb picking at the integrity of the cable for decades. Hana paused for a millisecond as she pushed herself to her feet and considered abandoning her husband. But the crazed look in his eyes sent her skittering away from him.

She forgot the concrete planter again as she turned to run, and it played its best hand. Her wrist bent backwards as she tried to save herself and flew face first over the low wall. The breath left her lungs at the same moment as a deafening crash echoed around the clearing. Birds screeched and leapt from the canopy at their rude awakening, glass clattering and tinkling to the floor on either side of the window. The ground vibrated as Logan landed beside Hana. He exhibited more control than his wife, snatching the back of her tee shirt and dragging her flat against the low wall. His heavy forearm pressed her head downward at an unnatural angle, an ache blooming in the tendons of her neck. Logan's stomach and chest heaved, and he held his breath as light flooded the grass in front of them.

"What the hell?" the nurse demanded. Grass crackled and crunched beneath his feet. A hiss escaped from his lips. "Oh, look at this. The cable snapped. We put that on the maintenance list months ago." Fabric rustled as he moved the curtains aside. Mabel's wail added an eerie note, her urgent tears of distress both ghoulish and pitiful. The male nurse swore, his attention divided between too many factors.

"I'll deal with her," Sally said, her tone decisive. "Call the front desk in the main hospital and get someone out to fix it." A glass bumped against a metallic surface, followed by the gentle patter of pouring water. "Have a nice drink, Mabel," Sally urged. "Bedtime drinks."

"I don't want it." Mabel's tears ended with abruptness. The sound of hurried gulping followed.

A swish heralded the nurse drawing the curtains across the abomination of the shattered window. The voices became muffled. Sally spoke again, a severity in her tone. “Did Mabel’s visitor sign the book?” she demanded. “I didn’t think she had any family. We’ve struggled to locate anyone.”

The nurse muttered something in reply, but another woman’s voice rose above them all. “I’ll take the other ladies to the day room,” she said. “Then we’ll need to check everywhere for flying glass. Let’s get Mabel up again. She can’t stay here.”

Sally’s voice held a curious twang of fear. “She can’t go anywhere. I’ll sit with her.”

“But what about cuts or glass in her bed?” the other woman demanded. “It’s sprayed as far as the back wall. Look.”

Sally sounded frantic. “She’s already asleep. It’s unfair to wake her. The glass would have hit me first if it came this far.”

“Come on!” Logan whispered to Hana. “Let’s get out of here.” He put his weight on one arm and rose, using a knee and the sides of his feet. Hana scrambled up beside him, clutching her right wrist against her chest.

“The bloody planter got me again!” she mouthed, her eyes wide.

Logan nodded and strode across the lawn. When Hana didn't follow fast enough, he gripped her shoulder and steered her ahead of him.

They reached the shelter of the bush canopy and Hana touched the fingers of her left hand to her collar bone. "Let me catch my breath," she begged. "No one's coming after us."

Logan sighed and bent at the waist, bracing his hands against his knees. "Utter stupidity!" he huffed. "There's no point in anything we just did."

"But there is!" Hana waited for him to stand up straight before placing her soiled palms against his shirt. "Don't you see?"

64

Wreck - pararī

Hana patted her hands against his chest as though trying to infuse him with her enthusiasm. He didn't get it, clamping his fingers around her wrists. "She mentioned a boat and a missing son. Sally doesn't know who she is. What if she came from the shipwreck?"

"That's a massive leap, Hana!" Logan complained. He set his hands on her shoulders and spun her around, sending her ahead of him. "Total strangers don't just pay other people's hospital bills."

"But she is!" Hana protested. She twisted on the balls of her feet like a dancer, ducking beneath Logan's left arm. "Weren't you listening? And Sally interacts with her at least twice a day. I saw her drop a pot of pills on the floor outside the front door. I think she's drugging her. Mabel is a prisoner."

"Nope." Logan wrapped a powerful arm around Hana and lifted her bodily off the ground. He flipped her over his shoulder and carried her away like a sack of horse feed.

"Put me down!" she wailed, pounding his back with her balled fists.

"Put you down hard or soft?" Logan asked, his tone even and filled with an eerie calm. "You choose." His flippant treatment of her triggered a flash of rage. She waggled her legs but caused only herself pain. She doubted he'd follow through on his threat to drop her, but a flicker of anticipation dulled her need for retribution while in a position of utter weakness. Logan bore her away through the darkness, his cowboy boots stepping over the knotty undergrowth. Fronds bashed Hana's cheeks and forehead. A cloud of gnats hung around her face.

"Soft!" she relented with a whine. "Okay, soft." He set her down with exaggerated care.

"Let's go back to the bike and we'll drive home." Tiredness lengthened his vowel sounds to a drawl.

Light burst across the sky as Hana parted her lips in protest. They turned to peer through the trees as a small engine revved. Gravel skittered in the distance, crunching and popping beneath car tyres. The vehicle slewed in a tight arc, the headlights dancing with only a slight delay as Sally sped along the bumpy lane. Hana bolted, her plimsolls pounding the floor of the bush as she headed toward the main hospital. A tap on her shoulder caused her to speed until Logan called after her. "Left, Hana! You've gone too far."

She skidded to a halt and tipped sideways, almost losing her balance. Strong fingers closed around her wrist and kept her upright. Logan yanked her arm high into the air as she righted herself. The moment stole her breath and robbed her of the apology she voiced only inside her head. Her chest hurt and pain blossomed from beneath her right rib.

"This way." Logan clasped her hand and tugged her along a hidden path. With the night vision of a fox, he showed no difficulty at navigating the darkness. He led her towards the hospital's welcome glow before halting on the periphery of the bush. Hana tugged her hand free and bent at the waist, pressing her palms against her knees. Her breath heaved, oxygen wrestled from the air and into her lungs. "Step back," Logan urged. He snagged a handful of her tee shirt and hauled her beneath the canopy of coconut leaves. Breathlessness caused her to move like a skittle, but he made no comment, offering support without judgment as her feet stumbled in the undergrowth.

Their straight trajectory through the bush meant they'd overtaken Sally. She'd traversed the winding downhill road from the dementia unit and arrived after them. Hana pressed herself against the trunk of a tree and held her breath as Sally blasted past. As her red rear lights bounced into the distance, Hana turned to Logan. "Do you think she's going home now?"

His lips pursed, and he allowed himself a light shrug. Hana tutted at the impossibility of the question. They possessed the same information and he couldn't know the answer any more than she did. "Sorry," she said with a sigh. "Thanks for stopping me from sprawling on the floor back there."

"All good." Logan left the cover of the trees and peered at Sally's retreating rear lights. He narrowed his eyes and frowned. "She's not going home, babe. She just turned right before the main building."

Hana stepped forward, linking her fingers around his elbow. "What fork?" she mused. "I thought the road bent around to the left and ran towards the main car park."

Logan released a sound like a low growl in his throat. "Tell you what," he suggested. "Let's walk along there a little way." He winked at her, creating the effect of a light flicking off and on as his lids shuttered his sparkling irises. "Just to satiate your curiosity."

"Okay." Eagerness fuelled Hana's depleted energy levels, and she stepped onto the road with an eagerness to get going. Logan seized her left hand, his fingers warm against her cool skin.

"We'll take it steady," he said, making it into an order rather than a question. "No more running from monsters."

Hana nodded. She'd agree to anything if he allowed her to track Sally. "Should we fetch the bike?" she asked, jogging to match his long strides.

"Na." Logan shook his head, the moon casting blue highlights through his raven hair. "It's too loud. This site isn't extensive. She can't have driven far."

Excitement joined the throng of confused emotions in Hana's chest. She pictured herself exposing Sally in an illegal counterfeiting ring, or at least another ill-advised flirtation. Instinct told her they'd stumbled on something far more sinister. She pitied poor Mabel, spinning for herself a narrative in which she uncovered a hostage situation and set the elderly woman free. Sally's naked image sprang into her mind, her nipples poking through the thin fabric of the sheet. She'd laid in the spot just vacated by her sleeping husband, his warmth still radiating from the mattress. A shiver caused by a spiteful spirit snaked through her. Logan belonged to her, not some chancer with a cute body and decent breast implants. Hana squirmed beneath the green eyes of jealousy which rocked her soul. The vengeance had become a little too personal.

They followed the gritty lane through the hospital grounds. It threaded behind the main building and cut across the bush from east to west. A faint glow encouraged them forward as gravel crunched beneath their shoes. Hana puffed as the incline grew. Despite the lowering of the temperature, the breeze worked against them. The road twisted to a south westerly angle and a cool wind blew off the sea, filling their eyes and mouths with stinging salt vapour. Hana braced her forearms against her eyes and paused for a moment, her side aching from the exertion. "We're getting rubbish weather to add to our woes," she complained. "What next?"

"There's a freak cyclone cutting across the bottom of the island in the next few days," Logan replied. He stood in front of her, his spine taking the brunt of the wind's constant pressure as he sheltered her from its ire. "It's not expected to make land, but we'll already be at home by the time it does. I overheard someone speaking about it at the night market."

Hana blinked up at him. "Is it five days away?"

"No." He stroked her fringe back from her face. The wind attacked her ponytail, yanking out long strands and thrashing them against her cheeks and chin. "I scored us an early flight out of here."

"When?" She pressed her palms against his chest. Her lips turned down as she regretted her eagerness. "What will we tell Mark and the children?"

"Nothing." Logan smiled down at her, his eyes sparkling. "I thought we'd go missing for a few days in Auckland. Nobody needs to know we spent our free time looking at the sights. We're leaving tomorrow night."

Hana closed her eyes and tilted her chin upward. As though taking offense, the wind shoved at the backs of her knees until her calves shook. "I'm ecstatic," she said with a grin. Her mood improved as relief passed through her like the warmth from a hot water bottle applied to frozen toes. She reached up and pressed a kiss to Logan's chin. "Now, let's mess up Sally's life before we leave."

No longer caring about maintaining secrecy, Hana linked her fingers through Logan's and they strolled along the centre of the narrow road. She spared a moment of sympathy for all the good people on the island who now wouldn't benefit from their trade. They'd intended to buy food, souvenirs and gifts. She doubted their meagre spending would make much of a dent in the local economy, but the island couldn't afford to treat too many holiday makers that way. She considered the pastor's lovely wife, Mary, and remembered her note still back at the villa. It seemed a wasted opportunity for friendship. She'd liked her.

An eerie glow cast a grey pall over the bush as the road wound again as though spiralling back on itself. And then the moment of happiness and satisfaction ended with as much speed as it began. A heavy diesel engine cut the air with its throaty rumble. Headlights dappled the surrounding trees with a strange blue light. Hana gasped as she shot sideways, her left cheek slamming against Logan's solid biceps.

"Down!" he hissed. He forced her off the road, half carrying her in his haste. He clamped a hand over her mouth and pressed her into the undergrowth. Insects buzzed with delight at their early supper. She didn't have time to catch her breath before the truck levelled with their position, exhaust fumes choking like a grey cloud from its ragged tailpipe. A low whine betrayed a worn fan belt, accompanied by the hiss of brakes rubbing against a tyre.

Hana's fingers sunk into the loamy soil as she tried to push herself onto her knees. A hard forearm maintained a bar across her spine. Logan crouched beside her. "Let me up!" she protested in a hiss of frustration.

"Stay down!" he ordered, his tone offering no room for discussion. The truck laboured on the slope. Gears crunched as the driver fought the clutch. Hana gnawed at her lower lip as the engine alternately strained and threatened to stall. It didn't appreciate either of the gears the driver forced the shift into, and it pranced and whined. Hana popped her head up, fighting Logan's left armpit to see the truck. She caught a flash of dull paint, flecks of rusted metal showing through pocks and dents on the vehicle's battered bodywork. Logan's muscles relaxed as it hiccoughed past them and continued up the hill.

"Blue ute," Hana said, forcing herself onto her knees. She slapped at the bugs, which made a meal of her bare arms. One flew into her mouth and she gasped and aspirated it. A moment of coughing failed to dislodge it from the back of her throat.

"Red." Logan patted her back until she admitted defeat.

"What?" she croaked.

"Red ute. Not blue. Darkness gives the colours a different appearance."

Hana peered at him, seeing only his irises glinting in the demonic glow from the ute's red tail lights. "That isn't right," she commented, dismissing his theory with a brutality she didn't mean.

"Yeah, it is," he maintained. "Bodie told me. It's a question they ask the car thieves when they roadblock them at night."

Hana reared back, her brow furrowed in disbelief. "They ask them what colour their car is?"

"Yeah." Logan nodded. He rose to his feet and brushed bark and loose soil from his knees. "Because they don't know. Red looks like blue under artificial light."

Hana stared at him. "Thanks for that." She had no answer to his ill-timed information dump. "So, why are we grovelling around in the dirt yet again?"

"Because they're going to the same place that your mate Sally went."

"She's not my mate." Hana accepted his outstretched hand and mimicked his brushing motion. "How do you know where they're going?"

"It's a dead end." Logan clambered up onto the road and held out his hand to Hana. "I memorised the map we saw at the reception yesterday. It's a collection of derelict buildings under renovation. They're fund raising to create an upgraded surgical ward." He flapped his hand behind him. "And an X-ray department."

"Of course they are," Hana grumbled. "And of course you speed read every poster in the place during the five minutes we queued there."

"I did." Logan nodded. He waited for her on the grassy knoll at the side of the road. "They only had one poster relating to men's health. There are more females on the island than males."

"So?" A knot of irritation burgeoned in Hana's chest. It occurred to her that he could have led them from the hospital to the dementia unit without her muddy detours. A brown moth fluttered in front of her nose. She vented her anger by slapping it out of the way. Its fragile body clattered against the side of her hand and she shuddered as it fell like a stone.

"So, Sally's on the wrong island." His tone held humour. "She'd have more takers on an island with inverted statistics."

"Nice," Hana breathed. She didn't want to think about Sally in any sexual connotation because then she'd have to kill her. The slimy green jealousy in her soul dictated it. Kill her and bury the body.

65

To drive off - arumakimaki

The road opened out into a wide cul-de-sac at the top of the ridge. Thick bush surrounded the buildings nestled there as the island's highest peak towered overhead. Its outline obliterated the beckoning stars and the silver light from the weak moon. It created a sense of nature encroaching on humanity as though it would only take a single word for it to spring forward and swallow the evidence. Panels filled the spaces which glass had once occupied. Chain-link fence rails kept local youths from entering three of the dilapidated structures, though graffiti still decorated the wooden surfaces. A heaviness filled the clearing, and Hana gave an involuntary shiver. She wrapped her arms around herself and pushed herself closer to her husband. "What happened here?" she whispered to him.

He looped his arm around her shoulder as they observed the neglected buildings from the safety of the bush. "I think it's cyclone damage," he replied. He pressed a kiss against her temple. "Let's go back to the bike now. It's a long trek down the mountain. Then we still need to drive to the villa and pack."

Hana's brows knitted into a troubled line. "But what about Sally?" she demanded. "Where is she?" She indicated the hatchback parked at an angle at the end of the cul-de-sac. The ute driver had abandoned his vehicle behind it, the heavy treads filled with grit and mud. His front wheels arced to the right from beneath the arches as though poised for a quick escape.

Logan released a heavy sigh. "She's having a bonk in the end house with some random who can't afford to fix his truck's transmission. I don't really care, babe. Let's go now. It's been fun, but it's over."

Hana gasped and turned to face him. "You went through this to humour me?" Her voice rose, filled with antagonism. "What the hell, Logan? I thought we were in this together!"

"We were, and now we're not." Logan's elbow brushed her shoulder as he turned his cowboy boots to face the downward camber of the road. "It's late. I'm tired and we're leaving the island. Let's go. I don't care who she's shagging. It doesn't affect our lives."

"But what about Mabel?" Hana set her hands on her hips. "What about that poor old lady? Sally is keeping her a prisoner."

Logan cocked his head and observed his wife. He hid a yawn behind the back of his hand. His shoulders lost their squareness as he considered his reduced options. Hana took a hurried step out of range of his powerful arms. "Don't even think about it, cowboy!" she growled. "Even you can't caveman carry me all the way back to the bike."

"Try me." The two word reply held enough bite for her to take another careful step backwards. It wasn't careful enough. The heel of her left plimsoll caught against a tree root and she overbalanced.

"No, no!" she hissed, righting herself against the rough bark of a coconut trunk. "Sally's up to something. She's the villain of this peace. I want to see what she's doing."

Logan raised a black brow, his eyes cast into heavy shadow. "Isn't that a little perverted?" he asked, his tone serious.

Hana stamped her foot, frustration building to a crescendo in her eardrums. Her vocabulary dried on the back of her tongue, leaving her with no smart retort. It left her with only one course of action.

She lowered her head and dived to the left, seeing the disbelief and anger in Logan's face. He grabbed for her and missed. Always a better soccer winger than a rugby halfback.

Hana snuck around behind him, squeaking as he spun and his fingers closed around the hem of her tee shirt. “I want to know!” she growled, her throat closing around the words. Logan’s teeth clamped hard together as he increased his grip on her tee shirt. He reeled her in, centimetre by centimetre. “One peep!” Hana begged as she crashed against his chest. “One little teensy weensy peep.”

“Why?” Logan lowered his chin as his arms enclosed her. Her wriggling made no difference to his grip. “Tell me why?”

Hana stopped fighting him and relaxed. The question permeated her desire to sneak up on Sally and find her in yet another compromising situation. Perhaps she wouldn’t care, but the urge to embarrass or humiliate her burned in Hana’s gut. So, she said it, the word tumbling over her tongue and lips. The cool breeze snatched it and tossed it over the mountain’s imposing crest. “Revenge,” she admitted. “I just want one moment of superiority over her.” Her shoulders sagged. “Maybe it’s not about her at all. I think we’re back to me, never feeling good enough.”

Logan pushed out his bottom lip and studied her through narrowed eyes. He ran his left hand along her arm until his fingers linked through hers. “Okay,” he said, his voice a low rumble in the darkness. He inhaled and stared off into the distance for long enough to confuse Hana about his meaning. Then his other hand snaked beneath her tumbled hair until his thumb caressed her cheek. "Hana," he said, his tone serious. "I'll go anywhere with you and do whatever you need me to do. I just need you to understand why you're asking."

She nodded. Her quest seemed less important somehow. What did it matter if Sally ran a brothel in the derelict building? She could entertain the entire island and catch every disease under the sun. Hana would still fly off into the distance with her husband and forget she existed. "You're right," she conceded. "Her actions won't impact our lives. This holiday experience is just a blip, an interlude. I'll still need to go home and face my demons. The cops haven't caught my attacker, so she's out there somewhere, biding her time to blow up my life again." She shrugged and squeezed his fingers. "Revenge is ugly and I'm better than this. Let's go back to the bike. Who should we talk to about Mabel? Sergeant Wally George?" She said his name with disdain. He hadn't admitted to his tryst with Hallie, but she knew in her gut she'd hit on the truth. She considered Mary, the pastor's wife, and sighed. "I've thought of just the person to tell," she realised. The heaviness in her heart lightened, allowing more oxygen to soothe her mind.

"That's great," Logan said. Hana sensed his smile through the darkness, his approval like nectar to her soul. He squeezed her fingers and led her back onto the road. "Let's go check out this spooky house."

"Wait, what?" Hana demanded. "Aren't we going back to fetch the bike?"

"Yeah." He nodded, a calm, definitive movement. "But you said you wanted revenge. I only asked for a reason, and that's as good as any."

Hana gaped for a moment and her eyes widened. "Ooh," she said. Her gaze raked the pebbles of grit beneath her feet. "You just reminded me of something."

Logan's cowboy boots ground against the road as he shifted to study her. He didn't speak, allowing her a moment to process the elusive thought. Hana stared at the floor until it came to her. "Craig said that," she mused. "I watched him take what I'm sure was a bundle of fake money from the cubby beneath our villa. Jared saw what he did and Craig said, 'This is as good a place as any.'" She wiped a hand across her mouth and frowned at Logan. "What did that mean? What's so good about the cubby underneath a random villa on the resort? Why share the existence of the cash with Jared, but not with his wife?"

"Sally might know about it," Logan reasoned. "They might both keep their dodgy stuff there."

Hana shook her head. "No. The pastor's granddaughter knows Craig circulates the fake cash. The community is searching for a culprit and he's right under their nose."

"But Sally pointed the finger at us." Logan shrugged his shoulders. "Isn't that protecting her and Craig's interests?"

Hana inhaled and drew her lips away from her teeth. "No. That was pure revenge. I saw it in her face. She hates whatever she sees in our relationship. That's why she climbed into bed with you. I went out for over an hour. She had that whole time to visit you and do her worst, but she made sure I'd arrive back and find her in position. She set me up."

Logan grinned. "You don't think she fancied a piece of me, then?" He clamped his teeth down over his lower lip and pressed his free hand to his chest. "I'm gutted."

Hana snorted. "No, actually. I think she had the sense to know you wouldn't touch her with a barge pole. It was all for my benefit. She watched me leave with the lawyer and knew our discussion wouldn't take more than an hour. Despite all the secrecy, I bet the locals know about the bar in the hills. Maybe she's the only female member who Charlie spoke about.

The bar man could have called her to let her know we'd left."

"Long shot," Logan agreed. "But possible." He jerked his head towards the dilapidated building not ringed by the chain-link fence. "Only one thing for it," he concluded. "We need to see for ourselves."

66

Conspiracy - kotivaka

They reached the nearest corner of the sprawling structure when another engine sounded. Logan swore and pulled Hana into an overgrown flower bed at the rear of the section. She struggled to right herself and peeked through closed, bobbing flower heads as they danced in the stiff breeze. A heavy vehicle rounded the last bend and navigated the popping gravel, the driver opting for sidelights instead of full headlamps. It coasted to a stop at the bottom of the rickety porch steps. The ratcheting of the handbrake echoed in the silence. The driver cut the engine and emerged from the cab, slamming the door closed behind him.

Hana held her breath as he tucked his shirt into his jeans. Muscles bulged beneath the fabric, and he held the confident stance of a boxer. Hana kept her body still, forcing her eyes closed against a bug which chanced a dash across her cheek before plummeting off her nose and into her lap. Logan shifted beside her. She sensed him readying himself to defend their position, sizing up the opposition and already sure of how he'd put him down.

But the other man set off up the steps. He didn't bother to lock his vehicle, taking more care over his footing than studying his surroundings. He rapped on the thin board hiding the glass of the front door and waited, his soles setting off a series of worrying pops on the borer beetle eaten porch.

The door opened inward with a long creak. Hana leaned sideways, pressing her weight into her right wrist. She ached to identify the person occupying the house, but Logan nudged her other elbow. When she glanced at him in annoyance, he shook his head. She lifted her hand, only then discovering the crisp packet stuck to her palm. Its plaintive rustle hadn't featured in her need to see beyond the front door. Her muscles trembled with equal parts excitement and fear. "Sorry," she mouthed, realising how much better her husband appeared to be at snooping.

Low voices issued from the narrow alcove which placed the door within its protective canopy. Both held a gravelled male quality. Hana's lips twisted and misgivings tortured her natural sense of curiosity. Perhaps she didn't wish to see Sally on her back for multiple men. She turned to speak to Logan, but he shook his head again. The front door closed with a decisive click. He leaned close so he could whisper into her ear. "We can move around the building." His breath tickled her cheek, making her want to swat at him. Irritation prickled at the back of her throat at his calm assumption of command. "We might find a crack in a board to peer through." He rose to a crouch, using both hands to balance. Yet still, his movements appeared graceful. She realised her mistake of setting the hunter after her prey. Logan Du Rose wouldn't stop until he caught it.

Hana tugged on his wrist. "That's the man who visited our villa earlier," she whispered. "The one with the pool guy."

Logan nodded. "Yeah. The dude from the night market." He set off without waiting for her reply.

Hana tried to copy his silent movements, releasing a grunt of alarm as a succession of woody Cape Daisy stems snagged her plimsolls and caused her to pitch forward onto her elbows. She forced herself up, bent at the waist, and followed his loping gait.

The tradesman who boarded up the derelict building must have invoiced the hospital by the quantity of nails instead of by the hour. He or she had used at least ten where one would have sufficed. Hana reached Logan as he studied the dull silver head of a nail intended to hold up roof joists. He pointed at it and wrinkled his nose. A simple tack would have clasped the board to the frame without difficulty. But the glazier had used nails longer than her middle finger, judging by the bent one abandoned on the jutting windowsill. Hana lifted her index finger to touch the smooth head, but Logan caught her hand and folded it into his palm. Fingerprints, she realised too late. Touch nothing unless absolutely unavoidable. He'd entertained a reconnaissance mission, not one which resulted in them facing opposite walls of a jail cell again.

They circled the building in an anticlockwise motion, stopping at each windowsill to search for a viewing point. The heady scent of decayed vegetation shrouded the structure. Hana's growing desire to cough signified an infestation of black mildew within the fabric of the property. She covered her mouth with her hand, pausing at intervals to banish the familiar sensation of choking rising from deep in her chest. Logan made many forays ahead of her, always returning within moments. "I've found a gap." He lowered his face and spoke against her cheek, pulling her against his side as he squatted on his haunches. Heat rose from his exertion, accompanied by the familiar musk of his shower gel, which overpowered every other smell. Hana ran her fingers over his strong shoulders and experienced a dart of desire which launched itself from her navel and plunged into her groin.

The exercise seemed at once futile and pointless. Her interest in Sally's downfall winked out like a spent bulb. They were leaving in less than twenty-four hours. The woman could go to hell with her insatiable libido, her fake money, and her sham marriage. Hana pressed her lips over Logan's, registering his blink of surprise. Though her conservatism had pushed their early years of love making into the bedroom, Logan's infectious need to court danger had driven them into far more hazardous places since. A bush track, their SUV, the bathrooms at the hotel, the hay barn, most of the paddocks on the mountain, and the kitchen counter at their house. Hana had discovered she quite enjoyed the riskier venues. As her need for Logan superseded any juvenile desire for one-upmanship of Sally, she experienced an overwhelming urge to bed down in the neglected flowerbed and kiss him. "I love you," she whispered. She twisted her body to face him fully, twigs and bark digging through the fabric of her jeans and deadening her knees. Her lips pressed against his, her fingers twisting together around his neck. Her breasts pressed against his powerful pectorals, her mind already running wild with the glorious promise of him naked.

"And I love you too."

Hana sensed his mouth lifting at the corners in a smile. She pushed her tongue against the seam and satisfaction sent a fanfare to her brain as his lips parted. Her eager fingers slipped beneath the waistband of his jeans and she tugged at the hem of his shirt. Warm skin acted as a balm to her soul and she shuddered as her cool palms coasted upward from his waist. She pushed her hands further under his shirt until they reached the firm plates of muscle covering his shoulder blades. Then the fun ended.

"Hana!" Logan breathed into her right ear. He kissed her soft cheek and groaned as desire warred with good sense. "Much as I love the idea of this," he whispered, "it's terrible timing."

Hana's shoulders sloped in defeat. Humiliation tapped a familiar condemnation into her mind and, for a moment, she fell silent. Logan tilted her chin with his index finger, forcing her to meet his gaze. "Something I didn't think to mention earlier," he whispered. His warm breath smelled of coffee and minty gum. "That guy carries a Glock 27 in an ankle holster. I noticed the bulge under his pants. Gantry Hosking is involved in this, and he carries a gun in his waistband. I don't fancy getting my nuts shot off in a moment of happiness."

Hana's lips formed an 'o' of dismay. "Right." She drew out the vowel as her mind scrambled for a retort. "You didn't think to mention it."

Logan shrugged. "I noticed it outside the supermarket. His shirt lifted as he climbed into his truck. He seemed like a nice guy who wanted to thank us for helping Jared. I had no reason to believe he'd ever turn his weapons on either of us." His lips arched downwards. "It seemed good information to know, in case we needed a weapon."

"But you think it's worth mentioning right now?"

Logan tipped his head sideways and narrowed his eyes. His grey irises glimmered in the silver light of the moon. "Sally isn't holding court inside this building, babe."

"You looked?" Hana's interest piqued. Her eyes widened, and she pushed herself into a crouch. "I wanna see."

Logan growled low in his throat. "Let's drive back to the villa," he urged. He snaked a hand around her waist, his fingers caressing her through the soft fabric of her tee shirt. "We can find another venue." His mouth twitched on one side, his gaze heady with promise.

But the bug had seized Hana again, and she dipped her chin. "Okay," she breathed. "But just one little peek."

67

Alarm - ārangaranga

The narrow view through the crack in a board offered an aspect of a darkened hallway. A wide hole in the inner glass allowed foetid air to ooze from the derelict building. The gap appeared jagged, the original knot in the board shrunken and gone. The wood had split outward from two points around its circumference, creating something wide enough to post a novel through if angled to fit. But the broken pane behind it shrank the aperture to little more than the width of a beer mat. Hana shivered, her enthusiasm doused by disappointment as she saw nothing unusual in the wood-panelled walls which decorated the interior. She pressed her eye to the hole again and held her breath.

"Where are they?" She turned and mouthed the words to Logan, who shifted to face her. He shook his head, keen to bear her away from the danger he sensed. His unease communicated itself to her, and Hana's heart rate ticked upward. "I don't see anyone. We know there are three people in this building."

Logan gave a long blink. He set his jaw as though realising she wouldn't leave if he didn't help her work it all out. He nudged her aside and peered through the crack. "I don't know," he concluded with a frown. "Wait here." He lifted his index finger and jabbed it towards her. Hana pursed her lips, recognising the strength of the command. She nodded, not wanting to relinquish control of the tiny viewing aperture. Then Logan disappeared, his long shape blending with the shadows stretching out from beneath the eaves of the building.

He returned in just under a minute, approaching Hana from the other direction. She screwed her face into a pout at his risk taking. He'd traversed the most vulnerable side of the building, which housed the front door. "There's a window on the gable end," he whispered into her ear. "They didn't bother boarding it when they abandoned the building. It's ajar. I can stand on the balcony rail outside the back door and crawl through it."

Hana's mouth dropped open in astonishment. "But why? You want to drive back to the villa? You said they had guns."

Logan shrugged. "I'll do it if you want me to. If it's going to eat you up so you can't think about anything else, I'll do it."

A bluff, Hana thought. He was calling her bluff. He'd spelled out the risks and knew she'd decline the offer. She bowed her head. "It's not worth it," she conceded.

Disappointment filled her chest with yet another failure. This had no relevance in her life, but still it piled its weight on top of the rest. The mountain of defeat wobbled and threatened to topple. But Hana's mistake had been allowing Logan to see her reaction and weigh it before she could consolidate her emotions. He pressed a kiss to her temple and blended into the darkness.

A gasp escaped Hana's lips as a whoosh. She clapped a hand over her mouth as her heart rate increased, thrumming a heavy beat in her chest. She'd driven her husband into her own futile madness and the weight of guilt seemed to bow her head towards the ground. The mental processing took too long. It gave Logan a head start as he circled the building. Hana felt her way behind him, the dead stalks of forgotten blooms tearing at her fingers as she crab-walked in his wake. A gentle scuffling from the bush in front of her culminated in an indignant squeak from an unidentifiable night creature disturbed for the third time. Hana gave the bush a wide berth, risking a foray away from the side of the building and placing herself in jeopardy. It would only take one occupant to skip down the front porch steps to spot her before she could run aground again.

Hana darted back into the flowerbed, her body listing and lurching with the ungainliness of her movements. She tripped over a root, which her bare palms failed to notify her of, and crashed face first into the dirt. Earth filled her mouth, coating her tongue with its horrid mustiness. She swallowed something which lodged in the back of her throat. A cough built, and she fought to control it. She jammed her mouth closed to avoid aspirating the crumbled loam. Wiping her nose on the hem of her tee shirt, Hana dislodged leaves and soil fragments. The moon shifted from behind a low cloud and revealed a grey stain across the light fabric. A gnawing sensation occupied the pit of her stomach, understanding her face plant had robbed her of any chance to stop Logan.

She took more care of her progress, the cough still burning in her chest. Spitting produced sound which seemed to carry in the stillness of the bush. So, she resorted to dribbling grit from between her lips as it rose to the forefront of her mouth. Hana paused at the far corner of the house, listening for sound before peeking around the splintered siding. The angle of the rising moon cast long shadows under the eaves. They stretched across the scrubby lawn and sent their long fingers into the fringe of the bush. She needed to crawl closer.

As Hana poised to move by building momentum in her aching legs, she heard a noise which caused her to halt. She tipped forward, her sore palms landing again in the soil. Tiny cuts set up myriad warning stings. It came again, a long, low shushing noise, like something heavy dragged across a concrete floor. A pulse beat in her neck, picking up speed as she imagined Logan's prone body at the mercy of the building's occupants. He'd said they might have guns. Her only comfort was the knowledge she hadn't heard shots.

Hana scrabbled in the dirt, pressing her fingers beneath the decayed runners forming a skirt around the pilings. She seized a length of rotten wood, which measured no longer than her forearm. Raising it, she hefted its weight, finding it less heavy than expected. Dried and crusted, it would smash against anything hard, crumbling to pieces without effect. She tried again, her fingers closing around something more substantial. The brick slid free with a little prising, slipping back beneath the siding with a sigh. Dehydrated earth piled back to fill its resting place with enthusiasm. Hana examined the split-brick in the moon's reluctant light in the seconds before it hid behind the next scudding cloud. Left over from a forgotten building project, it had slept under the house for decades. Soil cascaded through the holes formed in its centre. Hana closed her fingers around it and pictured her options. If the dragging sound related to Logan's comatose body, she could smash the brick against the side of the building and cause a disturbance. But what then? She had no weapon and no phone to raise the alarm. And who could she call?

A sound reached her ears, the gentle plop of something heavy hitting the earth. A tiny vibration reached her through her knees. She turned back the way she'd come, noticing something glinting in the dullness. Leaves and twigs obscured a bright light as a screen lit their shadowy undersides. Hana crawled towards the glow, brows narrowed in concentration as dirt lodged against the inside of her lips and crackled against her teeth like space dust. She dodged the hazardous section, which caused her earlier downfall, and arrived beside the eerie torch just as the light winked out.

Her fingers closed around the phone and she snatched it up. Shallow breaths broke free of her lungs, forcing her taste buds to acknowledge the dust on her tongue. She shielded the phone with her other hand as though attempting to blanket the light. The screen activated again at her touch of the side button and she held her breath. She input the code with a trembling index finger. Logan had opened a text to her and typed into the box, before slotting the device through the broken window and out through the board. A lack of signal meant he couldn't send the missive, but he'd known she'd find the device.

'I'm okay,' the message said. *'But you will not believe this.'*

68

Wait - tāpapa

Logan didn't emerge from the building. Hana gripped his phone in white-knuckled fingers, hearing the muted dragging sound more often as she crouched beside the building. An ear-splitting screech accompanied another round of noise. Hana closed her eyes and pictured the scene, pushing her mind towards scenarios. "Wood," she whispered to herself. "Wood dragged across concrete."

Not bodies then. Not Logan. She clutched the phone tighter, as though it represented a lifeline to him. The fingers of her other hand wielded the brick. As the sound grew almost continual, she cast around her for a safer hiding place. Her position against the right side of the building made her a target for another set of arriving headlamps. She paused for long enough to hear nothing unusual around her. The rustle of bush creatures and the lazy call of a morepork formed a gentle symphony which reminded her of home. Drawing in a giant breath filled with mildew spores, dust and fear, Hana dived across the lawn and hurled herself beneath the wide leaves of a kawakawa bush. There she stayed, waiting as her watch hands spun past one hour and then two.

Hana remained within the shadows of her chosen bush, resisting the urge to move even as her limbs protested against her stillness. She kept the phone face down in the dirt beside her, wishing it had a signal so she could call for help. But call who? Logan had trespassed onto hospital property. They were in the wrong.

Now and then, she brushed her fingers over the brick as though seeking a resolution from its rough surface. It offered her little comfort against a gun or a man with muscles sculpted upon muscles.

She closed her eyes and focused on her breathing, settling herself as she remained in her awful limbo. A bang around the two-hour mark caused her to jump and set the delicate heart-shaped leaves rustling and quivering around her. The heavyset man she'd hidden from earlier stepped onto the porch. He lit a cigarette and creaked down the rickety porch steps. Cumbersome combat boots poked from beneath the hem of his jeans. Logan's earlier revelation made Hana peer harder at him. The darkness exposed only his silhouette as he flicked on a torch and cast the beam around the building's exterior. The light bounced off the white flecked paint, and Hana noticed a tell-tale bulge at his left ankle. He scoured the area around the building as though searching for something. He stalked close to the slatted walls and swung his flashlight in wide arcs around him.

Hana held her breath as a spray of glittering white orbs backlit her vision. She jammed her eyes closed, praying the beam hadn't revealed her to him. She bowed her head, relying on the low visibility to mask her vibrant hair colour. A fleeting thought recalled the foxes of her childhood and the ghostlike quality of their pelt in the darkness. She didn't wish to put it to the test, her lungs protesting the carbon dioxide lodged in her chest as her body stole the oxygen. The flash light bounced away and then back again.

"Is that you, Po?" The man's voice held a growling quality and Hana's chest locked. She ached to release the breath but held onto it, knowing when she let it go its whoosh would wake the island. He'd seen her. Despite her best efforts, he must have seen her.

The beam scoured the scrubby grass in front of her and just as she figured her head would explode from lack of air, a dull click sounded from within the building. Another creak and a hushed whisper. "There's something outside." He qualified his expedition with a hint of guilt. "The wind is getting up again. It's forecast to turn nasty." The orange pin light from the lit cigarette danced behind his back, the real excuse for his foray outside. The other voice spoke again, the hint of a squeak in the low tones. Sally.

The man's shoulders drooped. "We don't know they've arrived," he said, his tone betraying his uncertainty. "It could be a coincidence. We shouldn't panic." His flash light bobbed across the grass and away from Hana, flaring up the narrow steps to the front door. Like a naughty child, he stubbed out his cigarette on the sole of his boot before shoving it into his pocket. Hana counted herself through an agonising four more seconds until he bounded onto the porch and into the house, the beam swinging before him.

She exhaled with relief as the front door clicked and darkness reclaimed the copse. Her lungs ached and her heart pounded as her body searched for a use for the spike of cortisol and adrenaline. Clutching her chest and shoving her fallen fringe from her sweating face, she worried for Logan. He'd entered the house to satiate her curiosity, like a schoolboy earning her approval. It seemed ridiculous in the retelling. She imagined herself confessing to Bodie that her husband risked life and limb because she believed a woman she disliked might run a brothel in a derelict building in the middle of an island. Closing her eyes, she pictured his raised eyebrow of disbelief and the inevitable glib comment. 'So, during your mini-break, he watched porn just for your benefit?'

The highest leaves and branches in the canopy bent and twisted in the uncharacteristic icy breeze, which chilled the night air. The man had spoken the truth. It could turn nasty. Though she'd registered no weather forecasts since arriving on Rarotonga, nature had broadcast its own intentions. The bite in the air contained water vapour. She pressed her trembling fingers together and dropped them onto her thighs. Her calves and ankles complained, tingles and darts of pain alerting her brain to their compression. Hana collapsed onto her left hip, her Achilles tendons at first reluctant to lengthen and release her feet into their normal position. Ragged breaths shuddered through her chest, her lungs still panicking about the possibility the next one might not arrive. She gulped air through her open mouth, picturing Logan's regal features and pleading with a silent God for his safety.

But by the third hour, Logan still hadn't emerged.

Hana pushed herself deeper into the foliage, using the giant fronds as cover in case the man returned to his feigned search to justify finishing his cigarette. She resisted the natural urge to fold her legs beneath her, instead sitting on her bottom and stretching them in the undergrowth. The next while held an unknown danger, and she didn't want to run on cramped, seized muscles.

As the minutes ticked by and midnight passed, Hana strained to listen to the surrounding sounds. The darkness hindered her vision and she couldn't rely on her sight to warn her of a potential threat until too late. The bullish man had responded to a noise, and it occurred to Hana that Logan may have caused it. She tuned into the familiar bush music, filtering out the chirp of nearby crickets and the ever present clucking hens. She caught it then, low but distinct, the female voice coming from deep inside the house.

Hana leaned forward, reluctant to leave the safety of her hidey. She shut off the mental queue of other sounds, waiting for identification and focussing with superhuman strength. The occupants of the house kept their voices below normal volume, but Hana heard the heavyset man's protest from inside the house. "I heard a noise," he hissed. The dragging sounds seemed louder. Wood scraping against wood this time. "I went to investigate. You wanted security, and that's what I'm doing. Guarding!" He spat the last word and the female voice rose.

"You left the front door open! Anyone could have walked straight in! I've told you, they're here. They found Mabel. We need to clear up and leave the island."

"Are we done yet?" The other male voice held a note of tiredness, as though he'd reached the end of a long rope. Hana squeezed her eyes closed and recognised the deep tones. The man who cleaned the pool at the Paradise Villas had driven the red ute through the hospital site to the derelict house.

The voices ceased. Hana stared at the building's faded slats and frowned. The dragging sounds continued, degenerating to a dull scratching. It reminded Hana of wooden crates wrapped in packing tape being dragged across floorboards. She shook her head in confusion, but acknowledged her gratitude that it didn't sound like a man's limp body being hauled anywhere. The house sported wooden floors. She'd seen them through the peep hole into the lobby. Closing her eyes, she imagined the layout of the building and figured perhaps the threesome had moved into the kitchen at the back of the house to drag their boxes and argue. She shook her head. That made no sense. Where had they been until now? She and Logan had skirted the entire building and seen no light from beneath any of the boards. Not even the bluish glow of a phone screen.

A gnat buzzed near her right ear, its movements lazy as it settled against her cheek. She fought the urge to swipe at it until it quit and buzzed off. She gasped as something crawled around inside her jeans and sank tiny pincers into her left buttock. So much for the bug repellent she'd covered herself in before leaving the villa. She wiggled around until the eerie sensation ceased, hoping she'd squashed it in her pants and dreaded finding it later.

Hana brushed her fingers over her face, gasping in shock as a hard bodied insect detached from her forehead and plunged past her left eye. She stifled a scream behind her palm. "Logan, where are you?" she whined to herself. "Where the hell are you?"

She sat in the dirt for another hour. The front door opened to reveal muted lights moving through the building, but she discerned no more sounds of heavy items shifting into position. And still Logan didn't emerge.

Bush insects turned her tender flesh into their supper, ignoring the stinky repellent as though she hadn't bothered. The whirr of heavy duty fans carried through the darkness from the hospital's main building as it filtered the chemical, bacteria laden heat on the wards and pumped it into the night. Hana shifted position again, mindful of her need to run if the necessity arose. She glanced back through the trees and saw the light distortion from the hospital stretching into the Payne's Grey sky. She blew out a frustrated breath, not sure how much longer to wait. They hadn't planned for this eventuality and it left her stranded and unsure.

A surprising number of cars drove along Sanatorium Road to the hospital's reception. Hana's heightened sense of alarm warned her of every single one. A scooter rasped in the distance, its protracted buzzing ceasing with an abruptness which made Hana concerned for the rider. Waves hissed onto the beach in the bay beyond Ara Metua and Ara Tapu Roads, its relentlessness a paradox to her statuesque state. And the breeze picked up until it bent the swaying coconut trees in a slam dance fit for a heavy metal concert.

Hana waited. And waited. And waited.

Still, Logan didn't come.

69

To drag along - kikakika

It would later seem ridiculous to admit she fell asleep. A thing of shame, of failing to guard her husband's back. Hana would only ever tell one person about her emotional bankruptcy. But fall asleep, she did. The constant alarm, the worry at every new sound, and the fear for Logan's safety should have kept Hana awake. Instead, it drove her to the point of catatonic exhaustion. Her brain flicked the switch for her.

Hana woke with a gasp just before dawn, the result of a sharp nip to her neck. An earwig slithered into the front of her tee shirt and nipped again, its pincers producing the sensation of stabbing needles. She groaned as she lifted the hem of her tee shirt and raised the underwires of her bra, slapping at her chest until the squished body cascaded into her lap. She flicked it away with a squeak, confused about her odd location and the crick in her neck. Her fingers ached with cold, their movements laboured as she fought to push her tee shirt hem back into the waistband of her jeans. Her full bladder complained, and a shiver radiated out from the centre of her being to occupy every muscle.

The confusion melted into horror as she roused enough to remember why she'd spent the night sitting in the dirt. The cloying taste on her tongue sent warnings of nausea to her brain. She ran soil-stained knuckles over her gritty lips. An eerie grey light oozed from the other side of the mountain, chasing the moon higher in the sky. Branches creaked and groaned, making her wonder that she'd slept at all. Her lips cracked when she muttered to herself, dehydration and the chill air working against her. "I need to find Logan," she said, her voice croaky and loud in the stillness. Even the birds had silenced as though in expectation of some coming disaster.

Hana scrabbled beneath the fallen leaves and silt to find Logan's phone. She shoved it into the back pocket of her jeans after checking the screen. No calls, no messages because no signal met the inaudible pings of distress it sent into the ether. She hefted the brick with no logical reason other than it seemed the right thing to do. A weapon, albeit a poor one. "What would Logan tell me to do?" she asked herself, pushing her aching body upright. The rustling she stirred with the kawakawa leaves hardly registered amid the gale, which tossed them around in spirals of chaos.

As though in response to a silent communication from her husband, Hana skirted the bush to where she'd last seen the two trucks and Sally's car. She remained behind the tallest of the bushes, keeping out of sight as the grey light failed to banish the shadows from around her. She stumbled and blundered through the undergrowth, keeping the roof-line of the boarded-up house in her peripheral vision. The chain-link fence rails surrounding the other three buildings leaned at odd angles against the pressure of the fierce wind, which rattled the sections like a metallic cackle. Coconut leaves conspired overhead like gossips in a school playground, trunks arched against the force of nature which bent them into elbows. Hana held on to anything she could to avoid being expelled into the clearing. Her hair whipped her cheeks and blinded her with its frenzied zig zagging.

Hana clung to the more solid girth of a totara tree, knowing from experience it would snap before it gave in to the compelling jig commanded by the wind. She pushed her hair from her face and surveyed the cul-de-sac to the left of the house. All three vehicles remained. So, they'd continued through the night, doing the strange and secret work which required a man to travel from New Zealand to guard it.

She worried about Logan, telling herself he'd escape as soon as the coast cleared. Her bladder's urgency increased from her walking around. She pressed herself deeper into the bush to relieve herself, never taking her gaze from the haphazardly parked vehicles. Hana used a dew dampened dock leaf to clean her hands before resuming her watching, focussing her attention on the peeling paint of the front door.

Day broke without fanfare, adding little to the eerie light. Heavy clouds gathered overhead, filled with foreboding. The mountain towered over the island like the head and shoulders of a giant, a mop of angry black cloud-curls whirling around it. The chaotic wind ruffled them into confusion, squally and furious as they tossed in every direction. Hana's hair lifted from her head as though electrocuted, the wind unable to choose its final destination. A fine rain soaked her clothing in minutes, released as delicate drops almost invisible to the eye. Her watch marked time passing as the new day failed to distinguish its hours by the light. A purple murkiness shrouded the island, and the rain increased in volume.

Hana stayed beneath her totara tree, eager to avoid the bulk of the deluge. Drips collected at the ends of the spiny needles and poured onto her head. She stared at the front door of the derelict house with such focus, she failed to move fast enough when it flew open. She gasped and slipped behind the hefty trunk, splinters from its rough surface pushing beneath her cold finger pads. A shiver ran through her as Sally emerged first. The medical scrubs appeared rumpled, dust accumulated in the creases. Her right pants leg had edged up her calf to create a lopsided effect, as though she had one leg longer than the other. She yawned and scrubbed her knuckles over her eyes. Her other hand towed a brown suitcase which followed her out, its wheels releasing a low rumble against the rickety porch.

The man who'd referred to himself as a guard stepped out behind her. He lifted the suitcase in one movement, sweeping it into his arms without effort. "I'll put this in your car," he said in his gravelled voice. "Will you give it to Po?"

Sally sighed. Hana peeked from behind the tree as she ran tired fingers through her hair. She glanced up at something overhead before using the back of her hand to wipe a drip from her forehead. "I will never understand why Hosking involved him, Henk. It doubled the risk."

The pool man emerged into the half-light, scrubbing at his eyes with his knuckles. "Because he got suspicious about the boat. That's why. He forced us to buy his silence."

The heavyset man released a low growl. "The stupid boat is the riskiest part of this whole venture. That's gonna come back to bite us in the ass."

"Na." His companion disagreed. "The fake cash will do that." He turned his feet in Sally's direction, though he sent his raised eyebrow towards his heavier-set friend. "That travel agent and her husband brought it onto the island. It's messed up all our plans." His gaze turned to Sally's profile and his fathomless pupils seemed to bore holes in her left cheek. Oblivious, she tugged open the boot of her vehicle and stepped back to allow Henk to dump the suitcase inside it. The leather bulged, the zipper resembling lips barely pressed closed around a damaging revelation. Sally slammed the boot lid over it and leaned against the bumper.

"Are we good?" she demanded. "Did you find out where that bang came from near the back of the house? Because I need to sort out the old lady. They'd put her to bed when I got there last night. She'd missed her meds and started talking. I can't risk that again, not when we're so close."

"It's just the wind on a loose board. Hey, how do I get my share out of there?" The pool man took a step towards her, flailing his right arm behind him towards the house. He'd seemed harmless while wielding his net full of vile things at the resort. But in this alternate setting, he appeared larger and more threatening. His brown irises flashed as Sally shrugged and turned towards her vehicle.

"Don't know, Ron," she said, her tone nonchalant. "But I suggest you do it before Henk torches the place. We've dragged enough pallet wood and plastic wrapping into the lobby to melt this site in five minutes."

"You promised we had more time," he urged. He stepped forward and grabbed Sally's right shoulder. She spun around under the force of his grip. A note of panic entered his voice. "You're all free and clear. I still have thousands to clean. You said we had longer. You promised you'd help me."

Sally lifted her hand and, with a deft, left-to-right movement, swiped the man's grasp from her shoulder. She caught the inside of his forearm with the side of her fist. "And whose fault is that, Ron? You had your chance," she hissed. The wind took her words and tossed them aside. They arrived at Hana's ears as a disjointed, warbling note. "We spread ours evenly. Henk's couriered almost one hundred and fifty-five grand back to New Zealand over the last year. That doesn't include what we've laundered locally. It's all sitting in the bank now, nice and clean. You didn't trust our methods. You wanted to find your own way." She jerked backwards as though her allegiance with him had been a temporary and distasteful thing. "That's just over sixty grand each for me and Henk that he's carried back to the mainland, minus flights and Po's fee. Nine thousand dollars every three weeks taken safely through customs, just under their maximum threshold."

Henk grinned. "Cash salary for security work on Rarotonga. Genius. The dogs flagged it every time, but the customs guys stopped counting it after the fifth trip. Genuine New Zealand dollars, which were all backed up by wage slips, just a little muddy from who knows what?"

"Drugs probably," Sally bit. "Or trafficking. We'll never know." She jabbed a sharp fingernail towards the pool man, the spikiness of her action betraying waning patience. "You had the same amount as us." She whirled away, her blonde hair lifting around her head like vipers on a gorgon. "You said you'd fix it. So now fix it."

"I thought we had longer," Ron whined again, following her to the driver's side of her car. "You shifted a heap of yours in Fiji and on the other Cook Islands. I bet you got rid of most of it by letting tourists draw cash on their credit cards at your resort. You need to help me."

"And why is that?" Sally demanded. She stuck her chin in the air and faced him, her breasts millimetres from his chest. "We knew they'd come after their cash eventually. Nobody loses a shipment like that and doesn't search for it. You understood that. It's not our fault you didn't plan for it. Why do I owe you anything?" She pressed her hands over her hips, all her angles jagged and harsh.

Ron leaned down and raised his voice, his shout causing Sally to stagger back against her open driver's door. "Because your husband screwed it up, didn't he? It's him who's passing the fake money all over the island. Him and his dimwit mate. And it's caused a chain reaction and messed up any chance of me getting my share out. Those tourists got arrested and now there's a judge, a lawyer, and a cop from the mainland asking questions. Because of your husband's sticky fingers."

A cop from the mainland. Hope budded in Hana's heart. Had Liza tipped off Bodie? But Hana quailed at the desperation in Ron's voice. It made him dangerous, catapulting him towards mania as he saw his dreams slipping away. By Sally's calculation, he'd had thousands of dollars to convert from dirty money to clean. They'd started with a fortune. Ninety thousand dollars seemed like a drop in the ocean compared to what they'd already shifted. She blinked at the memory of the sign on the reception door. Sally had given the dirty cash to unwitting tourists who'd paid her back on their credit cards. They'd legitimised her nefarious plan, probably paying interest on the transactions. The group had spread their activity over almost a year. And then Craig acquired his shipment of counterfeit cash three months ago. From Hallie and then Jared. That single act had tipped the balance.

Hana frowned as the trio argued in front of the house. The door slammed, and they didn't notice. Henk waded in on Sally's side and heads jerked and arms waved. The wind changed direction, skewering their words and tossing them aside. It seemed clear from her body language that Sally knew nothing of Craig's fake money. Her wild head shaking met Henk's awkward nod and Ron's angry gesticulation. And what had Hallie said the last time Hana saw her? *'Craig doesn't know the half of it.'* Which meant Hallie understood enough about Sally's illegal endeavour to believe Craig had no clue. Hana shook her head. What a mess.

She took a step backwards and her body shook with the impact of crashing into a hard object. A hand slid around her neck and clamped over her mouth. "Heard enough?" a harsh voice growled.

70

Murder - moeāana

The locking of Hana's lungs was immediate. She couldn't inhale with the large hand cupped over her mouth and nose. The faint scent of rubber mingled with that of fish, the mixture distasteful enough to make her recoil. Her crown smacked against something unyielding and her captor released a cry of pain. Sally and her companions looked across at Hana in a collective movement of jerking heads and widening eyes. Henk swore.

"How stupid are you?" the newcomer growled, lifting his voice to include them. His breath caressed Hana's right earlobe, but he didn't release her. Warm liquid seeped through her tee shirt and he spluttered at the end of his sentence. She'd made him bleed.

"What the hell?" Henk sounded aghast as he strode towards them, his bear paws folding around Hana's upper arm. He yanked her against his ribs, half turning her and threading his other hand around her throat. Her right shoulder reached only as far as his pectorals.

Hana's captor bent in half like an envelope. Blood dripped from a busted nose.

"Where is he?" Sally reached her at a run, her pupils tiny pinpricks in her blue irises. Her lips peeled back from her teeth like a snarling dog. Her fingers closed around Hana's upper arms, as though she sought to wrestle her away from Henk. Sharp nails dug into the soft flesh and Hana couldn't shake off her inflexible grip. Sally turned to look first at Henk and then at the other man. "These two travel as a pair," she stated, her tone choppy and agitated. "If she's here, then so is he." Her jaw flexed and her face tightened. "Who are you? Are you cops?"

Henk's voice rumbled through Hana's spine. "Gantry?" His breath ruffled the back of her hair. "Did you see him on your way up here? What do you need me to do?"

"Na, there's just her left. I dealt with her husband. Found him coming out of a window at the back of the house." He spoke to the scrubby grass, blood still soaking into the soil in heavy droplets. His clothing of three quarter length combat pants and a polo shirt stressed his grizzled appearance. Of them all, his hands belonged to a man used to salt water and the unforgiving grain of ropes. Black engine grease saturated the skin of his palms as he held up his right hand and waved it from side to side. “If he’s a cop, he’s a dead one now. I shot him straight through the chest. Give me a second,” he demanded. “She got me in the face real good.”

A flicker of satisfaction at his pain moved through Hana before the news about Logan hit her full in the solar plexus. She would claim Gantry’s broken nose as a victory despite the instinctive nature of the action. But Logan. Did he really just say he’d shot Logan? She needed to find her husband but had now missed her golden opportunity for escape. Had it ever really existed?

“What will we do with her?” Ron, the pool man, sauntered over with enough forced jauntiness to betray his anxiety. His gaze darted between the other men before settling on Hana. She discerned the pure fear in his expression. He’d got out of his depth and he knew it. “Look,” he said, his tone reasonable. He took a step towards her, close enough for Hana to notice the yellow flecks in his brown irises. Muscle rippled through the sleeves of his work shirt, *Paradise Villas* emblazoned across the right pectoral as a cheerful logo. “Why are you up here?” he demanded. Dropping his chin, he raised his eyebrows as though sending her a telepathic response which he expected her to parrot.

Hana swallowed as her mind searched for a plausible reply. She couldn't think of one.

"I saw the Harley," Hosking rasped. "It's parked down at the hospital."

"I never meant this to involve murder," Sally snapped. "But if you shot the guy, we'll need to get rid of her too now." The façade of geniality had never held much weight, but pure animosity replaced it. Sally cocked her head. "Why didn't we hear the shot from inside the house?"

Ron blanched, his complexion resembling raw chicken. "We did," he said, his brows drawing together. "Remember that loud noise? We thought the wind caused it."

Hana surveyed the group, and the desperation in Sally's expression caused her own mortality to wink back at her. These four individuals had come so far in their scam they wouldn't let anyone or anything ruin it now. This was game over for Hana and anyone else who got in their way. Her mind reached out to Logan, though slimy tendrils of fear sent it skittering away from the place where he should have been. "God," she breathed, unable to think of anything suitable to replace the arrow prayer. "God."

"We could fetch Po," Henk suggested, his sentence rising at the end as though with a forlorn hope. "Let him earn his keep."

"Na," Hosking replied, almost too fast. "We'll deal with her." He rose and used the hem of his polo shirt to wipe the blood from his nose. A trickle replaced what he removed and collected above his top lip.

Henk snorted. "What, another dementia candidate? How many more people can we shove in there before they get suspicious?"

"They're already asking questions," Sally bit. "It was a temporary solution which has gone on for too long. If that stupid Mary from the church hadn't found the old woman wandering on the beach, I could have kept her at the resort. Her charitable concern forced us to send her to the dementia unit. It exposed us too much."

"So deal with her now!" Hosking leaned towards Sally, his neck outstretched like an emu and his chin jutting forward. "Before she talks about the boat again." If Hana had imagined the other woman possessed any authority in this mess, she wiped the thought from the chalk board of ideas in her brain. The queen bee illusion had faded from Sally's visage like a waning moon. She fell into place as a worker in this twisted hive mind.

Questions about Logan's plight licked at the fringes of Hana's sanity and she pushed them away. If she waited, it might not be real. Logan would come for her. He always did. But grief might come first, and she'd danced with it before. Hana swallowed the pain blossoming out from a void in her core. It choked her, and she coughed. Hosking's blood soaked through her tee shirt at the back, but it seemed to go through her body and emerge at the front. Hana peered down at her neckline, confused at the damp lines there. Tears dripped from her chin. She hadn't realised she was crying.

"We could burn early?" Ron suggested. He offered Hana a glance which contained a hint of apology as shock consumed her. She shivered as her knees knocked together, incapable of holding her upright. "We spent the night sawing up the pallets and stacking them beside the stairwell. We could sit her in the plastic we removed from the bundles. It's just ready to go. All it needs is a match." His Adam's apple bobbed. "Help me to get my backpack out. It's mainly one hundred-dollar bills. I kept a couple of twenties back, though. For just in case."

Hana swallowed. Her quick calculations hadn't given her an accurate estimate of their fraud. She'd based the numbers on what she overheard Sally and Henk saying they'd taken into New Zealand. But more existed. Way more. She focused on the possible revenue of credit card transactions to distract her brain from calculating real life. And the possibility of spending the rest of it without Logan.

Hosking snorted. "You still have that?" he scoffed. "Why haven't you laundered it yet?"

Henk shook his head. "We just had that conversation," he said, his tone dull. "It's too late now."

Too late now. A voice echoed in Hana's brain and the sentence repeated on a loop. *Too late now.*

"No." Ron backed away from the group, his head shaking from side to side. "I'll fetch it. Dump it in my truck. It's fine. I'll deal with it."

Hosking rolled his eyes. The spite in his expression added to the boulder in Hana's chest made from dust and rubble. She suffered a further moment of alarm, as though a secret voice had whispered a warning into her soul. Ron, the fire starter. Did Hosking intend for him to emerge from the building unscathed? The darkness in his eyes suggested his plans did not include the foolish man who'd cleaned pools and guarded fake cash. Fake cash. Why were they going to so much trouble for counterfeits so poor that Logan had spotted one at a single glance? Logan. He shot Logan. Hana bent double, and Henk allowed the movement. She clutched her stomach and closed her mind.

Ron scurried up the front steps and into the house. His shoes slapped against the boards like drum beats. He dragged a backpack from the wood panelled lobby and towed it across the porch. Hana had envisaged a child's day pack, but the bulging sack belonged to a serious hiker. As tall as Sally's suitcase, it sagged towards the bottom like a melting snowman. After bumping it down the first step, Ron halted and turned, glaring at the red fabric in confusion. "Wait!" he cried. His knees hit the step and his fingers scrabbled to find the zipper. A rasping sound followed as he drove the zip around the top edge. His voice rose higher, a screech of dismay. "It's gone!" he yelled. "Someone's taken my cash. There's less than half of it here, but I packed it myself." His bemused gaze turned towards Sally and Henk.

Hosking snorted, his patience shortening by the second. He gave off a dangerous aura like a sparking electrical wire in the moments before it breaks free of its housing and begins its cycle of thrashing. "What a loser," he hissed. "Come on, let's get going."

Henk placed a heavy hand on the back of Hana's neck and forced her upright. He pinched the delicate tendons at the base of her skull and she cried out in pain. "Do as you're told then," he barked, as though justifying his cruelty. She lifted both hands behind her and snatched at his wrists. The action bent her body in a backwards arch.

"Put her in the house," Sally snarled. "Let's torch it with her and Ron inside it."

"It's too early," Henk complained. He sighed. "It's all too early. We're not ready. But seeing as the owners of the cash have arrived, we'll burn it just as the cyclone hits. Less evidence in the aftermath. We can't start it yet. We need the fire service incapacitated by the weather." He edged Hana from beneath the protection of the tree canopy and the wind seemed to delight with its new toy. It circled her legs like an excited puppy, pummelling her knees from the side and forcing her against Henk. He grunted and squeezed her neck, steering her towards the knot of vehicles at the end of the cul-de-sac. "Ignore Ron," he growled. "He's had a year to plan. Put her in the boot."

"The suitcase is in there. She won't fit," Sally complained. She stretched an arm around Gantry Hosking, her expression softening to one of sympathy. "You okay, hun?" she asked in a baby voice. The shrillness of the pitch ruined the effect, but he didn't seem to notice.

"Hurts," he grumbled. "This has got too messy. Let's head for the boat and get out of here before the worst of the weather arrives. We can drop her over the side when we reach deep water. Her husband is too heavy. But the building will bury him. It'll take weeks to identify his body from dental records." His gaze slid sideways to Hana and her chest clenched, though she wondered why. Apart from her babies, safely far away, what did she have left for them to take? "Are you still good to stay a few days more, Henk?" Hosking asked, altering his tone to convey less heaviness. "To smooth things over like we agreed?"

"What about the house?" Henk dug the fingers of his free hand into Hana's ribs. Pain bloomed over the surgical scar and she groaned. He jerked his head towards Sally's vehicle. "Take out the suitcase and put it on the back seat."

Sally kept one arm around Hosking, but placed her free hand over her hip. "I can't cart her around with me!" she snapped. "I need to visit the dementia unit and give Mabel her last dose of Fentanyl. This is the end. She's given us all there is now, I think. We have the boat and the money. We'll never know who the shipment belonged to. So, I'll put her out of her misery this morning and then we'll leave on this afternoon's high tide."

Henk halted on the gritty road, causing Hana's soles to slide. Her legs went from beneath her and she landed in the dirt. Something with hard edges dug into her buttock. It took her breath away, worsening an already painful bruise. The phone. She had Logan's phone.

Henk released her, and she balanced on one palm, her wrist aching. Grit dug into the skin to leave a raised graze. Her hair spun around her face until she couldn't see through the thick red curtain. It welded to her tear-streaked cheeks.

“We have trucks with open rear beds!” Henk’s voice rose as though shouting might help him make his point. The breeze stole it and tossed it away. “There’s nowhere to hide a body. What do you suggest? We sit her in the passenger seat with her hands zip tied?”

“He’s right.” Hosking raised his head to acknowledge Henk’s tantrum. “We can’t take her. She needs to travel in your boot.”

Sally shrugged and kept her arm around his bulky shoulders. It stretched her body at an awkward angle, her armpit extended as though disjointed. She showed more inclination to remain linked with Hosking than she ever did with Craig. Hana frowned and considered Sally’s play for Logan. She couldn’t see the point of it any more.

Logan dead.

She couldn’t see the point of anything.

“Whatever you say, hun.” Sally’s tone held an unfamiliar, soothing edge. “You’re the boss. We could swap vehicles just for now.”

Hosking grunted, and Henk’s rigid stance softened. His relief turned to cruelty, and he aimed a kick at Hana’s thigh. His combat boot connected with a sickening thud and she cried out in pain. “I can’t deal with this chick,” he growled. He pursed his lips as though he might spit on her. She no longer cared about anything but the possibility of finding herself enclosed in the boot. Without an audience. She'd use the phone as soon as she got a signal. Liza would think the call came from Logan. She would answer it.

Henk raged on, spittle flying from between his lips. The wind spattered it across the gloomy patina of his shirt as darkened polka dots. "You sort it out between you. I got my share of the cash out of the country. You got the boat." He jabbed a finger at Hosking. "We're done. As soon as we reach the dock, we're going our separate ways. Just as agreed." He turned towards the house and released a growl of irritation. Hana drew her legs out of range from another kick. "What is he doing?" Henk's voice rose to a shout.

Hana turned to see Ron emptying his red backpack under the cover of the porch. He'd opened each of the many pockets to reduce the bag to a sagging muumuu. "There's only half here!" he shrieked, waving a bundle held together by a narrow strip of paper. "One of you stole my share!"

"Really?" Sally kept her arm around Hosking's neck. "You think any of us had time to worry about taking your cash? We used the entire night to make a bonfire. When did Henk or I spend any time apart from you?" Her other arm waved around her. The wind snatched it and sent it dancing to its will. She forced it back against her side, her body rocking against the breeze, which drove at her horizontally. Her scrub pants flapped like flags around her thin legs.

"Well, someone did!" Ron rose, and the bundle fluttered in his white-knuckled fingers. He shook it and the papers made a shushing sound. "There's about half missing." He rose on shaky legs, staring into his pack in disbelief like a child who's had his lunch stolen.

"I'm sick of this!" Henk turned to face Hosking and Sally. "Let's go with the original plan!"

Crusted blood dried on Hosking's face and upper lip. Hana's position on the floor offered her no vantage point, and she couldn't fight three other adults at once. A sense of inevitability covered her in a blanket of passivity.

Hosking shot Logan.

He'd killed her husband.

Ron turned to her, pointing an accusing finger, and the mood of the group shifted. "Henk went outside by himself! I packed it up when we first arrived." He blinked at Henk's growl of dismissal and rewrote his dangerous narrative. "She did it!" he screamed over the pummelling of the wind against the rickety building. "She stole my share."

Four angry faces turned towards Hana. Four suspicious pairs of eyes already radiating judgement. And murder.

71

Wicked - kino

"Where is it?" Sally's question held an uncharacteristic reasonableness. She dipped at the waist as though speaking to a naughty dog.

Hana's lips parted, the icy wind and dehydration already making them crack as she tried to answer. Her mind filled with prayers for a phone signal and that they'd hurry and shove her in the boot so she could make her emergency call. It felt as though she stood at the edge of a shaking cliff with her toes already over the precipice. She would remain powerless until out in the nothingness. The void of the tiny car's boot represented her nothingness. Her words emerged as gibberish. "But, but," she managed. Then, "It's fake! Why would I want fake money? I have no use for it."

Sally and the three men surrounding her stared at each other, their eyes sliding left to right in a soundless conversation. Hana sensed she'd missed something important. A sly smile fixed on Sally's lips. She sighed and her rounded breasts rose and fell. Her shoulders sloped as an air of relief shrouded her. "Take my car," she said to Hosking. "It's unlocked." To Henk, she said, "Move the suitcase onto the floor behind the passenger seat. Cover it with a blanket. Put her in the boot and take it all to the boat. I'll borrow your ute and meet you at the wharf in half an hour."

"But what about my money?" Ron shook his fist in the air. Hana spun on her backside, grit popping beneath her jeans. The phone's rounded edge dug harder into her soft buttock as she watched the scene unfold. She anticipated the disaster before it came, the fragile currency strap containing the notes releasing as though in slow motion. Ron screamed again as the delicate paper wings spun around his head like attacking bats. The familiar face of Queen Elizabeth II landed on Hana's wrist, the kārearea, the New Zealand falcon on its reverse side as it flipped. Then it disappeared on the wind as though snatched by an invisible hand. She ached to fly with it, to soar into the angry grey sky and escape the coming grief.

Twenty-dollar notes rose in a crescendo of dancing motes in a swirling tornado around Ron's head. He jumped on the spot, snatching back a crisp bill only to lose it when he lurched for another. Hana held her breath as more peppered her where she sat. A thousand dollars in twenties filled the grey sky and turned it green for just a few quick seconds. Then they lifted as a flock and fluttered over the canopy, catching against top branches and coconut leaves before continuing their journey.

The irony lodged in Hana's chest as a suppressed, hysterical laugh. Ron had raged over his alleged missing share, only to lose fifty banknotes to the wind. Fifty fake twenties? The question remained with her, drowning out the much more important question. What happened to Logan's body?

"I'm so done!" Henk strode away from the group. His heavy boots carried him across the unmaintained cul-de-sac to where his red ute waited. He reached it and fought the driver's door open. The invisible fingers of the wind pushed and pulled until the hinges creaked. Henk raised his voice to reach over its cackle. "This weather is coming in faster than we thought. Do what you need to and get to the boat or you won't get out of the harbour. Don't forget to leave the suitcase with Po. We'll say our goodbyes and I'll come back here and set the fire."

He sank into the driver's seat, the door slamming hard enough to rock the vehicle. The diesel engine fired, and he spun in a tight arc, gravel spitting from behind the tyres. Sally raised her free arm as he sped past, her words snatched away by the wind. “But I needed his ute,” she cried. Her gaze slid to Hana. “What will we do now?” She addressed her question to Hosking. He wiped the dried blood from his chin and shrugged.

“Mine’s down at the hospital. I walked up here. It’s parked beside the Harley. You can take mine if you like.”

Sally tutted and flicked her sleeve from her wrist. She examined her watch. “I don’t have time to walk down there and then drive to the unit.” She spun in a circle. Her eyes narrowed, twin slits of deviance. “What about him?” Her cheek brushed Hosking’s shoulder. “He’s a liability.”

“Always was.” Hosking waggled greying eyebrows. Hana studied his overweight build, which contradicted Craig’s attempt at something more sculpted. Yet Sally’s adoration held no pretence. She’d sunk her life into this basket of poisonous delicacies without reserve. “You could take his ute.” Hosking’s statement held a world of pain for the vehicle’s owner. They both stared at Ron, tasting his death like snakes licking the air.

“Where’s my husband?” Each word lodged in Hana’s throat. “I need to see Logan.” She forced herself onto her knees, her movements lacking speed or strength. She tugged the hem of her tee shirt down over the outline of the phone. The ice-cold wind had seeped into her bones. Hosking's claim of killing Logan had turned the joints to cement. The landscape listed as she clambered upright. Thoughts of her husband filled her mind. All she could comprehend was the memory of resting her cheek against his strong shoulder blade just hours earlier as the Harley purred beneath her. It couldn't have just ended. Not like this. Her chest hitched and more tears funnelled down her cheeks to tumble from her chin. The wind snatched them with a greedy maw and spat them onto the earth. Her fingers twitched to touch the phone, but she resisted, clasping them together before her in prayer.

"Shut her up," Sally snarled, her top lip curling back from her teeth. Her hair rose around her head like coral tossed around a reef. "Let's tie up the loose ends and leave." She dipped forward and grabbed a hank of Hana's curls in her balled fist, using the pain to bend her to her will. "Where did Ron go?"

Hosking sounded tired. He sniffed, and the action caused blood to drip from the end of his nose. "I'll find him," he said in a growl. "Put a bullet in him and take his precious share."

Hana peered at him sideways as dismay and disbelief morphed into anger. This man who owned a local dive boat and ran tours for visitors had crossed a hidden line. He'd mowed down Jared and shot Logan with no visible sign of guilt. She didn't care about Ron, but she needed the killing to stop. Her brain ached for space to think, to collect her thoughts into a viable, Logan-worthy plan.

Hosking stepped in front of Hana, already lifting the hem of his stained polo shirt. His fingers closed around a Smith and Wesson 38 Special. He slid it from his waistband by degrees. Step. Tug. Step. Tug.

Sally gave another merciless yank on Hana's hair. Rage exploded in her chest.

Hana dug her heels into the grit, her mind in free fall. Logan's meticulous self-defence lessons played on a film reel through her inner vision, careful instructions and endless practice. Though her body faltered, her brain knew the dance steps.

Sally expected her to pull away from her and adjusted her balance to fit that assumption. Hana did the opposite. She launched backwards with everything she had, her muscles straining and something tearing low in her gut. She forced her shoulders into Sally's rib cage, dipping backwards and angling herself like a loose arrow. Her soles dug into the gravel until they found the compacted earth beneath, adding momentum to the reverse slalom. Every ounce of energy went into the movement, driving Sally backwards until she overbalanced and shuddered to a halt. A sickening crunch signified her head cracking like a coconut against the unforgiving trunk of the totara. Hana sprawled with her, limp arms tangling with Sally's flailing legs as she landed in a heap on top of her.

She struggled upright, Hosking already turned and striding towards her. Quick calculations revealed a probability little more than a remote possibility. Hana dived like a rugby forward, aiming for his chunky waist. She put everything into the manoeuvre, every spark of energy. Her brain fizzed with the insatiable hunger of fury and revenge.

He'd shot Logan.

He had a gun.

She wanted that weapon with every fibre of her being, already tasting the satisfaction of punching a bullet through his face at close range.

"Ron!" Sally clutched the back of her head and wailed for help to a man whose death she'd sanctioned only seconds earlier. With Henk and his muscles already half way down the mountain, it stripped her of possibilities. But Ron didn't come.

Hosking flew backwards through the air, with Hana splayed across his stomach. They landed together, both releasing a whoosh of spent air. Hana recovered first. She raised her hands as he flailed on the ground, digging her fingernails into his eyes and renting layers of skin from his closed lids. He roared in pain, tossing beneath her and hauling her head backwards, using her trailing curls. She turned her face and sank her teeth into his wrist, clamping down like a hound until a metallic taste alerted her tongue to his blood. She bit through the fatty layers as he screamed. He hauled on her hair with one hand while trying to release his other wrist.

Then he punched, reversing his momentum and driving Hana's head backwards. Her jaws released with the unexpectedness of the tactic, and his fist caught her cheekbone. Pain fuelled her furious rage and her vision bloomed white, adding a milky layer to every message her eyes relayed to her brain.

She heard the revolver land in the dust, the heavy thunk amplified in her mind. Hosking struggled to rise, and Hana dived over the top of him, landing in a muddle of arms and legs. He snatched at her ankle, his fingers squeezing the bone until numbness blossomed through her Achilles tendon and deadened her right foot. Her fingers scrabbled in the dirt, searching for the gun. It became her only focus, her single reason for breathing.

Hosking shifted his weight, sliding out from beneath her. Hana's knees crashed to the hard ground, but the jolt gave her a greater reach. Her left hand closed around the ridged wooden handle of the loose revolver. A skip of satisfaction coursed through her body. She spun onto her left hip, bringing her right hand around like the sail of a windmill to support her grip. Logan's phone gave a sickening crunch in her back pocket. But she levelled the snub nose barrel at Hosking's shocked face.

The familiar contours of the revolver infused her with confidence. She'd fired this model often and her muscles knew the weight and the recoil. Her index finger slipped through the tiny guard and closed over the trigger. Her lungs filled and then deflated, the sigh leaving her body in a hiss as she took aim.

72

Shoot - pupu 'i

"Don't do it." Logan's voice held an uncharacteristic wobble. He lumbered towards the knot of injured and soon-to-be dead. An awkward list to the left marred his gait.

"You shot him!" Sally's shriek held a criticism, and she glared at her partner in crime. "You said you killed him."

Hosking's lower jaw flapped as though unhinged. He didn't remove his gaze from the revolver's dark mouth. Though he raised his right hand in a sign of defeat, Hana sensed his mind whirring with calculations. His irises flashed as though inner scenarios pulsed before them.

"You've come so far, haven't you?" Hana's voice held an uncharacteristic rasp. She shifted backwards, flattening her right hand against the ground to brace her weight. Logan loomed in her peripheral vision, one eyebrow raised in question. Dirt and leaves spattered over his windblown black curls as he towered over the scene. Hana addressed Hosking but didn't lose track of Sally as the other woman sat forward and pressed a hand to her bleeding crown. Hana's mind refused to acknowledge the mirage which seemed to represent her husband. He looked like Logan and he appealed to her with Logan's familiar grey eyed gaze. But grief hovered beyond Hana's vision with enough threat to make her doubt.

"Yeah." Hosking shifted onto his bottom, a mini tornado whipping dust around his bare legs. "We've come a long way."

"You incarcerated a confused old woman," Hana began. She sent strength into her knees but didn't lock them. Her fingers curled around the gun as she took a determined stance and closed her left eye, sighting Hosking's forehead in her right. Breathe in. Breathe out. But she didn't fire. Not yet.

It occurred to her she didn't yet know the contents of the revolver. Hosking seemed unworried by her possession of it. Hana edged the chamber out with the index and middle fingers of her right hand and used her left thumb to turn the cylinder. It spun without resistance. No grime or dust clogged the dull interior. Four of the five cartridges glinted back at her, suggesting Hosking had fired one shot at Logan.

Hana's heart hardened, and she pushed the chamber closed with a satisfying click. With shaking fingers, she edged the barrel around to make her shot count. The light died in Hosking's eyes as he realised Hana Du Rose was more than she appeared. Not so fragile now. The thought caused Hana's eyes to lift at the corners in a wicked smile.

"So," she continued, settling into her stance. A sense of comfortable familiarity eased over her. "You imprisoned Mabel. I haven't yet worked out the relevance of that. You killed Hallie. Or is she also hidden somewhere? You mowed down Jared, cheated with Craig's wife, and planned an arson and two more murders." She cocked her head. "Make that three. Where is Ron-the-pool-man? Does he know he's next?"

Sally snuffled at the bottom of the tree and Hana shifted her left hip outward. She knew she couldn't hit both, not with the distance between them. And not from a seated position. The revolver was famous for its point and press capabilities, but it offered no opportunity to sight a target with any accuracy. You had it or you didn't. And Hana had fired Logan's illegal collection of revolvers often enough to understand that any tiny movement at the nose end could throw the shot wide by a country mile.

She didn't intend to miss.

Logan cleared his throat. "Hana." His tone held a warning. "I brained a guy inside the house. We didn't exchange names."

Hana slid her gaze towards him. The revolver bounced in her fingers. "This piece of crap said he killed you." Her voice wobbled. "You're a haemophiliac. Why are you still walking if he shot you in the chest?" A sob punctuated her sentence. She swallowed down her fear, turning her head to wipe her sticky cheek against the stained sleeve of her tee shirt. Sally moved to her right, a slow, deliberate slithering like a hungry python.

Hana shook her head and rose in a fluid movement as graceful as a rising dancer. Courage infused her legs with confidence, and she didn't remove her hands from the gun. Her vision filled with an eerie red mist. She arced the revolver's nozzle between Hosking and Sally. "I'm a great shot," she growled. "So try me."

Logan stepped to her left, covering the ground with the peculiar listing stride. He dug into his shirt pocket and held something up in front of him. Hana took a split-second glance before settling her attention back on Hosking and Sally. "See," Logan said. He shook the device and glass tinkled from the broken screen. "He killed your phone." The wind snatched the pieces like a child having a tantrum, throwing them far and wide as glittering crystals. Then it focused its destructive attention on Hana, buffeting her legs and ramming her outstretched forearms until the muscles became heavy. Her eyes filled with tears of relief and frustration. Her vision swam. Logan stepped in the way, acting as a wind break. He lifted his shirt to reveal a blue outline of her phone over his left pectoral muscle. Purple lines threaded outward, signifying his urgent need for medication.

"He said he killed you." Hana gritted her teeth and shifted the revolver's aim onto Sally. She ached to show them how it felt when someone threatened to strip everything of worth from their lives. "Why are they doing this?" She shouted against the wind and it tore her words from her throat. "All this over fake cash!"

Logan dropped the hem of his shirt and fed the destroyed phone back into his pocket. He held out his palm for the revolver. "Give it to me, babe," he said, his tone confident. "You don't want this on your conscience."

Hana ground her teeth in her jaw and shook her head. Hosking blinked, his expression enough to put her on notice. In her peripheral vision, Sally made her move. She snapped her body forward, her breasts bouncing against the neckline of her scrubs. The wind tossed her yellow hair like a dust bunny. Her movement appeared crablike, and Hana sensed Logan's giant inhale before she heard it. Sally covered the ground on her hands and knees, giving Hana the awful sense of being chased. It only took a second for the trigger to close against the guard. The cartridge left the chamber with a bang like the clatter of a brick hitting a tin roof. Hana welcomed the recoil, her lips sliding into a grim smile.

73

Wound - puputa

Sally's screams filled the clearing. They rose like an operatic chorus and the wind threw them back at her. Logan swore and snatched the revolver from Hana's outstretched hands. "Geez!" he cursed, adding other unrepeatable and choice phrases.

Despite the bone-deep shaking of her body, Hana stared down at Sally with a frightening absence of care. Next to her, Logan inspected the revolver with a raised eyebrow.

Gantry Hosking shuffled through the dirt to Sally. Together, they sheltered beneath the coconut tree, and he wrapped his arms around his stricken partner. "You shot her!" He glared up at Hana with a mixture of disbelief and respect.

Hana pulled her lips back from her teeth and snarled at him. "And you shot my husband. We both missed."

"You didn't miss!" He raised his voice to yell over the wind which attacked them from all sides. The air contained moisture which soaked their clothes and plastered their hair to their faces. Hosking pointed at Sally's shattered right forearm as she sobbed and cradled it to her stomach.

Hana twisted her lips. "I aimed for her face." The voice didn't sound like hers. It held an uncharacteristic hardness. She ached to snatch the revolver back from Logan and try again. The shot had come from a jab and stab reaction, rather than a relaxed point and press. Hana wrinkled her nose, viewing Sally's round face as a target instead of a fellow member of humanity. She lifted her right thumb and forefinger and practised her aim. Her words contained no hint of emotion. "I shot left-handed," she observed.

"Yep." Logan offered no critical appraisal. Hana frowned at him. He usually had such a lot to say about her missed shots. She reached out her left hand to touch him, but drew back.

"He said he killed you," she repeated. The knot of grief worked its way from her chest into her throat.

"Yep," Logan said again. "But he didn't. I'm the dude with nine lives. Remember?" The attempt at humour flew over Hana's head with the dust and leaves funnelling above the clearing. Logan stuffed the revolver down the back of his waistband after shuffling the remaining cartridges from the cylinder and into his jeans pocket. "We need to get out of here," he stated, tilting back his head to stare at the sky. "This is getting nasty real fast."

"She needs help!" Hosking's words swirled around his head like an impassioned echo. He dipped forward to look at Sally's right arm as she cradled it like a newborn. "Oh, hell!" he exclaimed. "Is that the bone?"

Sally wailed again, tears and snot coursing down her cheeks. But she glared at Hana with pure hatred pouring from her rotten inner core. Hana took a step towards her, but Logan's hand closed around the ball of her shoulder. He tilted her backwards and spun her to face the remaining vehicles. "No time for that," he called, his voice faint despite the proximity of his lips to her ear. "We need to go now!" He pushed her toward Ron's ute, shouting to her, "Go!" His movements appeared more laboured than usual and he clamped his left arm against his ribs. He staggered against the force of the driving wind as though unable to summon the energy to fight for much longer.

With a last glance at the couple bowed beneath the coconut tree, Hana obeyed her husband. She fell into step, using him as a windbreak and peeling off to round the rear tray of the ute. Her mind occupied her with visions of the tree squashing the spiteful pair, or of its coconuts raining down around their ears. But a shout from Logan called her back to the moment and the desperation of their circumstances.

"What?" she mouthed, halting with her right hand curled around the rail bordering the ute's rusted flat bed. The wind snatched the word from her mouth and whipped it away. Her body shook with the effort of resisting its constant tug. It had snuck up on her, the breeze turning to a buffeting wind which now resembled a gale.

"I can't drive." Logan's head shook, and it took a second for his meaning to land in the slot machine of Hana's brain. He tapped his injured pectoral with the opposite hand. Hana stiffened. Her anxiety went into free fall. He'd shown her the blossoming bruise, and she knew what happened next. He would bleed and bleed and bleed, the internal damage worsening with every passing minute without help.

Hana jogged around the rear of the ute, the wind forcing her forward fast enough to make her overshoot. She struggled back to Logan's side, reaching out with the fingers of both hands at the dawning realisation she couldn't stop. The wind renewed its tug on her legs, trying to spin her body into a reluctant waltz and take her with it. The scream died on her lips as Logan caught her with his powerful hands. He grunted as she cannoned against him.

Logan rived the driver's door open and waited until Hana got a firm grip on the metal rim provided by the partially open window. As her fingers closed around it, he swan-dived across the driver's seat and landed face first. His long legs crawled across the gear stick to the passenger side and he arrived in the seat with a bump. Raw pain narrowed his eyes to slits of agony. Hana blinked in surprise before understanding his reasoning. The angle of the wind as it ate up the clearing meant they'd never get the passenger door open against it.

Hana slid into the driver's seat and the sudden stillness inside the vehicle seemed to make everything from outside louder. She heaved in a breath and leaned out to close the driver's door. But the wind got there first, causing the hinges to creak as it tugged and tore at the metal.

"Leave it!" Logan shouted, and Hana nodded. She fumbled beneath the steering wheel to locate the key, relieved to discover it already plugged into the ignition. A keyring dangled from it. The logo from the Paradise Villa Resort covered the black faux leather. '*The holiday of a lifetime*', it read.

Unable to reach the pedals, Hana felt for the lever to alter the distance. She found it at ground level beneath her ankles and cranked the seat forward. Her stomach hit the steering wheel, and she groaned in pain, her scar tissue setting up one of many ignored protests. For once, Hana didn't bother with her regimental cockpit checks. She left the rear-view mirror in place for a much taller person and ignored those on either side. The engine fired with a frantic twist of the key and she shoved the gear lever into first. The vehicle shuddered in discomfort and she remembered the clutch, driving it down with her left foot. A lurch took the ute forward in an exaggerated bunny hop as Hana released the pedal. And its forward bull-bars ploughed into Sally's tiny hatchback.

"Sorry, sorry!" Hana found the marker for reverse gear and shoved the stick into position. As she released the clutch and the ute shot backwards, it took with it most of Sally's bumper. A catastrophic dent in the boot lid had twisted the locking mechanism, and Hana released a chuckle of hysterical proportions. "That suitcase of fake cash is never gonna come out!" she cackled. She spun the ute in a tight circle and the tyres bit into the sparse gravel. They spat it behind them like buck shot and peppered Sally's stricken vehicle. The driver's door swung with the grace of a broken wing as the vehicle turned. Then the force of the upgraded Cyclone Angela closed it with a slam. It fractured the half-raised window and sent crystals cascading into Hana's lap.

74

Hide - pipini

The downward slalom tested Hana's driving skills, and her heart spent too much time in her throat. It reminded her of a game of MarioKart, in those horrid moments when her tiny caricature lost control and a pixelated wall approached at speed. But the algorithm kept her graphic vehicle on the track and a glider appeared like magic from its roof. Hana wished for those robotic attributes as the wind bent the trees into knee joints and tossed the heavy vehicle like a toy.

She headed for the main hospital building and slewed the ute to a dramatic stop just short of the front porch. Her door seemed welded shut as she hauled on the release and shoved with her elbow. A man wearing a security uniform looked up from his task of fastening the left of the reception doors. He blocked the entrance on his knees as he hammered a bolt into its housing. Kind brown eyes blinked at Hana as he assessed her struggle and rose to his feet. He hurried out to the vehicle, his white hair lifting from his head like flames as the wind seized him. "I've got you!" he called to Hana. His greying eyebrows raised as he noticed the glass covering her jeans.

"The wind shut it!" She rived on the door handle again, glancing back at Logan. He lay back in the passenger seat, his complexion grey, and he clutched his chest. "I need to get help for my husband. He has haemophilia."

"Shift sideways," the man said. Hana ducked out of the way as he raised the hammer and gave the door's interior panel a healthy thwack. He hauled on the outer handle. The door gave a grinding creak and popped open. Hana's plimsolls touched the floor of the car park only seconds later.

A cardboard sign hit the top of the ute with its pointy end. *'Radiology patients use this door,'* it proclaimed as it continued its journey over the roof's gable end. Hana sped around to the passenger side and hauled on Logan's door, gratified when the guard joined in the struggle. They pulled it open against the wind, helped by Logan, who turned sideways and braced his feet against the panel.

"Watch out!" the old man called, dragging Hana towards his chest as the door popped open and the wind got busy wrenching the hinges the wrong way.

"I'm okay," Logan muttered, but he didn't seem okay. Hana wedged her shoulders beneath his left arm and the security guard mirrored the action on his right.

A slam echoed beneath the porch as the wind changed its mind and closed the passenger door. It moved on instead to peel away a section of loose corrugated tin at the edge of the roof. Hana thanked the security guard as they reached the reception desk. He helped Logan to a nearby seat as she cleared a space in her tangled fringe through which to speak. "My husband has haemophilia," she began, shouting against the wind which hadn't accompanied them inside. The receptionist blinked at her, his eyebrows rising in surprise. "Sorry." Hana took a breath. "It's a long story, but he got shot in the chest." The man's eyebrows climbed higher and disappeared beneath his black fringe. "He needs a Factor 8 injection. Octocog Alpha. Do you have that here?"

He stared at her with a blank expression and her heart sank, the withdrawing adrenaline coursing through her blood stream with no place to go. The shakes set into her fingers and worked their way to her knees. The damp of her clothes and the ice lodged in her exposed arms conspired to turn her to jelly. She glanced around at Logan, gratified to see his colour returning and the shock leaving his stormy grey eyes. He fumbled at the buttons of his shirt and the fabric fell away from pectorals worked into armoured plates. A black bruise overtook the left. The internal bleeding spread through the capillaries to create an image of multiple forked tree branches.

"I'll get someone." The receptionist reached for his phone, but he'd responded to the physical outworking more than his understanding of the disease. Or so Hana thought. "Police please." She saw his lips moving and realised her mistake. He'd focussed on her description of the injury and she'd used the fated word for a gunshot. Hana groaned and slapped her palm on the counter between them.

"We need to deal with his wound first!" she protested.

"Hana." Logan's voice roused her from the argument she'd begun in her head. Hana turned to see the alarm in his grey irises. "Yeah," he said, as realisation broke over her expression. "We should leave."

Logan had the weapon which shot him pushed into his waistband. Instead of summoning help for his injury, the receptionist had condemned them to another stint in the jail house. Hana crossed the short distance to stand in front of him, a million questions already on her lips. "But," she began, and he shook his head.

"Help me up," he growled. "I have pills at the villa. It's just a bruise. Not as bad as I thought." He blew out a laboured breath and raised his eyebrows in a silent apology. "I panicked."

Logan Du Rose never panicked. Hana sensed the lie, though he worked hard to keep it from view. She held out her arms and his weight caused her to tip forward as he used her for support. "Don't do this," she whispered. "Give it to me. I'll bin it."

Logan shook his head. "It's too hard," he whispered. "Let's go."

Hana glanced at the porch doors, observing the security guard as he finished hammering in his bolt. He gave the wood a sound shake as though testing his work. Her heart quailed. He'd shown them kindness, risking his own safety to help them from the car.

"Doug!" The receptionist rose and shouted to him. He shot a glance at Logan and then lifted his voice. "Doug!"

The guard turned, a ready smile on his lips. He took three steps into the reception area with his hammer clutched in his right hand, his expression still open and friendly. The affability died in his eyes as a crash sounded from the porch. Grinding metal squealed as it twisted, the gale renting the roof with the ease of opening a sardine tin. It peeled back the metal to expose the joists and beams, leaving them facing the blackened sky like the ribs of a carcass. Redundant bolts and screws rained like arrows on the porch floor and the security guard blinked at his good fortune.

When he and the receptionist turned back to the new patient, they saw only an empty waiting room.

75

Cyclone - 'uri'ia

"We can't use the Harley." Logan grunted with every step as they hurried away from the hospital. "Too risky. We'll get blown to Fiji."

"Sounds nice," Hana called, her tone wistful. They halted as a sandwich board flew past them. It twisted and turned in a dance to soundless music.

"We need to get back to the villa." Logan heaved in a shuddering breath and kept his right arm fixed around Hana's shoulders. "I have Desmopressin tablets. I can double them up for now. It's just a bruise."

Hana didn't believe him. But she'd allowed him to rush her through the rear door of the reception as the wind tore the roof from the porch. They headed towards the intensive care unit, not sure where to go.

At the first opportunity, Logan wiped their fingerprints from the internal workings of the gun. The handy table containing surgical gloves, hand sanitiser and masks sat at the end of the corridor leading towards Jared's ward. Logan pulled on gloves and used a mask to rub the sanitiser over the revolver's mechanisms. He finished by coating the handle and nozzle. He even focussed on the mouth of the barrel, balling the damp mask and stuffing it into each orifice. Logan covered all parts of the weapon, ensuring no partial prints or DNA would ever find its way onto a police database. Hana watched his deft actions, marvelling at the strategic clicking in his brain. She would have wiped it on her shirt. She would have handed Sergeant Wally George everything he needed to arrest her for shooting Sally.

Logan lifted the part empty box of masks and stuffed the revolver at the bottom. He covered it with discarded gloves and masks from the dustbin beside the table. Then he pushed it into the bottom of the liner and let the other rubbish cover it. He stuffed the gloves he'd used into his jeans pocket. "Let's go," he said, his voice a low growl.

"What about security cameras?" Hana asked. "We don't know where they are."

"There's one over the main reception door," he replied. "That's the only one which caught us."

With every passing moment, his movements seemed to regain their fluidity. The effects of haemophilia could incapacitate him. An intense sense of resignation accompanied any injury with cataclysmic possibilities. But he'd recovered enough to shake the fear and get moving. "I'm good," he said as though answering Hana's unspoken question. He rubbed his opposite hand over his chest. "It bloody hurts, though. Not just my chest. He shot me from ground level and I fell out of the window like a bag of spuds." Logan walked at a fast pace while rubbing his right buttock. Hana noticed a series of nasty grazes oozing on his forearm.

"I thought he'd killed you." She gulped at the magnitude of the sentence. Each word seemed dragged from the back of her throat. Logan slipped an arm around her shoulders, and they hurried through an exit door leading into a paved courtyard. As he held the door open for Hana to pass beneath his arm, he leaned down and pressed a kiss to her temple.

"You held your own back there," he said. Admiration laced his tone. "I'm proud of you."

Hana's heart swelled high enough in her chest to create a locking motion. It left her speechless. She hadn't known how much she needed to hear those words. Her lips moved, but no sound emerged. Seconds later, the moment for a reply had passed.

The courtyard led to another building and Hana rived on the handle to find the door wouldn't open. She gasped in horror and whirled around to face

Logan. "It's locked!" she said, her eyes wide in her pale face.

"It's okay." Logan dragged his wallet from his back pocket, the action slow and laboured. He winced as he stretched his injured pectoral. He leafed through his cards until he found the one he wanted. "It's almost expired," he said. With the deftness of a cat thief, he swiped the card along the gap between the lock and the jamb. It took two attempts and left the plastic ragged along one edge. But the mechanism of the lock released enough for Logan to push the door open. It sprang back out as they passed it and sealed behind them with a click.

Hana blew out a ragged breath. She'd underestimated Logan's ability to gain access to just about anywhere. She clung to his hand, trotting beside him to match his long stride. They dashed through another endless corridor until an external exit released them to the changed paradise beyond its doors.

The wind attacked them as though greeting a chosen victim. It shrieked with joy, cackling as it threw leaves and rubbish into their eyes. It pushed and shoved, tugged and tore, lifting Hana's tee shirt to expose her scarred side at the same time as ramming her against Logan. Their feet tangled and she would have fallen but for their clasped hands.

"You're good, you're good," Logan puffed, hauling her upright. The gale tore his words from his lips and shredded them. He forced Hana against a brick building and covered her with his body as an airborne rubbish bin flew past. It clanged against a parked truck, glancing off the windscreen and continuing its journey. The damaged screen hung like a curtain across the dashboard, shattered beyond repair. Trash eked from the flying dustbin, wrappers, and cans discarded across the car park like wedding confetti. Hana wrapped her arms around Logan and buried her face against the uninjured side of his chest. She ached to check his wound, to know what they faced. As though sensing her intention, he peeled her arms from around him and bent to look in her eyes as he spoke to her. "I don't know what to do," he said. His tongue poked into the corner of his mouth. "Nowhere is safe."

Hana nodded. They couldn't walk against the wind, the Harley wouldn't remain upright, and stealing a vehicle might leave someone else stranded. Someone with just as good a reason to get home. And another sound had entered the fray. High pitched and filled with alarm, a claxon piped a warning to locals to head somewhere safe. But what place on the island counted as safe?

Hana's thoughts shifted to the sight of the truck with the broken windscreen, and Logan turned to follow her gaze. "It's a delivery lorry," she called. He frowned at her words, despite the closeness of her lips to his ear. She blinked, wondering if he hadn't heard her. A hissing of leaves sounded nearby, followed by the almighty crash of a coconut tree decimating a vehicle parked at the end of the row. Hana tugged at Logan's sleeve. "I meant it's not someone's personal vehicle. We could borrow it."

He hissed as he surveyed the truck. Then he shook his head. His teeth dug into his lower lip as he turned to weigh their options. Hana gripped his forearm as the wind slammed sideways against her knees. "We need something else!" he shouted. Though the gale stole his words, Hana read his lips. "Something lower."

She peered past him and spotted an older model Mazda 3 parked two spots away from the squashed vehicle, now wearing the weighty plume of a coconut tree. Her head butted Logan's arm as she jerked her head towards it. He spun on the spot as he assessed the danger, sifting data through his brain as fast as the weather unfolded overhead. The rain from earlier resumed as a gentle patter, but the swirling black anger reflected from the sky promised it wouldn't remain so benign. A roll of corrugated iron, ripped from an unknown location, roiled through the air in a bizarre tailspin. Had Logan not folded himself over Hana again in an instinctive need to protect her, it would have parted his head from his shoulders. Hana clung to him as it ground and scraped along the wall beside them, rigidified by the deafening screech of metal roughening against brick. They needed to make a decision and leave. Neither of them wasted their words against the animalistic howl of the cyclone. But they moved together as one.

Just like always.

76

Steal - keiā

Hana pressed herself against the wall as Logan battled the driving wind. He broke into the low-slung silver vehicle without smashing the quarter light or affecting the integrity of their protection against the gale. It took seconds. Just a single kick against the panel beside the driver's handle and the system disarmed.

After double checking the wind's direction, Logan jogged to the passenger side door and pulled it open. He beckoned Hana towards him, catching her outstretched hand as it seemed she might fly past him. The action spun her in a wide arc, and she slammed against the rear panel of the car and left a dent. Every bone in her body conspired to ache, almost paralysing her. Logan stuffed her into the passenger seat as though kneading dough into a baking tin. The vehicle rocked beneath her as she caught her breath, but her side mirror revealed Logan's battle to cross back around the car.

It seemed for a moment that he wouldn't get the driver's door open. Hana spun in the seat and stretched across the gear lever, placing her soles against the inside panel. She pushed, forcing all her weight through her feet and supporting Logan's efforts against the wind. It pounded him against the side of the vehicle without mercy. The door popped open as the gale sighed and regrouped, preparing to finish him. Logan plunged into the driver's seat, squashing Hana's outstretched legs and catapulting across her. She cried out as her left knee bent the wrong way. The tendons stretched almost beyond their capacity.

"Sorry! Sorry!" Logan dragged his legs inside the car as the disgruntled wind shut the door hard enough to have sliced off his shins. He raised himself up by bracing his palms against the seat, giving Hana enough time to drag herself from beneath him. His crown brushed the vehicle's ceiling, and Hana noticed sweat on his brow. He looked sick again, as though the battle with the wind had depleted the last of his reserves.

"Are you okay?" She forced her feet into the footwell, her left knee already swelling in her jeans. She reached across and clamped a hand over his forehead, an action so familiar in relation to her children. A damp clamminess left her fingers slick. Not good. Not good at all. "We need your medication," she stated. Logan pursed his lips but didn't agree with her.

The wind rocked the vehicle. It resembled a rocket in the final desperate moments before lift off. Every second wasted put their proposed trip to the villa in even more doubt. Logan dipped forward and depressed the bar beneath his chair. The seat flew back at speed until it reached its full extent. Logan leaned back and dug in his jeans pocket until he retrieved the Harley's key. His deft fingers turned over the fob and extended a screwdriver. Hana clung to the door handle, buffeted by the chaotic rocking of the vehicle as Logan detached the plastic casing over the ignition, stripped wires and pressed them together. He glanced across at her with a victorious grin which made him appear boyish. "Don't try this at home," he advised with the seriousness of a voice-over warning about a dangerous sport. His first effort earned him a painful shock. He blew out a ragged breath and steeled his nerves to try again. "This doesn't happen on TV," he commented, his humour jarring against the perilousness of their circumstances. The engine spluttered to life on his second attempt, but his fingers shook. "Find me something," he demanded, clasping the wires to keep them apart and jerking his head towards the glove compartment in front of Hana's knees. "A peg, a clip, anything. I need to keep these wires away from my leg as I drive, otherwise I'm toast. The first zap woke me up, but I'm not game for a second."

Hana dug in the glove box but found nothing of use. A can of female spray deodorant gave her hope, as did a faded pink scrunchie littered with stray dark hairs. "It's a woman's car," she said, as though providing a running commentary. "A woman with long hair." A glance at Logan found him frowning at her, the wires held apart in front of him. The wind pounded the vehicle as though determined to lift it into its embrace. A concrete roof tile glanced off the bonnet of the Mazda and ploughed through a window of the brick building.

"I don't want to hurry you," Logan growled, his tone edgy.

"Got one!" Hana held the bobby pin aloft in victory. She handed it across to Logan, who avoided the frayed ends of the wires. He kept them separate as he folded them over and clipped the thick red one onto the plastic edge of the dangling panel.

"Fasten up!" Logan urged as he fixed the driver's belt around his chest and plugged it in. He groaned as it tightened over his wound. Hana fumbled with hers, tugging it from the housing with trembling fingers. She fastened it and sat back in her seat, distracting herself from the looming disaster with memories of home. It seemed only yesterday that a stray hair-grip had disabled her vacuum cleaner. The innocuous, almost invisible bobby pins were everywhere, courtesy of Phoenix and her fixation with ballerina hairstyles. The child danced with all the grace of a rhinoceros, but her fine Du Rose looks and her elfin body helped her to look the part as long as she stood still.

"Bobby pins," Hana sighed to herself. She would never again complain when stepping on one of the metal clips in the bathroom in the dead of night. Or when she knelt beside the stricken vacuum cleaner and hauled yet another from its bowels.

Logan cranked the gear lever into reverse and stamped on the gas pedal. The seatbelts hugged their torsos tight enough for him to release a hiss from between his clamped teeth. Hana gripped the door handle with both hands, twisting her body and causing her wound to give a warning gripe. The Mazda shot backwards in an arc, the tyres squealing as Logan jammed the gear lever into first. A liquid amber tree creaked to their left, its branches swirling with energetic leaves. The ground shook as the wind attacked it, tipping it from the roots with the glee of a naughty child. It groaned as its centre of gravity shifted and it lost the fight. A crash vibrated through the car park as the pretty star-shaped leaves added themselves to the flaxen foliage of the fallen coconut tree. They criss-crossed the stricken vehicle, already pounded almost flat beneath their combined weight. The longest branches stretched to touch the space where the Mazda stood just seconds before. Bolts popped and metal crunched on the unfortunate vehicle still clinging to the space where its owner parked it. Hana held her breath as the Mazda spun past the wreckage and Logan pointed the sporty bonnet towards the hospital's circular road.

77

Warning - ‘akamatakite

Logan searched for the headlight switch as the sky darkened to a furious, swirling black. It resembled the hungry maw of some celestial beast. A forceful wind pursued them down the mountain and onto the main road circling the island. The sea joined the conspiracy, the waves already lapping the edge of the asphalt. Cyclone Angela upped its anti, pounding the reef and driving its churning surf to ruin the quiet safety of the bay. As Logan battled with the steering wheel, Hana leaned forward to observe the choppy, threatening waters. Where yesterday she'd paddled in them, able to see her bare toes on the sandy seabed, the cyclone had obliterated every facet of its beautiful identity. The waves held a murkiness as they splashed on the road and spread beneath the Mazda's tyres. Sand and coral bounced against the tarmac, sending a filthy spray to cover the driver's side window.

Hana spread her left palm over her side, lifting her tee shirt to examine the fragile scar tissue. The surgeon had stapled the edges of the incision together, creating a line of white dots on either side of the wound. It had resembled something from a science fiction movie when Hana got her first look at it. She had recoiled in horror, though her children had gaped with morbid fascination. Though long gone, the staples had done their work, and the scar remained sealed. Bruising spread out along Hana's right hip and snaked towards her spine. She dug her fingers under her and pulled Logan's phone free. The hard edges had not played well with her tender buttocks as she fell at the mercy of Gantry Hosking and his twisted mate. But she imagined her backside fared better than the device. Shards of the screen fell like sparkling dust on her jeans from a monumental crack across its centre. The casing arced upwards from the point of impact, mirroring the curve of Hana's butt. She lifted it to show Logan, unsurprised when he ignored her in favour of battling the wind to keep the Mazda on the road. She pushed it into her front pocket as he straddled the centre line. They encountered no other vehicles. He used it as a marker as the wind snatched at the wheels and tossed sea debris onto the bonnet and roof. Any altruism Hana had felt at saving the Mazda from its intended crushing evapourated. By the time they reached the villa, it would be a write-off, anyway.

Boulders rolled inland from the beach, ambling across the road at a casual pace like migrating turtles. The wind drove them, pushing and shoving in a one-sided game of curling. A siren sounded a warning, its wail reedy as it cut through the violent cacophony of the cyclone. Hana held her breath, her knuckles white against the seatbelt as Logan slalomed through them. A smaller rock skittered from behind the covering of its mate and the driver's front tyre slammed against it. The rock pinged backwards and shattered into smaller pieces, which made lighter ammunition for the gale force wind. It hurled them towards the houses facing the ocean. A local man struggling late to board up his windows ducked. The wind snatched and scattered the shrill tones of breaking glass.

Rain and hail alternately plastered the windscreen of the Mazda. The wiper blades spun too fast to watch, bashing sheets of water from left to right. Logan hunched over the steering wheel, the familiar injury-greyness of his complexion exacerbated by the weak daylight. Sunrise had abandoned the island, rising above the chaos. Pinned to the sky, it watched nature's destruction like a powerless, benevolent parent.

Hana leaned sideways and rested her palm on Logan's left thigh. His muscles bunched beneath his jeans as he concentrated. He didn't acknowledge her contact, and the furrow gouged into his brow remained. Hana closed her eyes and prayed for mercy. Tributaries dashed across her side window as the rain intensified, making it harder for her to see her surroundings. She peered through the changing landscape of the glass as the tributaries fought the motion of the vehicle, forcing herself not to track the Mazda's hazardous progress through the windscreen. The bungalows she'd admired from the Harley no longer winked through mottled glass panes. Many wore pale particle boards like beige eyelids over their view. They already knew the power of a cyclone. They did not wish to see another.

Hana gasped at a bang beneath Logan's seat. The car lurched sideways and Hana squeezed her eyes closed, bracing for impact. Her teeth gripped hard enough to send pain from her clenched jaw to her temple. Another injury flared its displeasure, and she forced her eyes open. The view had altered. Logan's seat appeared lower than hers. He fought the steering wheel harder as an ear-splitting grinding sound emanated from beneath the vehicle. "What happened?"

Her answer came as black strips of rubber which coiled on the silver bonnet like eels. The forward motion of the car sent them clambering onto the windscreen and flopping onto the roof. "Two tyres!" Logan shouted. He didn't remove his grip from the steering wheel. "One from the rock near the golf course and the other one just blew." The car screamed as the rims dug into the asphalt, but Logan didn't slow its speed. He hissed once and Hana looked down, realising she'd dug her nails into his thigh. She withdrew her hand, regretting the loss of contact but not able to trust herself not to repeat the reflex action. Her hands pressed together between her own thighs, each palm registering the cold of its mate. She bowed her head and prayed for divine assistance. The cares of yesterday seemed juvenile and irrelevant. She'd wanted so much to prove their innocence, to find Hallie, liberate Mabel and implicate Sally. Now, she just wanted to survive the cyclone which attacked from the west.

It drove in from the ocean like an avenging angel, swirling and pressing as though determined to force Rarotonga onto a different grid reference. The cyclone would end because they always did. The weather front would shift it northwards and disperse it away from humanity. But what would it leave still standing behind its fury? She prayed it would be the Du Roses, and if not her, at least her husband would return to comfort their children.

The vehicle scraped its way towards the Paradise Villas. Eerie claxons piped their danger calls from positions mounted on buildings as they passed. The sound waxed and waned as they drove from one to the next as though guided by an all knowing hand. Logan dodged fallen trees and debris. In the final hundred metres, an upturned tin roof crashed onto the road, forcing him over the embankment and onto the beach to avoid its shuddering death throes. The Mazda ground to a halt, the rims buried deep into the sand. The engine cut out in sympathy, and only the cries of the wind remained. Logan still clutched the steering wheel, his fingers seeming reluctant to peel themselves free. His breathing sounded shallow, and the sweat had dried on his forehead. He looked sick.

Hana licked her cracked lips and released her seatbelt. The car listed as it struggled to find its level. The wind whipped up the surrounding sand into an impressive storm, intent on removing all traces of paint from the metal chassis. Hana reached across and touched Logan's shoulder. "We need to get away from the beach," she said. Her voice sounded loud in the silence of the vehicle, the wind forming the backing vocals of an eerie song. "Logan!" She shook his powerful biceps, the muscle still bunched and active as though his battle with the steering had continued in the absence of kinetic energy. "Get out!" She punched his thigh with the side of her right fist and his gaze turned towards her.

"Ow!" he said. "I'm thinking."

"Then think faster!"

Cyclone Angela had come from the west and it brought the South Pacific Ocean to play. The protective reef had disappeared, buried beneath the massive volume of water which soused yesterday's pleasant beaches. The choppy waves roiled and fought to reach landfall, crashing across the white sand with abandon. Logan's lashes fluttered as the first wave smashed his side of the Mazda and the vehicle rocked. He swore and rubbed condensation from the side window with his raised forearm. "We both need to get out of your side," he snapped. He unclipped his seatbelt and twisted towards Hana. She waited for his usual calm instruction, but he shouted at her, "Run!"

78

High tide - ʻakapī

"I shot someone. Oh, my gosh! I shot someone!" Why did the guilt choose that moment to torture her? It pinned her in place like a stranded starfish waiting for the tide. She gaped at Logan but didn't move.

Sounds like a sucking drain issued from beneath the vehicle. Rogue waves attacked the muffler, their swishing echoing back along the metal. The Mazda shifted again, sinking Logan even lower than before. He pushed himself onto his knees on the driver's seat and reached across Hana. His heavy torso compressed her abdomen and she cried out. She hated how this happened to her. The single random, ill-timed condemnation had dropped into her mind and caused it to fritz like a poor electrical connection. She ceased to function at the exact moment she needed every brain and nerve cell to operate at capacity.

Logan yanked on Hana's door handle and pushed. But he'd stretched his long body as far as he could and so lacked the force to shove the passenger door out and up. The vehicle lurched again as the waves sucked the sand from beneath it and threw the particles at the deserted road beyond the embankment. "Hana." His lashes flickered as he locked his impatience out of sight. "Get out of the car, Hana. Right now. Move." He braced himself against the passenger door with his right hand and cupped her waist with his left. Perhaps by accident or design, his thumb closed over her scar as he pushed her to move. She inhaled a ragged cry of pain, her eyes filled with accusation. "Get. Out. Of the car," he urged.

Hana reached sideways and depressed the button for the window. But without the charge from the stalled engine, it slid open and stuck with only a finger width to escape through. She spun onto her back, her head braced against Logan's left shoulder as she used her extended legs to force the passenger door open. She grunted with the effort. The door creaked upward, caught by the wind as it reached its highest point. The gale rushed around the rear of the tilted vehicle with a wail of glee and rammed the door, crunching it back on its hinges with the ease of snapping a twig. It didn't stop there. The door screeched and groaned as the wind set about it, tearing it like a broken wing from a stricken bird.

Hana dropped her feet into the slanted foot well and dived forward. Danger set every muscle and sinew zinging with the need for survival. She clambered forward onto the embankment, snatching at tufts of beach grass which detached in her fingers. Her knees hit the sand as the car grunted and slid sideways. "Logan!" She tried to stand, but the wind rolled her backwards and flattened her, leaving her staring upwards into the furious swirling sky. Sand blasted her cheeks, and she raised her forearms to protect her eyes. Flipping onto her stomach helped, but she kept her mouth closed to avoid choking on more of the rough texture which filled her tongue and throat. She crawled towards the Mazda and reached out her right hand. The vehicle pivoted on the embankment, waves sucking at its tyres and tossing it like a cork. She crawled towards it.

Logan's fingers closed around Hana's icy hand as he scrambled through the door aperture. His boot soles slipped against the wet metal of the upturned sill, and he used his powerful biceps to haul himself through the gap where the passenger door had once hung. He landed on the embankment on his knees. He kept a tight grip on her fingers, though he didn't need her assistance. The contact between them united their struggle. Logan spun onto his back and gazed up at the sky. Broken and useless, the passenger door hung from the vehicle by one hinge. Still, the wind showed no satisfaction with its cruelty. It pushed and tugged at the vehicle with relentless enthusiasm, easing it from the embankment like a child worrying at a loose tooth. Logan's emerging weight altered the Mazda's centre of gravity. His exit caused it to sink lower into the waves' embrace. Hana lifted her arms to cover her face as they shifted the stricken vehicle like a moored boat against a floating dock.

Logan rolled onto his stomach and pushed himself onto his hands and knees. His hair lifted above his head as though electrified, a lesser version of the tangled barbed wire mop which encircled Hana and beat against her cheeks. "We need to get away from the water!" Logan shouted the sentence, and despite their proximity, Hana caught only the first and last words because the wind stole the rest. Her shoulder bumped his as she attempted to stand. The squall tried to separate them, tossing her sideways so she hit the uneven sand with her scarred side. She cried out in pain as a tussock dug into the healing tissue. Logan's arm wrapped around her waist, and he hauled her to her knees and then to a standing position. Agony as heat exploded beneath her lowest right rib. It snatched away the last breaths not already vaporised by the wind. The nearest claxon died with a receding wail as the building it clung to disappeared from beneath it. The reception for the Paradise Villas dissolved with the crunch and groan of airborne construction materials.

A coconut tree fell with a whump ahead of them. The vibration ran through their soles from the impact of the heavy trunk hitting the verge. Its foliage followed in a delayed Mexican Wave, husky coconuts bouncing on the asphalt and rolling in every direction. The topmost reach of the tree took out the entrance sign to Paradise Villas, pummelling it into the surrounding flower border with a hammer of death blow.

Hana tried shallow breathing to conserve her energy. They limped across the deserted street at an angle to the entrance. Logan half carried her to the ditch between the road and the resort, hunkering down and turning to face her. "Are you okay?" he mouthed. He lifted his hands and cupped her cheeks. His thumbs coasted across the soft skin beneath her eyes, smoothing away tears she hadn't known she'd shed. "I love you." His lips moved and the familiar crinkles appeared at the corners of his eyes.

Hana's chest tightened and her lips fumbled over the reply as her brain told her she hadn't said it enough of late. Apologies burgeoned on her tongue, but the roar of the cyclone rendered them unspoken. She'd wallowed and now would pay the price. Hana gripped Logan's wrists and dipped forward. She wrapped her arms around his neck and held onto him. The fickle rain began again, showering them in painful, icy blades. Hana's tee shirt stuck to her skin and already frozen, the shivers consumed her until even her teeth chattered.

Logan unwound her arms from around his neck and observed her with eyes, which communicated calm assurance. "We'll be okay." He pressed his lips against her cheek. A bush zinged past their heads, rolling like a marble on the wind's current. Another joined it as Cyclone Angela screamed through the flower beds, ripping up the foliage and tossing it into the fray. Hana appreciated the moment's grace which Logan had given her, but recognised the stupidity of remaining outside. When he cupped her elbow in his left hand and tugged, she responded to his grip and rose onto all fours. They crawled along the fence line towards their villa, not knowing if it remained standing.

Hana's jeans scraped along the soaked grass, saturated and stained by sand and loam. Logan pushed her ahead of him, using his body as a wind break. Twice, it shoved him into her, his forehead glancing off her tail bone. When she risked a hasty glance back at him, she noticed blood flowing from his nose and collecting on his upper lip. She stalled, stretching her gaze towards the beautiful beach where she'd sunbathed just days earlier. The waves lapped at the road, a furious tempest of stained surf the colour of urine. They chased across the asphalt with tentative strokes of a destructive brush, rushing into the ditch and colouring in the spaces behind the scouting trickles. Hana held her breath at the sight of the Mazda, just the roof visible twenty metres beyond the place it ran aground. She mouthed a silent prayer for it, for its owner and for them, the car thieves they'd never intended to become. Logan jabbed her left buttock with his knuckles, urging her forward on their laborious journey. But another fleeting vision caused her to remain frozen in position. Beneath the charcoal sky, a bundle bobbed on the surface of the water. It slid from behind the Mazda's sinking chassis and floated towards the island.

Logan nudged her. His words whipped from his tongue before he'd uttered them. His fringe glued his left eyelid closed and water dripped from the end of his regal nose. Hana gulped and pointed at the passive object in the water, its relaxed appearance obedient to the whims of the unnatural tide. The wind renewed its efforts to tear the beach apart, altering its direction for a split second and confusing the waves. They tumbled over one another like confused players in a game where the rules had changed without warning. And the shape spread a pair of wings with the grace of a yacht's swinging boom. Hana screamed and pointed behind her, her lips parted in a soundless 'o' as the gale stole her voice.

Logan shook his head, and his next shove contained more urgency. Its violence rocked Hana's body. It roused her from the horror of Cyclone Angela's first claim. No one could help the victim now.

Hail fell from the sky, pelting Hana's head and shoulders with balls of ice which struck with the force of pebbles. So she turned back to her task, keeping the fence line to her left. A panel creaked as its screws loosened. It gave up the fight and fainted to the grass like a dying leaf. It fluttered as though breathing as the wind sought to lift it and carry it away to dance with the debris in the sky. Logan pushed Hana again, urging her to pass it before it gained lift and cannoned into them. She sped up like a child playing a game in which the players mimicked dogs and other four-legged creatures. Grass fragments coated her palms and dotted the tops of her fingers. Dirt seeped through her jeans and turned her trailing laces to squirming brown worms. Ice balls clung to her hair and massaged her scalp with a relentless ache. She skirted the fallen fence panel as another screeched from its anchor. It sagged and dipped too close for comfort. As Logan's heels passed it, the one still reclining on the grass became airborne and flew. It cleared the villa to their right, soaring high above the shining tin roof. But its journey ended with a collision. The concrete power pole held, but the wires did not. Something sheared off and blue sparks cascaded from overhead and fluttered to earth like lighted snow.

Logan scrambled to his feet and snatched Hana along with him. His fingers dug into the soft flesh of her elbow and she lifted into the air by one arm. Her knees and feet trailed like twin back stops as he dragged her along the lawn like a sack of meat. The wind slapped their faces with sandy fingers and tore at their hair and their summer clothes. And the power line arced and gained momentum like a Guy Fawkes' Catherine Wheel.

Paradise had vanished and the maw of the persecuted natural world retook its throne.

79

Wreck - pararī

A fire flared into weak existence on Hallie's porch as another power line sagged and then slithered onto the covered deck. Sparks encouraged it, the wind fanned it, and the poorly maintained decking with its faded patina and dry splinters fed it. Only the rain and the hail dampened its ardour. The fire nurtured itself in lieu of a break in the persistent spray.

They both saw its beginnings as they crawled onto their porch, but Logan just shook his head and yanked Hana's elbow. She couldn't make out what he said. He propped her against the siding beneath the cover of the shaking porch as he searched in his pockets for the key. His fingers shook as he withdrew it, the nail beds already blue with cold. The typhoon ran at Hana, pinning her against the wood like a poster glued to a wall. Her lungs ached as each breath drew in more air than she could cope with. Twice, it smashed Logan against the building as he dug in his pockets.

The screen door proved almost impossible to open. The original design of the resort had positioned the villas like a giant had rolled dice. And the one leased by the Du Roses ran perpendicular with the beach. The force of the cyclone pounded the porch and the front door. Even Logan's might couldn't tear it from its position. No matter how his biceps bulged and his jaw clenched, he couldn't match the brute force of the wind. Another coconut tree added its wail to the creak of its struggling neighbours as it crashed head first through Hallie's roof. Hana released a sob and closed her eyes. She couldn't bear the pointless damage but worse, she feared the weakening greyness of Logan's complexion as his disease fed an internal bleed. She hated her own fragility at that moment. Poor little Hana. She knew what people thought of her. What had Liza called her? Ginger Barbie.

Hana fought the wind's violent pressure against her chest to turn her body towards Logan. She edged closer, stretching out her arms towards him. A deep line creased his brow and his head moved from side to side in an automatic denial. But some inner battle prevented him from finishing the rebuke. He seized Hana's wrist and hauled her into the tiny entranceway set further into the villa's frontage. His spine pressed against the glass of the lounge window with its strange right angles and frame-less design. Hana saw it shudder in her peripheral vision and worried what might happen when they got the front door open. Would the cyclone enter behind them and snatch the villa from its pilings with them inside? She clung to Logan's ruined shirt and prayed they survived long enough for her to tell him how much she loved him.

For a split second, the wind changed direction again. Just a matter of degrees, the occurrence would prove minuscule in the grand scheme of things. But for the Du Roses, it meant a breathing space of several seconds. Logan's fingers shook as he closed them around the handle, the keys still dangling from the lock. The screen door gave. It opened faster than either of them anticipated. Hana grabbed the keys and rushed beneath Logan's arm, fumbling with the next barrier and aware of the wind's ability to snatch the screen and smash it against their backs. For once, she didn't flap, focusing on her task with superhuman movements. The lock clicked, the door swung open, and she stumbled through, unable to retrieve the key and not caring. Logan tumbled after her, but the wind spotted their subterfuge and came after them. It took both of them to force the front door closed. They leaned against it, the sudden silence of the villa both strange and eerie. Hana's ears rang with a high-pitched whine, as though the wind had taken residence inside her head. Logan blew out a ragged breath. His head dipped and his shoulders heaved. The door shook behind them. Cyclone Angela demanded entry to continue its mischief.

With a groan, Logan slid down the door and sank onto his bottom. He wiped his nose on the back of his hand, and Hana spied blood as he withdrew it. "Your medicine?" She still needed to lift her voice as the cyclone raged outside. "Where is it?"

"Wash bag." His lids hung low, reducing the aperture of his eyes to slits. Hana's breath caught in her chest, and she nodded.

"No!" Logan's shout halted her as she reached for the light switch. "Don't risk it." He licked his lips, and Hana saw more blood on his tongue. Fear tapped an urgent beat in her mind and she bolted towards the bathroom. Her feet moved with a familiar heaviness. It had hounded her since the surgery and throughout her recovery. It wasn't just the aftermath of trauma, anaesthetic, or physical weakness. Dread dogged every step, causing her to trip over her flailing laces and clatter into the door frame before entering the bathroom. Hana didn't stop to examine the wash bag or empty its contents. She pictured herself scrabbling in Logan's personal items, her frozen fingers scattering the useless along with the essential.

Instead, she snatched the bag from the windowsill and cradled it against her chest. She ran back to him, collapsing to her knees on the tiles beside him and placing it in his lap with exaggerated care.

Logan fumbled with the zipper, his freezing hands unable to grip enough to pull it aside. Hana leaned over him, aware of the universe's ticking clock even though the digital timer on the night stand had ceased when the power failed. She slid it back for him, taking the bag and upending it in the narrow gap between his thighs. A bottle of aftershave gave a sickening clunk as it hit the hard floor. Liquid pooled beneath it and eked a dark, fragrant stain through the grout beneath the tiles. Logan dug through the wreckage with fingers which worked like a bunch of bananas. He lifted a box, a white pharmacist's label obliterating the patterned cardboard. His head seemed too heavy for his neck, and Hana snatched it from him. She smashed her thumb through the upper lid, not bothering to waste time opening it. A glass vial slid out as she tipped it into her palm and pushed it towards Logan. His head shook and dread grabbed her heart and squeezed.

"Me? No!" A groan exhaled from between her lips as she recoiled. "Into a vein?" Her voice squeaked as though matching the wind's howl as it crashed against the door. Logan's body vibrated with the force of it.

"Anywhere. Subcutaneous is fine." He didn't sound like he cared. His cheeks had the pallor of cooled porridge and his fingers seemed unable to grip as he sifted them through the debris on the floor. A nasal spray skittered sideways, another valuable tool in the haemophilia armoury.

Hana dug beneath a roll-on deodorant and a bottle of shaving cream. She picked up the syringe and liberated it from its crinkly packet. Her hands trembled, but her jaw remained clenched and determined. Ginger Barbie. She'd show the judge what she was made of.

Hana knew she should wash and dry her hands before unwrapping the needle. But the wind pounded the door in a growing demand for admittance and robbed her of the time for niceties. She wiped her fingers on her soaked jeans and pulled the needle free, careful not to touch the junction where it would fit onto the syringe. A twist secured it. She blew out a ragged breath as she removed the needle's plastic cap and jammed it between her teeth for safe keeping. It took two attempts to plunge the sharp edge through the bottle's foil lid and ensure it reached the liquid. A curious light-headed sensation caused her to rock on her knees as she sucked the precious Desmopressin into the syringe. Logan reached out and rested his hand on her knee. "Breathe," he instructed, his eyebrows raised as he observed her struggle.

Hana released the held breath, pulling the needle from the empty bottle. The glass container dropped to the tiles and rolled a short distance before coming to rest on its side. She held the syringe, so the needle pointed towards the ceiling. Depressing the plunger dispelled the air collected on the surface of the medication. Droplets slid down the needle like condensation on the glass of a summer drink. Hana tugged up Logan's shirt with her free hand, careful to keep the sharp needle away from his face as she scrabbled with his waistband. The damp fabric clung to him and left mottled patches on his skin as she shoved it aside.

"You need more fat," Hana joked, her words clanging into the grey silence of the villa. The echo of the roaring wind provided eerie backing vocals. She pinched a wedge of skin from his toned abdominals and jabbed the needle through the layers. Her thumb wavered on the plunger, threatening to deliver the medication too fast. Hana had watched her husband and countless nurses enough times to use the underside of her metacarpal joint and not the ball of her thumb. It offered more control as the liquid sluiced through the needle and into her husband's body. Hana set the cap back on the needle and cast it onto the floor.

She replaced his damp shirt before wondering if he'd like a clean one.

Logan lifted the nasal spray and jerked his chin towards her. She obliged, covering his left nostril while administering the spray and then repeating the action as he inhaled. Droplets collected on his upper lip. Digging through the contents of the wash bag unearthed the tablets, and she tipped two into her palm. Logan opened his mouth, and she sat them on his tongue before realising he needed water.

Hana rose to her feet and ran to the kitchen, her plimsolls squelching against the tiles. She seized an upturned glass from the draining rack and lifted the tap handle. Nothing happened. It took a moment for her to register that the lack of power meant the water pump couldn't work. A second later, she realised Logan shouldn't drink it anyway. She whirled around and opened the fridge. Something heavy smashed against the kitchen window and it rattled in its frame. Hana ducked, seeing the torn floral fabric from a sun umbrella splayed across the glass. She sighed and turned back to her task.

A single bottle of spring water rattled in the door shelf and she snatched it and loosened the lid. Despite the darkness of the fridge's interior, the bottle still felt cold. Condensation oozed over her fingers.

Logan coughed as his dry mouth and throat battled the tablets. Hana threw herself back onto her knees and held the bottle to his lips. He drank, the excess running from the corners of his mouth and along the tendons in his neck. Hana apologised and withdrew it, gratified, as he offered her a small smile. "How long?" she asked. Her nose wrinkled at the futility of her question. She knew the answer.

He gave it anyway. "Soon," he promised. "An hour for the tablet or spray. Fifteen minutes for the injection."

Hana pursed her lips and sat back on her heels. She knocked the bottle with her knee and cursed as precious liquid leaked onto the tiles.

"You drink," Logan advised, his voice betraying his exhaustion. "You're dehydrated too."

Though reluctant to deprive him, Hana fought the desire to upend the bottle of cool water into her mouth and guzzle until she choked. As the liquid trickled through her system, the need to use the bathroom gained a painful urgency. "Can you manage for a minute?" she asked, crouching beside Logan and setting the bottle on the tiles beside him. "Don't knock this over. It's next to your hand."

"I'm feeling better." He lifted his left hand and waggled his fingers before dropping it back to the floor. "It's psychosomatic, I know. It can't work that fast. But it's there in my system and it'll halt the damage."

"You're still gonna hurt afterwards, though," Hana said with a sigh. "Want me to look at your chest?"

"No." Logan gave a definitive shake of his head. "It won't change anything. Go to the bathroom and then we'll work out what to do next." As he spoke, the wind redoubled its attack on the door. It rocked against him, causing Logan's body to shudder.

Hana ran to the bathroom and used the toilet. The flush wouldn't work without the power serving the water pump. She couldn't wash her hands either. Digging in her wash bag, she retrieved a hand sanitiser bottle and wished she'd had that when she injected Logan. She took it back to him and found him leaning forward, his head between his knees.

80

Lies - kana 'ete

The plastic bottle skittered across the tiles as Hana crouched beside him. She set a steadying hand on Logan's shoulder. "Talk to me," she ordered. "What do you need?

He shook his head, the action almost negligible. "I'm okay," he lied. "Just sore."

Hana lifted the water bottle and pressed it into his hands. "Drink," she urged. "Let's get those tablets dissolving." On a whim, she snatched up the pill bottle and the nasal spray and held them out to him. "Put these in your pocket. We don't know what the next hour might bring." Logan finished drinking and swapped the bottle for the medication. Hana lifted it to her lips, her lashes fluttering as her lids closed in pleasure. She almost dropped it as a crash sounded against the front door. A crack appeared in the topmost wooden panel, the wind whistling its fearful tune through the gap.

"It's just the chair from the porch," Logan said. He laid a fortifying hand on her knee. "Everyone else seemed to know this cyclone was brewing. You'd think Craig would secure all loose items at the resort."

Hana rolled her eyes and her lips tightened. "Yeah, but his maintenance guy spent the night up at that derelict house, remember? It probably left him short-handed." The chair ground against the door as the wind released it long enough to smash to the ground somewhere near the doormat. Hana cocked her head and stared at Logan. She lifted her right hand and pressed the palm over his forehead. "You're less clammy. I'm guessing everything will work faster because we basically gave you an overdose." She sank to her bottom beside him, their thighs touching as she rested her back against the door. It trembled with the force of the wind, the stricken chair still emitting feeble taps as though calling for help. The vibration ran through Hana's bones, alarming and yet soothing at the same time. She tapped the bottle again to remind Logan to drink.

"No, you have the last," he said, his tone gruff. "I know how you enjoy the backwash."

Hana grimaced and gave an exaggerated shiver. Phoenix refused to share drinks with Mac after she discovered crumbs in an orange juice he'd slurped. Wiri told her it was a backwash, and she'd claimed the trauma had ruined her life. Hana closed her eyes and created mental images of her children. She prayed they'd stayed safe, wishing she could reassure them. Her eyes popped open and her gaze shifted to Logan. But they weren't okay, were they?

"At least tell me what you discovered last night," she asked, her tone jovial. She edged the bottle back towards Logan. "I don't want it," she lied. "If we're going to die, at least tell me what's going on with the fake cash and what they meant when they talked about a boat."

"It's not about counterfeit cash." Logan set the bottle to the right side of him. He leaned forward and dug his knuckles into his eyes. Dirt lines showed beneath his fingernails.

"It's not?" Hana pulled her knees up to her chest, her damp curls leaving dark trails on the front of her tee shirt. "But they had fake money."

Logan blew out a breath and shook his head. "Someone diversified, but in a very minor way. They've drip fed the local economy, without swamping it. Dropping a few fake notes here and there and waiting to see what happens never showed signs of professionalism. After what I've seen, I know it isn't."

Hana settled on the cold tiles. She pushed her fingers into Logan's left palm. It didn't matter that his stained clothes reeked of salt water and mustiness, or that the dirt embedded in the scratches on his arms had a greenish hue. He'd come back to her, like she'd hoped, like she'd prayed he would. Hana sniffed her left armpit and wrinkled her nose at her own unwashed scent. "What's the green stuff on your arms?" she asked as he remained silent.

Logan shook his head, dust cascading from his hair to speckle the tiles. "Attic insulation. Maybe asbestos." Exhaustion laced his tone. "I'll throw my clothes away when this is over." The wind hammered at the door and he sighed. "I don't think we're flying home tonight."

Logan's hair stood up in black fronds, a dusting of grey adding highlights. The eerie light from the lounge window cast a shine onto the raised strands. Rain water and sweat stained his shirt, following a natural line between his pectorals and over the defined ridges of his stomach. A rush of love and gratitude left Hana shaking, comprehending his agony as he'd discovered her in a pool of blood on a bathroom floor just a month earlier. She got it. Her heart lurched as though a curtain had fallen away to expose a nasty secret. This is how he'd felt. "I thought I'd lost you," she stammered, her fingers vibrating in the safety of his wide palm. "I couldn't bear it. You told me to wait and I would have stayed there for the rest of my life. A pitiful old lady wearing rags and waiting for her husband to return."

"The cyclone would have blown you all the way to Australia first." Logan wrapped his damp arm around her shoulders and kissed her temple. His attempt at humour failed. He crushed her against his ribs, grunting with pain as it constricted his bruised chest.

"Please tell me about what you found," Hana reiterated. She turned on her side and nestled against his armpit. Her left arm rested across his stomach.

Logan exhaled. "I took photos on your phone. But I did that before Hosking turned it into a banana."

"Well don't chuck it. They might save to the cloud as soon as we get data," Hana suggested, and Logan nodded.

He ran the edge of his right hand beneath his nose and inspected the result. Dried blood flaked away and satisfied, he relaxed against the door. The vibration lessened as though Cyclone Angela also waited to hear the details. Logan sighed, his chest rising slower than it fell. Hana sensed pain and reticence in the action. "I crawled through the window and ended up in a hallway at the back of the building. It's an incredible space, really ornate with loads of historical features."

Hana struggled with the pace of his story. Usually, she laboured and waffled as he fidgeted. The curious role reversal seemed wrong, but dissecting it was also pointless. Her mind drew her back to the sight of the body floating in the bay, its clothes swirling like a shroud as the ocean tossed it from wave to wave like a bullied child in the playground. Hana shivered, gratified when Logan's arm tightened around her. "Sounds gorgeous," she mused. "What were Slutty Sally, Ron and Horrible Henk doing there?"

"They're using the building to store cash," he said.

Hana frowned. "We know that. Fake cash."

"No." He shook his head. His crown bumped against the door. "Not fake cash, Hana. It's real, but it's dirty. They're laundering it. Henk takes it back to New Zealand as wages, with payslips from a security job on the island. Sally is using it to refund credit card withdrawals at the resort's reception. They've shifted millions in a brief time. Sally and Henk took trips to the Philippines and moved a heap more. There are two stuffed bank accounts with their names on them."

"Laundered cash?" Hana frowned. She straightened her legs, her brain registering muscular pain from her long night. She glanced at her watch, alarmed to find the morning slipping away even though the sky hadn't lightened. "Where did they get it?"

"Remember that cyclone I told you about from last year? It wrecked a boat just outside the harbour."

"Yeah." Hana closed her eyes. "The Salty Fish or something similar."

Logan ran the back of his hand over his lips. He held the water bottle out to Hana and, when she refused, slugged the rest. "Well, that's the boat which brought in the dirty money. The Sail Fish. I saw wooden crates and enough plastic wrap at the house to suggest someone prepared the cash for an extended period sitting on the ocean floor. I guess they planned to drop it, and someone else would fetch it at a later date. If you think about it, it's a brilliant plan for hiding hot currency for a while."

"Around here?" Hana squeezed her eyes closed, aware of the grittiness of her lids. "But the water is crystal clear and there are diving tours all the time. That's a dumb idea."

"I don't think they meant to end up here," Logan added. "The cyclone blew them miles off course, and they wrecked near the island. Hosking's crew salvaged the cash and stored it up at the hospital in that derelict building. He's the only dive boat operator in this region. But that's the interesting thing. The crates and the plastic show no sign of ever being in the water. They're clean."

"Maybe they dried it all," Hana mused. "How long would that take?"

Logan shrugged and hissed under his breath. "Not sure. The owner of the cash must have planned for that." He shook his head and winced. "Nah. The crates are bone dry. The plastic should smell like salt or seaweed. I didn't see a grain of sand in the building. The money didn't leave the boat."

"Okay, so why launder it?" Hana asked. "Why not just spend it openly? Like a lottery win?"

"They don't know where it came from. The distributor might have marked the notes. An organisation which goes to that much trouble to hide it knows it's dirty. Why would Hosking take the risk? It's possible someone missed it and came looking. Or may still come. This island has few resources. It's taken almost a year to identify the captain's body. The New Zealand police would help by circulating dental records, but the Sail Fish hailed from the Philippines, so it's all taken time. It's possible whoever watched for any bodies to reappear will work out the yacht sank in Rarotongan water. They'll come looking for their product. Hence the rush."

"Ohhh." Hana tutted. "That explains something. I think your visit to Mabel spooked Sally. That's why they're running. They believe the owner of the cash has arrived on the island." She tapped her teeth with the fingers of her left hand. The loamy taste made her wince. "But Craig used fake money. He and Sally are both scamming the island and don't realise the other is running their own scheme." Hana turned to observe her husband's strong profile. His colour improved with each passing minute, but dark circles still underlined his stunning silver irises. "The pastor's granddaughter saw him do it. And I watched him retrieve bundles of it from the cubby behind our villa. Jared used it too. I'm guessing Craig gave it to him for the poker game but expected him to win and not to lose every cent."

Logan tutted and his chest deflated. He rubbed his right hand across his injured pectoral. "This is where it gets complicated. The fake cash is a red herring. Even Hosking didn't know where it came from until recently. But I heard Sally and Henk talking about Hosking's dive boat. And I don't think the Sail Fish wrecked. It's possible the ship at the bottom of the ocean is actually his original vessel. The Ellie Marie."

"Piracy?" Hana turned to face him. The wind increased its battering of the porch. A tearing issued from the balustrade like bones breaking. She cringed. "How could they get away with that? Each boat is different."

"Not necessarily. There are makes of scuba boat, just as there are cars. The wreck on the ocean floor is almost identical to the boat we toured on. So what if the Sail Fish answered a distress call from the local dive boat after it hit underwater rocks? One man's body got washed overboard and never turned up." He tapped his sternum. "I'm repeating a version of the story Hosking's diving instructor told us as we got ready to snorkel. But he told it the other way around. He said the Ellie Marie answered the visiting yacht's call and gave assistance. It contained three occupants. The man overboard never showed up, but the authorities recently identified the captain. In the instructor's version, a woman died too and has also remained missing."

"Mabel!" Hana's eyes widened. "She's the female occupant! Is that why Sally is keeping her drugged at the dementia unit?"

"I think so. The dive instructor told us the Ellie Marie suffered damage in the cyclone and they sailed her to the Philippines for a refit. I think they stripped any identifying serial numbers off the Sail Fish, and someone here did the same for the sunken Ellie Marie. Remember, I saw only one name plate when I swam around the wreck? It struck me as unusual."

"They planted it." Hana's eyes narrowed. "It seems like an elaborate ruse. And why would Hosking and his partner encourage you to dive around it? I'd take all future divers to the other side of the island and never mention it again. Why tempt fate?"

Logan twisted his lips. The action opened a cut, and a droplet of blood pooled along the scarlet line. "Because they're reinforcing the lie in case anyone ever asks. It's self-reassurance. Imagine how many divers this year have heard that tale and noticed nothing untoward in their story. It's becoming a legend."

"Okay," Hana mused. "So, who took the Sail Fish to the Philippines, and who remained in Rarotonga to strip the wreckage of the Ellie Marie? One requires an experienced diver, and the other doesn't. And what boat did they use in the interim?"

"Someone else who's good in the water, I guess."

A memory returned to Hana. She saw a yellow kayak with a scrape across its hull. Ron had spoken about Craig's insatiable need for sex and said Hosking had seen him with a woman in the bay. She let the information fall into place for a moment, sifting through the separate facts until she achieved clarity. It led her in a different direction. "Ron," she said, her tone dull. "The pool guy. He'd only need a small fishing boat with a tiny motor for diving there. Or a kayak. So that's why they kept him around. But they're all leaving today." She glanced sideways and ducked as another heavy object tested the strength of the lounge window. It clattered against it and a loud crack echoed around the villa.

81

Fall - tātopa

"It's not safe here." Logan grunted as he leaned forward. The lounge curtains flew skyward in the cold air, which vented through the crack.

Hana nodded, but her mind whirred. "Po," she mused. "Sally put a suitcase of cash into her boot. She intended to deliver it to someone named Po."

"Hana! We need to get to the back of the villa!" Logan warned. He dipped forward onto his knees and the bottle tipped sideways and skittered away from him.

Hana shook her head, stubbornness making her foolish. "I waited all night for you to come back out. You haven't told me everything yet!"

Logan's left hand closed around her upper arm and he almost hauled her shoulder from her socket. "I scouted the house after I first entered it. There's a basement level below ground. A kind of bunker.

They stored the cash in there. That weird noise was them dragging the remaining crates across the concrete floor. The entry point is in the lobby. Sally walked up the steps and I slipped into the room to the left. There's a closet with access to the attic. I pulled myself onto the shelf and hid in the roof space. It gave me freedom to move about the entire building if I walked on the joists and didn't make a sound. Their voices carried from the basement. I heard everything." His grip on her arm hurt as he gave another valiant tug. "Now, let's go!"

But they'd wasted too much time. *She'd* wasted it, actually. Logan yanked her to her feet and hauled her past the bedroom and kitchen. Her wet plimsolls slid against the smooth tiles, turning it into a skating rink. With the balance of a man who'd spent his life in the saddle, Logan kept moving, his feet pointed towards the square bathroom jutting out from the rear wall. The open doorway beckoned like a yawning mouth.

Hana screamed and dropped to her haunches, covering her head with her forearms as the lounge window smashed, showering hazardous droplets of glass onto the sofa beneath it. A padded recliner from beside the swimming pool followed, jamming itself through the gap like a burglar attempting to clamber through the aperture.

"Hana!" Strong fingers curled beneath her armpits and the veins showed in Logan's forearms as he dragged her backwards across the floor. Her heels squealed over the tiles. "Where are you hurt?" Logan raised her up and spun her around, his irises flashing as he ran gentle palms along her arms and shoulders. "Did it get you?" Glass cascaded from his tee shirt, hitting the floor like tinkling snow.

But the lawn chair hadn't finished. It shuddered, raising itself up as it continued its mission to enter the property, egged on by the driving gale force wind.

A crack shook the building and the front door groaned as something heavy pressed against it. A metallic searing heralded the demise of the fly screen beyond it. "We need to get out!" Hana shook her head and glass shards tumbled from her hair, entering her clothing and scoring her delicate skin in the places it touched. Rain spattered the sofa beneath the window, darkening the fabric in seconds.

"Yeah." Logan crunched across the debris to the front door as another crash sounded. The pill bottle had slipped from his pocket and he bent to retrieve it. He took a single step backwards. The front door flew open, the wooden architrave rent from its housing. The concrete base of an umbrella stand blocked the gap like an arm stretched out to prevent the entry of something far worse. Pinned diagonally across the doorway, it funnelled the wind into two narrow spears of icy air. The wood surrounding the remains of the architrave groaned. "Go!" Logan shouted the words, the whistle and screech of the wind drowning them.

Hana struggled to remain upright. The wind rushed her with the force of a rugby tackle. She dipped at the waist, edging sideways with agonising steps until she reached the frame for the bathroom door.

Logan swore as the wall to the left of the open front door peeled away like a banana skin. The heavy umbrella stand shifted until the edge of its base almost slipped past the remains of the splintered door frame. One more giant push and it would hurtle free across the villa, a missile fit to shatter bones. The lawn chair groaned and drove itself further through the window. "Bathroom!" Logan yelled as Hana clung to the architrave with white-knuckled fingers. The laces draped on either side of her plimsolls like ribbons. He covered the distance between them with difficulty, the pill bottle falling from his hand and gaining lift until it smashed against the rear wall. The tablets fell like hail against the floor before joining a frantic dance commanded by the wind.

Logan reached for her, his body acting as a break. He gave her a valiant shove into the bathroom, forcing her through the gap and piling through after her.

Even his mighty strength couldn't close the bathroom door behind them. His fingers clawed at the wall as he heaved himself across the room. A hungry vortex yawned after him, pulling and sucking at his shirt. His body weight hit Hana full in the spine as he cannoned into her, catapulting her into the vanity. He seized the ornate pottery cylinder which housed the toilet brush and hurled it through the bevelled window behind her.

The wind seemed to cackle with excitement at the through-draught, blowing and screaming until the bathroom door slammed hard of its own accord. The building creaked overhead with the piercing shriek of metal nails releasing their hold on the aluminium roof.

"Out!" Logan yelled. He braced his back foot against the skirting board and dragged Hana across his body by the elbow. She tripped over her laces and head butted his chest. She twisted her body to stare up at him, not sure how he intended her to get outside, or what he expected her to do once there. The wind filled her open mouth as she attempted to complain.

Logan lifted her one handed, his forearm clasping her around the waist. His other clung to the towel rail, and Hana saw a gap appear beneath its flimsy supports and the wall. "Out!" he commanded again, his voice hoarse in her right ear. Her left knee hit the vanity, and she understood. "Get under the building." And then he propelled her upward, flattening her against the windowsill as her plimsolls struggled for purchase against the smooth ceramic sink. His muscular arm pinned her there as his other hand appeared in her peripheral vision. He'd snatched a towel from the rail and used it to create a safe passage through the remaining jagged glass. Logan shoved her into the narrow space and she screamed against the pain which sliced across her midsection and thighs.

And then she felt herself falling, falling, falling, until she contacted the floor like a bag of bones. The impact stole her breath and agapanthus petals showered her with their purple scent.

The angry sky glowered above her, its eerie, glittering light a portend of worse to come. Hana raised herself up on her elbow and oriented her body to face the back of the villa. She needed to get out of Logan's way if his descent mirrored hers. Her fingers clawed at the shiny leaves. Stiff stems batted her forehead as she obeyed his last request. As the wind careened around both corners of the building in search of her, her fingers pushed through the foliage into nothing. Hana forced her body to follow, looking back as she edged beneath the creaking structure. "I'm through!" she yelled, the tendons in her neck aching with the strain of sending her voice over the wail of the wind. "Come down!"

But he didn't. Hana watched from the murky darkness beneath the villa as the roof, angled like a witch's pointed hat, screeched past her and crashed into the structure behind theirs.

"Logan!" she screamed at the top of her lungs. But he didn't come. She prayed for the soft thud of his cowboy boots to signify his undignified landing in the flower bed, but the cyclone denied her anything but the hoot of its maniacal laughter as it tore the resort apart. Bit by bit.

82

Separation - ʻakatakatakakē

Hana cowered between the villa's pilings as the gates of hell opened and swallowed Rarotonga. The deafening sounds numbed her ears as she failed to distinguish one destructive screech from another. She couldn't discern time and her smashed watch face told only lies. The hour hand stuck forward in an unnatural elbow joint, its comrades silent and unmoving. Hana covered her ears with her palms and squeezed her eyes closed. Discarded bricks and loose rubble dug into her stomach and chest. Stinging sensations from her midriff indicated wounds sliced open by her hasty journey through the broken bathroom window.

Hana jumped as something moved against her left arm. The dimness beneath the villa offered little visibility. She turned her head to see what new demon had invaded her hiding place, her gaze landing on a set of beady eyes peering back at her. A tufted head darted forward and pecked at her exposed wrist. Pitiful sounds emitted from a pointed beak. Hana swallowed. She'd made an early enemy of the chicken hoard and didn't trust it at such proximity. She grunted as it pecked at her armpit, as though seeking admittance. Hana lifted her arm as the villa before her vanished. She kept it raised, shock rippling through her body. Where did it go? Empty space remained, the chunky round pilings sticking from the ground like bones. The cyclone had ripped the villa from its awning with the ease of a child snatching up toys.

The chicken pushed its way beneath Hana's armpit, its head popping out and hovering close to her cheek. Hana dropped her arm and its feathered bottom wiggled as it settled in the dirt beneath it. They waited together for the cyclone to pass.

It seemed to rage for hours. Hana's myopic view from beneath the underside of the villa changed every few minutes. Objects whizzed across her vision at dizzying speed. She ceased trying to recognise the broken pieces of sheared metal or the complete panels of walls. The vacant space before her filled with debris. It caught against the raised pilings before the wind urged it on to more flight, more damage and destruction of any structures impeding its way. The area filled and emptied, filled and emptied with the regularity of a ticking clock. And she couldn't think about Logan. Any attempt to conjure his handsome features in her memory reduced her to tears. Logan pressing the wedding ring over the fourth knuckle of her left hand. Logan holding their babies with tears speckling his silver irises. Each snapshot only intensified her panic.

Rain funnelled from the heavens like spears. They lashed the dirt in front of her face and created a river, which cascaded into her makeshift hiding place and collected in a puddle beneath her stomach. The chicken appeared to sleep, its eyes closed and its neck bowed. The proud plume on its head remained plastered flat to its crown as though withdrawn in protest. Hana rested her right cheek on her fingers and closed her eyes.

Her subconscious maintained a vigil as her surroundings changed with the constancy of a film reel. But Hana's mind switched off as though to keep her safe. The chicken's faint body heat warmed her left armpit. Its damp feathers smelled of wet grass and a flora Hana couldn't recall. The cyclone continued for what seemed like hours, wreaking havoc over the resort. It ripped, tore, stripped, and levitated almost everything in Hana's narrow view. The changing scene made her dizzy in those brief moments when even louder crashes or bangs caused her to gasp and turn her head. Many times she imagined the floor of the villa above her, abandoning its role as her temporary ceiling and flying off into the distance. But it held. Somehow.

Logan had joked about his nine lives, but he'd already used up more than that. Hana prayed he'd found somewhere safe to hide, but a numbness occupied the space where her connection with him resided.

Cyclone Angela had systematically dismantled the villa they'd shared. Hana had glimpsed her open pink suitcase whizzing east hours before, her clothing and underwear deposited far and wide. The bathroom window she'd clambered through lay in a tangle of twisted wood and glass shards just metres in front of her. She removed her hand from beneath her chin and stretched her arm out wide. Her exhausted mind conjured an image of Logan hiding beside her. She ran her fingers over his imaginary broad shoulders and silky black hair. But the dust and the soaked ground shocked her back to reality as her palm hit the floor. And the precious picture of Logan winked out. Hana cradled the chicken tighter. The dryness of her mouth caused her tongue to stick. She doubted she could speak to a potential rescuer.

Rescuer.

Her hope plummeted further at the notion that anyone else had survived the onslaught. She hadn't seen or heard another soul for hours. A blue spot showed at the apex of Hana's view, and she risked edging forward to peek out. The chicken released a squawk of irritation and hopped alongside her, determined to stay close. A hailstone the size of a golf ball puttered against the soil, flattening the last tendrils of a struggling agapanthus. It rolled towards Hana, bumping against her chin as another landed a metre away. The chicken complained again as Hana reversed back into her hole. When she lifted her arm, it shuffled back into position. "It's not over," she whispered to it with a sigh.

A hailstone rolled into the hidey and Hana grasped it in fingers which defied dexterity. She blew off the dirt and licked it. "Ironic, I guess," she mused. "I wouldn't drink the tap water, but I'll take a hail stone off the floor." The ice numbed her lips and tongue, but it at least melted to a drinkable liquid on her palm. She offered it to the chicken, and it pecked at the water, its beak creating a light bump against Hana's icy skin. She repeated the process with more ice balls until the chicken turned its face aside in refusal, and her stomach set up a nauseating growl.

The hail gave way to torrential rain again, and the lawn's sheen disappeared beneath a murky puddle. Water ran in meandering tributaries beneath Hana's body until even the ache from inactivity faded to a dull, icy burn. The chicken shivered against her, their bodies sharing in a cacophony of rattling teeth and beak. And as the sky grew darker still, and the cyclone remained overhead, Hana ceased fighting her circumstances with mental images of those she loved. Her cheek rested on the fingers of her right hand, her shins and feet submerged in the growing flood waters. Consciousness lost its grip on her and dire circumstance proclaimed itself the victor. She mentally christened the chicken Winston.

83

Save - pu 'apinga

"She's hypothermic. Careful with her neck until we know what we've got." The male voice held a tired urgency, the strained notes of someone who'd worked beyond their available resources.

Hana's chin hit the floor as the warm fingers gripping her right hand tugged her arm further forward. A woman's soft hand pressed against the artery on the underside of her wrist. "Slow pulse and shallow breathing. Just wait, she's regaining consciousness."

Hana groaned at the pain which bloomed from the glass cuts on her chest and stomach. Her body edged along the ground by degrees, moving forward through the dirt as the fingers closed around her right wrist and pulled.

"Grab her other arm," the female voice ordered. "Steady."

Hana clamped her left elbow against her side, her icy wrist slipping free of the man's grasp. The chicken's cold, feathery body shifted through the dirt with her as though glued to her ribs.

"What the hell is that?" A man's voice rose, high pitched and startled.

"A hen." The tugging on Hana's right wrist ceased. Warm, foetid air filled her nostrils and open mouth as she blinked up into a watery light. Cyclone Angela trailed a tropical breeze, which ruffled the woman's brown hair as she gazed down at Hana's upturned face.

"Winston." Hana's voice croaked from thirst and lack of use. "Winston." She tried again. "Help him."

"Is she talking about the dead guy over there?" The man lowered his voice.

Hana held her breath and clasped the chicken around the middle. She thrust it forward as though presenting it on stage. "Winston." The cockerel lay lifeless in the dirt, its wing feathers brushing Hana's nose. Her eyes filled with tears as she dealt with the chicken's death and the slow realisation someone had mentioned a dead guy. "Logan," she rasped. "Logan."

"Is that another chicken?" the woman asked. Her voice held a ring of familiarity.

Soft brown hands appeared in Hana's vision as the man stroked her hair away from her forehead. "Where's the blood coming from? Roll her onto her back, but careful. We might need the spinal board." Heavy tan walking boots filled Hana's peripheral vision as he rose and shouted to someone nearby. "Hey, bring the board over here."

Running feet heralded instant obedience. Hana groaned as her rescuers rolled her onto her back. Her eyes watered against the brightness of the sky. It still held the greyness of trauma, but the clouds had lost their ebony anger. Light rain fell like mist, coating Hana's cheeks and chin. "Logan," she said again, but no one replied.

"What's your name?" The woman remained on her knees beside her. Deft fingers examined Hana's nape and dug beneath her to run across the geography of her spine. "It all feels okay, but you'll need scans and X-rays at the hospital," she concluded.

Hana turned her head sideways, taking in the green scrubs and yellow vest with *Medic* printed across it in block serif font. A badge pinned to the green fabric explained the sense of familiarity. Karla, the nurse from Jared's ward. "Hana. But my husband," Hana begged, her throat hitching. "Where's Logan?"

Karla winced and lifted Hana's tee shirt. "I remember you. I'm not sure where your husband is," she replied. "The police are collating all the information about missing people. They can tell you more."

"But he has haemophilia," Hana pleaded. "I need to find him."

The medic shook her head and glanced up at her colleague. "Three cuts are deep. They need excising and stitching. We can't mess around with them here. Is that second ambulance back from the hospital yet?"

"But my husband," Hana protested as willing hands shunted her sideways onto the board designed to restrict the worsening of back or neck injuries.

A hiss of fury erupted from nearby and the stretcher listed sideways. Hana gasped as the protective strap tightened across her forehead. Karla bounced beside her as though her feet had joined in an involuntary jig. "Bloody chicken!" she shrieked.

A violent flap of wings carried Winston upward, and he clattered with the side of the stretcher. His plume half rose, ratty and frayed, the feathers bent at odd angles. It lent him a crazed appearance, his tawny colours dull in the weird silver light. His grizzled feet clutched at the stretcher's edge and he waddled onto Hana's thighs.

"Winston," Hana breathed. A tear slipped sideways from her right eye. The strapping prevented her from lifting her hands to cradle him, but the cockerel settled on her legs. He tucked his clawed feet beneath his body as though roosting and gave the stretcher bearers the benefit of his black, beady eyes.

"We can't take a chicken to the hospital!" The man supporting the head end of Hana's stretcher hardened his jaw. "Can't you lift it off?"

"You lift it off!" A male voice came from the other end, sounding incredulous. Then, "Ouch! It bit me!"

Karla exhaled and shook her head. "We don't have time for this. Take the chicken to the hospital with Hana. Radio for someone from the vet clinic to meet you there if they're free. It might need attention or euthanasia." She paused, and Hana forced her eyes far enough to the left that they ached in their sockets. Karla shook her head. "It just looks irritated to me."

"Logan?" Hana asked again, her cracked voice rising. "My husband. He sent me through the window and told me to hide under the villa. He promised to follow."

The medics glanced at each other, and Hana saw Karla swallow. "We know nothing," she ventured. "We only found you and one other person so far."

"Why didn't you head inland with everyone else?" The man above Hana spoke to her, his lyrical tone gentle. "Didn't you hear the cyclone warnings?"

"We heard the claxon but didn't know where to go." Her heart rate increased and her chest rose and fell with shallow breaths. She'd shot Sally and would have to face the consequences alone and without Logan's wisdom. Sally might at that very moment occupy a hospital bed and would delight in pointing Sergeant Wally George in Hana's direction. "I don't want to go to the hospital," she insisted. Her wrists flexed against the bindings, keeping her in place. An angry pain bloomed across her stomach. "Put me down. I want my husband. I'm not leaving here without him."

She cranked her eyes to the right, her head pinned to the stretcher by the taut strap. A man wearing a hard hat appeared beside her, a needle and syringe extended in his left hand. "We don't have time for this," he barked. Hana inhaled in protest at the sharp scratch on her right arm just below the shoulder joint. She tried to speak, but numbness spread across her tongue and down through her neck. The eerie sky crossed her vision last, streaks of silver and white like wisps of wood smoke as her eyes rolled back into her head.

84

Protect - auau

Hana woke to the sound of rapid gunfire. She threw up her arms to protect her head and a bleating wail added itself to the mix. A second later, firm hands closed around her wrists. "Steady, steady," the hand's female owner urged. "You're safe. We're giving you intravenous fluids. Don't pull out the tube. The cannula is in your right hand, look."

Someone had glued Hana's eyelids closed, and she panicked, unable to see. She yanked her wrists upwards, hitting herself in the nose as they pinged free without resistance. Then came the other noise, a high-pitched scream which ended in a hiss and what sounded like a fanfare.

"Why is that chicken still here?" A male voice lifted above the fray, tired and irritated. It held the musical twang of the local accent beneath the grave unhappiness. "Where's the bloody vet? Get that

IV line back in and silence that machine's bloody clicking!"

Hana sensed the flutter of wings, a soft stirring of the air and then the light pressure points caused by two splayed feet traversing her left thigh. Winston skirted her wounds by stepping onto the mattress and scurrying to her face. He appeared less bedraggled with his feathers dried out. His red comb stood upright again, a permanent kink in the plume between his eyes. He shook himself and his bulk increased, his cape and chest fluffed like a puffer fish. Only one blue sickle feather remained in the sad tail display. His beady eyes observed Hana, and he blinked, creating an expression of permanent surprise.

"The vet said he's fine," the first voice remarked. "He just wants to stay with the patient."

"Winston," Hana rasped. "His name is Winston." A curved straw appeared beside her mouth and she drank, the cool liquid easing her sore throat. The warnings about not drinking the local water burst into the forefront of her mind and she released a sob. "Logan," she pleaded, water cascading from between her lips and soaking her neck. Her memory conjured an image of their last moments together, sharing the bottle of spring water while hunkered behind the villa door. "I want my husband! I want to go home!"

"Mrs Du Rose?" The familiar baritone silenced Hana as though a hidden hand had flicked a switch. Her body stiffened as she awaited Sergeant Wally George's prognosis. He'd either found Logan or worse, he hadn't. It no longer remained within her list of concerns that he might arrest her for shooting Sally.

"Where's Logan?" Her chest hitched, her lungs restricted by the waterproof bandages taped to her stomach and chest. The adhesive plastic prickled against her skin. A curtain fluttered around her cubicle, a gaudy seventies sunburst of chocolate brown and mandarin orange. The nurse finished re-attaching the tube to the cannula in Hana's hand before leaving with a promise to return.

"You gained a chicken." Sergeant Wally George edged closer and Winston turned his beady eyes on the police officer. The man sighed and took a cautionary step back. "Didn't you hear the sirens?" he asked. That question again. How could the local officials not see that a wailing claxon with no instructions held little value to a stranger on the island?

"We didn't know where to go." Her reply sounded flat, her emotion walled behind it, waiting for release. "Logan got hurt. We needed his medication from the villa. He has haemophilia."

He got shot in the chest, her brain reminded her. And her phone saved his life only for him to lose it to a gale with no conscience.

“I remember.” Sergeant Wally George relaxed his stance. He stared down at her, his expression quizzical. “We found your friend’s body. She washed up onto the beach in the cyclone.” Hana watched his Adam’s apple bob in his brown throat as he turned aside to collect his thoughts.

“I know,” Hana replied. “I saw her floating near the resort as we tried to get to safety.” Bile rose into her mouth at the memory of Hallie’s splayed arms, her hair trailing from her skull like seaweed. She gulped. “Logan didn’t see her. We just needed to get out of the weather. I couldn’t help her.”

Sergeant Wally George exhaled and studied Hana for a long moment. “I had nothing to do with her disappearance,” he said, lowering his voice. “But you’re right, she visited the station on the day she vanished. She’s travelled to Rarotonga for years and we’d all run into each other countless times. It’s a small island. Her child wasn’t mine. But I know her pregnancy was new, around six weeks. That’s not why she came here.”

Hana clenched her jaw. Thoughts of confession rampaged through her mind, but she needed Logan to provide the clarity. He’d planned their strategy for escaping this faux paradise without Hana ending up on trial for shooting Sally. "Why did she visit you?" Her voice wavered. "Was it to tell you Craig had counterfeit cash or something else?"

Shutters crashed over Sergeant Wally George's brown eyes. "To apologise," he said. "For her animosity." He pursed his lips with no intention of revealing any more secrets. Winston infused Hana with warmth as he snuggled between her left arm and her ribs. He pushed his beak into the downy fluff of his chest. His head disappeared as though it had never existed. Hana stared at the apex of his shoulders and the seamless way in which his feathers covered the arch of his neck. "How many dead or injured?" she asked.

"One dead," Sergeant Wally George replied. "Over twenty decent injuries, such as yours. Tens of minor cuts and bruises."

"But the death isn't Logan's." The numbness returned to Hana's voice. "Otherwise, you would say so." Her gaze cut to the police officer. "Where is my husband? Is he injured then? He must be somewhere." Fear rose into her chest, stretching the aching muscles covering her ribs and locking her lungs on an in-breath. Would she know if he'd left this life without her? Surely her heart would shatter like the glass from the bathroom window and send her after him. "Where is he?" she demanded again.

"I don't know." Sergeant Wally George's tone held genuine sorrow. "I wish I did." He sniffed and gazed towards the fluttering cubicle curtain and the gap where it met the wall. "I should crack on," he said, turning his feet to face his escape.

"Wait!" Hana demanded. Her fingers absent mindedly caressed Winston's wing bows. "You found Hallie's body, but she didn't die in the cyclone. She isn't the death you referred to. I heard the paramedics talking about a man's body. Whose is it?"

She thought she knew the answer before he said it, the weight lying like a brick in the pit of her stomach. But she'd got it wrong. She knew that as soon as the police officer opened his mouth. "I don't think you know him," Sergeant Wally George intoned. "A man named Henk Roibos. He's registered as staying at a different resort but may have sheltered with friends at Paradise Villas before the cyclone got going." He tapped the side of his nose. "Please don't share that information. We won't make it public until New Zealand police have notified his family." He dipped from the waist as though bowing. "I'll get back out there and keep an eye open for Mr Du Rose."

Hana swallowed, confusion filling her brain. It forced out the realisation that Logan might not come back to her. "No," she breathed for Winston's hearing only. "He's lying. Why would Hallie apologise for her animosity towards him in the afternoon and then repeat it that same night after she got drunk? I don't believe that's why she went to see him. I think she told him about Craig's cash and he upset her somehow." Sergeant Wally George's footsteps tapped away on the tiled floor. Hana pursed her lips to stem the scream pressing up from her chest. "And Logan isn't dead. He still has lives left. And if he's anywhere on this island, he'll come for me."

85

Roost - ‘ata ’ata

A vet removed Winston during the night. The cockerel protested his ejection with a mighty doodleoo, which woke everyone on the hastily created emergency ward. Hana woke as a brown skinned man with smiling eyes scooped the creature into a metal cage. “I’ll take care of him,” he promised in a whisper.

“He’s called Winston,” Hana croaked, and he responded with a nod. A nurse stuck her head in and smiled at Hana before swishing her cubicle curtain closed. Silence settled back over the ward as lamps flicked off again, but Winston’s disappearance left an ache in Hana’s soul.

The medication soothed her into a heavy sleep before betraying her to vivid nightmares induced by trauma. Dead bodies flew past her vision as she gripped Logan’s outstretched fingers. But in each painful rerun, her grasp failed and a sucking sensation ripped her away from him. They became separated by hazardous flying objects which obscured her view of his face in the ruined bathroom window.

Hana woke with a sad hiccough. Lifting her left hand to her face, she discovered fresh tears on her cheeks. She'd reported Logan missing to a police officer she hadn't recognised. He'd followed close on Sergeant Wally George's heels and nodded with sympathy, scratching Logan's full name onto his notepad with a failing pen. Several times he'd scored over the L as the ink depleted on his page. Hana feared he might poke the nib right through and had closed her eyes. He'd mumbled promises and then left, stalling to shoot the breeze with the man in the next bed who'd suffered a concussion when his garden shed became airborne with him inside it.

An eerie darkness hung over the makeshift ward, a dim light filtering through from the corridor. Cobalt shadows smothered Hana in the lea of the hastily erected cubicle curtains. The rustle of fabric coming from her left accompanied the heavy presence of another. Hana held her breath, her lashes fluttering in a pretence of sleep. The high buzz of static filled her ears as she strained to listen, needing to discern the snores of the woman in the next cubicle from her awareness of this new presence. It hadn't been there when she last woke, but screaming herself sick didn't seem smart without evidence. Her throat locked at the thought of a night-time visit from Ron, Hosking, or Sally. Or the mysterious Po.

Hana inhaled, relying on her senses for clarity. Her brain relayed recognition of the elements, sea salt, sweat, dust and the faint, familiar scent of home. She exhaled, a sob bursting from between her clenched teeth. "Logan?" she whispered, her chest hitching.

Turning onto her left side brought a fresh burst of pain from the stitches holding together the spiteful cuts to her torso. He'd pushed her face-first through the bathroom window, but her deceitful memories had conjured alternative horrors in the aftermath. She had fleeting visions of his bereft expression as Cyclone Angela whisked the villa into its maw like Dorothy's house in the Wizard of Oz. "Logan?" she begged, her voice rising.

A breathy sigh accompanied the movement. "Yep," he whispered. "Most of me, anyway." His warm hand closed over her wrist, halting her flailing grabs into mid-air. She inhaled, pitching forward and met by the chrome safety rail keeping her in the bed.

"I thought I'd lost you." Tears ran in rivulets from a well in her soul. They pattered onto the starchy sheets and soaked the sleeve of her gown. Logan rose with a grunt, releasing her wrist for a moment. The bed rail gave a guttural groan as he released the mechanism and guided it down until it clicked into the housing. Logan's right hip nudged Hana aside as he edged onto the mattress. His arm reached around her shoulders and tugged her close. Hana pressed her nose against his ribs and cried, muffling the sound against his shirt. The tube attached to the cannula in her right hand pulled taut across the sheets. A stinging sensation issued from the needle plugged into her vein. It proved enough to prod Hana from her misery and banish the bone shaking sobs from her chest. She sat up and edged her bottom across the mattress to allow Logan more room. "Tell me what happened?" she demanded, wiping her nose on the back of her hand.

Logan's head sank against the pillows, and he released a gargantuan sigh. Hana reached for his right hand as his arm looped around her shoulders. He settled but gave a hiss of pain. The rough fabric of a bandage met Hana's questing touch. "I broke two fingers," he said, his tone lacklustre. "I also have a fractured rib where the phone took the impact of the bullet. There's a cut on my forehead and two marvellous black eyes. I'm glad you can't see me."

"Turn on the light." Hana pushed herself upright, but Logan forced her back against the pillows.

"No," he replied, his tone severe. "I'm not supposed to be here. They said no visiting. It's chaos out there."

"How did you get in?" Hana whispered. Her gaze shifted to the faint light blooming from the corridor and fanning out above her cubicle curtains. "How did you find me?"

Logan sniffed and shifted on the mattress. "I repeated the trick with the sash window, but this time I managed it with more grace. Then I just walked around until I heard you."

Hana swallowed. "Heard me?" Her voice emerged as a squeak. "Doing what?"

Logan's shrug rocked her body. "Just little noises you make when you've gone to sleep upset. Anyway, who's Winston?"

Hana groaned. "My rooster. The vet took him. I need to get him back."

"Right." Logan didn't sound amused. "Well, that's a relief because you said his name twice."

Hana snuggled against his side, wincing as he grunted with pain. "Can you listen for someone coming? I think the cyclone wrecked my hearing. My head is filled with background noise."

"We're good," he soothed. "The staff use pen torches for light. The nurses check every thirty minutes. You can see the glow over the curtains. I'll shift under the bed and hide when they come back."

"Logan," Hana breathed. "I can't believe you're here. I'm so relieved. Tell me what happened after I climbed through the bathroom window."

Logan snorted. "Armageddon. The cyclone ripped off the roof of the villa and then picked at the siding, tearing it plank by plank. It played them like a caber tossing competition, smashing them through the bathroom wall. The door burst open and caught me in the face. It knocked me out for a spell, but I'm not sure for how long. I woke to find our two-seater sofa pivoted on its end above me. One more gust and it would have crushed me beneath it." He used his left hand to scrub at his eyes. "I crawled along the far wall and remembered Craig's cubby beneath the floor. We didn't realise you could access it via a trap door under our bed. The frame and mattress by that time were airborne. The gale prevented me from standing up straight, so the only safe alternative was to head lower. I squeezed through the trap door and it slammed shut on my fingers. My head pounded like a jack hammer and fun fact, the cubby door doesn't open from the inside. I tried kicking it, but the building had twisted on its pilings, so I gave up. There seemed no point climbing back into the villa until the cyclone passed over."

"So you were near me the whole time?" Hana's voice rose. A man's voice shushed her from nearby and she froze.

Logan's torso shook with his emphatic nod. He lowered his lips to her ear. "I didn't know for sure. If you'd made it underneath the villa, then yes. If not, you could have ended up anywhere on the island. I tried shouting to you but the cyclone drowned out my voice. I lost consciousness for a long while and woke up to hear yelling and banging. Someone mentioned a woman called Hana, so I crawled back out through the trap door. I terrified one of the civil defence guys picking through the rubble. He screamed like an opera singer when my head popped through the floor. A nurse said they'd pulled you free and sent you here. She insisted she put butterfly stitches over my head and strap my fingers before she'd let me leave. There are only two undamaged ambulances left, so I walked to the hospital."

"Oh my gosh!" Hana breathed. "You should tell someone you're okay. I reported you missing."

Logan grunted. "I'm not quite ready for that yet, babe. That big dude, Sally and Hosking, are still out there. It's best I locate them before they find us."

Hana shook her head, her matted hair brushing against the pillow. "The big guy is Henk," she whispered. "Well, he was Henk. He died at the resort."

Logan tutted. “So, that’s one less to worry about.” His tone contained no shred of compassion.

“What about the pool guy? Ron.”

Logan made a low sound in his throat, like the growl of a feral dog. “He’s nursing a worse headache than mine, babe.”

“When did you do that?” Hana demanded. “While he searched for his money? I think the others ripped him off. Hosking spoke about him as though they thought him surplus to requirements.”

“I figured as much,” Logan agreed. “The big guy planned to start the fire and leave on the next flight out. Hosking and Sally were sailing away. I don’t think any of them thought the cyclone would do this much damage. And the pool guy had no exit plan. Not of his own making, anyway.”

“Do you think Ron’s still out there?” Hana breathed.

Logan shook his head. He rested his cheek against Hana’s crown. “He’s not functional, babe. If he’s anywhere, he’s on this ward or Jared’s. But not in any condition to go after anyone. I hit him hard.”

Hana exhaled through her nose. The whooshing sensation sent pain into her forehead. “Can I come with you?” she begged, her tone tight. “Where can we hide until our flight leaves? Do you still have our passports and tickets?”

Logan's laugh rumbled through his chest and into her jaw. "Yep." He tapped his waistband where the bag nestled against his abdomen. "The passports will need drying out before we leave, but I'm guessing the airport staff will understand. We can replace them once we get home. They will hopefully reprint our tickets, especially as both our mobile phones are buggered."

"My clothes are in a bag at the end of the bed," Hana said. "Your phone is in my jeans pocket. It might work."

Logan pressed a kiss to her temple and hugged her against him. "I doubt it will."

Another loud protest issued from the cubicle across the corridor. "Some of us need to sleep!" a gravelled bass tone insisted.

Hana clung to Logan as he rose. A silver light spread across her sheets as dawn kissed the island. "Don't leave me!" she begged, her chest hitching. "I'm coming with you!"

"No!" His tone held authority as he kissed her forehead and peeled her grasping fingers from around his wrist. "I have stuff to sort out and you're safer here. Get some sleep. I'll come back for you." The curtain swished, and he'd gone before the next round of shushing provided the only disturbance to the endless night.

Hana rubbed her index finger over her cracked lips and burrowed into the sheets. She rebuked herself for not once telling Logan how much she loved him. Eight hours ago, she'd have traded anything just for that chance.

86

Navigate - kaveinga

Despite her angst, Hana lay back against the pillows and closed her eyes. Logan's survival lessened the rock in her chest, but she wanted him with her. She imagined the nature of the 'stuff' he needed to do, putting her needs into context. News of Cyclone Angela would have made the New Zealand media by now. Logan needed to contact Mark and then Toby. Perhaps he'd ask Liza to make the call to Alfred.

Her raw fingers coasted across the crisp sheet until they contacted something soft and light. She struggled to grasp it in her left hand, huffing in frustration as it fluttered out of range. When a darting lurch crushed it between her index finger and thumb, she lifted it to her nose. One of Winston's downy chest feathers tickled her skin, and she sighed, rubbing the delicate softness across her cheek. She hoped the vet would show him kindness and not allow the cockerel's officious manner to repel his efforts.

Hana lay in bed until a bright new dawn lit the ward and highlighted the stains and rips in the curtain surrounding her cubicle. The clear liquid drained from the sack suspended from a hook beside the bed, entering her veins and providing life giving fluids. People stirred around her, disjointed grunts and muffled complaints drifting towards the ceiling as they examined their injuries.

Exhausted nursing staff, conscripted from days off, pushed trolleys laden with drugs. Hana watched through a rip in her curtain as they doled out antibiotics and pain medication in pairs. One read from a list of doctor's notes and the other handed out tablets as they crawled past the sea of beds.

"How are your stitches?" The voice made her jump, and Hana's eyes shot open. Only then, she realised she'd fallen asleep amid the gentle rustling of the hospital's inhabitants coming to life. She blinked up at the male nurse she'd last viewed through Mabel's window. He smiled down at her almond-shaped eyes in a russet complexion.

Hana swallowed. "I'm not sure," she replied, her voice a strained croak. The man frowned and reached beside him for a glass of water.

"You suffered from hypothermia and dehydration yesterday. The drip will rehydrate you, but you must take sips as often as you can manage."

Hana gulped, choking on the excess fluid which slipped from both sides of her mouth. The nurse gave her a sympathetic smile of consolation and replaced the glass with a wad of tissue. Hana performed the clean-up, her pale cheeks flushing pink. She kept her gaze down as she asked, "How's Mabel? Is she okay after the cyclone?"

The nurse blinked and stared at her. He tilted his head to one side and narrowed his eyes. "Do you know Mabel?" he demanded. His tongue clacked against his teeth. He set the glass on the cabinet with a heavy thunk. "Do you know who she is?"

Hana sighed, aware that chance and exhaustion had taken her down a path she hadn't planned. She mopped at her lips and considered her reply. "I know of her," she said, lowering her voice. "I know a woman called Sally visits her, adding Fentanyl to her food or drink each morning and night." Hana swallowed, forcing out the words through a tongue which felt like sandpaper. "I know she means her mortal harm."

The nurse edged closer, dipping his torso as though proximity might assist him in comprehending her words. "Who told you this?" he demanded, his tone high. Concern had replaced the kindness in his hazel irises.

Hana bunched the sheets in both hands on either side of her, two of her most painful fingers refusing to bend. "I overheard Sally talking." She stuck to the truth, hoping Logan might approve. He would understand she sought to protect the captive old lady. Wouldn't he? She pursed her lips and pressed on with the revelation. "I saw her drop the pills when she entered the dementia unit. Later, I heard her saying she gave Mabel fentanyl. She's planning to overdose her this morning before she leaves the island."

The nurse reared back, a repeat of his reaction when Mabel spat at him. He muttered a curse and pressed his fingers over his lips. "Her son visited her," he babbled, the words piling free from loose lips. "Sally didn't like it." He whirled away on soft-soled shoes, blasting through the curtains in haste. The flimsy curtain rings snapped in three places and left the tired fabric hanging like bunting. "Wait there!" he shouted over his shoulder.

But Hana couldn't wait there. Not now. Her hands trembled as she clambered over the rail on the right side of her bed. Crinkles from her sodden hiding place beneath the villa still lined her toes. She stripped off her gown, finding her battered body naked but for a pair of paper hospital knickers. The wheels of the drip clattered against the cupboard as Hana towed it behind her. She located the plastic bag containing her soiled clothing. Upending it onto the bed, she found it damp to the touch, shivering at the realisation she needed to force her reluctant limbs into it.

"Try the phone in the reception," someone called, perhaps in answer to the agitated male nurse. A wave of relief tore through Hana at his conscientious concern for Mabel. He would call the dementia unit and halt her execution.

She remembered too late putting the bullet through Sally's arm. Would the wicked woman possess the energy or ability to kill Mabel? Hana imagined her turning up with Hosking on her heels. One of them would follow through to remove the last living person able to identify their clever switcheroo with the boats. And the money. Mabel knew about the money. Worse still, perhaps the owner of the laundered cash had employed her to transport it. The identification of the missing captain's body meant they were possibly already on their way. They would come with losses, questions and violence. No wonder Sally and Co had brought forward their plans for escape.

Hana yanked up her wet jeans, wincing in discomfort. The stitches across her stomach dared her to fasten the buttons, so she left them open beneath her soaked tee shirt. A shiver of discomfort rippled through her body, not helped by finding only one lonely plimsoll sitting in a puddle at the bottom of the bag.

She delayed the moment for removing the needle from her right hand. Her stomach roiled with the likeness of sea sickness as she peeled off the plaster and withdrew the plastic lure. She hung the dangling entrails over the drip's metal spindle and didn't look at it again.

Logan hadn't removed the phone, perhaps reluctant to search for it in the dark. Hana pressed the power button and despite the crystallised screen, a faint glow appeared behind it. She rammed it into her back pocket, releasing a hiss of pain as it nestled like a puzzle piece into the painful bruise on her buttock. Pushing her fringe from her eyes, she peeked around the curtain into the ward.

A hotchpotch of beds greeted her. The nursing staff had amassed the injured, adding the beds like a game of dropped sticks. Only a few patients had curtains, the screens retrieved from assessment rooms and pushed together into wonky three-sided squares. A woman's reedy voice piped from behind one of them and Hana realised the staff had provided screens for the females and ignored the men.

Beds lay head to foot beyond her cubicle, male faces pressed against the pillows. Some were empty, the occupants shuffling towards the bathrooms, naked buttocks showing through the vents in the rear of their gowns. A man with a grizzled beard fiddled with a patch over his left eye. He still wore a stained floral shirt sold at the Saturday market, and he frowned and watched her through his good eye as she slipped past him. The distance between the beds admitted only a skinny person side stepping, and Hana's thigh brushed his knuckles as she passed. She lifted a finger to her lips and pleaded with him not to raise the alarm.

Her bare feet padded against the icy tiled floor until she reached the far wall. There seemed little point exiting through the busy main corridor. Mabel's nurse relayed his story in a loud voice to someone on the phone, drawing the attention of the other staff. They moved past the door of the ward as though sucked into a vortex.

Hana's fingers closed around the bottom of the nearest sash window and heaved. Fresh morning air gushed into the gap and the frame rose on its pulley. Hana gave it a determined shove, and it stayed in place, the flimsy curtains rising to touch the top of the nearest patient's bald head. He turned to face her as Hana forced her knees to bend and carry her through the gap. Wet fabric stuck to her chapped thighs and hampered her movements.

Stones dug into her soles as she landed on the path outside, but she kept moving. Morning dew dampened the grass shoots as she stepped onto a lawn, not bothering to close the window behind her. Mabel's nurse at least possessed the information to ensure her safety now. The blood tests Sally's wallet had previously refused would reveal the truth, but then everyone would come for Hana.

The Rarotongan police force would want to speak to her. And Hosking and Sally? Yeah, Hana bet they'd love a chat, too.

87

Persuasion - tāporoporo

Parted from Logan once again and left to make her own way, Hana skirted the main buildings of the hospital. She avoided notice as she padded towards the exit road, still uncertain where she wanted to go. The concrete heated beneath her bare feet as though the island had already forgotten Cyclone Angela's visit. Hana edged onto the verge, hiding the peeling skin of her toes within the blades of spiky grass. She listened out for vehicles, slipping behind trees at their rumbling approach. An electric BMW took her by surprise, creeping level with her before she registered the gentle hiss of its battery.

Hana jumped, tripping over her own feet before falling sideways into a woody bush. The branches snatched at her bare arms, showering her with leaves and debris. The passenger window lowered as the vehicle stopped beside her. "Mrs Du Rose?"

"I'm fine!" Hana called, forcing a false brightness into her tone. She brushed the crispy shards of leaf matter from her shoulders and tangled hair. But the car didn't move away, and it took a moment of panic for Hana to notice the driver had used her name. She gasped, her dry mouth failing to emit the squeak which built in her chest. Spinning on the spot, she ran at the bush, hoping to batter her way through it. Brittle branches crunched and snapped, but it repelled her like a trampoline. Hana landed on her bottom on the concrete pavement. The air left her lungs in a painful whoosh and she lacked the energy required to pick herself up again.

Shiny shoes appeared to her right, their patent surface filled with the reflected bright spots of the treacherous sun. Flared suit trousers the colour of sour cream spilled over them, encasing chunky legs which met in the middle. "Mrs Du Rose." The male voice rumbled over her, backed by the unmistakable twang of humour. "Why are you running away from me?"

Hana clutched her chest and gazed up into the florid face of Charlie Clay. "Hi," she croaked, as though lying on her back, on a pavement, in broad daylight, constituted normal behaviour. "I hope you don't expect me to get up." The fingers of her right hand sought the raised edges of the pacemaker nestled beneath her left collarbone. Her skin had a disconcerting paper-thin quality after her long wait in the puddle beneath the villa.

Charlie's hand appeared in her peripheral vision. Hana clutched his sausage-like fingers and listened to him huff and puff as he hauled her to a sitting position on the pavement. She groaned as her weight rested on the painful bruise to her buttock and Logan's phone set about driving its effects deeper. It took an age for her to pivot onto her knees and stand, using Charlie's wrist and forearm for support. She dipped forward to catch her breath before hauling Logan's phone from her jeans pocket. "Well," she concluded as the remains of the screen tumbled like falling stars to the pavement and vanished. "That's torn it."

"No matter, no matter." He glanced around him as he led her towards his vehicle. "Let's get you to safety before someone thinks I ran you over." He waved to a passing transit van. The driver slowed and bobbed forward to stare at the odd scene of a lawyer wearing a safari suit and stuffing a vagrant into his expensive vehicle. Charlie waved him away with an authoritative flick of his left hand. The transit's engine roared, and the driver sped downhill towards the island's outer ring road.

Hana sank into the passenger seat with a groan. Brown dried blood crusted the stomach area of her tee shirt, and she lifted the fabric between finger and thumb. It stuck to the packing covering her stitches, and she struggled to peel it free. "I'm bleeding again," she observed to Charlie as he slumped into the driver's seat. The vehicle listed on the right side as his weight stress tested the suspension.

"Try not to get it on the seats, dear." He patted the dash board. "This is my work vehicle." No sympathy radiated from his voice as he turned to her and paused. "Seatbelt."

Hana leaned back against the seat and closed her eyes. Each turn and bump of the vehicle alerted her to scrapes and bruises she hadn't known existed. The crown of her head ached, as did her poor buttock. Her stomach and chest smarted from the glass cuts and her filthy toes with their crusted, peeling skin revolted her. "Did Logan send you?" she asked, a sigh disturbing the cadence of her sentence.

"No," Charlie answered. "The judge. Your husband is a one-man wrecking ball."

"What?" Hana sat upright and turned to face the lawyer. The seatbelt clicked into place. "What is he up to?"

Charlie's fluffy eyebrows rose and fell in a hairy Mexican wave, which he'd perfected with years of practice. "Nothing at the moment," he concluded. "Mr Du Rose is in jail."

Hana blinked through eyes which held the scratchiness of physical and emotional exhaustion. “No!” Words spilled from her lips like a torrent spewing from the dam gates at Karapiro. She pressed her right palm against her chest as though swearing an oath. “I shot Sally, not him. What fresh hell is this?” Her left hand raked through her curls, getting stuck before the fingers reached her scalp. “Take me to the police station!” she demanded. “Take me there now, or I’ll jump out of this car.”

“No.” Charlie dipped his right elbow, and the doors locked. “Those are not my orders.”

“Liza thinks I’m Ginger Barbie!” Hana unfastened her seatbelt and rived on the door handle. “She has no faith in my ability to do anything useful!”

“And right now, you’d prove her correct.” Charlie’s jaw line showed through his sagging cheek as he ground his teeth. His career on Rarotonga had perhaps never featured an angry woman wearing bloodstained clothes and threatening to death roll from a moving vehicle.

“Ginger Barbie.” He licked the words with his tongue and grinned. “Oh, she’s such a dag, isn’t she?”

Hana gaped at him. “You like her more because she thinks of clever, bitchy names for me?” Her voice rose in the silence of the moving vehicle as Charlie turned right onto Ara Tapu Road and drove clockwise towards Avarua. She grew still and quiet at the sight of the damage which lined the western side of the island. Coconut trees lay like tumbled skittles at the edge of the beach and across the outer lane of the carriage way. Men in yellow vests wielded chainsaws, the cacophony of their labour drowning out the gentle hiss of the lapping waves. The water had receded from the road, retaking its place in island life with a degree of shame. Debris littered the white sand, the remnants of its unreserved fury just hours ago. Hana spotted two wrecked boats, one on its side with a man-sized hole in its wooden hull. The other, the remains of a yacht, leaned as though drunk against one of the few upright coconut trees still standing on the west coast. Its snapped mast and rigging hung like a hairnet over the bulbous head of the tree. Both boats held the dejected sag of failure.

Hana remained silent as Charlie navigated displaced boulders, fallen trees, and an army of community volunteers tasked with taping the island back together. The task seemed impossible with beach facing houses missing their roof or porch. Many had lost both. An upside down shed balanced on the flat bed of a truck. Hana pursed her lips, unable to discern whether it flew there itself or human hands had loaded it for removal.

Hana saw more locals in the brief journey than she had in the busyness of the markets. They commiserated with each other. Many wielded brooms and spades, already getting to work and believing the rigorous strokes of their bristles could make a difference in the tumult of a battered life.

"It's happened before. Often," Charlie remarked after a glance at her wide eyes and ashen face. "Our island spirit is strong. Those with untouched homes on the east will help. They'll offer shelter, labour and materials. Resilience is our way." His giant knuckled left hand reached out and patted Hana's writhing fingers, as though attempting to draw away a little of her pain. "You are my concern now," he soothed, his voice low. "I'm taking you to safety."

"Where?" Hana edged away from him, aware her ill-advised reliance on a comparative stranger had left her exposed. "Where are you taking me?" Her voice rose as she demanded answers. "I want to see Logan. Take me to Logan!"

"All in good time," Charlie replied. "I'm afraid you'll need to trust me."

88

Abundant - nui

Charlie continued on his clockwise journey around the island, making small talk as though Hana cared. "The pylons on the golf course survived," he remarked. "So, at least we have electricity for now." He patted the shiny walnut dashboard with a chubby hand and beamed. He lifted it and jabbed his index finger towards the Trading Post.

Hana blinked in surprise at the sight of a shipping crate in the space where she'd eaten hot chips and drank soda just days earlier. "Where did it go?" she gasped, shock stripping away her own concerns for a moment.

"It's all packed away," Charlie chortled. His lips curved upward, enjoying her surprise. "After successive cyclones destroyed the original buildings, they designed everything for 'plug and play'. The balustrade for the deck is the only part not detachable, but the owner found the long pieces across the street. He'll get it all fixed back in place by tomorrow. The damage at the airport is superficial. No planes will fly in or out for a few days, possibly a week. Part of the roof lifted and crashed down into the arrivals hall. There is debris on the runway." He leaned forward to stare at the sky through his windscreen. "Angela won't return, but a couple of minor friends might hazard a visit. Her following wind is still high. The airlines won't return until the risk is lower."

"We might get another cyclone?" Hana's chest tightened and her muscles clenched. "I can't live through that again," she breathed. "Just kill me now."

Charlie's pinched expression revealed all of his chin and its dangling counterparts, flattening his lips into thin lines. "I'd rather not," he murmured.

Hana leaned back against her seat and forced herself to relax. Her circumstances couldn't get any worse even if she followed through and dived through the window of the moving vehicle. She shook her head, wondering how Logan ended up in jail on top of his double disappearance. Closing her eyes, she imagined his gentle kisses on her forehead and telepathically promised him she'd sort it all out.

The digital clock on Charlie's flash dial revealed the time as early morning. Hana counted back the hours but found herself lost. "Is it Monday or Tuesday?" she asked in defeat.

Charlie frowned across at her, deep lines scoring his forehead. "Tuesday," he announced. "The cyclone hit land yesterday morning. I think you remained trapped for a long time. You spent last night in the hospital."

"Thank you." Hana blew out a ragged breath. She watched Charlie through the corner of her right eye, observing his capable hands on the steering wheel as he drove her to a point of disembarkation known only to him. "Can I tell you everything that happened in the last few days?" she asked, her tone soft. "Just in case something happens to me."

"Oh, Mrs Du Rose." Charlie's tone held an element of sadness. "Why do I suspect you're about to do more damage in a few minutes to our little paradise than Angela did in twenty-four hours?"

Hana maintained a respectful silence for a few moments to allow Charlie to steel himself. She figured she needed to condense the story into the time it took for them to reach their destination. "Where are we going?" she demanded. "You can at least tell me that."

Charlie wiggled in his seat, shimmying like a blancmange against the leather upholstery. "Remember how I told you we had a woman in our little club up at Nui Ngaro?" One bushy eyebrow rose, flattening the wrinkles in the lid to create a mounded plate of flesh. In response to Hana's nod, he continued, "Well, I'm taking you to her. I have no wife and my understanding of women's needs proves limited. She's waiting for you with fresh clothing, food, and a different perspective. Her connections are far reaching and she has mana within our community. I'll leave you there and head to the police station to speak to your husband. She lives ten minutes away from here."

Hana nodded, the movement tugging on the painful joint where her spine met her skull. "Okay," she conceded. "There are things which you should know."

Charlie listened, the outline of his jaw protruding more through his fleshy cheek with every new revelation. Hana told him about Craig's possession of the counterfeit cash, and how it had thrown an unwelcome light on the bigger crime involving Sally, Hosking, the resort's maintenance man, and the now deceased Henk. She told him of Logan's theory that the Ellie Marie lay wrecked on the ocean floor and the Sail Fish hosted diving tours and fishing parties in her place. "And Mabel," she added, waving her right arm as they passed through the Matavera District, which looked no worse for wear. "Her son and the captain of the Sail Fish died. Sally kept Mabel at the dementia unit, paying her bills and making it seem like an act of benevolence. I don't know why she kept her alive. Perhaps there's something she still needed from her." Hana edged her gaze sideways to study Charlie's stricken expression. "Sally intended to kill her last night. I told Mabel's nurse this morning at the hospital. He's raised the alarm, so I hope he'll keep her safe." Hana cleared her throat. "But Sally has a gunshot wound to her arm. I did that, not my husband. The gun is gone. The police won't find it. Also, our missing neighbour from the resort is dead. Her body washed up on the beach during the cyclone. I saw it. I also know who killed her."

Charlie's lips parted with the first hint of a smile since Hana began sifting through her long list of incidents and theories. He turned to face her, his irises sparkling like cut glass.

"Now that is helpful," he said, his tone light. He tapped the steering wheel with his index fingers in a joyous dance. "Tell me more about that."

89

Powerful - ririnui

Mary stood on the porch of a cute villa. With the siding painted in a shade of butter cream and the sills and architrave a deep forest green, it mirrored the wholesomeness of a chocolate box cottage. The cyclone had battered the trees and flowerbeds wrapped around the house, leaving a trail of strewn leaves and misplaced sticks in its wake. But the east side of the island had suffered none of the relentless wrath evident in just a short drive around the coast.

"Welcome." The pastor's wife took Hana's hand as she struggled to extract herself from Charlie's low vehicle. Stones and grit dug into the soles of her painful feet, causing her to limp. She kept Logan's phone in her right hand as though it had formed a lifeline to him, gratified when Charlie bid them goodbye without entering the house.

"Please get my husband out of jail?" Hana begged, her lower lip cracking as she spoke. "Whatever it is, I'm his alibi." The metallic tang of blood settled on her tongue and caused her to wince in disgust.

Charlie nodded, settling back into his vehicle and reversing onto the main road. Hana watched him leave, praying he had what it took to relay her story in all its ridiculous surmising.

Mary led her up the steps and through her green front door. A blessedly empty house greeted her, and Hana's shoulders slumped in relief. She hadn't realised until that moment how much she wished to avoid the scrutiny and curiosity of others. Mary turned to Hana and rested her palms on her shoulders with exaggerated gentleness. Her tawny complexion revealed myriad wrinkles, which gave her face a delicate patchwork. Hazel irises studied Hana with concern. "I'm a retired nurse," she said, her voice tender. "Let's get you clean, and I'll look at your injuries. There isn't much I didn't see in thirty years in the emergency department. Charlie thought most of them were superficial when he spoke to the hospital, but I'd rather assess that for myself."

Hana swallowed the lump rising into her throat. Mary's kindness touched a raw section of her soul, which Sally's cruelty hadn't flayed. "I think my suitcase is in Fiji," Hana murmured. "I have no clothes." She frowned. "So, he went to the hospital to see me this morning?" She nodded, finding an explanation for Charlie's presence on the site. "I used my mother's maiden name, MacGillivray."

"What does the name mean?" Mary leaned closer, as though desperate for the reply.

Hana swallowed. "It's actually Scottish Gaelic, though my mother came from Ireland. Mac Gille Bhràtha. It means 'servant of God's judgement,' though believe me when I say I don't feel equipped for the task."

Mary patted her cheek. "You'll do just fine. I'm guessing your husband gave Charlie a series of names you might use. And don't worry about clothes. My granddaughter dropped some of hers around this morning. She's on clean-up duty at the supermarket after the cyclone. I'll show you to the bathroom and leave you to sort yourself out." She stepped through an archway into a vintage kitchen. Hana remained on the spot, unable to summon the energy to follow. A fridge door closed with a suctioned hiss and water sloshed into a glass. Saliva leaked into Hana's mouth at the thought of a cool drink. She'd almost begun drooling as Mary pressed the glass into her sore fingers.

"Thank you," she gushed, water sloshing from between her lips as she choked and guzzled it down. After draining the glass, she wiped her mouth with the back of her hand and allowed Mary to take it from her. Logan's phone dug into her other palm. "Doesn't it worry you I used a different name to the authorities?" Her lips twisted as she thought of Wally George and the waif of a police officer who'd taken her missing report for Logan. It seemed ridiculous to have lied to the hospital staff to protect herself from Sally, when the police officers had found her just by swishing aside cubicle curtains.

"No." Mary's smile didn't waver. "People come to Rarotonga for many reasons. Some need a break and others a hiding place. It's my business to love them better and give them space to heal." She pressed smooth skinned fingers over her breast. "Now. Take a shower, but try not to disturb any stitches. Then I'll see if I can remember how to patch up a patient."

She led Hana to a family bathroom and closed the door after slipping two fresh towels over a heated rail. They hung there looking fluffy and welcoming, the colour of mint. Hana jumped as Mary knocked on the door and called to her. "It will sound daft, but use some of the Rotorua mud on your hands and feet. They look very sore."

"Thanks," Hana called, galvanising herself for her big reveal. When she'd dressed in the dim light of the hospital ward, she hadn't examined her injuries. But in the brightness of Mary's apple green bathroom with the image of the crucified Lord watching her undress, Hana's attempts at denial doomed her to failure. The floor to ceiling mirror on the wall opposite the shower condemned her vagrant appearance.

She peeled off her jeans and winced at the ebony bruises dotted across her knees and hips. Removing the tee shirt proved harder, as fresh blood had leaked from beneath the waterproof covers and welded the fabric to her chest. Her wrinkled finger ends, pruned from the extended water immersion and vasoconstriction of the blood vessels would heal. But it made her hands behave like unwieldy bunches of bananas. Once she'd shrugged herself free of the tee shirt, it forced her to examine yet more bruises and five long lines of stitches across her stomach and ribs. One line caught the rounded upper curve of her left breast but just missed the raised edges of her pacemaker as it snaked as far as her collar bone. Tufts of black thread showed beneath the clear waterproof tape, but crusted blood turned them to blurred lines. Hana's numb fingers stroked the raised pink edges of her surgical scar, which curved beneath her right rib. She shook her head. "Wow," she breathed. "At least that stayed shut." The ramifications of it opening over her already damaged liver would prove grim. Hana patted it and reminded herself she'd put distance between the surgery and the trip to Rarotonga. She negated her concerns with a shrug. Arriving with a damaged organ and a scar reluctant to heal seemed the least of her worries right then.

She emerged from the shower with hair which smelled of grapefruit and a body devoid of filth. Disobeying Mary, she'd stripped off the waterproof packing and washed the area around each of the wounds. The blood beneath the tape had painted a gruesome picture of the damage, but a good, though painful, clean-up operation had removed the illusion. The medics had done their best work under cyclone conditions, and Hana resigned herself to some scarring, though minimal.

She pulled on the borrowed underwear. The knickers fitted, but Hana lacked the ability to fill the bra which Mary's granddaughter provided. The plain grey sweatpants hugged her bottom and thighs, but didn't press against her painful bruises. Hana pulled the simple sweatshirt over her head and washed sand and debris from the shower tray. She cleaned the wide-toothed comb, which she'd tugged through her matted hair.

"Feel better?" Mary asked her, as Hana emerged from the bathroom with a sigh.

"Much," she replied. "I'm so grateful." She turned her fingers over and stared at her wrinkly pads. "You're right about the Rotorua mud. I think it helped." She sank into the dining chair, which Mary pulled out for her, and slurped another welcome glass of water. Removing her sweatshirt, she sat in the kitchen in her bra, shooting anxious glances towards the front door.

"No one is coming," Mary soothed. "Mike went out early to clear debris with congregation members and organise places to stay for those with damaged homes. I locked the door, anyway. Visitors will need to knock first." She tutted at Hana's attempt at wound cleaning, using saline to finish the job. "No more wetting them," she insisted. "You don't want an infection." She spread manuka wound gel over the cuts and enclosed them beneath more waterproof patches. Then she stood and smiled down at Hana. "Charlie called from the police station. The mobile phone mast came down in the cyclone, but the land lines are still working. He's meeting with your husband soon, but he said to prepare yourself. It doesn't look good."

90

Kindness - ngākau

"Is it about Sally?" Hana demanded. She leaned against the counter while Mary fixed sandwiches for them both. Her stomach growled, as distressed by Logan's plight as her gnawing hunger. The hospital staff had offered dry crackers amid all the chaos during the night, but they'd caused Hana to choke with her dehydrated mouth and throat. A lump rose into her chest and she let it settle. Tears wouldn't help. "I shot Sally," she reiterated. "Charlie will tell them that, won't he? And Logan only attacked Ron because Sally and Hosking planned to drown me out at sea." Her words spat from between her lips like buck shot, anxiety making her unable to stand still. She moved from foot to foot, each bare sole as sore as its twin.

Mary carried two plates to the dining table and sat them next to each other. She replaced Hana's chair and jerked her chin towards it. "You need to eat, Hana. I'm sorry it's not soup, but the bread is soft and I've removed the crusts." She waited for Hana's compliance before seating herself. Pressing her hands together, she blessed the food. If she noticed Hana's reflexive fidgeting beside her, she kept the observation to herself. Mary lifted a neat triangle in a delicate finger and thumb before smiling at Hana. "I don't think the police know you shot anyone," she said. She nipped at a corner of her sandwich and chewed.

Hana stared at the perfect geometrical shapes on her plate, but reached for the refreshed glass of water instead. "So, why did they arrest Logan? We had nothing to do with the fake cash, the actual cash, the kidnapping and elder abuse, the boat switch, or the cyclone. Why is my husband in jail? Again!" she added, her tone harsh.

Mary mopped a crumb from the corner of her lip with a floral napkin. She turned to face Hana. "Charlie says it's a murder charge." She lowered her voice as though afraid the empty house might overhear and form judgement. "A woman is dead."

"Yes! Hallie!" Hana slammed her palm onto the table and regretted both the action and the sentiment. A vase of vibrant orange blooms wobbled, the water sloshing within its crystal depths. It also hurt her fingers. She shook her head. "Is it Hallie? Are they trying to pin her death on Logan?"

Mary sighed. She dropped her sandwich triangle onto her plate with a dull thud. "I believe so." She stretched a tentative hand across the distance between them. Its gentle weight rested on Hana's shoulder as she shifted in her seat with agitation. "Charlie says he didn't do it and that's good enough for me," she stressed.

Hana hung her head, her chin resting against her chest. She sighed. "I thought I knew who killed her," she mused. "I felt so sure. But what if Sergeant Wally George murdered her and Logan is the scapegoat?"

"Why would our local police officer kill a tourist?" Mary mused. "I changed that boy's soiled underwear in Sunday school.

Hana stared at a section of blank wall painted a neutral beige. She projected her inner thoughts onto it, organising the puzzle pieces into a workable list. "Hallie was pregnant," she breathed. "Her last round of IVF had failed just as Jared lost his job. They couldn't afford any more attempts. He told me the child wasn't his. But she lost the baby that afternoon and attended the emergency clinic at the hospital." Hana frowned and turned to face Mary. "We met her at the Trading Post that evening, and she already seemed drunk. I figured the prescription painkillers made her super intoxicated." Another puzzle piece slotted into place on the screen of her mind, but she didn't voice it. "Sergeant Wally George said she visited him at the police station for something else. When I pressed him, he claimed she'd apologised for her aggression to him."

Hana clicked her fingers and groaned. "Ouch! But I witnessed Hallie's anger towards him when she saw him outside the resort on the night she disappeared. She didn't seem like a woman who'd made peace with him."

"So, what does that mean?" Mary edged Hana's untouched sandwich towards her, the plate scraping against the wooden surface.

"It means he lied about the reason for her visit," Hana concluded. Defeat rounded her shoulders. "And we saw him just outside the resort, performing traffic stops minutes before Hallie's disappearance."

"Alleged disappearance." Mary offered the remark. "How do you know she went missing, then?"

Hana blew out a breath laden with exasperation. "I don't. The only part I can verify is that we left her safe on her porch. She became abusive and Logan wouldn't let me stay. Sally went to fetch her spare key from the office and I thought I heard the door bang as she returned. Craig stayed with Jared at the Trading Post but then hitched a ride and appeared moments after we got home to discover Hosking's men had tossed our villa. Craig asked where we left Hallie and mentioned Sally couldn't find her. That's the best time stamp I have. Around eleven o'clock last Friday night."

"You think Sergeant Wally George nipped into the resort and what? Killed her without leaving evidence? How did she die?"

"I don't know for sure yet." Hana folded her arms. "I guess Carrie, his off-sider, could also have done it. Why though? The only thing she's guilty of is a dodgy extra-marital affair with Craig. Her and most of the island's female population. I can't see how that involves Hallie." Frown lines scored a deep groove above her nose, and her chin jutted in a determined grimace. "The only thing I'm certain of is that my husband had nothing to do with poor Hallie's death. He didn't leave my side for a millisecond, and I'll tell that to any court!"

91

Satisfied - ma'a

Mary allowed Hana to make an expensive international call to New Zealand using her land line. After a quick conversation with Charlie Clay's assistant to get the correct number, Hana wrapped the curled cable of the telephone around her index finger and waited for Liza to finish ripping into her. With each passing hour, her waterlogged skin improved, her body performing its own chemical miracle and replacing the oily sebum required. Her swollen toes still resembled overripe apples as she peered down at them, but the pain in her soles couldn't rival the prickling ache of her many stitches.

"Are you a complete moron?" Liza raged. She raised her voice to a high, grating squeak as though reinforcing her poor impression of Hana. "Let's go on holiday, babe. The stabbing seemed lame, so let's see how a cyclone and a murder charge feels!" She growled at the end of her sentence, and Hana cringed. "Why do you expect me to know anything?" she continued. "You're right there! The island fits into a bloody teacup! How far away is the police station?"

Hana swallowed and took a deep breath. "I understand Logan called you when he reached the police station. You sent Charlie to represent him. I'm not allowed to see Logan, so I wondered what he told you."

"He told me, and I quote, *'I'm in deep shit, sis. Send the cavalry. I'll pay you back when I leave this hell hole.'* And I did exactly as he requested and sent that lawyer." She made an indistinct sound as though retching. "I refuse to call him again on your behalf. And you can tell him from me, it's unethical to have coffee, drinks, or engage in a raging affair with a legal inferior. Tell him I am not interested! He's a great pudding of a man and once in a lifetime is enough!" Hana gasped as Liza's hissed breath terminated, as though a giant hand had smudged her from the earth. A dial tone buzzed in her ear to replace Liza's bile.

Hana gnawed on her lower lip as the plot thickened. The judge's last comment revealed more than she'd intended. "So, Charlie Clay, barrister-at-law," she mused, "Your interest in my sister-in-law is a little more than just hero worship, isn't it? Someone enjoyed one of Liza's famed conference bunk ups." A reluctant smile lit her lips. It must have happened years ago, before Liza shot up the greasy pole of the New Zealand legal system. "Go Charlie!" she marvelled. "You're really not what you seem."

"Ouch!" Mary winced and pushed another glass of water towards Hana as she sat the phone receiver in its cradle. "I didn't intend to listen, but she shouted throughout the conversation. Your sister-in-law is one bitter woman."

Hana nodded and lifted the glass. Condensation dribbled across her fingers. She sank into the dining chair with a sigh, grateful for the loose fabric of the sweatpants across her bruises. "She is." The water slipped down her throat. Guilt set up a steady tick in her chest as she thought of Logan. "I hope the police officers give him enough water," she said with a sigh. "He spent just as long as me hiding from the cyclone. What if they don't think about it? They put me on an IV line in the hospital. He didn't have any such help. What if he's dehydrating right now? He must be so hungry and thirsty." She rose, sending the chair skittering backwards in her haste. But once upright, her choices receded.

"The officers at the station are good people, Hana," Mary soothed. "They have a duty of care. Your husband has access to a doctor if he needs one. And they buy food from the cafe at Avarua for all the inmates." She laid her hands on Hana's shoulders. "And Charlie is with him. This will turn out just fine. Prayer and patience, that's what we need."

Hana nodded, but the angst remained and it locked her knee joints. They refused her command to bend, so she could retake her seat. She shook her head, and a yawn escaped from behind her hand. "Sorry. Gosh. How embarrassing." She scrubbed her eyes with her knuckles. "I'm keeping you from helping your husband. And your community." Rapid blinking didn't help.

"He'll call if he needs me," Mary replied. She led Hana into a lounge soaked by yellow sunbeams. The jagged leaves of a banana tree sheltered a paved courtyard, a bench nestled beneath it. Open French doors allowed the warm breeze to filter through the room. "Why don't you take a seat there?" she asked, nudging Hana towards a long sofa. It faced the open doorway, offering contemplation of the mountain's bush covered summit.

Hana nodded and edged towards the seat. The soft cushions embraced her bruises, and she sank into them, already fighting to stay awake. But as Mary's slippers whispered away against the floorboards, her eyelids slid closed and she listed sideways against the sofa arm. Birdsong and a gentle wind filled her mind. The distant lapping of the soothing waves against the beach added the backing vocals. By the time Mary returned with the refilled glass of water, Hana had plunged into an exhausted slumber.

She woke two hours later with a start. The heavy thud still rang in her ears. Her arm ached with the remembered recoil from Hosking's revolver. The image of Sally's pained indignation faded from her mind's eye as Hana forced herself to rouse. She'd fallen asleep sitting almost upright, her dead weight supported by her left arm, which she'd crushed against the sofa. Sharp, agonising tingles ripped from wrist to elbow, coursing up and infecting her shoulder as the blessed numbness faded. Hana lifted her right hand, touching the wetness on her cheek before rubbing her eyes. Her first glance failed to recognise the room, and she panicked. Her heart rate increased, pumping blood through her eardrums to deafen her. But her legs wouldn't obey the command to stand, and so she remained sunk in the cushions like a brick.

The sun had shifted position, laying its yellow rays over an antique writing desk and a squashy armchair. Hana calmed as her mind returned to reason, plotting the sun's former angles and bringing with it the memory of Mary and of comfort and safety. And Logan.

Hana rose without grace, her limbs moving as though a puppeteer had cut her strings and cast her aside. Her toes hurt less. She peered down at them, no longer seeing the deep grooves and wrinkles caused by her waterlogged skin. She wiggled them before hobbling across the room to the door. The purple bruises caused by Logan's cowboy boot brought only more regret.

A left turn took her into the dining room. The changed angle of the sun had darkened it, casting long shadows beyond the table and its occupants. The low rumble of conspiratorial voices ceased.

"Sorry." Charlie Clay turned to face her, the dining chair squeaking a complaint as he altered his weight. His bottom spilled over the seat pad, squishing it flat beneath him. "I dropped my briefcase." He jabbed a chunky finger towards a bulging leather bag leaned against the table leg. "Didn't mean to wake you."

"More water?" Mary rose from her seat, patting the shoulder of the man beside her. "You remember my husband, don't you?"

Hana stared at the pastor's gentle face. He'd removed a cap from his head, leaving his grey hair flattened at the front but cresting at the crown. Dirt streaked his face and extended to cover his striped shirt. "Hello Hana," he said, tapping his temple in a lazy salute. "Nice to meet you again."

She nodded, unsure if his use of the adjective cut through the chaos she'd brought with her. Charlie appeared comfortable with his presence in the man's home as he snatched a sausage roll from a plate in the centre of the table and scarfed it whole.

The fog in Hana's head remained. She couldn't seem to get past it. "I shot Sally," she stated, her tone dull. Her brain reminded her she'd shot her more than once in her sleep. The recurring dream had robbed her of any time for healing. She shrugged, a child making an earth shattering confession of sin to parents too busy to listen. "I shot her," she said again. "Her bones stuck out."

Strong arms caged her from behind, fixing her in place. The forearms crossed over, fingers covered in scars and cuts clasping her waist and tugging her backward. Damp warmth shrouded her, the same grapefruit scent from Mary's shower enveloping her. When the stitches in her stomach complained, Hana wriggled free, spinning on her bare soles and pressing her face against Logan's brawny chest. "I lost my chicken," she sniffed into the fabric of his tee shirt. Her fingers didn't reach far enough to touch each other as she wrapped her arms around his bulk. Logan's laugh rumbled through his chest wall and shook her body. His chin rested on the top of her head.

Just like always.

"Hey Pastor?" He lifted his voice to speak to Mary's husband, and the man jerked his chin upward in response. One grey eyebrow lifted in question. "Who do I have to punch to get my wife's chicken back?" he asked.

92

Shake - ueue

Winston arrived at Mary's front door, tapping the wood with his beak. She drew it open and greeted the vet with a smile as the cockerel struggled for release in his arms. "Thanks for coming by, Claude," she said, as though usual island behaviour meant turning up at the vicarage with a rooster in tow.

"Glad to get rid of the darn thing," he admitted, bending his knees to give Winston a softer landing. "No long-term damage, but annoying as hell. He got into the dog food and put away more than his body size in kibble." His bushy brows met in the middle as he winced. "No offence intended with the hell reference," he growled.

"Come in for a brew, my friend." Pastor Mike joined his wife at the door.

The vet shook his head. "Thanks, but I need to get back to work. I'm on my way to the stables. A couple of horses spooked in the cyclone and cut themselves. Lucky escape if you ask me."

Winston checked out the kitchen and wove like a drunk around the dining room. He leaned forward as he ran, his wings tucked behind him. Hana tensed as she watched his progress, wondering if he'd revert to his former attack mode once he saw her. She drew up her knees and balanced her heels on the edge of the dining chair just in case. Logan rose and joined the group at the door, promising a donation to the veterinary clinic for his service to Winston.

"Hey," Hana said softly as the cockerel nibbled at a house plant under the window. His head jerked around almost completely, so he studied her over his shoulder. Then his beak opened wide and, with a squawk of rebuke, he became airborne. Loose feathers cascaded from his scruffy body as he cleared the dining table and clattered against Hana's chest. His claws raked her arms in his haphazard landing. He greeted her with chattering and clucks, forcing his beak beneath her left arm and wiggling his raggedy tail feathers. Unable to decide on a comfortable position, he perched on her left thigh and batted her breast with the side of his head. She lifted her arms and cradled him. His body became limp, much like it had when they sheltered beneath the remnant of the villa as it took its direct hit from the cyclone. Joyful sounds issued from between the points of his yellow beak. "You're one crazy dude," Hana said with a sigh. She smoothed his trembling crest and relaxed. Dust and feathers cascaded like snowfall onto the chair and the floorboards.

Hana glanced up as the front door closed. Logan leaned against the archway, his brows furrowed into a single dark line. "You know we can't take that home, don't you?" he said, his tone serious. She nodded and cupped her hands on either side of the rooster's head so he didn't hear the awful prognosis.

"I know," she agreed. "Biosecurity won't let us. I hoped we could find a suitable home for him. He's too tame to have spent his life feral. There's something different about him."

"If you say so." Logan pursed his lips and shrugged at Mary.

Charlie Clay wandered from the other end of the house, his hands still damp. "Thanks for the use of the bathroom, Mary," he remarked. "I need to speak to my client and then I'll push off. Things to do, people to upset." His lips parted in a wide grin. "Will I see you up at Nui Ngaro later today? The damage is minimal, but the members want to organise a working bee for the clear up of the car park."

Mary tapped her chest as though her concession involved a heart decision. "I'll see you up there," she agreed. She directed a slow wink at Hana. "Do you intend to supervise again, Charlie?"

"Oh yes," he replied without catching her inference. "It's what I do best."

Pastor Mike suppressed a snigger as he snatched up his ball cap from the table. "I'll see you guys later." He pressed a kiss to his wife's soft cheek. "Bye honey. Not sure when we'll finish. We started with sixteen trees down in properties on the main road, and we got four squared away."

"Text me?" Mary said, patting his cheek. Her eyebrows drew together as she remembered her mistake. "Oh yes. No mobile station. I forgot." She shrugged. "I'll drive by later and check you're all working." Her lips smoothed into a smile. "I'll bring cookies."

Pastor Mike gave a cute giggle and his shoulders tweaked up to touch his earlobes. "Look forward to it," he replied with evident enjoyment.

Mary closed the front door behind him and turned to face the remaining occupants. "I'll leave you to chat," she said with a wave of her hand. "Logan and Hana, you're welcome to stay with Mike and I until you leave the island." Before they could refuse her generous offer, she strode into the narrow hallway behind the kitchen. Hana recognised the click of a cupboard door and Mary turned aside, just visible as she carried a pile of clean bed linen.

Logan took the dining chair beside Hana, keeping his fingers away from Winston's threatening beak. A battle of wills ensued between the two males for Hana's affection. It centred around dirty looks and low growls, but also spelled the end for Hana's relationship with the stray chicken.

Charlie settled into a seat opposite them. He reached sideways for his briefcase and thudded it onto the table. Clearing his throat, he began jabbing his index finger at Logan. "Now, Sergeant Wally George believes you killed the woman in the villa next to you. Hallie Clarke. He's released you on police bail, but made it clear he intends to charge you once they have more evidence."

Hana leaned forward, cradling Winston like a baby. "I told you Craig killed her. Did you tell Sergeant Wally George we overheard Ron, the pool boy, describing how Hosking saw Craig disposing of her body? He murdered her on Friday night and hid her body in the resort until early Sunday morning. Craig used the kayak to row to the reef. Hosking misinterpreted Craig's struggle with Hallie's dead weight as him entertaining a lady, but I believe he dumped her body into the ocean. I saw deep scratches on the front of his kayak later that day." She rested her right hand on Logan's thigh beneath the table. Winston lifted his head and awarded Hana's husband the full, beady stare. "I'll alibi Logan. He didn't leave my side for the whole of Friday evening."

"The tale of Craig and the woman is hearsay. Unless Ron saw the incident for himself and we can question him."

"But you still told them what I said, didn't you?" Hana cradled Winston tight against her breast. He wriggled in protest and craned his neck to snatch at Logan's tee shirt sleeve, as though blaming him. Hana faced Logan, fear widening her eyes into glittering emeralds. "Their incompetence will make my head explode!" she complained.

"I told them." Charlie's chins wobbled as he pressed his palms against the smooth table top. He rose, snagging another cookie with the deftness of a pickpocket. He quirked an eyebrow at Logan and wagged the crumbling biscuit. "You're bailed to this address. You mustn't leave."

He shambled towards the front door in his shroud-like cream suit. The shivering fabric resembled custard trembling in a bowl before dribbling onto the handle of the briefcase. The door clicked as he closed it behind him, his heavy tread carrying him down the steps and into the driveway.

Mary returned with a pair of trainers dangling from her long fingers. She set them beside the front door. "They belonged to my daughter," she said, jerking her chin towards them. "She had tiny feet like yours." An air of sadness bent her shoulders into a gentle slope as she offered up the footwear like a tribute. Hana worried at the past tense in Mary's statement in the same way Winston had nibbled the plant leaf. She turned it over in her mind, too afraid to ask what happened to Mary's daughter and the checkout operator's mother.

Logan sighed and blew out a breath. He stretched his legs beneath the table, borrowed socks fluffy with wear encasing his feet. "What do we do now?" he said to Hana.

"Nothing." She dipped her head and her brows furrowed into a line. "You can't leave the house."

"No, he can't," Mary reiterated. "It's unjust, isn't it?" She turned to Logan. "You should rest," she advised. "Take more of your medication and allow your body to heal."

Logan shook his head, but Hana leaned forward to study the livid purple circles spreading beneath his eyes and the crusted cut to his forehead. "You look like a panda," she said without softening the announcement. "Go for a nap. Do you still have your nasal spray?"

Logan nodded and dug in the sweatpants pocket. The fabric clung to his powerful thighs. Taller than Pastor Mike by at least half a metre, the cuffs secured around Logan's calves instead of his ankles. He tugged the bottle free and set it on the table. Painful welts and cuts to his fingers still wept as he released it. The bottle wobbled from side to side as though thinking about making its escape. "What about you?" Logan demanded, frowning at Hana.

"I'm fine," she lied. "I slept in the lounge."

"If you're sure?" The words held an element of doubt, though his gaze slid towards the hallway door.

"I am." Hana rose, tucking Winston beneath her left arm. She followed Mary past the bathroom and through a door to a double bedroom at the end of the corridor. Net curtains fractured a soft light across a patterned bedspread, their weightless fabric lifting in a gentle breeze. Hana set Winston in the centre of a patchwork square, and he clucked and burbled.

"I don't want the chicken," Logan stated, a drawl of exhaustion in his voice. "I'll wake up without eyeballs."

"Okay." Hana kept her tone light as she fussed over her husband.

Mary pulled the covers back to expose a neat triangle of fresh, welcoming sheet. She smiled at the hunger in Logan's eyes as he gazed at the pillow.

"Just an hour," Logan conceded. He dipped forward and smoothed the bottom sheet with his fingers, as though testing a mirage for clarity. "Will you wake me?"

Hana nodded, not trusting herself to speak. She blinked at Mary, who stepped into the breach with remarkable ease. "We'll only disturb you if something happens," she promised. She stepped back to allow Logan to sink into the mattress. "But sleep is the best thing for you right now." She glanced across at Hana's stricken expression, but didn't voice their shared thought. *Better to sleep long in a mattress than not at all in a jail cell.*

Logan sighed at the deliciousness of comfort, having never expected to discover it in a Christian woman's home on a remote island in the South Pacific. He shifted onto his right side, avoiding the worst of his injuries. Mary drew the sheet up to his chin, her tender maternalism more than his mother had ever exhibited to the boy-Logan. She skirted the bed, stepping into the hallway to offer privacy as Hana pressed a kiss to her husband's forehead. "I love you, Mr Du Rose," she whispered, her breath ruffling his fringe. He murmured something in reply as sleep sucked him into its tunnel of nothingness.

Mary waited as Hana closed the bedroom door behind her. "Let's go," the pastor's wife mouthed. "We don't have long."

93

Fishing net - rerekue

The trainers proved a little tight, nipping at Hana's baby toes and aggravating her bruises. But the wisdom of wearing footwear became obvious as she limped onto the front porch, carrying Winston. In just a few brief hours, Cyclone Angela's following wind had taken the debris and spread it across every surface. It appeared she sought to remind the unscathed eastern side of the island of its lucky escape. Evidence of the broken west littered every surface. Document pages fluttered past Mary's cottage, their edges frayed and tatty. They waltzed while airborne before impaling themselves on the knotty branches of a rosebush. White paper butterflies seeking sanctuary. Other rubbish continued its energetic shimmying throughout the street, finding no rest but sounding a constant alarm. *Your island is wounded. Send help.*

A child's lone sock rested on the lawn, the toes tapping as though to inaudible dance music. And sand. Sand everywhere. It coated the chassis of the yellow Volkswagen parked beneath a carport, adding a heavy layer of frosting. It banked its shifting grit against the rungs of the balustrade and created dunes beneath the porch. Hana exhaled through her nose as Mary pulled the door closed and joined her. She slipped a comforting arm around Hana's waist. "Cyclone Angela has left a reminder," she soothed, her tone lyrical. "The responsibility belongs to all of us to rebuild one another. The loss for one, is a loss for us all."

Hana nodded and her shoulders shifted level with her ears. "I don't want to stop you helping your community," she said, her voice flat.

"You aren't," Mary replied. "You are my community today."

Hana dropped her chin. She left the porch, taking care over the three steps. Mary's gentle palm pressed against her spine, coaxing her forward. "Where are we going?" Hana asked, smothering a yawn with her hand. Winston shifted against her ribs as though afraid she might drop him. His claws scrabbled for purchase in the wrinkles of her sweatshirt.

Mary said nothing. She unlocked the bright yellow vehicle and slid into the driver's seat. Sand cascaded from the roof and sills as they slammed their doors and waited for inspiration. "I don't know," Mary replied, a knot of worry forming between her eyebrows. She turned to face Hana. "But we can't sit indoors and wait for the police to arrest your husband."

Hana nodded, grateful for the other woman's simple faith and solidarity. She considered the evidence for a moment before presenting her case. "Please, can you drive me to the hospital?" she asked. "Jared and Mabel are there. I should also check the clearing to make sure Sally didn't die with my bullet in her arm. But first, will you take me back to Paradise Villas?"

"Okay." Mary started the engine and used wiper blades to clear a space through the rear window. Their efforts produced a semi-circle of partial visibility. "I can't spray the glass," she said as she reversed onto the main road with extraordinary care. "The sand will clog."

She changed gear and pressed on the gas just in time. The anticlockwise bus overtook her with an angry blare of its horn. It sped onto the other side of the road, almost wiping out a stationary vehicle before careening into its own lane. Still fastening her seatbelt, Hana squeaked and slapped herself in the mouth.

Mary frowned across at her. "Everything runs on island time," she declared, "But it always runs."

Hana managed an indistinct sound in her throat. She gripped the seatbelt in shaking fingers. Winston balanced on her thighs. His craggy claws wrapped around her knees. He pitched and tossed with the momentum of the vehicle, his pointed talons digging into Hana's skin. She watched him, marvelling at the ease with which he accepted everything. Just days ago, he'd wandered the resort as a chicken. And yesterday he'd become a pet.

Mary drove to the resort, following the bus as it made chaotic stops to disgorge its occupants. The tourists heading for Avarua and the supermarket appeared shellshocked, trooping down the bus steps like automatons. Hana sympathised, making up scenarios in her mind for how they'd spent the cyclone. But then her brain stalled and threw her back beneath the villa as Angela tore it apart. Winston spun to face her, his beady eyes all-knowing and his chest feathers fluffed. Hana smoothed the wonky crest on his crown, grateful for his warmth spreading across her thighs.

They passed Charlie's office and the Trading Post. Like a pop-up card, the bar emerged from the destruction like a beacon promising hope. People already gathered at the benches assembled on the deck, though the balustrades could no longer stop them from pitching sideways into the harbour. They sipped from pint glasses, many of their bowed heads and stooped shoulders betraying their exhaustion.

A bank of sand occupied the entrance to the hospital. Men pushed it aside with heavy spades, their torsos clad in bright yellow vests to indicate their authority. Hana shuddered, not enthusiastic about her later trip to the derelict house on the outskirts of the site. Or at what she might discover there.

But Cyclone Angela had saved her worst fury for Paradise Villas.

Mary stopped the car on the side of the road, unable to proceed through the wrecked entrance to the resort. "Wow!" she breathed as though unable to believe her eyes. "It's gone."

And it had.

Hana had witnessed the reception's destruction as she and Logan battled to escape the borrowed Mazda. The building had flown into the air, taking its whining claxon with it. But she hadn't expected to return to a resort hollowed out by nature. All traces of humanity drilled into the dirt.

She pushed open the passenger door of Mary's car, half expecting Winston to flee at the sight of freedom. But he clucked and complained, digging his claws into her leg in protest. "We need to get out," she told him. "I want to see where Logan hid." Her lips pursed.

"And perhaps find the necklaces we bought for the children."

Winston tucked his head into his breast as Hana clasped him in her left arm and clambered free. His legs dangled like spaghetti strands from beneath her elbow. Mary walked beside her. An impassable sand bank rimmed the resort, cleared only where the linemen had begun their task. Cyclone Angela had filled the ditch, which Hana and Logan hunkered in just a day earlier. The unhealthy sheen of murky water topped the dense layers of sand and pebbles. Mary skipped it, lither than her sixty-odd years suggested. She held her arms out for Winston, but he set up a protest loud enough to draw the attention of nearby workers.

"Stop it, you idiot!" Hana rebuked. She shook her head at Mary and instead picked her way through the mess. Her left foot sank to the ankle, filling her trainer with a rank mixture of water and grit. Hana clenched her teeth, unable to bear Mary's look of knowing. She felt pure gratitude for the woman's wisdom as the pastor's wife said nothing.

They limped along the fence-line. An internal monologue reminded Hana of the treacherous journey of the previous day. They'd crawled the same route as panels crashed from their fixings and took to the sky. The renting, tearing sounds occupied her head in a hidden cavity of horror created for no other reason.

The strong wind chased them into the resort, as though desperate to show them its work. Winston grumbled and complained as it blew his feathers against their natural grain. He pecked Hana's cheek as though willing her to turn her back on it. But she ignored him, unable to drag her gaze from the destruction.

A fallen coconut tree formed a bridge across the swimming pool, smashed tiles and a crushed pump house beneath its waving fronds. Men rode a cherry picker beside the hefty pole supporting dangling electricity wires. They, too, wore the bright yellow vests of a community in trauma.

A single sun umbrella remained upright like a dutiful soldier. It stood beside the pool as though feigning normality. Hana shook her head. How could the cyclone have destroyed so much while leaving odd things untouched? Like the many kinds of death, it had chosen one victim while inexplicably sparing another.

A charred husk held the remains of Hallie and Jared's villa. It had burned itself out during the torrential rain which accompanied Angela's onslaught, but not before it ate the couple's possessions. Nothing remained to show Hallie ever visited the island. Just a damaged husband, a lost child, and a drawer-for-one in the morgue.

The walls and roof of the Du Rose's villa no longer existed. The tiled floor appeared surreal as a neat, shiny patch of normalcy exposed to the elements. Some furniture remained. A soaked two-seater sofa lay upside down beside the open trap door. The dining table sat exactly where they'd left it, the chairs still gathered as though for a bizarre alfresco feast. Hana picked her way up the splintered porch steps and onto the deck. The balustrade had left with the furniture, its absence adding to the eerie sense of openness.

"You ladies need something?" The rough shout caused both women to jump.

Hana rallied first, addressing the man who'd appeared from nowhere. He stood on the grass, his hands pressed over his hips in a veiled challenge. "We stayed here." An outstretched arm encompassed the wreckage. "Have you seen Craig today?"

The man wore the current fluorescent uniform of yellow vest and work pants. He lifted a cap from his head and scratched at a scalp as smooth as an egg. "Hey Miss Mary." His head bowed and his tone lost its edge. "Pastor Mike stopped by with donuts from the bakery earlier."

"Hello Dom. What a terrible mess." Mary twisted on the spot to take in the piles of wood and building materials gathered on the far side of Hallie's missing villa. "You're doing great work here. Have you seen the owner?"

"No, Miss Mary," he replied. "He and his wife are among the missing."

Hana gritted her teeth, unable to tune into the conversation between Mary and her parishioner. It seemed impossible that Craig had disappeared. How could she prove Logan's innocence without him?

The man left and Mary joined Hana in the remains of the dining room. Silent and brooding, Hana picked her way through the debris. "It left the kitchen sink." The smile didn't reach her eyes and her attempt at humour fell flat. Winston wriggled as though asking for her to put him down, and she obliged. His claws scratched against the tiles as he stood beside her, a lone sentry on a redundant duty. Hana gazed down at the cavern beneath the trap door and shook her head. She pointed, withdrawing her hand as she noticed how her finger trembled. "Logan hid in there." She tapped the tiles with the filthy toe of her trainer. "I was under here."

The pressure built in her chest, throttling her with the force of the sob. They sheltered so near and yet deaf and blind to each other's pain and terror. Numbness crawled up her calves and overtook her knees. The sensation of powerlessness dumped her onto the shiny tiles without warning. Hana fell forward, cradling her stomach and holding back the awfulness coursing up her throat and into her mouth. Winston skittered sideways with the force and suddenness of her collapse. He retreated to the fallen cushions of the two-seater sofa and observed her with concern. His crest rose and fell.

Mary settled beside Hana on the sandy floor. She didn't just squat, she folded onto her bottom, her knees bent and her legs drawn beneath her floral skirt. And in that moment, Hana knew the pastor's wife wasn't just good and kind. She was in it for the long haul. And afterwards.

94

Strength - pakari'anga

Hana blew her nose on the tissue Mary tugged from her sleeve. It fluttered in her fingers as Cyclone Angela's minions followed in her violent wake. Winston clucked and pecked around the remains of the Du Rose's villa. He seemed unsettled, returning to bite Hana's sleeve before stalking to a different corner to scratch and investigate. "What will you do with him?" Mary asked as Winston inspected the upturned sofa.

"Don't know," Hana replied. "Logan's right. I can't take him home with us."

"My friend keeps chickens," Mary said, her tone thoughtful. "I can ask if she'll take him, but few people want the roosters."

Hana pushed out her lips as she watched Winston fly onto the side of the kitchen sink. The missing portion of the cupboard beneath it revealed copper and plastic pipes funnelling below ground level. The silly chicken missed his footing and fell into the basin. He strutted around, his head appearing dismembered as he tapped at the plughole and the stainless steel for answers they didn't possess. "I wonder why they don't," Hana mused, her tone sarcastic.

Mary considered her reply as though assuming the question raised a serious matter. "The noise," she said. "And they keep fertilising the eggs."

Hana focussed on her crossed legs and her damp left shoe. "I've ruined your daughter's trainer. I'm sorry." She flicked at the trailing laces covered in green sludge and grit.

"She won't need them again," Mary replied. The bottomless ache behind her hazel irises filled Hana with an insurmountable dread. It erected a wall between them with the speed of a blink, barring Hana from probing further. Mary's fingers twitched in her lap and she gathered her skirt into a flowery puddle between her legs before standing. "We should leave," she advised. "This site isn't safe."

Hana pushed herself upright, using the saturated sofa for support. The fabric had already acquired the greying patina of early mould spores and inevitable decay. Her fingers still smarted and her toes ached within the small shoes. A sense of futility swept indolence through her bones. She wanted to set the sofa back in place and lie down, close her eyes and send herself back in time to Sunday's Hana. Her mind filtered a list of advice she would give to herself. *'Take Logan, hide beneath the villa together. Stay there.'*

Her curls tapped her cheek as she shook her head in disbelief. Sunday's Hana would have dismissed all warnings because Sunday's Hana knew best. She ran a shaking hand over her face and sighed, hating herself.

The creaking of the trees which remained standing heralded a warning. Mary edged towards the space where the front door had stood as a weak and illusory sentry. The missing walls meant she could have stepped out anywhere, but habit and discipline sent her to the narrow lip of the threshold. She crossed it and halted on the deck, her left foot just centimetres from a gaping hole where Angela peeled up the planks and tossed them into her frantic rumba. "Oh!" she exclaimed. She lifted her hand and pointed.

But Winston had already heard them. He hopped onto the slippery side of the sink, struggling to grip against the wet metal. His wings spread, cartilage and tendons creating a span wider than Hana had imagined. The bedraggled crest sprang upright, torn and wobbling, but still majestic. His tufty tail feathers pointed like a rudder. And when his beak parted to reveal a snakelike tongue, he released an immense "Cock-a-doodle-doo!"

Hana jogged towards Mary, tripping over the smashed carcass of a drawer and sliding on the wet tiles. She righted herself in the same moment, her mind filled with the eerie swish of a thousand moving feathers and the grunt and chirp of chattering beaks. Chickens sped from hidden corners of the debris. Brown ones, white ones and a speckled variety which resembled tie-dyed fabric. They magnetised towards the croaky doodle-doo, which Winston repeated until the adoring crowd assembled in a jostling throng before him. Hana held her breath as he lifted into the air on shaky wings and crash landed in their centre like a feathery missile. Bodies rose and alighted like children on a trampoline around his descent. And then they surged away. As though sucked into an estuary by a visiting river, they jockeyed across the grass like white and brown and speckled clumps of art.

Winston had gone. Without a backward glance at Hana.

Mary turned to look at her, sympathy in her down-turned lips. "I guess that answers that question," she soothed. "He has a family."

Hana snorted. "You mean a harem?" She struggled to keep the disgust from her voice. "I should have named him Michael. Or Tama!" She scuffed the tiles with the toe of her trainer and spun to stare at the wrecked villa. Nothing of hers remained in view, and she lacked the energy to hunt through the debris for the trinkets bearing her children's names. But it felt wrong just to leave them there. She'd chosen the seashells strung on cheap leather thongs with *Phoenix, Wiremu, Edin* and *MacGillivray* engraved into the delicate surfaces by a cursive hand. A gnawing emptiness bit at her stomach and she dropped to a crouch. It seemed a gargantuan struggle to remind herself she hadn't lost them. And she still had Logan. For now.

"We should leave." Mary flicked her wrist and frowned at the dial of her watch. "I muted the sound on the landline and answering machine, but we shouldn't stay out for too long."

Hana nodded and rose on stiff limbs. Mary's implication reinforced her fear that Sergeant Wally George and his tiny entourage might descend on the vicarage. They could whisk Logan away before she returned. She spun her reluctant feet towards Mary and stepped over the threshold.

A single brown feather lay on the spiky lawn. Hana bent and snatched it into her left hand, smoothing her fingers over the splayed quill and fragile, directionless fronds. Without speaking, she stuffed it into the long pocket of the sweatshirt and followed Mary back to the road. She needed answers. And soon.

95

Recovered - māro 'iro 'I

Rarotonga rose like a phoenix from the devastation of Cyclone Angela. Hana watched as crews swelled with more yellow vests as workers and willing chainsaws added to their numbers. She pursed her lips and stared through the window as the island redeemed itself in the face of her scrutiny. It hadn't shown them kindness, though its capacity for it surpassed her expectation. She glanced across at Mary as the pastor's wife waved to Mike's parishioners and drove a stranger to bury a body.

Sand drifts still billowed into the hospital's tree lined entrance, but men waited to fight the never-ending battle. Like the punchline to a poor joke, the wind blew the debris over the invisible boundary and the men swept it back out again. They piled it to one side, where more hands shovelled it into plastic sacks.

Hana looked down at fingers which lay empty in her lap. "I miss the chicken," she admitted, her tone dull.

Mary glanced at her and nodded. She offered no trite words of well-chewed wisdom. She just drove as far as the damage to the site allowed, before pulling over and parking in a layby. Arborists in harnesses dealt with fallen trees, leaning trees and those which prolonged their labour by peppering the road with an unpredictable barrage of coconuts. Mary locked up her yellow car and waited for Hana. "Where should we start?" she asked.

"Charlie came to the hospital this morning." Hana lowered her voice. "I saw the trees leaning, but the entrance looked clear of sand. We drove straight out onto the main road. Why is it filling now? Cyclone Angela left in the night."

"Wind direction." Mary jerked her head towards the road, not visible from the layby. She shrugged. "The west coast took the brunt of the storm, but then Angela moved north and east. It's not over until it's over. The following winds will loosen everything she left hanging. They forecast rain for this afternoon. The crews will work for as long as they dare, but gusting wind and driving rain will send them home."

Hana's shoulders slumped in defeat. "So, this could get worse again?"

Mary nodded, and her lips flattened into a line. "Sorry. Let's get any outdoor destinations checked first, shall we?"

Both women puffed as they walked to the derelict buildings sheltering in the mountain's shadow. Mary prevented her from making a wrong turn at the end of the gravel road. "I think you're referring to the old maternity buildings," she said, her tone heavy. "The midwives saw patients in the one at the far end of the cul-de-sac. The three other buildings held a surgical unit, a theatre and wards." Her steps faltered, slowing as though an invisible force held onto her ankles. Then she rallied, matching Hana's pace again.

"Logan said he found an underground bunker," Hana stated. The wind snatched her voice and tossed it behind her.

Mary nodded and turned her face aside to avoid a mouthful of sand and dust. "Yes, that's the old theatre. The concrete floor offered more stability for operations. There seemed no point leaving all the equipment down there after the buildings wrecked."

"What happened here?" Hana's nerves jangled as she grew closer to the clearing. The four stricken structures loomed over the horizon like magistrates overseeing the bench.

"A cyclone tore them apart a decade ago." Her lips pursed and a vertical line grooved a gulf in her forehead. "My daughter worked the night shift so she could spend time with my granddaughter during the day. She married a local boy who worked on the boats. They were happy. But the Cyclone dropped a tree on the building as Cheyne helped a woman to deliver her baby. A joist fell, and she didn't stand a chance." Her fingers writhed before her as they entered the doomed space where so much misery had found its voice. Her feet dragged beneath her, already transformed into heavy iron blocks. "A freak wave washed her husband overboard the same night. Both gone. Just like that." Her lashes fluttered as remembered pain lit an unquenchable fire behind her irises. She clicked her fingers, the sound stolen by the wind as though to emphasise her powerlessness.

"Don't come any further." Hana pressed a hand against Mary's shoulder. "Stay here. I'll look for Sally and Hosking."

The haunted expression didn't fade from the lines of Mary's pain-mapped face. But she shook her head. "No," she breathed, lengthening her sigh. "I haven't visited this place for too long."

"So, the hospital authorities just left it like this?" Hana kept her voice light as she emerged from the trees. Despite the wind's relentless hammering against the west coast, it had spared the neglect by its forebears to continue rotting.

"No." Mary gulped. She lifted her arms before her like a sleepwalker. "They tried to rebuild, but the Trust ran out of money. They fixed the roof and repaired the siding." She performed a slow pirouette as though devouring the scene with her eyes. "I didn't realise it looked like this." Her fingers fluttered to her mouth, the pads white as she pressed them over her lips.

"Stay here!" Hana ordered her, sensing the fragility of her resolve. She added her involvement of the pastor's wife to her long list of regrets entitled, *'Things not to do in paradise.'*

They'd approached the buildings from an alternate direction. Seen in daylight and from a different angle, they appeared even more derelict. Hana edged closer with care. She skirted the three structures surrounded by the leaning safety fencing and headed for the rear of the fourth.

The tiny window through which Logan had entered and left the building seemed higher than Hana remembered. Someone with shorter legs wouldn't have made the climb, unable to brace their weight against the balustrade and launch themselves into space. Only a man over six feet tall with biceps like work-hewn boulders could make the manoeuvre with any hope of success. The local glazier who used a million nails to secure the boards over the windows had not factored in Logan Du Rose's determination.

Hana wanted to applaud and slap the glazier in equal measure for not barring her husband's entry.

Hana stepped onto the low deck, careful to keep her hands away from surfaces able to collect fingerprints. She stooped to inspect the wall beneath the window and the rickety deck onto which Logan had plunged face-first. A glance behind her showed how Hosking had crept up on him, hiding in the shadows as he took aim. The heart shot had hit its mark, causing Logan to slip from the window and fall. Hana's lips pursed as she considered the twist of fate which had placed her phone in his shirt pocket. His momentary kindness to relieve her of a burden had saved his life.

Hana stared at the deck, keen to retrieve the bullet. The planks had dried and eased apart after years without maintenance. She dropped to her knees and peered through the gaps, spotting mud and weeds below, but no bullet. "It doesn't matter," she promised herself, as disappointment took root in her thoughts. She couldn't carry spent ammunition across the New Zealand border any more than they'd have waved through her chicken.

Hana circled the building, noticing the sag of the roof on joists no longer able to support it. Daylight betrayed the deception of the darkness in keeping the Du Roses from seeing the hazards of their mission. Hana regretted many things about that night, but it surprised her to discover that shooting Sally didn't feature on her growing list. The silver hatchback still sat with its nose buried in a neglected flower border to the left of the building. Cyclone Angela hadn't smudged out the deep tyre gouges in the gravel from where Hana rammed into it from behind. A twenty-dollar note fluttered like a trapped moth from beneath the left wiper blade. Hana's memory filled the silence with the echoes of Ron's cries as his hoarded currency took flight like a murder of crows into the furious sky.

Turning, Hana pushed her feet onward around the stricken vehicle, frowning as she saw the boot lid twisted but open to the elements. She peered into the vacant space, noticing a shopping bag containing Sally's scrubs, one high-heeled sandal and a discarded tyre wrench. But no suitcase stuffed with cash.

Using the creaky steps to the front porch, Hana wrapped the hem of her sweatshirt around her fingers before trying the door handle. It turned, and the door pushed open with little effort. She waited for her eyes to adjust to the gloomy interior before stepping over the threshold. Dread tapped a beat in her chest as she forced away imaginary pictures of Ron lying dead in the hallway. But her senses told her the building remained empty of the living and the dead. It whispered its sad song of pervading loneliness replayed by places devoid of human occupancy. Wooden pallets stood floor to ceiling in a hodgepodge stack guaranteed to topple at the slightest provocation. Plastic wrappers glinted in the light from the doorway, threaded in long strands throughout the makeshift bonfire. It awaited Henk's designated flame, which would not come.

Hana turned away, and the question sprang into her mind as though prompted by the fire set for his match. Why had Henk travelled to Paradise Villas? How had he died?

Mary remained in the clearing, her body stiff and unyielding as Hana approached. She slid an arm around the other woman's narrow waist, sensing the bone-deep chill seeping through Mary's clothing. "I'm sorry," Hana whispered. "We shouldn't have come." It seemed of little consolation that she'd known nothing of Cheyne or her traumatic death. She still bore the responsibility for a kind woman's devastation as Mary shivered and moved on faltering steps. The walls of her ruined heart shook, but no tears fell, the well long since barren and neglected.

They passed the tree where Sally had slumped after the gun recoiled in Hana's grip. She still heard the echoing report, though she spotted no bloodstains still in the scrubby grass. Cyclone Angela had sanitised the area as though the crime scene's brutality disgusted her more than her own systematic shredding of homes and businesses.

Mary's steps dragged as they walked. Hana clung to her elbow, chastened by the other woman's distress. She imagined Pastor Mike's anger at her thoughtlessness after he'd opened his home to the Du Roses without judgement. It seemed futile to plead ignorance of their loss, even though it was the truth. Boughs creaked and groaned around them, backed by the dull percussion of lonely coconuts plopping into the undergrowth. Even the island condemned her ingratitude. Hana stopped at the turn leading to the dementia unit. She lifted her hand to stroke the escaped strands of hair behind Mary's ear. "Go to the car," she said, infusing her tone with gentleness. "Wait for me or leave. I'll understand whichever you choose." She glanced towards the tin roof glinting from between the trees. "I need to check on Mabel." She pursed her lips, reluctant to put the agonies of the living before those of Mary's dead.

Hana wavered, contemplating taking Mary into the unit with her for safe keeping. It seemed a gross dereliction of duty to send her walking alone towards the main road. But Mary nodded, and before Hana could change her mind, her sensible shoes carried her away. Mary's feet and nose pointed at a future which occupied her activity, but not her heart. Hana sensed the invisible umbilical cord tying her to the abandoned buildings and what she'd lost there. "I'll be quick," Hana promised, whispering into a breeze which stole the words from her tongue.

She'd planned to visit Mabel as Logan had. To stand before her and coach free an explanation. But Mary's emotional catatonia had swiped the item from the list. And so, Hana retraced her steps of a few nights ago, satisfying her curiosity by peering through windows into a different darkness.

96

Clean - tāmā

Hana navigated the dreaded concrete planter outside the dementia unit, but found the broken window shrouded by a thin wooden board. It robbed her of a view of Mabel's bed. The glazier had used another fifty thousand nails to secure it to the frame, and Hana hoped she never met the man on the road. Judging by the twenty flat headed screws littering the ground beneath the windowsill, the man had a vision impairment.

She contented herself with sneaking around the outside of the building, peering through windows and drawing a map in her head. Just as she'd almost admitted defeat, she discovered a room containing a television. A local news channel blared into a space designed like a dental surgery. Chairs lined the walls in a waiting-room-formation. Patterned curtains the colour of vomit fluttered against the breeze leaking through the gaps in the frame. And Hana saw three occupants in the room. One watched the TV. Officer Carrie's body turned towards it in a high-backed chair. Her hazel eyes drew into slits of concern as she watched a newsreader interview the jovial owner of the Trading Post. Litter and stray foliage dive-bombed their conversation from every direction as the weather turned once again to usher in a low-pressure front.

But the other two occupants sat with their heads bowed, deep in conference. Sergeant Wally George scribbled in his notebook, his hand moving fast enough for his fingers to blur. And Mabel spoke in full sentences, which evaded Hana's ears. But she wore slacks and a cardigan, her hair pulled into a tight chignon. She appeared tired, but sane. And furious enough to spit bees.

Hana had only wanted proof of life and of safety for the elderly woman. Having seen that for herself, she jogged away from the unit and headed towards Jared's ward. The downhill slalom in trainers too small for her forced Hana to take more care of her footing. A steady tick in her chest marked time, infusing her with urgency. The sight of Mary's grief had pricked at her soul. Losing a child was an abomination. No parent ever equipped themselves to pick their way through an existence without them. It was life turned on its head. The grieving became pitied, though sympathisers risked staining by association as though their loss might contaminate and spread.

Hana paused at the entrance to the high dependency unit. Her fingers scrabbled in the box of disposable masks, her loyalty split, and her heightened sense of responsibility confused.

Mary had given Hana sweetness and generosity. Jared had displayed only selfishness and pain. Hana's feet turned, her mind already decided on their direction. If she ran, she could catch Mary before she reached the car. They would return to the house and drink coffee and talk about Cheyne and the family's terrible loss. She would forgive the granddaughter at the checkout who had set the terrible events into motion. Jared could answer Sergeant Wally George's questions. She'd leave it all to the police officer born and named for his duty. Though no one had ever asked him what he wanted.

Hana dropped the mask onto the table, a sigh of relief filling her chest. The soft click of the unit's door closing caused her to glance up, already planning her excuses. But it wasn't a tired nurse who tended to the sick on a paltry wage. It was one who pretended to do it, but who only ever wrought illness and insanity on the least of them.

"You've ruined everything." Sally's eyes shone like black pebbles in her angry face. A lack of makeup stripped her face of its fading bloom. The fluttering lashes she'd used with such liberal abandon on Logan were no longer in place. A blob of glue dotted her cheek as a blockage in the tear tracks. Her blue irises glared through fine dyed hairs in need of a root touch up. The lack of bright war paint reduced her lips to thin pale worms around clenched teeth. "And I knew you'd come here. You just can't leave things alone, can you?"

A natural inclination towards compassion troubled Hana, battling against a naked fear sparked by the bottomless hatred in Sally's blue eyes. She took a step backwards, her trainers squeaking against the tiled floor. Faded terracotta slabs marked the path beyond Sally to the high dependency unit. From where she'd just come. Hana squared her shoulders and set her feet in a solid base. She didn't want to hurt Sally again, recognising the other woman's irrational desperation fuelling her actions. Dried blood stained her sleeve, and she carried her right arm like a broken wing. A metal splint poked from the filthy, frayed edges of a bandage. Someone had provided temporary relief through basic first aid, uniting the two fractured edges of the bone until a better solution presented itself. It looked like something Logan might pull together in haste. But Hana's internal organs gave a twinge of pain as a reminder she'd lose any coming battle involving physical strength versus mania. Even against a one-armed woman. She knew that because she already had. She'd laid in her own pooling blood on a bathroom floor and felt the devil's touch.

"I've lost him!" Spittle sprayed from Sally's lips to create shiny crystals on her cheeks and chin. "It's all gone. The boat sank, and he went down with it." The fathomless pits of Sally's pupils held a familiarity which cooled Hana's blood. She'd also seen it in Flick and in Jack.

Sally had stepped over an unseen line into murderous territory when she administered Fentanyl to an elderly lady and formulated a plan for a final, fatal dose. Once across, she'd discovered no return route existed. Only onward into more lies, more covetousness, more desperation, and the cloying need to win her errant lover's respect. Craig. Not Hosking. Not really. And more death. Because once across the line, the rules governing morality faded.

"I should leave." Hana backed away, testing scenarios in her mind as though playing one of Mac's video games. But as she edged away, Sally moved closer, her weight already forward, and prepared to chase her. She herded Hana into the long corridor leading to the construction site beyond the double doors, backing her up like a sheep dog. "The police are here," Hana said, keeping her voice calm. "They know what you did to Mabel." She lurched sideways, grabbing for the door handle she'd entered through only moments before. But Sally's solid presence loomed beside her, and Hana's fingers missed their mark. Sally crashed into her, pinning her to the safety glass. The air left Hana's lungs in a whoosh and her chest locked. Terror launched from her stomach to her throat, rendering her speechless. How could she have ended up here again, at the mercy of another's depravity?

Sally grabbed Hana's trailing curls and yanked her head back hard enough to drop her to the unforgiving tiles. Hana landed hard on her coccyx, still unable to breathe in enough air. She writhed on the worn linoleum and waited for the blow which would rattle her teeth and bring the darkness. But Sally took a step away, as though not trusting herself. It bought Hana enough time to scramble away on her hands and knees, putting distance between them. But not enough. Never enough between the fragility of life and pure, acidic rage.

97

Recovered - māro 'iro 'I

Spittle landed on Sally's chin as the mania extended its roots deeper into her psyche. She sidled like a crab, winding towards Hana with her left hip leading. She carried no obvious weapons, but her journey over the morality line meant she didn't need one. Sally sneered, and her thin lashes flickered. "Her name isn't Mabel! I made it up. The cops are idiots, and she can't remember anything about what happened." Her left hand crashed to her side, strands of Hana's hair floating from between her balled fingers.

"You can run," Hana suggested. "Before they work it out and come for you. Leave. Start again. You have a fortune in laundered cash somewhere in the world." Her words chuffed free of her lips as she staggered upright. She placed her palms behind her, stretching out her aching arms until she touched the double doors to the construction site.

Sally snorted. “Money isn’t everything,” she snarled. Hana had heard the statement many times and always from someone with their name attached to accounts bursting with it. But Sally had dismissed her own reason for waking each morning and living her careful subterfuge for the past year. Money had driven it. Collecting it. Moving it. Disguising it and laundering it until it became clean enough to slide unchallenged through a banking system. It had occupied every waking moment and most of her dreams. Hopes and desires for a better future away from the island provided an energy source. A chance affair with a local diving instructor had netted a bounty. And netted her. Yet Sally had disregarded its lure and influence in a single moment of regret. Now she needed a scapegoat.

Sally lifted her left hand and jabbed her index finger at Hana. Her injured forearm shifted against her, and she winced. “You’re the catalyst. Everything unravelled from the moment you arrived on this island. It’s all your fault.”

“No.” Hana realised her mistake much too late. She pressed her palms against the double doors behind her, willing at least one of them to open. Her body tilted backwards, and she leaned her weight into the effort. The hinges creaked in response, but the wood held. Locked. The busy workmen used their tools to rebuild the island alongside their community instead of dismantling a disused hospital ward. And she'd inadvertently allowed Sally to corner her with the rage in her blue eyes seeking an outlet.

Sally took a calculating step forward. Hana's mind plunged her back to the bathroom, to the knife, and to the calm smile of the woman who'd wielded it. She hadn't seen it coming, hadn't sensed the danger until the blade slipped through her blouse and into her side. She hadn't felt it either. A mere scratch, a paper cut, just enough to make her start, but nothing to worry about. Numbness had spread across her stomach, lulling her into a false sense of security as the woman backed away. But the satisfied smile caused Hana to look down and witness the blood trickling across her thigh and soaking her jeans. At that moment, everything had changed.

The tremor in her legs felt the same. Hana faced Sally, her body vibrating with the rumble which coursed through her limbs. It seemed to originate from her knees, as though they'd always owned their own source of fear but chosen this moment to activate it. Her palms pressed against the doors, her fingers rising at their knuckles to join the battle until they whitened. But the doors stayed locked and unyielding.

"You forced our hands," Sally declared. Ice laced her voice like barbed tips. "You made us believe the cartel had arrived. But your husband visited Mabel, didn't he? We rushed everything, and it all went wrong. Gantry drowned. My brother is dead. All the people I cared about died because of you. This was my chance to prove myself. Mine." She tossed her head, but the glossy locks of just days before had disappeared beneath a matted haze. Humidity had crimped the roots nearest her face to wire wool, the dampness of sea salt exaggerating the crazed illusion. She took another step forward. "Craig wanted you from the first moment he saw you. Did you know that?"

Hana shook her head, the notion nauseating and abhorrent. In the back of her mind, Sally's statement reverberated. Her brother. Henk. Tall and blonde and invested in Sally's crazy scheme. His presence on the island had never made sense. The returning tourist with a bogus job. She wondered how he'd died. An image of Craig sprang into her inner vision, his full lips leaving wet slug-like trails across Officer Carrie's cheek and neck. She gave a visible shiver. Had the ageing playboy killed Sally's brother and then made his escape? "I don't want Craig," Hana stated. Her voice wavered, and she detested the weakness in it. A head shake accompanied her impassioned denial. Then a shrug. "Why would I? Have you met my husband?" The sarcasm escaped before she could prevent it. She didn't want to die in the deserted hospital corridor, but still couldn't tread the path of least resistance.

"Craig sleeps with anyone who shows an interest in him. He's disgusting!"

"But he still wanted to add you to his collection!" Sally snarled. "Right on my doorstep."

"You had Gantry Hosking! You're not spotless in all of this." Hana shoved her bottom against the doors. Still no movement. Sally's face crumpled, her tongue poking through her lips as though she'd tasted vomit. Hana ceased her futile fight with the door and forced her limbs to relax. This time, she'd defend herself. The thought entered her mind without knocking, giving her words to battle with instead. "Wait?" Hana cocked her head and studied the other woman. Sally appeared dirty and dishevelled but not wet. Her scrubs didn't contain the stains and creases from an unwelcome dip in a cyclone-muddied ocean. They didn't resemble Hana's ruined clothing, soaked and dried and then soaked again. She inhaled and released the unwise barb. "Oh, my goodness! Hosking left you! The boat sank, but not with you on it."

Sally's jaw showed through her cheek as a hard line. "Because of you." She dragged her words across invisible grit. Her left hand cupped her right forearm and caressed the injured bones beneath the dirty bandage. "Because of this," she hissed. "It made me a liability."

Sally spread an empty hand before her in a placatory gesture, her injured arm still clamped against her ribs. Her head cocked to one side, her sweating brows drawn into lines and shadows. "Don't worry. I'll console your husband after you're gone. I know how to please a man." Shades of the old Sally returned. Her body straightened as her former confidence flooded it with thoughts of her sexual allure and prowess. Her thin lips lifted into a smile.

Then Hana detonated her momentary good humour. "You know how to please a man, but not the one you always wanted to satisfy."

Sally's face morphed into a blank mask, but her eyes burned with an intensity which came from deep within her soul. Hana counted another dangerous step closer, and then Sally stalled. Her heady perfume reached Hana with a stale backing of sweat and dust. "Shut up!" the woman hissed. "Just shut up."

Hana sensed her losing concentration. Sally lacked a plan and possessed no obvious weapon. She'd ceased moving closer, as though she needed all her faculties to formulate a coherent idea and follow it through to a conclusion. Yet every other move Sally ever made had a purpose. She'd fooled an entire island population into believing she worked at a hospital unit, which didn't exist. The money she'd laundered could add up to millions. Hana figured the only things she'd done on the spur of the moment involved her craving for Logan. His alpha maleness had attracted and beguiled her. Those attempts to seduce him reeked of sloppiness and a lack of planning. Hana pressed the tiny advantage, hoping to force Sally into a rage or panic-fuelled reaction. Those she could deal with.

"I saw Craig," she said, her tone light. "I walked in on him making out with Officer Carrie against the reception counter. He had his hands under her shirt. She turned him on so much, he needed to scurry behind the desk to hide himself. Did you know about that?"

Sally's teeth ground until her jaw showed through her cheek. Her eyes bugged as though shocked at who Craig had dallied with more than the fact that he'd done it. "He didn't use to be like that." Her rigid shoulders deflated. She exhaled, her chest caving. "He didn't need to whore around," she muttered. Her use of the past tense showed she knew something of Craig's disappearance.

Hana assessed her surroundings. She'd left it late but forced herself to accept the doors and the partially derelict ward beyond them offered no escape. With the corridor of three metres in width, and Sally occupying a third of it, she estimated her chance of slipping past and running for the high dependency unit and help. Screaming. She added a scream to the plan. Perhaps someone would hear her. If that failed and Sally grabbed her, she would defend herself. Logan had shown her a hundred times how to react if someone attacked her from behind. But her liver ached. Her poor severed liver.

Sally's nostrils flared and her lips peeled back from her teeth. "This is it." Her jaw squared as she dropped her chin. "Your widowed husband is my ticket off this island." Her body rocked with laughter like a mad woman. But she hadn't descended into insanity. Shades of dementia were an illusion. Mabel had demonstrated that. Sally was a stone-cold killer if she had a plan and a way forward. And she'd made one. But it didn't include Hana's longevity. Or apparently her own husband.

Hana swallowed and balled her fists. She shifted her thumbs to the outside of her bunched fingers. Logan's voice echoed in her mind, offering silent instructions she could no longer decipher. "I could die tomorrow, and Logan still wouldn't pick you. And by the way, your last little charade lacked decent planning. My husband is a bear of a man. He'd have eaten you for breakfast. Only he wouldn't because you didn't do your research. He can't abide anyone to touch him but his closest family. Not even a hug."

"I'll work it out," Sally boasted. But her lashes flickered, and Hana sensed her flailing. "I always do."

"But you don't do you?" Hana drew her hands from behind her and readied them at her sides. "You always end up getting used. Even by your own husband. What happened there? He's searching for something. Was it a drunken one-night stand which became an illusion of perfection in his head? Is that what you're up against?" Her heart hardened like a brick in her chest. "Or was it just his affair with Hallie? Did it begin as a one-off to get her pregnant and become a regular thing? She told me he'd stayed with them in Auckland just over six weeks ago and I didn't make the link." Hana clicked her fingers. It hid her lack of control over her trembling limbs. "Oh, wow! He and Jared roomed together at university. Craig always loved Hallie, but Jared married her. Were you the consolation prize? He wanted to divorce you and escape the island, but you wouldn't let him. That's why he punished you by seducing other women. Is that also why he fenced the counterfeits? Because he knew about Hallie's pregnancy and wanted to support her? The fake cash was his one-way ticket back to New Zealand and his child."

"Shut your mouth!" Sally's feet barely moved, but she gained ground as though riding an invisible segue. Her lips pulled back from her teeth. "Hallie didn't want him! She loved Jared. Stupid Craig. He was just the sperm donor. Gantry stole the Sail Fish and found the money in the hold last year. Crates of it were ready for hiding on the seabed. I played my part. Craig would have come with me to start again after that bitch died. That was my grand plan. We could live in luxury anywhere we fancied."

Hana pushed her hands forward, palms facing outward in a gesture of peace. "I've been there, Sally. You can't win against an attraction like Craig's. You should have cut your losses while you had the chance."

Sally blinked and her chin shot up, her head teetering on her wrinkled neck until it shifted her centre of gravity. "Your husband cheated on you?" Glee sparkled in her irises, Hana's well-intentioned advice cast aside and wasted.

"Not Logan," Hana replied. She shifted her weight into her left knee and stabilised the sole of a dead woman's borrowed training shoe against the tiled floor. Her right leg waited for use as a pivot, the knee stable and her hips loose. The scent of leaf matter and warm soil sang its siren song to her. She would go home soon. Home to her children, her brother, and her cranky in-laws who weren't relatives by blood at all. Those who had become her family. So, she kept speaking, words falling from her lips as she readied herself. "My first husband dumped me for his office manager." She kept talking, filling the airwaves with pointless prattle. "He planned to leave me, but fate conspired against him, and he died in a car wreck. His mistress' relevance faded in less than a day and she got nothing. No recognition for her loss. No sympathy. And no happy ever after. That's how it ends, Sally. How it always ends. I don't even remember her surname."

Sally had stopped moving two metres out from Hana. Her scuffed ballet flats stilled against the lino disguised as fake terracotta tiles, her feet together as though she planned to perform a graceful pirouette. Trailing laces tied them to her ankles, the only reason she hadn't lost them in her chaotic fall from grace. The agony in her expression caused a mix of emotions to vie for dominance in Hana's soul. She pitied her, but hated what she'd tried to do. What she could still do.

Sally's left hand snaked into the pocket of her spoiled linen trousers.

Hana didn't wait for Sally to reach her and raise that uninjured hand with the nails manicured into crimson talons. She didn't want to see the object the hand collected into her palm. Because everything Sally did was part of a plan, and Hana had underestimated her. The weapon appeared small and angular, glinting in the fluorescent glow from the overhead strip lights.

And Hana had been here before. Only this time, she wouldn't leave in an ambulance.

She shifted her weight over her knee, back and then forward like a marathon runner in a lazy standing start. Her clenched right fist moved forward to contact Sally's surgically altered nose. She shouted, as Logan had taught her a long time ago. "Nose!" she yelled. She drew her hand back and administered a sharp jab to Sally's throat. The woman didn't have time to dip her head in pain before the second blow landed. A gargle of shock punctuated her open-mouthed scream. Hana had forgotten to yell, 'throat,' but she remembered the rest. "Guts! Nuts!" Two more punches hit Sally, one to her stomach and the other to her groin. Hana's second knuckle smarted on her right hand from the impact as the guts-blow glanced off Sally's turning hip. Hana angled her body at speed and used her balled left fist against Sally's pubic bone, incapacitating her despite the lack of nuts. It was a low blow and one she'd prayed she'd never need. She could have used it many times in the past, always shying away from a tactic which appeared abhorrent. It had cost her. So, she used it. The impact ricocheted up her wrist and into her elbow. For Hallie. And for Craig's despised baby.

Sally crumpled forward and her weapon of choice clattered to the tiles. Not a knife or a gun, but a syringe. The exposed needle sparkled in the sunlight, a bead of fluid dappling its stainless-steel surface. As Sally hit the hard floor, its twin spewed from her pocket, the container empty and the needle encased in a plastic lid. Two syringes. One already used.

Hana ran, knowing in her heart what Sally had done. And not sure she could do anything to change the outcome.

98

Bedrock - papa

Naloxone. Karla drew it into a syringe with a competent tug and plunged the needle into the cannula already plugged into Jared's vein. Hana waited by the door to his room, her fingers pressed against her mouth to keep in the scream. Her mind warned her to look away from his waxy skin and static chest, but her gaze stayed fixed on his plight.

The medic at Karla's side appeared too young to save a life. His white coat brushed her bare arm as she bent to listen to Jared's breathing. The doctor's tawny skin had a smooth quality that assisted the mirage, which projected youth and inexperience. Hana watched him as he lifted a stethoscope from around his neck and plugged the stiff ends into his ears. None of those shortcomings had unnerved him as Hana screamed into the unit. He'd comprehended her stuttering sentences, putting together *Jared* and *Fentanyl* and staring at her in veiled indifference.

Hana pressed her spine against the door frame, grounding herself through the wood's solidity. A pulse raced in her eardrums, obscuring the frenetic activity in the room and detaching her from its seriousness. Thank goodness Karla had remembered her, clasping Hana beneath the elbow and leaning close to discern her hurried ramblings. Thank goodness Karla had listened to and believed her. She had vouched for Hana's sanity and spurred the doctor into action as though putting him under starter's orders. He had sped to the treatment cupboard and returned bearing a vial and a syringe. But he hadn't administered the life-saving medication, perhaps deferring to Karla or just leaving her to take the blame.

Jared had appeared already dead, his arms corpse-like by his sides. A line of foam dribbled from one side of his mouth. A gurgle accompanied each slow breath, ten seconds between the rise of his chest and its almost imperceptible fall. His open eyes and glassy gaze stared at a damp patch on the ceiling. Time seemed to pause as they all waited for the Naloxone to work. The doctor kept his stethoscope pinned to Jared's chest. Then the air whooshed from the room as though sucked into a vacuum and the medics synchronised their movements. Karla covered Jared's grey face in an oxygen mask, its energetic hissing cloaking her snapped instructions. The doctor snatched up the chart at the end of Jared's bed and lifted a pen from his top pocket. His hands shook.

"Sally did it." Hana's voice wavered. The sentence shoved her back in time to her childhood and the horror at a broken vase, which her mother had adored. Mark smashed it with a football and blamed her. The older boy's pointed index finger had seemed to condemn her, but for the ball still rolling towards the bottom of the stairs. "Sally did it," she whispered. She covered her mouth with her shaking hands and pressed her fingers against her lips to seal in the scream. Her legs had turned to lead blocks, fear and the tiny trainers cutting off her circulation. And then she dropped her bombshell, the words muffled. "Sally killed Jared's wife. And she's outside in the corridor."

"For real?" The doctor's eyes widened by degrees like the opening of a rosebud. "Outside this room?" His voice squeaked. Karla's brow furrowed as she scorned his panic.

Hana shook her head. "Outside the unit," she replied. "She has another syringe. She tried to inject me too."

The doctor's glance flicked to Karla and his white coat's authority faded in the glare from this new and unfamiliar crisis. "What should I do?" he demanded.

A rigidity crept into Karla's shoulders, and she stepped away from Jared. The oxygen mask pumped pure air into lungs, which rose and fell with comforting regularity. But his eyelids had closed, secured shut against the rallying cry of his brain. "We'll implement a lockdown," she said, her tone calm. "Start the procedure and use the landline to call the main reception."

"How?" His professional courage had fled with Hana's revelation, knocking him from his self-made pedestal and plunging him into doubt.

With a snort of disgust, Karla pushed past his rigid body, clattering his shoulder with hers in a movement which held a deliberate shove. Hana slid aside from the wide doorway and edged towards the visitor's chair. Karla's worn shoes turned her left and squeaked towards the unattended reception desk.

A sense of devastation filtered through Hana's exhausted brain. A lockdown would pin her inside the high dependency unit and keep her away from Logan. And away from poor, struggling Mary and the void which had consumed her when she tried to help a stranger. Hana's right knee clattered with the chair and she felt her way into the hard plastic seat without looking. Her mind ran through scenarios and painted images of a different outcome. The doctor's soft question made her jump, and she sank her teeth into her tongue. “What?” she demanded in a painful hiss.

“I asked why?” He cocked his handsome face as though entitled to demand answers from the interloper who’d carried such damaging news.

“Why what?” The answer evaded Hana, as though it had hidden itself in a distinct reality from hers. She pressed her right palm over the scar beneath her borrowed sweatshirt. It ached, adding its protest to the cacophony of her combined injuries. Together, they formed a symphony of dull, throbbing pain.

“Why did she kill this man’s wife?” The doctor’s question dragged Hana back into the moment, and she floundered.

“Because she said she did,” she replied. Hana jerked her head towards the corridor. “She said so.” Her mind replayed the scene and Sally’s apparent confession. ‘*Craig would have come with me to start again after that bitch died. That was my grand plan. We could live in luxury anywhere we fancied.*’ Her lips moved as she ran the sentence through her truth filter. “That was her grand plan,” she whispered. “To kill Hallie and give Craig luxury.” The doctor watched her as she cocked her head and ran the scene again. She closed her eyes, and the images cleared, gaining none of the clarity she’d thought they contained.

"Ah well, if she said so," the doctor commented. He crossed the room to place a cool hand over Hana's forehead. "Are you okay, miss? You don't look so good."

Craig and Hallie. Hallie and Craig.

The signs were there, and she'd missed them. Craig loved Hallie, and she'd fallen pregnant with him. Perhaps the swinger vibe which her astute husband had picked up contained more truth than Hana had allowed. Logan had spotted a sexual tension, which her muddled mind failed to recognise. So many tiny clues lined up as though wishing to provide the final nails in Sally's coffin of doom. Only six people had access to Hallie that night if Hana discounted the resort filled with guests and an island bursting with strangers. If she also discarded Ron, Henk, and Hosking as suspects. Logan had seen Henk at the Trading Post with a group of other males. They'd remained there after the Du Roses exited the bar. Ruthless Henk, Sally's brother, who hours before Hallie's death had ransacked both their villas with Ron. Hosking just wanted his boat. He'd seemed to care little about the cash. Hana doubted he'd kill for Sally, not when he'd abandoned her on the island. And Jared had remained in town, alibied by unwitting witnesses, when Hana and Logan overheard Henk and Ron talking. Ron had seen him at the poker game.

Hana's right arm lifted as though tugged by an invisible string. A blood-pressure cuff slipped over her sleeve. But her mental sifting continued.

She and Logan had left Hallie on the porch. The bang of the office door closing heralded Sally's return with a master key. Craig appeared moments later, arriving on their doorstep.

Pressure increased in Hana's forearm and wrist, cutting off the circulation and shocking her free of her thoughts. The doctor held the bell of his stethoscope, its diaphragm cold against Hana's warm arm. He'd pushed up her sleeve, and she hadn't noticed. "Wait," he commanded as she tugged against his grip. Hana stared down at the rounded bell as his fingers shifted. A flower covered its clinical surface, the sticker peeling upward on the edge of a yellow petal. Someone had stuck it there, perhaps this man who hid his lack of courage beneath brusque authority. Someone had intended to soften the edges of the medical intrusion with a yellow daffodil.

Hana gasped. "The flower," she hissed, staring at the doctor's fingers with an eerie intensity in her green eyes. Because she knew where she'd seen something floral and delicate, evidence of a murder. And she'd seen it twice.

99

Slap - popoki

"I'm fine." Hana pushed the doctor's hands aside and got to her feet. The room spun, and she blinked against its peculiar tilt. Karla had returned, ministering to Jared with her quiet assurance. "Is Sergeant Wally George coming?" Hana demanded. She stepped across the room and gazed down at Jared. He'd lost the complexion of a cadaver and his lips twitched. Tear tracks glittered against his brown skin as they dived towards his pillow.

"The hospital is in lockdown," Karla said. She finished checking Jared's pulse and laid his limp hand on the crisp bedding. "The police will arrive soon."

"But Sally is out there," Hana said. "She's still a threat."

"Why?" Jared croaked, the words grinding from his throat without energy. "Why did she want me dead?"

"You have very low blood pressure." The doctor stepped behind Hana and tapped her left shoulder. "Are you experiencing faintness or disturbed vision?"

Hana's pointed gaze sent him retreating a few paces. He shrugged and looped his stethoscope around his neck. She focussed on Jared, needing answers he perhaps didn't possess. "Did you bring in the counterfeit cash?" she demanded. "Or did you send it with Hallie?"

"Both." He cleared his throat. His words slurred as though dragged across broken glass. "She's dead, isn't she? Sally killed her too."

Hana paused. She wanted to let his logical conclusion flood over her, but something about it jarred. Hatred for Sally clouded her judgement and created a crown of guilt around the woman's head. But it didn't fit, not with ease. She'd missed an important detail, and the coronation stalled. Her fingers twitched as though she played an invisible piano. Unable to confirm his accusation, she steered him back to the fake money. "Did Hallie know?" she demanded. "Did she realise you used her as a courier three months ago when she visited the island?"

"No." His voice cracked, and another trickle of saline tracked from his eyes to his ears before plopping in giant drops onto the pillow. "I asked her to take a gift to Craig. Told her he'd got a load of flyers delivered to our place because it was cheaper. She carried a bundle of hundreds. He visited and stayed with us for the Auckland travel show six weeks ago and went home with fifties. I brought the twenties across with me last week."

"Where did you get them?" Hana's tone held more bite than she intended.

"Can't say." Jared turned his face aside and closed his lids against her prying.

"Why did you lie to her about the diving tour?"

Jared released a sigh long enough to have exhaled the cares of the world. "Craig asked for help. He'd caught out Sally in a lie about her wages from working at the hospital. She said they paid her in cash, but he found out from someone else they didn't do that. They can't. So, we followed her around the island all day. She visited some derelict buildings on the hospital site. The pool guy's ute was there, but she didn't stay long. Then she drove to a dementia unit. While she nipped inside, Craig used the spare key to open her car. She'd filled a bag with a couple of thousand dollars in loose cash. He stole some of it and hid it."

"Under our villa with his fakes." Hana finished his thought for him. "And he swapped it for some counterfeit twenties, which he later used at the supermarket." Jared didn't reply, and Hana continued without his assistance. "You came clean to Hallie, and she caught the bus to the police station." She jutted her chin in the air. "But she told Sergeant Wally George, and he dismissed her claims."

"I don't know." Jared sniffed. "What does it matter now? Sally killed her and tried to drug me."

Hana sighed. It mattered to her. It mattered very much.

The Rarotongan police arrived in a hail of sirens and chaos. Sergeant Wally George and Officer Carrie took copious notes with scratching pens, dispatching their subordinates to search for Sally. They carried ancient satellite phones with aerials held on by tape. "Lightning hit the radio tower," Sergeant Wally George explained. "We keep these for emergencies."

Hana perched in the visitor's chair, which she'd pulled alongside Jared's bed. She sipped a lukewarm cup of tea which Karla had fetched for her. The quiet ward bustled with an unfamiliar noise. Marching feet clattered heavy boots over the worn linoleum while disjointed voices offered echoed sit-reps over the satellite phones. She winced as the doctor exaggerated his role in the heroism to a stoic, silent Officer Carrie. Scratch, scratch. Her pen transposed his words onto her page.

"Hallie lost the baby before she died." Hana leaned forward and pressed her fingers over Jared's. Did uttering the statement make his wife's death seem better or worse? She wasn't sure, but dealt only with the truth. His chest hitched, but he didn't speak. His fingers flickered beneath her palm as though wishing to shake off her ruthless kindness. Hana sighed. "The baby was Craig's. You knew that, didn't you?"

Jared's jaw showed through his cheek as a harsh line of grinding bones. He turned his face aside and spoke to the heart monitor on guard by his side. "Why him?" he whispered. "I would have coped with anyone's child but his."

Hana left him to his misery and sought permission to return to Mary's house. Sergeant Wally George frowned at her and shrugged. "I'll check," he offered. Then he stopped and turned, his shoe soles squeaking against the smooth floor. "I don't have time to drive you anywhere though," he added.

Hana shook her head, lacking the energy to reassure him. She'd find her way back to Logan somehow, even if it meant walking for kilometres in dirty, too-small trainers. "Have your officers found Ron, the pool guy from Paradise Villas, yet?" she asked. Logan had given the man a headache but not killed him. Ron's absence when she visited the derelict house earlier meant he'd gone to ground with his backpack.

"We're searching the area," Sergeant Wally George replied.

"Sorry." Hana raised a hand to delay him further. "And what about Craig? I saw him disposing of a hair scrunchie which belonged to Hallie Clarke. Ron pulled it from the swimming pool at the resort in a net. Craig confiscated his bag of rubbish before he could finish the job." She took a tentative step towards him. "Hallie drowned, didn't she? In the swimming pool. I believe Craig hid her body in case the police searched the resort for her that night. But Hosking ran Jared over and, without him willing to file a missing report, no one would listen to us. The police wouldn't search." The words ground free, the accusation deliberate. Sergeant Wally George's lips flattened into thin lines against his square chin. But he didn't comment, giving Hana licence to continue. "Craig deemed it safe enough on Sunday morning to row his kayak out to the reef and tip Hallie into the ocean. If the cyclone hadn't come into shore, no one would have found her."

Sergeant Wally George sighed and nodded his head. "I'll make a note of everything you've said," he promised. His shoulders slumped and after a cursory glance around the clinical hallway, he lowered his voice. "Hallie Clarke died from drowning in chlorinated water." He seemed to falter over the next sentence as though battling a hidden pain for the fallen woman. "A massive dose of fentanyl meant she didn't stand a chance. Someone drugged her and then dumped her into the resort's swimming pool."

He left Hana with that revelation. He returned within minutes to instruct the man guarding the main door to allow Hana through them. She stepped outside into the rain and it doused her in seconds, plastering her hair to her scalp. So, Sally had drugged Hallie, perhaps beginning earlier in the evening, as she ferried fresh drinks to the table. It explained Hallie's extreme reaction to the alcohol. But her drowning made no sense. Why carry or drag her between the villas to a more exposed part of the resort? Why not leave her to die on the porch? Her misery over the miscarriage would account for the impetuous drug overdose. Hana considered all the people who'd walked past the swimming pool that night. But they'd approached from the main entrance, cutting across the lawns between the villas. They had no reason to glance across at a deserted pool marked by subdued lighting.

The relentless rain soaked through Hana's borrowed clothing in minutes. Her bra sagged against the water and created awkward wedges through the wet sweatshirt. Hana trudged through the hospital site, picking her footing with care to avoid puddles and fluttering debris. Apart from Sergeant Wally George and Officer Carrie, civil defence volunteers and local wardens made up the island's emergency police force. They trotted around the hospital site wearing high visibility vests and sharing the decrepit satellite phones. “They’ve found a body!” a grey-haired man shouted to another volunteer carting a metal detector up the slope. “Someone buried him in the bushes behind the old maternity unit.”

Hana released a groan of dismay, whispering under her breath, “Logan Du Rose. Please tell me you didn’t.”

100

To plug or stop - pōpani

Hana caught the clockwise bus from the hospital to Mary's house. She saw no sign of the pastor's wife or her vehicle on the bumpy ride around the island. The driver hadn't asked for a fare, but pointed at the blood soaking through her sweatshirt from the glass cuts. "Cyclone?" he asked, his bushy eyebrows raised in sympathy.

"Yes," Hana replied, her voice small and weak. "A broken window."

In a spirit of community empathy, the driver waited for Hana and two elderly passengers to take their seats before he clumped on the gas pedal. The couple had less difficulty than Hana in getting comfortable on the plastic covers. Every swerve or slam on the brakes caused her to slide forward, banging her knees on the metal bars of the seat in front of her. She staggered off the bus at the stop nearest Mary's house, her legs turning to jelly with every step.

Logan met her at the front door, his grey eyes blazing, and his lips set into thin lines. "What the hell, Hana?" he demanded. He spread his arms wide to encompass her dishevelled state. "Are you limping? Is that blood?"

Hana groaned and closed the front door behind her. "My chicken left me. Mary abandoned me and then I bumped into Sally."

Logan ran his hands through his hair, leaving it sticking up at the front. But in true Logan Du Rose fashion, he pulled Hana towards him and crushed her against his chest. He kept his own counsel for long enough to create an air of expectancy. Hana shivered beneath his warmth.

"I'm sorry you woke to an empty house," she murmured, pushing her nose against his shirt. He smelled of sleep and citrus fruit with the faintest hint of toothpaste. "We only intended to leave for an hour."

Logan rested his cheek on her tangled hair. "You're freezing," he said, his tone soothing. "Let's get you cleaned up and into dry clothes." He bent to unlace her trainers and with them in his hand, opened the door to sit them outside beneath the porch. They shed crusty leaves and clumps of mud in a circle. Guilt tightened Hana's chest. Cheyne's precious trainers, now soiled and unloved.

"No," she said, tugging on the door as he closed it. "I can't leave them there. They belonged to Mary's daughter. She died up at the derelict houses where Sally kept the crates of dirty cash. We walked up there, and Mary couldn't cope. I can't let her daughter's ruined trainers be the first thing she sees when she arrives home."

Logan nodded and retrieved them. He carried them to the bathroom and while Hana repeated her shower, he washed away the traces of destruction from their soles and their fabric uppers. She sat on the side of the bath in a fluffy towel while he picked the debris from the plug hole and tossed it into the nearby toilet. "Thank you," Hana said, admiring the trainers as they drip-dried on the bath rack. "That's much better."

He sighed and slumped onto the narrow ledge alongside her. Exhaustion still nipped at his frayed edges, lining the purple bruises beneath his eyes with a more permanent darkness, which went soul-deep. "So, Craig is missing, Hosking drowned, Henk died at the resort, Sally drugged Mabel, killed Hallie, and then tried to finish Jared." His tone contained a flat, dull quality.

"Apparently so," Hana replied, but her reservations remained. "But why not just leave Hallie to die on the porch? Sally gave her enough Fentanyl to make her fall asleep forever. Why drown her in the swimming pool as well?"

"I'm at a loss," Logan admitted. "I can't think straight." He tugged away the towel from her chest and pursed his lips at what he found there. Relief flared in his tired irises. "That top one's stopped bleeding," he said with a sigh, allowing Hana to pull the towel back into place. "That's something, anyway."

"I need to find Mary." Hana looked to him for answers, just like she always did. "I feel responsible for her."

Logan dropped his chin and nodded. "Okay," he agreed. "Someone left a bag of spare clothes on the porch. The note said they're for Pastor Mike's visitors. We'll assume for now they meant us. Let's see if we can muster up a complete outfit for you and we'll catch the bus around the island. I'd like to check on the remains of the Harley and assuage the horrible pictures in my mind." He wrinkled his nose. "I loved riding that bike."

Hana cocked her head and frowned. "Okay," she replied, drawing out the word. "But we need to take care. You're bailed to this address, remember?"

Hana switched the plasters on two of her deepest cuts and dressed in clothing from the plastic bag. She matched a floral muumuu with grey sweatpants, which she rolled up at the ankle. A knitted cardigan completed her ensemble. The kind donor had added a pair of worn flip-flops, and Hana pressed her sore toes into them. She gathered the flowing muumuu fabric and wedged it between her thighs so she could inspect her footwear. "I look strange," she announced as Logan raised an eyebrow. He appeared distracted, eyeing his cowboy boots still drying in the lobby with wads of newspaper poking from their zippers. "I already got a free ride on the bus," Hana said, letting the swishing fabric cascade from her thighs like a burst dam of blue and pink and purple water. "Did you lose your wallet in the cyclone?"

"Nope." Logan lifted his shirt and patted the pocket of his sweatpants. "It's in here. I still have the passports too. They're a little damp, so I spread them on the table to dry." He tugged his wallet free and grinned at the fluttering ticket pinned beneath his index finger and thumb. "Oh look, I bought two concession tickets at the start of the holiday. Remember? We can ride round and round all day."

Hana groaned at the sight of the other note which came with it. "Is that the fake twenty from the Trading Post?"

"Yep. I might make a gift of it to Sergeant Wally George."

"Please don't!" Hana begged. "He'd love to blame everything on the tourists instead of the locals."

Logan grunted, and his tone held a warning. “That’s kinda fair though, babe,” he said. “Jared started it, and Craig kept it going.”

“Then let’s leave it as a joint venture which doesn’t involve us!” Hana protested. “Eat it or burn it. You choose.” She snatched it from Logan’s fingers when he didn’t reply. “I’ll get rid of it.” She disappeared into the bathroom and the sound of tearing paper echoed into the hallway. Then the flush of the toilet followed it.

They tidied until the bedroom and bathroom looked as neat as when they arrived. Hana folded the clothes from the bag and piled them at the end of the bed. Then she sat down beside it, causing it to list like a toppling spire. “What do we do now?” she asked, picking at the dry skin on her fingers. “I can’t remember if Mary locked the front door or if she mentioned a spare key.”

Logan stretched out on the mattress in a pretence of trying to remember. His eyelids fluttered closed. “Not sure,” he said, his words slurred.

“Maybe I’ll just have a little think too.” Hana spoke around the yawn which involved every facial muscle. She lifted the pile of clothing and placed it on the dressing table. The muumuu obstructed her progress as she clambered onto the bed beside her husband. The flip-flops poked upwards, her feet hanging off the end of the mattress. “Just a little think,” she whispered.

But her head emptied of all thought, and nothing remained.

101

An attachment - piri

Hana woke to something cool pressed against her forehead. She lifted her left arm and flapped at it. “No!” she protested as the action dragged her from sleep. The comfy pillow beneath her right cheek shifted. “Earthquake,” she mumbled, jamming her face harder against the rolling surface. Then Logan swore, using one of her least favourite terms. The sound echoed through her cheek.

“Everything is fine.” The mattress dipped beside Hana. “But you’re boiling in all those clothes. Let me fetch you a drink. Perhaps take off the muumuu.” The mattress shifted again, rolling and pitching as a weight lifted.

“Muumuu,” Hana muttered. She giggled, the word unfamiliar and strange. Her mind painted an image of home and the four-poster bed they’d shared since the start of their marriage. “Muumuu,” she repeated.

A groan erupted from her pillow, and Hana jerked her head aside. Her eyes opened wide and as her focus returned, it relayed a different picture. A pretty, unfamiliar room surrounded her. But she recognised the groans of her husband. "Just kill me now," he murmured. "Shoot me in the face and have done with it."

"No!" Hana forced herself onto her right elbow and covered Logan's mouth with her other hand. "I already shot my quota for this holiday. What's the matter?" She leaned over him, compressing his left shoulder until he groaned again. "Apart from the obvious. And stop swearing. We're in a vicarage."

But Logan did swear again. "I need my meds," he gasped. "My ribs are killing me."

The muumuu wrapped around Hana's calves as she slithered from the mattress and bumped over the wooden footboard. Her feet seemed heavier, as though an invisible hand had filled the flip-flops with lead while she slept. She stumbled to Logan's other side and found his nasal spray on the night stand. His fingers shook as he took it from her and used it.

Mary reappeared with a turquoise tea tray. Ice cubes clinked in time with her footsteps, bounding on the surface of two tall glasses of water. "Here we go," she said, as though speaking to errant children. She edged aside the pile of clothing on the dressing table and set the tray beside it. "It's hot in here. You both looked as though you fainted. I panicked." She walked to the window and levered it open far enough for the air current to suck out the net curtains. They billowed freely beneath the frame as though believing they could fly away from the island. Hana knew how they felt. She tamped down the uncharitable thoughts and sank onto the bed beside Logan.

"Sorry," she said, the simple apology covering a multitude of sins and offences. She held out her hand to Logan, offering support while he forced himself to a sitting position. They sat on the bed and faced their host as though awaiting a reprimand.

Mary handed them each a glass and leaned back against the wall. "No, I'm sorry. I abandoned you at the hospital and then someone tried to kill you." She blew out a ragged breath. "The entire island is talking about what happened. Someone attacked you, and you still saved a man from being murdered." She flapped her hands as though desperate to gain flight, her body language betraying her desire to be anywhere else but here.

Hana slurped the water and patted sweat from her forehead with the back of her hand. It brought her time to consider her reply. When it came, it held generosity and sisterhood. "I didn't know about Cheyne. And I can't imagine your grief at ending up right where it happened. Any grieving mother would react in the same way, and I had no right to expect anything different. My biggest regret is not just leaving with you." She exhaled. "I should have."

Logan cleared his throat beside her, and their curious marital telepathy carried his rebuke. *'Yes, you should have.'*

Hana patted the bed beside her, and Mary sat, though her movements held reluctance. "They caught the woman," she said, unaware of the relief which darted through Hana's chest. "Sergeant Wally George and Carrie have her locked up in the police station. They caught her husband too. He tried to bribe a fisherman to take him to Atiu. But he used counterfeit cash, so the man reported him to Officer Carrie." She shook her head and her greying curls bounced against her ears. "They seemed like such a pleasant couple. I found this poor old girl wandering on the beach in her nightdress a while ago and Sally drove her to the hospital. She seemed so desperate to help her. It's such a sad story. What kind of person takes their elderly mother on holiday and leaves without her? I later heard Sally paid for the woman's treatment and visited her often in the dementia unit. The congregation offered to raise funds, but Sally took care of everything." Mary picked at a hangnail and funnelled her concentration into the action. Hana recognised her pain avoidance and let her ramble. "So, why would Sally turn on her guests like this?"

Hana swallowed at Mary's assumption. She sensed Logan shift on the mattress beside her. She tuned into the gentle sounds as he sipped his water. Hallie, Jared, and Hana all stayed at the resort. It seemed a logical conclusion that Sally had turned on the tourists in a fit of madness. Hana pursed her lips and shrugged. "I'm sure the police will find the answers," she said.

"I hope so." Mary tutted. "The counterfeit notes have damaged trust on the island. We kidded ourselves tourists brought it with them, but it came from a local after all."

Turning, Hana pressed her free hand over Mary's. "I'd love to hear more about Cheyne if you'd like to tell me. Do you have some photos?"

Mary blossomed like a marigold beneath the noonday sun. She nodded, and the crinkles returned to the corners of her eyes. "I'd love that," she whispered. She jerked her head towards Hana's torso. "Do you need the cardigan and the muumuu? The sun is coming out. You'll get too hot."

Hana dropped her chin and considered the huge red flowers covering the chintzy fabric. She shrugged and grinned. "I don't need underwear beneath it," she stated with a chuckle. "I kinda like it."

Logan aspirated his next mouthful of water and coughed. He choked and groaned in equal measure. Hana showed no sympathy for him. She left him to make himself decent and followed Mary to the lounge to keep her promise.

Charlie arrived as Hana poured over a second photo album containing images of a teenage Cheyne. He clumped up the porch steps and Mary responded to his weird tapping on the door. She opened it and caught him as he pitched backwards, still in the process of removing his left shoe. He joined them in sifting through the albums, recalling his memories of a smiling girl who became a loved and valued member of their island community. "We finished clearing the car park at the bar," he commented as Mary set a mug of coffee in front of him. His words held no rebuke.

"Sorry." Mary slumped into the chair beside Hana. "I returned to the old maternity unit on the hill. It's such a mess."

"Weren't the police crawling all over it?" Charlie's eyes bugged and his many chins wobbled.

Mary shrugged. "They didn't mind. I sat on the grass and prayed." She tapped a work-worn finger on the polished table. "We need to do something about that site. It's a disgrace. And a poor memorial to Cheyne." An air of determination shrouded her, and strength radiated from her quick movements as she waved an agitated hand. "Let's do it!" she stated. "I'll speak to Mike. We'll get the congregation involved and build a new maternity ward up there."

Hana studied Charlie's expression and discerned the faintest grin tug at the corners of his lips. He saw her watching him and raised a bushy eyebrow. Hana couldn't decide if it communicated a warning or a question. But she'd suffered enough from the latest intrigue, and she stuffed her curiosity back into its box.

Another knock on the door heralded Sergeant Wally George. He accepted a mug of coffee and asked to speak to Logan.

"I'm not sure about that," Charlie sputtered, but the police officer lifted a hand in dismissal.

"We know he didn't kill Hallie Clarke," he stated. Exhaustion weighed every movement and his head bobbed like a daisy on his thin neck. He sighed. "Please, just let me speak to him."

Hana roused Logan from another uneasy sleep. She discovered him still sitting where she left him, the glass half full and listing to one side. "Babe?" She took it from his fingers and set it on the night stand. "Sergeant Wally George is here to speak to you."

"No!" Logan dipped forward, balancing his elbows on his thighs. A deep groan accompanied the action as his painful ribs complained at the compression.

"I need to sleep!" he protested. "Can't he arrest me tomorrow?"

"I don't think he's here to charge you," Hana stated. "Come on, sweetie. Let's get this over with."

Sergeant Wally George got to his feet as Logan entered the room. Awkwardness oozed from every pore. "Mr Du Rose," he began, and Hana's nerve failed her. The formality of the sentence suggested she'd misrepresented his visit.

"You're not taking him," she insisted. A sidestep put her across Logan's path, and she spread her arms like wings to block his progress. Logan grunted as he walked into the back of her, clutching at his chest and his ribs simultaneously.

Sergeant Wally George lifted his left hand in a gesture of peace. "It's okay," he promised, his tone emphatic. His body dipped at the waist to emphasise his meaning. "I'm here to explain."

102

Poetic justice - ‘uā‘o

Hana didn't believe him. Her faith in the Rarotongan police force had diminished with each interaction until none remained. She stood guard over Logan as Sergeant Wally George stepped forward and offered his outstretched hand. Charlie Clay rose also, shambling across the room with incredible speed. "Explain first," he insisted, nudging the police officer's shoulder until he returned to his seat.

"The owners of Paradise Villas killed Hallie Clarke and disposed of her body." His tired eyes tilted downward at the edges as though desperate to close in sleep. "Officer Carrie charged them both this afternoon. There are other pending indictments, including false imprisonment and drugs related offences."

"What about the counterfeit cash?" Hana demanded. She relaxed her posture and allowed Logan to slip between her and Charlie. He sank into a dining chair and arched his spine the opposite way, as though attempting to negate his pain. Mary smiled with indulgence and plonked a mug of strong coffee in front of him. Hana slunk into the adjacent seat, resting her palm on his left thigh.

Sergeant Wally George lifted his mug and took a deep slurp. “It appears Craig Henderson imported it with the help of Jared Clarke.”

Hana’s lips parted to ask about the crates of dirty money until Logan’s foot landed on hers beneath the table. She frowned and stared at him, detecting the slightest, imperceptible shake of his head. Gratitude filled her chest as Mary placed a packet of biscuits in the centre of the table and enquired about Mabel. “Sally and Craig seemed so kind,” she commented again. “I admired how they paid her hospital bills and searched for her family.” She frowned and turned to Charlie. “Didn’t her husband travel to New Zealand recently to follow up on leads relating to her identity?”

Logan snorted, and Mary’s forehead creased in confusion. “I don’t think that’s why he went,” he commented. He smudged spilled coffee over his sweatpants with a scarred finger.

“Oh.” Disappointment shrouded Mary, all the fizz of her earlier enthusiasm dwindling. She exhaled and slashed the biscuit wrapper with a pair of lethal looking scissors. The action conveyed her hidden misery.

Sergeant Wally George took a swig of his coffee and observed Hana through lowered eyelids. It created an intimidating effect. "Funny thing," he mused, his tone circumspect. "Sally Henderson has a bullet wound to her right forearm." His bushy brows drew together into a line. "She says you shot her."

Hana forced the air from her lungs to produce a convincing shrug. "That's weird," she replied, adding enough disinterest to cover the lie.

The officer leaned forward. He propped his elbows on the table and studied Hana over the rim of his mug. "The receptionist at the hospital swears a couple fitting your description asked for help after a firearms incident. And the woman requested Factor 8 for a haemophiliac." His chin lowered and his gaze held a new intensity. "That's two reports involving guns. What do you want to tell me?"

Logan kicked Hana beneath the table again. She sighed with relief as he stepped into the breach. "We visited the hospital," he conceded. "I fell and injured my chest. We didn't think we could return to the resort in the cyclone, but the storm hit the hospital and so we risked it." Logan tugged his nasal spray from his pocket and set it on the table. The last few days had damaged the label. A dent marred the bottle's structure. Logan pushed it across the table until Sergeant Wally George tugged it towards himself.

"I see," he concluded. "Are you able to show me your injuries?"

"Oh, come on!" Charlie protested. He leaned over Logan's head and slapped the polished wood with his palm. "This is ridiculous. Most unprofessional."

"It's fine." Logan lifted his tee shirt to reveal the abomination covering his left pectoral. Hana's mobile phone had created a raised indent, which ran in a horizontal line. It looked nothing like a gunshot wound and more like something flat and thin had exploded above his left nipple. Sergeant Wally George's lips peeled back from his teeth in a reactionary grimace.

"I'm sorry," he muttered. "I'll feed that back through the investigation."

Seeming satisfied, Charlie rounded the table and dropped into the seat beside the police officer. The wood groaned beneath him as he reached for a biscuit. It fitted into the slot in his face whole.

Logan dropped his shirt and raised an eyebrow at Hana as the atmosphere calmed. She pursed her lips to stop herself from blurting something inappropriate or criminal. But her potential for honesty knew no bounds, and it fuelled a suicidal curiosity. She leaned forward and noticed Logan's eyes widen in her peripheral vision. Despite his light kick to her right ankle, she addressed the police officer. "How did you know Hallie was six weeks pregnant?" she asked, her tone soft.

Sergeant Wally George blinked at her, the action guileless and showing confusion. He tapped his pen against his chin. "I'm not sure," he replied. He pushed out his lower lip and shrugged. "I just did."

Hana stared at him hard enough to consider it rudeness. But unless Sergeant Wally George had graduated from acting school with honours, he hadn't lied. And that begged the question. How did he know that small but essential fact? It plagued her as the others sipped coffee and ate biscuits. Hana sat in silence, her mind sifting through details. It busied her to where she lost track of their conversation. Sergeant Wally George and Charlie rose, and Hana jerked in surprise. Logan gave her a curious side glance.

"Enjoy the rest of your stay," Sergeant Wally George said, shaking their hands. His smile held an element of desperation, as though the thought of never seeing the Du Roses again would help him sleep better at night.

"Oh, what about Mabel?" Hana's cheeks flushed at having forgotten about the old woman at the dementia unit. "What did she tell you?" She forced herself to stand on tired, aching legs.

Sergeant Wally George winced. "A fantastical tale of piracy involving our local dive operator."

"Gantry Hosking?" Hana took a step towards him, confused when she overbalanced and pinged against Logan's chest. He grunted in pain but didn't release the handful of her stretchy muumuu clutched in his fingers. "Sally believes he died."

Sergeant Wally George raised a speculative eyebrow and side-stepped the statement. He left Mary's house and took his information with him. Charlie left next, after extending to them an invitation to visit the secret bar in the hills. Logan declined with good grace and hid a yawn behind his hand.

"I don't get that," Hana began, rounding on him as soon as Mary closed the door. "Sergeant Wally George definitely told me that Hallie was six weeks pregnant. It's what convinced me he'd had a relationship with her. She must have told him. And why would she tell anyone but the father?"

"No idea." Logan bopped the end of her nose with his forefinger. "Let them sort it out, Hana." His tone held a warning, which she resented. But the mystery burned in her chest for the rest of the day. She woke thinking about it the next morning and pondered it while she helped Pastor Mike's parishioners to clear debris from an elderly couple's front garden. It ate away at her for the rest of their trip until it was all she thought about. Like an electrical charge which had failed to complete its circuit, the issue remained open and sparking.

Cyclone Angela had stripped away the island's false veneer, and the community embraced the Du Roses with genuine affection. No one mentioned the fake money or their wrongful arrest. They pushed the event into the past and gave it no more airtime. Hana and Logan helped with Rarotonga's healing. They dug and cleared as their injuries allowed, letting their earlier misery dissipate with the bad weather. The Harley turned up at the hospital. Sand had blasted the paintwork, but a falling coconut tree had just missed crushing it. The feathery fronds had both covered it from view and protected it from further damage. Logan's elation seemed limitless until his ribs made it too difficult for him to ride it. A brief trip up the street left him gasping for breath.

The Mazda 3, which had saved their lives, washed up on a beach near Arorangi. Pastor Mike tracked down the owner and Logan apologised, paid his insurance excess, and offered compensation. The elderly resident had shaken his head and waved away Logan's generosity. The fallen tree occupying the Mazda's parking space had already doomed its existence. "I'm glad it saved you both," he'd said, shaking Logan's hand. Hana had watched from a distance as the men talked. Shame still filled her at having stolen the vehicle. Regret followed. They could have stayed at the hospital in safety if she hadn't shot Sally. But for fear of apprehension, they might have saved themselves a world of trouble. Hana replayed the moment over in her mind and the result stayed the same. Her greatest irritant was still at having missed Sally's face.

And then the other knotty issues raised their heads. Who made Sergeant Wally George aware of Hallie's pregnancy and its duration? And who moved her dying body into the swimming pool? The cruel and unnecessary action plagued Hana. As did the identity of Po, to whom the group had owed a debt of gratitude and cash for unspecified services.

Hana slumped onto a nearby rock and brushed sand from her fingers. Her feet ached in the flip-flops. A coconut lay between her feet, rugged and brown like a giant hazelnut shell. She'd collected hundreds of fallen coconuts over the last few days. The appointment for their boat cruise had come and gone, the harbour still damaged from the cyclone's battering and the vessels landlocked. So, Hana and Logan had used their time to assist the local community with their clear-up operation. As Hana rested on the rock with a warm sea breeze ruffling her red fringe, Hallie's words returned as an echo. *'Craig doesn't know the half of it.'* What had Hana missed?

"Scoot over." Logan's rumbling voice snapped her free of her thoughts. She shifted sideways so they could balance together on the rock. "What's the matter?" he asked, wrapping an arm around her shoulders. His fingers appeared gritty, and Hana knew if she licked his skin it would taste of salt. "Do you want to go back to Mary's?" Logan asked. "We've finished dumping the sand back on the beach for today." He nudged the coconut with the toe of his cowboy boot, and it rolled like a weighted egg. "The market traders are collecting these to sell at the weekend. Want me to carry this one across the road?"

Hana shook her head but didn't reply. Logan had adapted to island life with surprising ease. A sun hat woven from coconut leaves by an elderly and adoring parishioner cast his handsome features into the shade. He still moved with difficulty. Pastor Mike had restricted him to broom-duty as they collected sand from the island and returned it to its rightful place. When he nudged Hana's shoulder, she sighed. "Who is Po?" She turned to face him, studying the familiar shutter which crashed over his expression. "Someone is still at the centre of this. They started on the outside, a casual blackmailer, or perhaps providing a necessary service specific to their skills. But I know they dumped Hallie in that swimming pool."

"How do you know?" Logan asked, his tone level.

"Because Sally already drugged her and put distance between herself and the Clarke's villa. She sent Craig to ask us if we'd seen Hallie, inferring she'd already checked the obvious places. He wouldn't go back to the villa again. He's too lazy. It's the only logical solution. Jared stayed in town, so no one would find Hallie until housekeeping visited the next morning. Sally didn't put her in the water."

"Craig then?"

Again, Hana shook her head. "No. He fished her out and hid her body because he thought Sally killed her. Sally wanted her dead because of the baby. She didn't realise Craig had followed her and found the money and the hiding place. It wasn't about the money for Sally, but at Hallie's effrontery in getting pregnant by Craig. Sally also didn't know about Craig fencing the counterfeit notes. Ron told her up at the hospital. I heard him. She wasn't aware of it."

"So, someone else moved the body into the pool." Logan's tone held no heat or enthusiasm.

"Yes." Hana sighed. "They've caught everyone else except for Po. Hosking mistimed his exit from the harbour and the coastguard found the Ellie Marie destroyed on a reef out to sea."

"Oh." Logan dipped forward and ran his left hand over his face. "I hadn't heard about that."

"Po killed Hallie," Hana stated. She swivelled on the rock to face him. "Just hear me out, please. He killed Hallie because of the baby or because she told the police about the money. The police, Logan." She snapped her fingers. "Sergeant Wally George is involved somehow. He knew about Hallie's pregnancy, right down to the last detail. How? And he's in a perfect position to divert any attention from the laundering operation." She sighed and shook her head. "The only thing which doesn't fit is what Hallie said that night. *'Craig doesn't know the half of it.'* Since her death, I've believed she referred to Sally's moneymaking scheme, but I think she also knew Po's identity and his involvement in it." Hana circled the index finger of her right hand. "Because Craig and Jared discovered the dirty money that morning, so that's not what she meant. Jared told her, perhaps out of spite after she confessed about the baby." Hana's shoulders slumped beneath the scorching sun. A red blush tinted her bare forearms and freckles dotted her toes. "And I'm back to Sergeant Wally George," she concluded. "I know he's Po."

"You can't solve this, sweetheart," Logan soothed. His tone held genuine sympathy. "We leave early tomorrow morning. It's time to let go."

Hana rose and dug her left hand into the muumuu's copious pocket. She tugged out the battered feather, which Winston left behind for her. She didn't need Logan to state the obvious, but he did it anyway. "You can't take that back to New Zealand," he said, no emotion in his voice.

Hana nodded. She'd put off the dreaded moment. After rescuing the feather from her sweatshirt as Mary dropped it into the washing machine, she'd kept it with her. "Winston is the king of Paradise Villa's now," she said, whispering into the wind. With its owners in jail, the resort would remain abandoned and destroyed, a blot on the stunning island landscape. Winston's chicken family would reign supreme, pecking and scratching without distraction. Hana lifted her palm, and the wind snatched the feather, sucking it into its maw and tossing it around her head. She closed her eyes, not wishing to see where it went.

Only Logan noticed its direction as it pitched and rolled on the breeze. It headed north towards Nikao and the airport. Perhaps it would race them home.

103

Abrasion - pakiko

Hana followed Logan's gaze, watching Sergeant Wally George striding across the arrivals lounge. Carrie spun on her heel and fell into stride beside him. A group of male passengers walked behind them, faces tired but their bodies ramrod straight and authoritative. Reinforcements from the mainland, perhaps, sent to relieve the exhausted police officers.

Hana shook her head as Logan led her towards the departure gate. She couldn't just leave, not with so many unanswered questions set to drive her insane. She wanted to tell someone what she'd worked out and perhaps find some peace. "I need to go back." Her fingers scrabbled at his grip over her wrist, trying to shake him off without drawing blood. "It's Po. I know who Po is."

Logan's grip intensified. "Don't do it, Hana," he urged, lowering his voice. "Get on the damn plane."

"Let go!" She wrestled against him, using her other hand to prise his fingers upwards.

"No!" He leaned sideways and hissed into her ear. Their wrangling attracted the attention of other passengers. A man wearing a severe expression approached them, his gait slow and tentative. He sported the navy uniform of a security officer and his fingers hovered over the radio clipped to his belt. "And I know who Po is, Hana!" Logan growled. "Leave it. We'll sort it out, but not this way."

Hana swallowed, and her scrabbling ceased. She stared into his solemn grey eyes and matched her steps to his. She resembled a bouncing child, running to keep up with his loping stride. But her gaze strayed over her shoulder to the departing police officers. "How long have you known?" she whispered.

Logan's lips twitched. "That's the thing about staying with local folk, isn't it? You hear things which mean nothing to them and everything to you. Everyone made us call him Sergeant Wally George, but it seemed like a crazy mouthful. I can't believe he grew up here with his classmates trotting out a nineteen letter name every time they wanted to borrow a pencil or kick a ball. But they did. No one shortened it, never. Not to Po, not to anything."

Hana nodded. Her fingers rested over Logan's wrist. "It's okay, you can let go. I won't make a fuss," she promised. "Po. I've heard the nickname used in connection with Bodie. The Po-po. Police. I worked it out days ago." She forced a smile onto her lips for the benefit of the security officer who'd followed them. Her boarding pass fluttered in her shaking fingers as she presented it to the airline representative.

"No luggage?" The woman bobbed sideways and stared at Hana's scruffy attire. Sympathy radiated through her sharp features at Hana's shallow headshake. "Sorry, love," she soothed. She waved her through, the koru pattern on her uniform jacket and skirt reminding Hana of home.

The Du Roses walked together onto the apron and queued at the bottom of the steps. "Because his name is Sergeant, we always assumed he ran the department," Hana said. She turned to face the mountain, which towered over the island's centre. Its forbidding glare hid the secret bar in the foothills while rumours of an ancient, angry resident chased away the curious. Hana sighed. "After Sally drugged Jared, I asked Sergeant Wally George if I could leave the hospital. He said he needed to check and came back a few minutes later."

"Yeah." Logan squeezed her hand. "Their uniforms are so casual and understated, we didn't know which of them was more senior. Carrie murdered Hallie because she asked too many questions at the station that afternoon. She couldn't risk her telling anyone else about the stash of currency."

"But why did Sergeant Wally George lie to me?" Hana mused. "He said she visited to apologise to him, but it wasn't the truth. She told the most superior officer about the money laundering. Carrie."

Logan shrugged. "He repeated what she told him. Even if it made no sense, he had no reason to doubt a senior officer."

Hana wrinkled her nose. "I had it all wrong? Hallie knew she'd made a mistake in telling Carrie. That's why she got so upset at seeing the police scooter at the resort. Running into the cops on the way home didn't help. Carrie brushed off her report, and it irritated Hallie. I wonder if she realised she'd signed her own death warrant."

Logan raised his eyebrow, but shook his head. "Let someone else worry about the details," he suggested, his tone soothing. "We're going home."

Their seats vibrated with the ramping of the engine as the plane eased forward onto the taxiway. The pilot paused for clearance. With so many displaced tourists, the airlines had sent extra repatriation flights. Too many. No one occupied the aisle seat on their row, allowing Logan to stretch out his legs. Three very sick passengers took up the business class spaces behind the cockpit. New Zealand medics had made the round trip to accompany them to mainland hospitals. A female patient wailed as the air pressure during take-off aggravated her injuries. Nobody begrudged them the expensive seats, not when they'd already suffered so much.

Hana kept hold of Logan's wrist, gratified when he shifted position to entwine their fingers. The ocean slid into view, serene like a cornflower blue tablecloth. A pile of debris left behind by Cyclone Angela marred the scene. Collected beside the terminal building, the pile of wood and twisted metal awaited collection by the overstretched refuse trucks responsible for expunging the remaining chaos from the island. The community had made light work of the clean-up operation, revealing a united spirit rarely witnessed by tourists. They'd cared for one another, fed, laboured, shared, rejoiced, commiserated, and loved. It created a unique vision of paradise from the one Hana had experienced. It reminded her of home and Logan's formidable Matakitaki mountain. Hana squeezed her husband's fingers as the force released them and the plane banked away from Rarotonga. She closed her eyes, enjoying the peculiar sensation in the pit of her stomach. It culminated in a rush as the plane settled into its course for New Zealand.

"What will we do?" she asked, turning to face Logan.

His lips flattened into a thin line and a dent appeared and then receded from beneath his right eye. "It's already in hand," he said, leaning towards her.

Hana jerked away from the kiss he'd aimed for and narrowed her eyes. "What did you do?" she demanded.

Logan's large hand cupped the back of her neck, and he pulled her closer. Their foreheads touched in an intimate huddle which cut out the rest of the world. "Charlie contacted Liza. She got a message through to the chief commissioner. It needs an outside investigation by the New Zealand police. Officer Carrie thinks she's got away with it right now. I hope she enjoys the next few days because it won't last. Sally left Hallie to die from a drug overdose, but Carrie saw her staggering in the street and assumed she was drunk. She dumped Hallie in the pool to drown and then Craig disposed of the body." His kiss landed, his lips warm and familiar.

"Why would Craig protect either of them?" Hana demanded. "And which one?"

Logan's lips flattened, a dimple appearing in his chin. "My money is on Sally. With Hallie dead, he needed to protect his livelihood at least. Perhaps he felt guilty about the baby and how it drove Sally over the edge."

Hana closed her eyes and released a painful sigh. "What horrible people," she breathed. "She'd already moved on with Hosking. Why should she care? And yet after he abandoned her, she believed she could just pick up with Craig again like nothing happened." She dipped forward, running her right hand over the surgical scar. "Where do you think Craig hid the body from Friday night until Sunday morning?"

Logan winced. "I'd rather not think about it, seeing as I spent time there during the cyclone."

"Oh!" Hana covered her mouth with her hand. "Under our villa! That's why Craig didn't want us to have the one behind it overnight. It gave us a perfect view of his antics. It's also why he went crazy when he found me standing there the next morning."

Logan nudged her elbow, his lips parting in a reluctant grin. He didn't want to dwell on having shared the same space as a dead body. She couldn't blame him. "Some good news. The hospital is due for a windfall. Charlie's taking care of that, too."

"Did you donate?" Hana's eyes sparkled with curiosity. Her heart swelled with love and appreciation for her generous husband. Until he spoke and the illusion burst like a soap bubble.

"You shit!" she breathed. She pressed a hand over her heart. "Please tell me you didn't kill and bury Ron?"

Logan's chin jerked into his shirt collar, indignation turning his irises a stormy grey. "Hana! I think you'll find Po did a little tidying up of her own during the cyclone. It made the perfect cover for disposing of unwanted co-conspirators. Think about it. They didn't plan to leave her with much, even though she'd stalled the identification of the Sail Fish's captain, and kept their secret. Every dead person increased her share, especially if she'd already gained access to their accounts."

"You think she's smart enough to do that?" Hana cocked her head.

"I think she's devious enough, for sure. This entire island runs on dodgy Wi-Fi. It's a hacker's dream. You don't think she'd fallen for Craig, did you? Liaisons with him in the office gave her access to his computers, maybe even his phone. She only needed to swipe Sally's bank details once, didn't she?"

Hana leaned closer, her lips brushing his cheek. "And Craig told her about Hallie's pregnancy. That's where Sergeant Wally George got his information. Carrie killed Ron and Henk? We don't know how they died, though."

"Head injuries. Blunt force trauma. Marks on their torsos suggested she used a taser to incapacitate them first. Maybe she tried to make them look like deaths caused by the cyclone."

"And you stole from Ron's backpack. Did you also move Sally's suitcase from the car?"

He smiled, his expression switching to indulgent as he gazed at his wife. The lost twinkle reappeared in his eyes. "I might have taken a slight detour after visiting you in the hospital. And I may have given something to Charlie for safekeeping before Officer Carrie picked me up on the main road. But it wasn't a suitcase, Hana. That was already gone, probably in the back of the police truck and hidden right behind me. Why else would she use the truck instead of her scooter if not to collect a heavy bundle of currency? I left Charlie with enough funds to rebuild the maternity wing. The local tradesmen use cash, anyway. And the money looked unmarked. I checked, and so did Charlie. Sally and Co technically never needed to launder it. I believe that part was taken care of before the Sail Fish left port. The idiots wasted a year mucking around with it and didn't need to."

Hana frowned and lay her head back against the seat. "So, Officer Carrie killed Ron. And she used a tyre wrench to hack open the boot and take the suitcase." She leaned forward and released her seatbelt as the red overhead sign switched to green with a lyrical ping. "Sally isn't safe in the island's jail. Do you realise that? She's the only one who can verify Carrie's involvement."

Logan nodded. "The New Zealand investigators arrived just as we left. Charlie's kept vigil, but he won't represent Sally. He just made it difficult for Carrie to harm her."

"That group of official looking men in the arrivals lounge were investigators?" Hana conceded with a nod.

"Pretending they're providing cyclone relief for the existing force."

"But regarding your plan, Ron didn't have that much money in his backpack," she mused. "Not enough to build something like a maternity unit. I saw it, remember?" She turned in her seat, the donated muumuu restricting her movements. Logan hated it, but she'd kept it to wear home. It seemed essential to always remember their drama filled trip. The giant shroud would act as a reminder of all her reasons to feel grateful. "You spent a long time in that house, Logan Du Rose. What did you do?" When he ignored the question, she thought for a while. A trolley rolled past them, pushed by a male air steward. He eased it along the narrow aisle towards the front of the plane and the injured passengers. Hana watched and then clapped a hand over her mouth. Her squeak caused the steward to pause mid stride and glance back at her. Pursing her lips, Hana apologised and waved a conciliatory hand.

Once the man had reached the end of the plane, she leaned sideways to whisper in her husband's ear. "Ron wasn't just screaming about his backpack, was he? What did he say?" She clicked her fingers as the images tumbled past her inner vision. "He'd shifted none of it yet. That means he'd hidden it." The answer sprang into her mind like a red stain, and she shook her head at her husband. "The attic. But you moved it so he couldn't find it in a hurry." She closed her eyes and pictured the green powder on Logan's arms from his sojourn in the loft. "You buried it under the insulation. And now you've donated it to the hospital for a new maternity wing in Pastor Mike and Mary's daughter's name."

A laugh rumbled through Logan's chest, filling their narrow row and rising into the aisle. Her horror caused him extreme enjoyment. He sniggered to himself until the air steward pushed the refreshment trolley alongside their seats. And above the vast blue South Pacific Ocean, he ordered himself a neat whiskey.

Dear Reader

I would love it if you could leave a review at your usual retailer.

I find the opinions of readers helpful and constructive. Reviews are the Holy Grail to an author as they cause our work to sink or swim. It is the bench mark for other readers and can determine whether our work will be successful and reach many or none. It doesn't have to be an essay or a literary criticism. A few words about what you liked would be most appreciated. The shortest review I ever received for my work was, 'Great,' accompanied by five stars and the longest was a whole video from a gorgeous woman in the USA. My favourite to date has to be the lady who said, '*I read until my eyes fell out.*' I keep looking at that one because it makes me laugh.

You can review on my website, ktbowes.com.

Go to the book's buy page where you can follow through to your own retailer and leave a review for me.

And hey, let me know when you've done it. I'd love to hear from you.

About the Author

K T Bowes is a bestselling teen and women's author. Her novel, *A Trail of Lies*, was the winner of the genre award for Author's Cave in 2014.

Phoenix Du Rose was considered for the prestigious Ngaio Marsh awards for 2021 and *Her Quiet Legacy* in 2022.

K T Bowes is an Englishwoman in exile in New Zealand, swapping rugged cosmopolitan for mountain ranges and terrifying rivers. She loves Māori culture and has learned to weave flax using traditional methods. Her other passion is Rongoa Māori, which involves creating medicines from native plants. She is a student of Te Reo Māori.

You can find her hanging out on social media in the following places.

Check in and say hello. Maybe suggest she gets back to writing and stops watching cat videos.

FACEBOOK

https://www.facebook.com/NZauthorKTBowes/

INSTAGRAM

https://www.instagram.com/k_t_bowes

Also by the Author

The Hana Du Rose Mysteries Series:

Logan Du Rose

About Hana

Hana Du Rose

Du Rose Legacy

The New Du Rose Matriarch

One Heartbeat

The Du Rose Prophecy

Du Rose Sons

Du Rose Family Ties

Du Rose Vendetta

Du Rose Blaze

Du Rose Paradise

The Hana Du Rose Mysteries; Generation Z

Phoenix Du Rose

Wiremu Du Rose

Mac Du Rose

The Calculated Risk Series:

The Actuary
The Actuary's Wife
The Actuary in Trouble
The Heart of The Actuary

Troubled series for teens:

Free from the Tracks
Sophia's Dilemma
A Trail of Lies
Gone Phishing

Escaping the Back Country NZ Series:

Pirongia's Secret
Deleilah

Standalone novels:

Artifact
Demons on Her Shoulder
All Saints
Her Quiet Legacy

Humorous Cozy Mystery Series from New Zealand

Dead Straight
Bad Hair Day
Side Parting

Join our In Crowd

This is another opportunity for you to join my VIP readers.
You can do that by signing up on my website ktbowes.com
In return, you'll receive four free eBooks sent to your inbox and an email from me once a month.
I'd love for you to join us.

Love from Kate x

www.ingramcontent.com/pod-product-compliance
Lightning Source LLC
Chambersburg PA
CBHW010358310726
48979CB00006B/1092

* 9 7 8 1 9 9 1 0 3 6 1 2 4 *